A Going Down in Flames Novel

Bridges
Burned

D1602819

OTHER BOOKS BY CHRIS CANNON

Going Down in Flames

A Going Down in Flames Novel

Bridges
Burned

Chris Cannon

Entangled Publishing, LLC
2614 South Timberline Road
Suite 109
Fort Collins, CO 80525
Visit our website at www.entangledpublishing.com.

Entangled Teen is an imprint of Entangled Publishing, LLC.

Edited by Erin Molta
Cover design by Starla Huchton
Cover art by DepositPhotos

ISBN 978-1-50756-810-1

Manufactured in the United States of America

First Edition January 2015

This book is dedicated to my family for all their love and support.

Chapter One

On the drive back to school, Bryn reflected on how her life had recently gone to hell. It had all started when flames shot out of her mouth on her sixteenth birthday, proving she wasn't completely human. Since then she'd been shipped off to a secret school for dragons — the Institute for Excellence — where she was learning how to control her shape-shifting dragon powers. She'd faced discrimination, death threats, and poisoning. She'd been blown up and involved in a battle to the death with a radical Revisionist member — and she'd been there for only a few months.

Though not everything about her new life was bad. She had a sexy boyfriend, Black dragon Zavien Blackthorn, and two good friends, Clint and Ivy. Being a crossbred dragon meant she had both the Red and Blue dragons' breath weapons, fire and ice, and even though she was the *only* crossbreed, she could still outfly even the fastest Blue. Of course, that's why some of the other Clans hated her. She'd upset the natural order of things in this color-coded world, where the Directorate dictated what Red, Black, Green, Orange, and Blue dragon Clan members could do as a profession and whom they could marry. It was absurd. Yet most dragons didn't question it.

Part of Zavien's appeal lay in the fact that he headed up the student Revisionist group that petitioned the Directorate to change outdated laws. Bryn glanced at Directorate lawyer Merrick Overton, who was driving the Cadillac SUV hybrid she was riding in. Her classmate and former nemesis Jaxon Westgate rode shotgun. She and Jaxon no longer hated each other. Scratch that: he no longer hated her based on his father's vendetta against her mother, but that didn't mean they were friends. Funny how saving someone's life could turn you from enemies to…what? Not friends. Frenemies, maybe? Who knew? It's not like she wanted to hang out with him, but there was a weird level of trust between them now that she didn't know what to do with.

God, what she wouldn't give to close her eyes and wake up at home with her mom and dad, sitting in the living room eating popcorn and watching bad television. But the Directorate would never let that happen. She was stuck. Stuck in this weird shape-shifting dragon world where she still didn't know all the rules. And half the rules she did know were total crap.

Time to concentrate on happier things. Zavien's black spiky manga-like hair and his dark eyes came to mind. The hypnotic buzz of the tires on pavement lulled her to sleep.

. . .

"Bryn, you're home." Merrick Overton's voice woke her. Her feelings toward him were mixed. He was a lawyer for the Directorate, yet he'd helped to protect her life. When they'd first met he'd offered to act as her benefactor, which meant keeping her as his mistress and supporting her after graduation. The reason he was still alive and breathing? She hadn't known what the word "benefactor" meant at the time.

"Home?" She sat up, expecting to see her parents' apartment. Instead, they were back at school. She covered her disappointment with a yawn.

"Good-bye. I hope we won't see each other again soon." Jaxon nodded like he hadn't insulted her and headed for his dorm.

"The feeling is mutual."

Merrick chuckled. "Come. I'll escort you to your room. I want to check the new security."

Not many students were out wandering the sidewalks or flying in the sky. It was Sunday evening, so everyone was probably relaxing or finishing up homework. She yawned for real this time. More sleep. That's what she needed.

Auburn-haired men with the muscular build of Red dragons walked the campus wearing uniforms that matched the guards at the front gate. That was new. The fact that her grandfather had swayed the Directorate to increase security on campus for her protection was amazing. Then again, most of the Directorate had family members at the school, because no one escaped attending the institute. Every single shape-shifting dragon had to attend from junior year of high school through college graduation, which sucked.

Not that the campus was ugly. Far from it. The old stone buildings and the meticulously kept grounds were almost too perfect—Stepford-creepy-level perfect.

A light wind ruffled the leaves, which looked like they were ready to turn. Bryn inhaled the crisp air. "It smells like autumn."

Merrick smiled. "Winter is around the corner."

"Do all Blue dragons love winter?"

"We do." He winked. "It's in our blood."

"Maybe that's why I like fall. It's between the hot and cold seasons like I'm between the Red and Blue dragons."

When they reached their destination, Merrick opened the door to the dorm. A small camera above the door pulsed with a tiny red light. "The surveillance cameras appear to be functional."

Each hallway had its own camera. Good to know someone was taking note of who entered the building. Maybe that would cut down on people breaking into her room and leaving her poisoned carrot cake, because almost dying from a dose of Dragonbane was not something she wanted to experience again. Once was enough, thank you very much. When they reached her room, she opened the door with the key and flipped on the overhead light. Two wooden rolltop desks sat on opposite ends of the room with their uncomfortable wooden chairs. A black couch and gray chairs flanked the mahogany coffee table.

She wandered into her bedroom and saw the four-poster beds with the gray comforters, the armoires, and the dresser. More furniture than she needed, since she'd never have a roommate. She'd grown used to living alone because no one wanted to live with the only known hybrid.

Nothing appeared out of place. She breathed a sigh of relief and joined Merrick in the living room.

"You don't have to babysit me. I feel safer with the cameras."

"I believe you *are* safer since your grandparents recognized you. Anyone feeling vengeful will think twice about crossing Ephram Sinclair."

"I think my grandmother is scarier."

"That's only because you don't know your grandfather very well. Now lock yourself in. I'm sure Zavien will be by to check on you soon."

She followed him to the door. "Thanks for watching out for me and for knocking off the benefactor crap."

"You're welcome." A smile played across his lips. "It's for the best that I rescinded my offer to act as your benefactor, because if my sister and your grandmother have their way, and if your lineage check to Jaxon comes back compatible, I might end up your uncle."

"That's not funny." She might not hate Jaxon anymore, but she had no desire to be shackled to him in a Directorate-sanctioned farce of a marriage. She crossed her arms over her chest. "If they try to set me up with Jaxon I'm claiming lesbianism."

Merrick laughed.

She might be worrying about nothing. "Now that I've been recognized by my grandparents, do you think the Directorate will really take me off the 'unfit to marry' list?"

"Your grandfather wants the Sinclair line to continue. He'll work toward that end, but it will take time."

"I turn eighteen in two years. What happens if I'm not approved by then?"

"Fortune-telling was never my specialty. Concentrate on your studies and the rest will work itself out."

Once he was gone, she headed to the bedroom to

change clothes. Dressed in her standard after-class attire of yoga pants and a tank top, she felt much better. Now what? A quick check in the mirror showed a tired girl with red, blond, and black striped hair. That wouldn't do. She focused her life force, or Quintessence, and imagined it as a ball of white light in her chest. She allowed the ball to drift upward, darkening her lips and cheeks, using it as makeup in a way that few students her age could do. It was a source of pride that she was so skilled at manipulating Quintessence. She couldn't wait to start her classes in Quintessential medicine next year. Becoming a medic, being able to heal other dragons, was her dream job. Once she was satisfied with her newly enhanced and far more alert-looking reflection, she wondered what to do next.

The new book bag Jaxon's mother, Lillith, had given her lay on the bed. And…she had no books. How was she supposed to get new textbooks when she wasn't allowed to tell anyone about the explosion at her grandparents' estate that had incinerated her book bag and almost killed her? Maybe Zavien would know what to do. For now, she grabbed the spare notebooks and pens she kept in her room and tossed them in the bag. The final step was adding the silver pen with the tracking spell Zavien had given her the first night they'd met. The pen that had allowed him to find her at her grandparents' estate where he had helped fight off Alec, the crazy radical Revisionist dragon who had wanted to kill Bryn and make her a martyr for his cause.

Knock knock. She shot across the room and yanked the door open. Her best friends stood there grinning at her. Ivy greeted her with a hug. Clint walked in balancing several cartons of take-out food.

"We heard through the grapevine you were back." Ivy released her and headed for the couch. "Tell us everything that happened at the Directorate meeting."

She'd love to share with her friends, but by Directorate law, it wasn't allowed. "Did Zavien tell you anything?"

"He showed up at camp this afternoon and said you'd been officially recognized by your grandparents because you tried to help save Alec."

"That's the *official* version of the truth," Bryn said. "There isn't much else to the story. Although my grandmother did invite me to Christmas Eve dinner."

"That's great." Clint set the take-out boxes on the coffee table. "Are your parents invited, too?"

After running away to escape arranged marriages, her parents had been banished from dragon society, and her grandparents had refused contact of any kind since. They had even refused delivery of any cards or photos her parents had tried to send. Now she might have a chance to mend some fences. "I'm working on that. How was the camping trip?"

"The only good thing we ate was s'mores," Ivy said. "We're starved."

The savory scent of french fries filled the air. "That smells awesome."

"Cheeseburgers and fries from the dining hall." Clint offered her a white box. "I grabbed enough for Zavien. I'm surprised he's not here."

"I haven't seen him since he left to go back to the campground." Bryn sat on the couch and ripped open a ketchup packet with her teeth.

Ivy removed the pickles from her hamburger and passed them to Clint. "When we left, he was talking with Nola and some of those radical Revisionist dragons."

Nola was the friend the Directorate had decreed Zavien should marry based on lineage. Even though Zavien swore they were just friends, the dark-haired Barbie still got under Bryn's skin.

"Did they seem upset?"

"They seemed sad about their friend, but they weren't angry," Ivy said.

"Tell me more about the camping trip." Bryn didn't want to think about Nola or the radical Revisionist members. For a while, she wanted to pretend she was a normal person with normal problems and normal friends rather than a shape-shifting, fire-breathing dragon at the mercy of an archaic society.

"Sleeping on the ground in human form sucks," Clint said. "But sleeping as a dragon feels strange."

"Some of the extreme Revisionist guys spoke to us. They're intense and sort of scary." Ivy dipped a french fry in ketchup. "The Directorate may have too much control over our employment and schooling, but I don't think they're evil."

Were they? Bryn remembered the men she'd pleaded her case in front of attempting to prove that while she was unique due to her forbidden Blue/Red dragon Clan heritage, she wasn't a threat that needed to be neutralized. "Some of them could pass for evil. Some are nice. It's the fact that they're so sure they're right about *everything* that pisses me off."

Ivy frowned. "I hate that there aren't any women on the Directorate, even though they claim women are allowed to be Directorate members. In the history book there is the occasional woman mentioned, but it's always as a footnote."

"I'd love to ask my grandmother how she feels about that." And then she remembered her grandmother's plan.

"Right now, I'm glad she doesn't have a vote. She and Jaxon's mom have lost their minds. They want the Directorate to check my lineage to see if Jaxon and I are a match."

Clint laughed so hard he fell off the couch.

Ivy clamped a hand over her mouth and worked at swallowing her food without choking. When she achieved that feat, she said, "You can't be serious."

"Since my mom and Ferrin were a match, Lillith thinks Jaxon and I might match up, too. She's enlisted my grandmother in her scheme. That's what terrifies me. My grandmother is almost scarier than Ferrin. In a one-on-one battle, I'd give them even odds."

"What about Rhianna?" Ivy asked. "What would happen to her if you and Jaxon were paired up?"

"If fate hated me that much, then I guess Rhianna would be matched with someone else."

Clint shook his head. "She'd have to go with someone younger. Most of the top dragon families already have agreements in place. That's why Ferrin had to marry someone much younger when your mom ran off with your dad. All the contracts with females of his own age had already been worked out."

"Then I shouldn't have anything to worry about. Rhianna's and Jaxon's families must have their agreement in place. Nothing could change that, right?"

"For Red, Orange, Black, and Green dragons, nothing supersedes an agreement between families," Ivy said. "In the Blue upper-class circles, things change if a family loses its wealth or status."

"So, what was your grandfather's house like?" Clint asked, completely changing the subject.

"Huge and cold. My grandparents have their own separate wings."

"I guess if you marry someone you don't like you can hang out in your own wing." Clint winked at Ivy. "We're going to have a small ranch house, so I'll always know where you are."

Ivy shook her head. "I want a two-story house like I grew up in."

A goofy smile spread across Clint's face, making Bryn chuckle. It had taken Clint years to make Ivy fall for him, even though they'd been friends forever. Before she could comment, another knock sounded on the door.

That must be Zavien. She hopped up, dashed across the room, and swung the door open. Jaxon and his friend Quentin stood there. Not who she wanted to see. If the way they were frowning was any indication, neither of them was pleased to be at her door.

"What's up?" She stepped back so they could enter.

Jaxon shoved a box wrapped in blue paper at her. "My uncle insisted I deliver your new textbooks in this ridiculous manner. The Directorate didn't want anyone to know why you needed the replacement."

She accepted the box and set it on the coffee table, but she couldn't help needling him. "Thanks for playing errand boy. What reason would you have for bringing me a gift?"

"My mother sent you an early Christmas present." He shrugged.

"That doesn't make much sense. And why is Quentin with you?"

"He missed me," Quentin said in a dry tone.

Clint cleared his throat. "What happened to your books?"

She hated keeping secrets from her friends, so she didn't. "I signed a paper saying I wouldn't talk about it."

Jaxon scowled. "You can't tell them that."

"It's not like I told them what happened. I kept my word. What did you tell Quentin?"

"That you can manipulate Quintessence. When Alec collapsed before the Directorate, you assisted Medic Williams." Quentin checked his watch. "Not to be rude, but I don't have a burning desire to know anything about your textbooks, and our dates are waiting."

"Thanks for the books." Bryn opened the door so they could leave.

Zavien stood in the hall with his hand raised to knock. His eyebrows went up at the sight of the two Blue males. "What are you doing here?"

Jaxon wore a serious expression. "I stopped by to talk to my future wife about names for our offspring. Sadly, your name didn't make the list."

Zavien's gaze darted back and forth between Jaxon and Bryn. "Tell me he's joking."

Before she could speak, Quentin said, "Sorry, it's true. Your name didn't make the cut. I believe they settled on Leonard and Beatrice."

"They were just leaving." Bryn pushed Jaxon out the door and then grabbed Zavien's arm and tugged him inside.

He caught sight of the present on the table. His eyebrows slammed together. "What's that?"

"Nothing exciting, it's my new books."

"Really?" He crossed his arms over his chest. "Open it."

Where was this pissy attitude coming from? "Open the damn box yourself."

Chapter Two

In two quick strides, Zavien crossed the space, and he ripped the paper off, revealing a white gift box. He removed the lid and frowned.

Clint leaned closer to peer inside. "Bryn, you might want to take a look in here."

"It's not books?" A small jeweler's box sat on top of the textbooks. Nabbing the blue velvet box, she snapped the lid open. Dime-sized sapphire earrings gleamed on the silk liner. "Wow."

"There's a card taped to the bottom," Ivy said.

Bryn opened the card and smiled. "They're from Jaxon's mom, Lillith."

Zavien leaned over her shoulder and read the message aloud. "I thought these would make a suitable thank-you gift. Love, Lillith."

Ivy touched the sparkling stones. "She's generous."

"I like her. She's more like a friend than someone's

mom." Her gaze moved to Zavien. "Feel better now?"

He ducked his head and shoved his hands in his jeans pockets. "After spending time around all that Blue Clan money, I thought you might be ready to move on."

Moron. How could he not know how she felt about him? "Money isn't important to me."

Zavien pointed at the earrings. "It buys pretty things."

She set the earrings down and moved closer to wrap her arms around him and lay her head on his chest. "I don't care about things. I care about you."

Clint stood and pulled Ivy toward the door. "I sense a heartwarming moment coming on. Call Ivy later to share."

Ivy objected as he tugged her out the door.

Zavien's heartbeat filled the silence. Why wasn't he saying he cared about her? Her throat became tight. She lifted her head and met his gaze. "Don't you have anything to say?"

He leaned down and pressed his mouth against hers. Happy warmth filtered through her chest. He may be too much of a guy to say he cared, but his actions proved he did.

Knock knock. Was that the door? Too bad. They were busy.

Knock knock knock.

"Damn it." Zavien stepped away from her. "You better see who that is."

Bryn opened the door ready to tell whoever it was to go away. Nola on her doorstep made her grind her teeth.

The dark-haired Barbie sniffled. "Is Zavien here?"

Zavien pushed past Bryn so fast, he shoved her into the doorframe.

"Nola, what's wrong?" He wrapped his arms around the

other woman.

What the hell? Heat fanned the flames in Bryn's gut. She engaged in a brief fantasy about ripping every hair from Nola's pretty little head.

Zavien led Nola to the couch and sat with his arm around her shoulders.

Why was he touching her? Smoke crawled up the back of Bryn's throat. If this went much further, she might *accidentally* blast Nola to a cinder.

"I'm sorry." Nola sniffled and dabbed at her nose with a lace-edged handkerchief. "I didn't know who else to turn to."

Zavien pressed his lips to Nola's temple.

Bryn gritted her teeth and forced the flames down. She had to get out of there, but it was *her* dorm room. She needed a reason to leave. "I was going to grab a soda from the vending machine. Do you guys want one?"

Wiping a tear from her cheek, Nola nodded. "That would be great. Thank you."

Pretending she wasn't on the verge of losing control, Bryn walked out the door. Once out of their sight, she stomped down the hall and bought three sodas. "They're just friends," she stalked back to her room muttering to herself.

Hand on the doorknob, she took a deep breath. "You can do this." The knob was yanked from her hand as Zavien opened the door from the inside. She lurched forward and stumbled against him. He caught her with his free arm, while he kept his other arm around Nola.

Trying to be a better person than she was, she stepped away from him and held a can of soda out to Nola.

"Thanks, I can see why you and Zavien are such good

friends. You're a sweet girl."

"That's me," Bryn shoved the other soda into Zavien's rib cage. "Were you leaving?"

"Nola needs me," he said.

"Right." *Asshat.* "You should go." *And don't come back until you figure out what the hell you want.* As he walked away from her, she fantasized about beaning him in the back of the head with the last can of soda.

She slammed the door as loud as possible, stalked to the phone, and dialed Ivy's number. Her friend picked up on the first ring.

"Tell me everything," Ivy said.

"The jerk kissed me and then left with Nola."

"Crap. I'll be right over."

True to her word, Ivy showed up in five minutes. Once they were seated on the couch, Bryn relayed the story of Nola showing up out of nowhere. "She stole him right out from under my nose. One minute he was kissing me, and then he's hugging her and kissing her forehead. What does that mean?"

"I don't know." Ivy hesitated. "They have been friends forever."

Smoke shot from Bryn's nostrils. "I hate her."

"No, you don't."

"Fine." She kicked the coffee table. "I hate that she showed up and he abandoned me. He could've at least kissed me good-bye." She kicked the coffee table again. "She called me a sweet girl...made me sound like I was five."

"I guess Zavien hasn't told her about you," Ivy said. "She needs to find her own guy."

"According to the Directorate, Zavien is her guy. My life

sucks."

"She may be his intended, but he chose you," Ivy said.

"Right." Zavien had sworn that he and Nola were friends who wanted to put off marriage as long as possible, and he was working to change the law. Still, being abandoned hurt.

"Come on." Ivy stood. "You need chocolate. We're going to the dining hall to binge on dessert."

They walked through her bedroom to the floor-to-ceiling window between the armoires, which provided access to the terrace. Once they were outside, Bryn shifted. It was second nature now. All she had to do was tap into her dragon essence. She could feel the power unfurling inside her, transforming her human body into a powerful beast with leatherlike wings and scales bigger than her palm and flames blazing in her chest. If she concentrated, she could change the flames to ice due to her Blue heritage, but fire came first. She was predominantly Red, like her father.

Stretching her wings, Bryn inhaled the crisp autumn air and launched herself into the sky. Freedom. That's what flying felt like.

"Let's fly for a while," she called out to Ivy.

Ivy's black scales flashed in the moonlight as she swooped in close and slapped Bryn's flank with her tail. "Tag, you're it."

To make it more of a challenge, she gave Ivy a head start. Using her wing muscles she powered up above the cloud line and aimed for the Black dragon several hundred yards ahead of her.

Catching her was too easy. She bumped Ivy with her shoulder. "Try to keep up."

Tucking her wings, Bryn dove through the clouds. She aimed for a grove of trees and skimmed above the branches.

A glance over her shoulder showed Ivy trailing behind. Time to slow down.

Ivy panted. "You're too fast. Let's play follow the leader. Maybe I can outmaneuver you." Ivy flew a lap around Bryn and then performed a midair somersault.

Cool. "Do it again," Bryn yelled against the wind. "I need to see what you did with your wings."

Ivy worked up some speed, tucked her wings against her body, and tumbled head over tail.

Looked simple enough. Bryn flew in a circle to build speed, pulled her wings in tight against her flank and flipped. The world spun over and over and over. Too fast. She couldn't stop her momentum. Laughing, she managed to stop flipping after four complete revolutions.

"That was a pathetic display," a male dragon's voice said.

Where had the Blue come from? Sneaky jerk. The outline of Jaxon's features flashed across the Blue dragon's face. At least it was a sneaky jerk she knew. Just for fun, she huffed a fireball at his head, which he dodged with ease. "Show me what you can do, Jaxon."

He accepted the challenge and demonstrated a precise diving roll.

"How feminine of you." She attempted to copy him. Considering she'd never tried the maneuver, she didn't do too badly.

"How inept of you," he shot back.

Ivy imitated the move with ease. "I thought Blues were supposed to be better fliers."

Jaxon yawned and managed to look bored. "If I had any competition I might try harder."

He could outmaneuver her, but he couldn't outfly her.

"See the roof of the dining hall? First one to touch down wins. Ivy can start us."

Frost shot from his nostrils. "You're on."

"Ready, set, go," Ivy said.

Pumping her wings, Bryn gained speed and barreled forward. Blue scales stayed in her peripheral vision. Jaxon winning was not an option. She pushed harder, moving ahead a fraction of an inch. He gained ground. She gritted her teeth and pushed harder. The rooftop came into view below. Her claws scraped the asphalt seconds before Jaxon's.

Momentum carried her forward. She had to fly a lap around the building to slow her speed. Jaxon managed to stick his landing.

The Blue dragon lifted his snout into the air when she landed next to him, her claws scraping the asphalt as she stumbled forward. "You have speed, but no finesse," he informed her.

"Nice landing." She copied his snooty snout-in-the-air maneuver. "Too bad you're so slow."

Ivy set down on the rooftop. "Enough flying, I'm ready for chocolate."

Right on cue, Bryn's stomach growled. "We're going to eat our weight in dessert if you'd like to join us."

Inviting Jaxon to join them felt strange, but not asking him seemed rude.

For a moment, he seemed at a loss for words. Then he cleared his throat. "I've eaten already. Thank you."

"This is weird," Bryn said.

"I could insult you before I leave, if you like."

"No thanks. Let's go, Ivy."

They flew down to the entrance and shifted back to

human form. It was a neat bit of magic that whatever clothes or jewelry a dragon wore had been spelled to shift with them, because ending up naked after a shift would be way too embarrassing.

They entered the building. About half the tables were full, since most students liked to eat in Dragon's Bluff on Sunday night.

"What's Clint doing?" Bryn asked as she checked out her dessert options on the buffet and grabbed three slices of apple pie.

Ivy reached for a piece of chocolate cake and then hesitated. "Is it rude to eat this in front of you?"

"I doubt I'll ever find cake appetizing again." A carrot cake laced with Dragonbane had ended her love affair with that entire line of baked goods. "Go ahead. It doesn't bother me."

"Thanks. When I left, Clint was about to start on his homework. He asked me to bring him a pizza at eight."

"Homework. Wait a minute, I had three completed assignments in my book bag." She groaned and headed for their usual table. "I wonder if the Directorate would write me a note so I won't have to do them again."

"What happened to your book bag?" Ivy asked.

"Legally, I can't tell you. But watch." She pantomimed an explosion.

Ivy's jaw fell open. "Your bag blew up?"

Bryn nodded.

Her friend scooted closer. "Were you hurt?"

Bryn batted her eyelashes. "How do you like my new eyebrows?"

"It sucks that you can't tell us what happened."

"Later, we can play charades. The Directorate never said anything about that." Bryn took a bite of pie. "Do they offer cooking classes as an elective?"

"My sister used to gripe about being paired with a Blue who couldn't cook to save his life, so there must be a foods class somewhere in the curriculum."

They chatted as they ate. Bryn tried not to look for Zavien, but his absence gnawed at her. *Where was he?*

"You've checked the door every time it's opened." Ivy licked chocolate icing off her fork. "Did Zavien say when he was coming back?"

"No." Bryn finished off her second piece of apple pie. One major perk of being a dragon: a much faster metabolism, which gave her the ability to eat whatever she wanted and never gain weight. "Once she appeared, he never looked back."

"He cares about you."

"I know." She smacked her fork down on the table. "He swore they were just friends. What if that changes? I know they're not into the same things, but she's so freaking perfect."

"I don't think she's perfect," Ivy said. "Her look is too contrived. No one walks around in those flowing dresses in real life. It's like she's putting on a show."

"For whom?"

"I don't know." Ivy toyed with her cake. "Now that your grandparents have recognized you, do you think an arranged marriage is in your future?"

"My grandfather wants the Sinclair line to continue." Bryn slumped in her seat. "He told Ferrin to have me declared eligible for marriage. I don't even want to think about what a nightmare that might be. On a happier note, Merrick retracted his offer to be my benefactor."

"That must be a relief. Now you don't have to wonder at his motives when he's helping you."

"Exactly. My grandmother wanted me to accept him. She doesn't think the Directorate will declare me fit to marry."

"You'd think she'd want what's best for you."

Bryn leaned closer. "In the human world, no one assumes a woman needs a man to support her. I told my grandmother that if Zavien and I don't work out I'll become a medic and take care of myself. She didn't approve of my answer."

"Growing up, we were taught that only a small percentage of petitions are denied based on lineage. About half of those denied are offered an arranged marriage that would be more suitable. The unlucky ones with undesirable genes are offered a benefactor."

"And everyone just accepts that?"

Ivy shrugged. "It's the way things have always been done, but if you told your grandmother you'd be happy single she should respect that."

"Happiness isn't a big part of the Blue Clan's belief system. 'Honor and loyalty above all else even if you're miserable' seems to be their motto." Bryn sipped her soda and tried to focus on the positives. "My grandfather was warmer while I was there. The only time my grandmother showed any emotion was when she warned me about being involved with Zavien. She said he was just amusing himself—gave me this whole 'only those you love can truly hurt you' speech."

"Falling in love with anyone is a risk," Ivy said.

Bryn finished off the third piece of pie and ignored the

nervous feeling in her stomach.

. . .

Back in her room, Bryn picked up one of the legends books she had checked out of the library based on a time when dragons were allowed to fall in love by instinct, before the Directorate mandated arranged marriages to keep dragons in line. She curled up on the couch and lost herself in the battles of love and war. Funny how the war part seemed easier to negotiate.

The Directorate had wanted to ban these books from the library, but Miss Enid the librarian had fought them fang and claw. The Directorate probably didn't want anyone reading these stories because they might inspire dragons to think for themselves. In her mind, she imagined small communities of dragons living under the radar. There had to be other hybrids out there. Her parents couldn't have been the only ones to ever defy the law.

A knock on the door had her up and running. No. She stopped herself. She would not run to him. "Who is it?"

"It's Zavien."

By the clock on her desk it had been five hours since he'd ditched her. She pulled the door open a few inches. "What's up?"

Hands shoved in the front pocket of his jeans, he had the good sense to look sheepish. "Can I come in?"

She stepped back, crossed her arms over her chest, and waited for him to explain.

He entered and leaned against the closed door. "Sorry about earlier. Nola needed me."

Not what she wanted to hear. "Really? What did she need you for?"

"I knew you'd be like this." He rubbed his hand over the stubble on his chin.

Flames roared in her chest. She tamped them down. "Don't patronize me. She's your friend. I get that. What if Valmont dropped by and I left with him. How would you feel?" Valmont was her own personal knight, who had become magically bonded to her when he'd protected her from a perceived threat. It was an added bonus that he was smoking hot and had made Zavien jealous enough to kiss her and admit his feelings.

Zavien bristled at the knight's name. "You have a point, but what did you expect me to do? She was crying."

"What was the emergency? Why were *you* the only person she could confide in?"

"Can we sit?" Zavien asked.

Shadows stood out under his eyes. In fact, now that she really paid attention, he looked like crap.

She waved him toward the couch. He sat close enough that his thigh brushed against hers, creating a frisson of warmth. Hormones would not distract her right now. At the moment, she'd rather kick him than kiss him.

"Nola is having a hard time dealing with Alec's death. She always felt like she should've been a better influence on him."

"Why would she think that?"

"He was her brother."

Chapter Three

Bryn sucked in a breath. "Does she know?"

Zavien gave a bitter laugh. "Does Nola know I killed her brother? No."

"Why didn't you tell me?" She wrapped her arms around him. "I'm sorry. You must feel awful."

"He wouldn't stop." His shoulders slumped and his voice sounded hollow. "If Alec would've stopped attacking, I wouldn't have been forced to kill him."

Guilt rained down on her. He'd killed Alec to protect her. How could she have forgotten that? Needing to look him in the eyes, she sat on the coffee table and placed her hands on either side of his face. "It wasn't your fault. Alec was crazy with grief over his marriage petition being denied."

The pain in Zavien's eyes made her heart ache. It was stupid not to worry about the effect this might have on him. The Directorate's only concern had been to cover everything up. No one had thought to offer him counseling.

"I'm so sorry." Bryn pressed her lips against his forehead. "What can I do?"

"Promise me you'll never tell anyone what happened that night. I don't want anyone to know. Nola can never find out."

The other woman's name sliced into her heart like a dagger. Ignoring the pain, she stroked his cheek. "I promise."

Zavien's body relaxed. He leaned his forehead against hers. "I don't want to think about anything right now. Talk to me. Tell me what you did tonight."

He'd been strong for her when she'd needed him. She could be strong for him now. "Let's lie down." They settled onto the couch. He wrapped his arm around her waist and she laid her head on his chest.

"Ivy and I flew for a while. Jaxon showed up to mock me, so I beat him in a race. Then we went to the dining hall for dessert, and I ate three pieces of apple pie to celebrate my victory." So what if it was a skewed version of her evening; it wasn't an outright lie.

She continued talking, weaving together unimportant details from past conversations with Ivy. When Zavien's breathing became regular, she stopped talking and thought about their situation. In two years she'd finish her high school classes. The degree in Quintessential medicine could take four to six more years. Zavien was in the first year of his bachelor's degree. He could work toward a master's degree and extend his time at school.

Originally, he'd told her Nola didn't want to marry until they had to. The thought of Zavien marrying Nola was like a splinter under her skin. It was always there, annoying her. If she came upon it unexpectedly, it jabbed deeper, causing true pain.

Zavien assumed Nola was dating someone, but if Nola had someone else in her life, why had she come running to him? If she didn't have someone else, then where did that leave Bryn's fledgling relationship with Zavien?

Frustration fanned the flames in her gut. And then a ray of hope... He'd agreed to take her to the fall dance. That was a victory not easily won. He'd told her over and over again that asking someone to the fall dance was akin to declaring intent to petition for a lineage check. Legally, his contract to Nola was already in place. Even though everyone knew he and Nola were just friends, he'd refused to take Bryn to the dance until she had threatened to go with Valmont. That had changed his uncooperative mind-set. Then he had agreed they could go to the dance with Clint and Ivy.

Feeling better, she inhaled Zavien's summer rainstorm scent and watched the rise and fall of his chest. Zavien's scent differed from Ivy's and Clint's. While all Black dragons smelled of rain, Ivy smelled of a lush rainforest, while Clint smelled like wet grass.

She'd never been close enough to other dragons to detect individual scents. Scratch that. Before she and Zavien had gotten together, Keegan had kissed her. Like all Red dragons, he had smelled of smoke and flames. His scent had reminded her of a cozy fireplace. The only other scent she might recognize would be Jaxon's. Blues smelled of ice and snow, but Jaxon had an undercurrent of something crisp and clean. He smelled like a fresh-cut pine tree on a snowy day.

Funny, how Jaxon no longer sat at the top of her most-loathed list. Since she'd sent her life force through Jaxon's veins to burn out the poison meant to kill him, they'd developed an odd camaraderie. It was a strangely intimate procedure to heal somebody with Quintessence. Now his insults were more of a joking nature.

Knock knock knock.

Who was that? She wiggled out from under Zavien's arm and answered the door.

An auburn-haired security guard stood scowling in the hall. "Curfew is in ten minutes. Mr. Blackthorn needs to return to his room."

His rigid posture and clipped tone implied she'd been up to no good. She opened the door wide enough for him to see Zavien. "He fell asleep on the couch. How'd you know he was here?"

The guard relaxed his stance. "What do you think all these cameras are for? We're trying to keep you safe." He winked. "As far as your grandfather's concerned, that means your friend needs to sleep in his own bed."

Her face heated. "Is my grandfather monitoring all my friends?"

"He thinks Zavien Blackthorn deserves special attention." The guard chuckled.

Great. "Give me a minute to wake him. I'll send him on his way."

The guard pointed at the camera across the hall. "I'll know if you don't."

Despite her irritation, she was grateful someone was looking out for her. "Thanks for checking on me."

The guard strolled away, whistling.

This new development could put a crimp in her social life.

She brushed her fingertips along Zavien's cheek. "Wake up. It's almost curfew, and the security guard says you have to leave."

He stretched and frowned. "What security guard?"

"One of the men my grandfather hired stopped by to say you needed to sleep in your own bed."

One corner of his mouth turned up. "I wonder if the guards are susceptible to bribes."

She laughed. "We'll investigate that later. Right now, you need to smile for the camera in the hallway, or my new friend will be back."

• • •

The sound of a piano worked its way into Bryn's dreams. No. It couldn't be morning already. She pulled the pillow over her head.

The music became loud and discordant. Her blood pressure rose as the alarm clock fulfilled its function of causing stress in students who didn't immediately wake up and turn the damn thing off.

Stumbling to the dresser, she whacked the top of the alarm. In the shower, she used extra tangerine-grapefruit shower gel, hoping the sharp scent would wake her. No such luck. Her orange bra and underwear set covered with fat yellow bumblebees made her smile. She pulled on gray thigh highs she wore in place of the outdated dress-code-mandated panty hose and moved to the armoire to choose an outfit.

Dressed in the first skirt and blouse she laid hands on, she grabbed her new book bag and headed for the dining hall.

Coffee. She needed lots and lots of coffee.

In the dining hall, she yawned her way through the buffet line. Students kept glancing her way and making comments to their friends. *What is that about?* She had managed to wear her underwear on the inside of her clothes, hadn't she? She glanced down. Yep. No bumblebees were visible. Must be her fancy new book bag.

After filling her tray, she joined Clint and Ivy at their regular table. "Mondays suck."

"They do," Clint agreed.

"Cool new book bag." Ivy ran her fingers along the leather. "It's soft."

"Lillith gave it to me."

Clint snorted. "She's trying to bribe you to accept her son."

"There aren't enough book bags in the world for me to accept that proposal."

On the way to class, a blond female Bryn didn't know fell in step beside her. "That's a lovely bag. Where'd you buy it?"

"It was a gift. I'm not sure what store it came from."

"I see." The blond girl drifted back to her friends. Rhianna was among them.

When Bryn reached Elemental Science, the seating chart on the board had her seated next to Jaxon. What the hell? Had her grandmother blackmailed Mr. Stanton? A quick check showed the entire class was no longer seated by Clan, so Mr. Stanton maintained his spot as her favorite teacher.

Jaxon ignored her, so she smiled at Keegan, who sat to her right. He returned the smile and then yawned, which made her laugh.

Mr. Stanton entered the room from the adjoining classroom-turned-storage-room that he always seemed to lurk in and gave an approving nod. "I hoped you'd notice the new chart. Since it's Monday, I had my doubts."

Students chuckled.

"Pair up with two other students with different breath weapons. I've seated you in an alternating pattern, so it shouldn't be difficult."

To her right, Keegan huddled in a group with two other students. She looked front and back to find the same thing.

Great. She faced Jaxon. "Do you have room for one more in your group?"

Octavius, the only male Orange dragon on campus, spoke from Jaxon's other side. "You're welcome to join us, Bryn."

"Thanks."

Jaxon sighed as if the situation caused him great pain. "Haven't we spent enough time together?"

"You're such a joy to be around I couldn't stay away," Bryn mocked.

"Something's changed between you two." Octavius's deep voice carried through the room.

"We learned to tolerate each other at the Directorate meeting." Bryn turned her desk to face them and tapped her pencil on the desktop while she waited for further instructions.

A moment later, Jaxon's hand flashed out and smacked the pencil down. "That's annoying."

Unable to help herself, Bryn raised the pencil and tapped it one more time. Childish, but fun.

Mr. Stanton cleared his throat. "Our elemental breath weapons were obviously designed to be used as weapons.

While we've become more civilized over the centuries, it's a good idea to know how to protect yourself if the need arises. Just a reminder, since we are inside, don't blast your classmates full force. Use an emissary, and by that I mean a small *controllable* amount, and aim it at one of your partners. Your partner in turn will deflect it back. Learn what it feels like to defend against ice, fire, wind, lightning, and sonic waves. You never know whom you might face in battle."

That's a cheery thought.

Octavius frowned. "My sonic waves are invisible. I don't wish to hurt either of you."

"You hit me before by accident," Jaxon said. "I fell out of my chair, but no harm was done. Maybe you should use a smaller amount than you normally would."

"I'll try. Why don't you and Bryn start?"

"Ladies first," Jaxon said.

"This isn't as much fun when I have your permission." The first time he'd verbally attacked her, she'd retaliated by shooting a fireball at his head. Remembering his expression of surprised terror still gave her a warm fuzzy feeling. She allowed heat to build in her chest, took in a measured amount of air, and shot a much smaller fireball at Jaxon's head.

He exhaled frozen flames and the fireball fizzled out in midair. The ice went up in a puff of steam. Water droplets drifted down and spotted their desks.

"Ready?" Jaxon asked Octavius.

The Orange dragon nodded. Jaxon held his hand palm out toward his classmate and concentrated. Frozen flames shot from his hand.

Show-off.

Octavius opened his mouth, and the ice disintegrated

into snow.

"Your breath weapon is the coolest," Bryn said.

"I believe that's why the Directorate deems us such a threat." Octavius's tone was bitter.

"What has the Directorate done?" Bryn asked.

"Ask him." Octavius pointed to Jaxon.

Jaxon squared his shoulders. "The decrease in your Clan's numbers is not the Directorate's fault."

"Really?" The muscles in Octavius's forearms flexed. "Then whose fault is it?"

"I don't know. Perhaps you should address the Directorate and find out," Jaxon said.

"If I addressed the Directorate I'd probably die of an aneurysm like Alec. His death was rather convenient, don't you think?"

Bryn froze under Octavius's questioning gaze.

"She tried to save him. Don't blame her," Jaxon said.

Guilt flooded her system. Alec had tried to kill her and Jaxon, but he'd been wronged first. Since she'd signed that stupid paper, she couldn't explain any of this to Octavius. "We're supposed to be working. Whose turn is it?"

"Why don't you go against Octavius?" Jaxon said.

"Can you repel flame? I don't want to hurt you."

He snorted. "You don't have to worry about me, hybrid. Maybe you should scoot back a bit so we have more time to react."

She moved her chair a few feet from her desk, took a deep breath, and huffed a fireball toward his shoulder.

Octavius exhaled, and her ball of fire broke into shimmering individual flames, which winked out of existence.

"That is so—" *Wham.*

Something slammed into her chest, knocking her backward,

chair and all. She windmilled her arms, but momentum threw her to the floor. *Smack!* Pain shot down her spine as her head whacked the floor. "Damn it." Cradling her head, she rolled to her side.

Jaxon draped his jacket over her legs. "Can you sit up?"

She gritted her teeth as he helped her to a seated position on the floor. "Tell me I didn't flash the entire class."

"About a third of them know you wear stockings. I'll keep the information about the bumblebees to myself." His smirk spoke volumes.

"Wonderful."

Octavius appeared by her side. "I'm sorry. I thought the lesser amount was safe."

"It's not your fault." Bryn rubbed the sore spot on the back of her head. "I thought my fire would disintegrate your sonic waves like Jaxon's ice did."

Mr. Stanton knelt next to her. "The mass of the ice stops the waves. Fire has no mass so the waves travel through."

"You might have mentioned that before," she snapped.

"Sorry. Do I need to call a medic?"

"No. Only my pride is wounded."

"Let's get you back in your seat," Mr. Stanton said.

Holding Jaxon's jacket in front of her, she stood and took her seat.

"Thanks." She passed the jacket back.

He nodded. "I reserve the right to antagonize you about this later."

After Elemental Science, Bryn headed to the library while the rest of her classmates attended history. Being banished from history class because she'd argued with the teacher—in her very first class—had its perks. She had an hour in the library to outline the history text or work on one of the term papers for Mr. Stanton.

First things first, she approached the librarian, Miss Enid, who sat behind the front desk. Bryn pulled out the legends books she'd finished reading, and placed the story about the Red and Black dragon falling in love on top. "This one was my favorite."

"I wonder why?" Miss Enid grinned as she picked up the books and placed them below the desk. "How are things progressing on that front?"

Miss Enid was one of the few who knew about her relationship with Zavien. "It could be better. I'm never sure where I stand."

"You never are, dear. That's why love is so complicated." She pulled two books from the depths of her desk. "Try these. I already checked them out for you."

"Thanks." On the cover of the first book, a woman with red hair swung a torch at a blond man who resembled Jaxon. "I feel her pain." The second book showed a dark-skinned woman blocking a sword thrust from a male member of her Clan.

Bryn climbed the stairs to the third floor and walked past the intricate stained glass windows depicting dragons in flight. Each dragon was blasting its breath weapon into the heavens. The Blue's ice, Red's fire, and Black's lightning were easily recognizable. The Green dragon's wind and the Orange dragon's sonic waves were more abstract. The artist had probably done the best he could. In the far back corner, she set her things on the table and began to work.

Ten minutes later, the chair across from her was pulled out. Now what? Without looking up from her history text, she asked, "Friend or foe?"

Chapter Four

"Associate," a male voice replied.

"That's an interesting category." She gripped her pencil and raised her head. Onyx, the leader of the Revisionists, sat across from her dressed impeccably, as usual. The silver tie he wore with his black suit matched the silver at the temples of his hair. And it made him look like he was trying way too hard. Even though Onyx had given her a key pendant with a protection charm, she didn't trust him. He was too slick.

"What's up?"

"Zavien informed me you've used up the protection charm." He chuckled. "Those normally last ten years. You're a lot of trouble."

"It's not like I *ask* people to try to kill me."

His smile widened until she could count his molars. "Too true. If you'll return the key to me, I'll have the charm replaced."

Her fingertips touched the dragon locket Zavien had

given her as a birthday gift, where she kept the key. "Do you think I still need it? My grandfather did recognize me."

"That was an unusual turn of events. I fear there may still be those who wish you harm."

Alec's wild eyes flashed in her mind. Maybe Onyx could answer a few questions. "How well did you know Alec?"

"He was a brilliant but misguided young man." Onyx's face clouded over.

Nice vague answer.

"I'd appreciate if you didn't put the anxiety spell on it this time." Bryn popped the locket open and retrieved the small golden key with the red and blue stones. "Since I know what it is I won't take it off."

"Of course."

He reached to take it, but Bryn pulled her hand back. "Where did the key come from?"

"It's something I had lying around." Onyx's fake smile came on full beam. "Given the color of the stones, I thought it suitable. Why do you ask?"

Did he really expect her to believe that? "Someone told me a legend about keys like this." She opened her hand and let the stones sparkle in the light. "They claimed the key would unlock treasure chests containing secrets the Directorate wanted to hide."

"An amusing fairy tale, and that's all it is, I assure you. Jewelers made these keys to promote that sort of story. They considered it an act of rebellion because they knew such stories would annoy the Directorate."

That made sense, sort of. "So there are other keys out there with different-colored stones?" She sighed. "No magical treasure chest waiting in my future?"

"Sorry to disappoint you." He snatched the key from her palm and slid it in his jacket pocket. "I'll be in touch, once the protection charm on the key is restored."

Onyx stood and headed for the stairs. Black material billowed out behind him. Holy crap, was he wearing a cape? She stifled a laugh. Who wore a cape rather than a coat? It was absurd, and it reminded her of Nola and all her flowing dresses. He and Nola would make a fabulous fake couple. And that would solve one of her problems.

Bryn gathered her things and set out for Basic Movement. It was the dragon equivalent of gym class, but far cooler. Next to Elemental Science, it was her favorite class.

"What do you want to do today?" Clint asked as he climbed onto a treadmill.

"I want to joust." Ivy punched the buttons for a fast warm-up walk.

Bryn warmed up on her own treadmill while she checked out the raised platforms where students did battle with what appeared to be giant cotton swabs. At the moment, a blond and a dark-haired boy faced off. When the dark-haired guy knocked his opponent off the platform, she gave a silent cheer. Sometimes, the whole color-coding system made it easy to know who to root for. Not that she hated Blues, but Reds, Greens, Blacks, and Oranges had been far nicer to her during her time on campus. She couldn't help but think that Blues were behind the carrot cake poisoning, and she'd bet money it was Jaxon's father who'd arranged it. Not that she had any proof.

At the far end of the room, Octavius and his mate, Vivian, the only two Orange dragons on campus, attacked and parried with wooden swords. It looked like fun.

"I want to learn how to use a sword."

Clint chuckled. "No one fights with swords anymore."

Bryn pointed across the gym. "The Orange dragons know how to use them."

"Ask Octavius to teach you," Ivy said.

"I might."

When she reached the ring, Octavius and Vivian had ditched the swords and moved on to the hollow stick drums unique to their Clan. As thick as Bryn's forearm, the drums were two feet long and decorated with black swirling lines.

The Orange dragons performed a choreographed dance, slamming the wooden instruments together in a manner that made it look like they were still fighting with swords. The resulting noise was a resonant sound that reminded her of bongos.

Vivian called to Bryn. "Would you like to learn? I need a female to perform the Chosen Dance."

That could be fun. Bryn climbed into the ring. "What's the Chosen Dance?"

"The women of my Clan have performed this dance for hundreds of years. Let me show you." She passed Bryn a drum. The hollow wooden stick was heavier than Bryn expected.

"First, do this step." Vivian stepped wide with her right foot, and then stomped her left foot. She brought her right foot in close and then performed the move leading with her left foot.

"It's like a hula dance," Bryn said.

Octavius laughed. "Where do you think our bronze skin and brown hair comes from?"

Huh. She'd never noticed that the two Orange dragons

resembled Hawaiians.

"Try your feet," Vivian suggested.

The foot pattern was easy enough. Swaying her hips side to side, not so much. Then again, it wasn't like she was trying to impress anyone.

"Now, hold your drum out and I will hit it," Vivian instructed.

Bryn held the drum steady and concentrated on her feet. Vivian swung her drum at Bryn's. The force behind the blows caused the sound to resonate around them.

A melody rose out of the drumbeats. Bryn hummed along as Vivian swung her drum harder and harder. A bead of sweat ran down her back as she held her drum firm in order to withstand Vivian's blows. The tempo of the song increased.

"We will stop after ten more blows. When we finish, look to see who is watching you. They are the males most likely to choose you as a mate."

How scientific was this process? She surveyed the area around the ring. Zavien talked with Mrs. Anderson by the joust. What was he doing here? Didn't matter. If he didn't look her way, she'd hit him over the head with the drum.

"Get ready," Vivian said.

Vivian smacked her drum against Bryn's one more time, and then Bryn checked the area for interested parties. Jaxon glared from across the room. Zavien walked toward her with a smile on his face. Keegan waved from the weight lifting area.

"You have broad appeal," Vivian said with a laugh.

"How do you know they aren't looking at you?" Octavius asked.

The bronze-skinned beauty reached up and traced her

fingertips across his lips. "It doesn't matter if they're looking at me. I only see you."

Sparks practically flew between the two. Not wanting to feel like a third wheel, Bryn placed the drum on the mat and backed away.

"Thanks for sharing your traditions with me."

"You're different than the others," Octavius said. "As are we. If you ever need a Clan, we would take you in."

"Thanks. That means a lot."

She climbed out of the ring, ignoring the backflips her stomach performed while she waited for Zavien to reach her. His black hair stood out in the usual three-inch spikes, but it seemed wilder than normal today. One corner of his mouth quirked up and her heart beat faster.

"That was interesting," he said.

Interesting good, or interesting she looked like a dork? "Vivian needed another female to perform the dance. It was fun."

He reached out to tuck a stray piece of hair behind her ear. "Was it for a special ritual?"

Unsure of how he'd react to finding out he was her chosen one, she avoided the question. "I don't know if I'm at liberty to say. The Orange dragons are a secretive bunch."

"Yes, they are. It's good you're friendly with them. They make formidable opponents."

Her fingers itched to touch him. Going with it, she straightened his tie, allowing her hand to linger on his chest. The impulse to kiss him made her lips tingle.

Zavien moved closer. "Have you seen the addition they're building to house the new ice rink?"

She shook her head. His warm fingers wrapped around

hers. "It's this way."

He pulled her behind the ring, out a door, and down a side hall. Where were they? She didn't know and she didn't care. Zavien opened another door, which led to a partially finished and deserted locker room. Before the door closed behind them, she found herself backed against a cold metal locker with Zavien's lips pressed against hers. She fisted her hands in his shirt and held on as heat and electricity built between them. A low growling sound filled the room. *Holy crap. Is that me or him?*

Zavien stepped back, breathing heavily, and stared into her eyes. *What? Did I do something wrong?*

"Did you use Quintessence when you danced? Was there some sort of magic involved?"

"What? No. It was just a dance."

"Sorry." He studied her like she was a puzzle he was trying to solve. "I don't understand why I feel so strongly for you right now."

Splash. His words were like a bucket of cold water. "What the hell does that mean?"

"You're always in the back of my mind. Right now, you're all I can think about."

"That's not a bad thing." After all, she spent a lot of time thinking about him.

"I suppose not." He stepped away from her. "You should return to class."

Cold air rushed in to replace the heat of his body. Goose bumps broke out on her arms. Why was he acting so suspicious?

She wanted answers to big questions, but would settle for something more practical. "What are you doing here?

Why did you come see me?"

"I stopped by to tell you I wouldn't be at lunch. I have errands to run."

Okay. That was nice of him. Her fear receded.

He laced his fingers through hers. "Come on. We better go."

Zavien left her at the entrance to the gym. Just walked off. Why didn't he kiss her good-bye? Was he afraid someone would see them? *Ugh*. She would not do this to herself. He'd come to see her. Even if he'd acted weird, he'd sought her out. That was a good thing.

She found Clint and Ivy waiting in line to joust.

"Where'd you run off to?" Clint asked.

"Zavien showed me the new addition for the ice rink. The locker room is…nice."

"Right," Ivy said. "The locker room put that smile on your face."

Before she could confirm or deny Ivy's suspicion, Jaxon spoke from behind her.

"Did Zavien grace you with his presence before he ran off to see Nola?"

What the hell? Clenching her fists, she turned to reply. "What business is it of yours?"

His eyes shone like shards of ice. "I thought you didn't want to be someone's mistress."

"I'm not."

"His marriage petition has been approved." Jaxon's voice held a mean edge she hadn't heard in a while. "That means you're officially the other woman."

"What is your problem?" Smoke drifted from her mouth. The line moved, forcing her to retreat a step.

He moved closer, crowding her.

Ignoring the line, she stood her ground. "I'm not a mistress. This is different."

"Is it?" He tilted his head like he was confused.

That old *I want to set his hair on fire* feeling returned with a vengeance. "It *is* different." She had proof. "He's taking me to the fall dance."

"Is he?"

The air of disbelief that radiated from him pissed her off. "Yes, he is."

"If you say so." He pointed behind her. "It's your turn."

Good. She needed to vent some frustration before she gave in to her natural instincts and shot the mother of all fireballs at Jaxon's stupid head. Climbing onto the podium, she accepted the jousting stick. Her opponent was climbing the ladder to join her when Jaxon approached and said something that made the boy climb back down, allowing Jaxon to take his place on the opposite podium.

"What are you doing?" she asked.

He spun the jousting stick in his hand. "Isn't this your dream come true?"

Why was she arguing? Crouching in a defensive position, she swung at him. He blocked the blow. She braced herself for the return strike. He stood there smiling.

"Hello? Aren't you going to swing at me?"

"No. I plan to deflect your blows. Eventually you'll become overconfident, swing too hard, and fall off all by yourself."

She wanted to shove the jousting stick down his throat. Instead she swung at his shoulders. He blocked her blow, knocking her jousting stick downward. Since he wasn't striking back, she turned in a circle and used the momentum to hit his thighs. Take that. He wobbled.

Noise from the students below caught her attention. They had an interested audience. She spun again and struck at his hips. He deflected the blow with more force, and she had to shuffle to maintain her balance.

"This is stupid," she said.

He laughed. "Class ends in ten minutes. Try again."

The corners of her mouth turned up. *Wait a minute. Why am I enjoying this?*

She swung again and aimed at the middle of his jousting stick. One of his hands came loose, but he didn't lose his weapon.

"Well played," he said.

"It was worth a try." Her shoulders ached from using the drum earlier, and jousting was beginning to wear on her.

She swung at his hips. He pivoted and brought his weapon down on top of hers with force. Caught off guard, she slipped and fell off the podium.

"Dammmmn itttttt." She landed in the pit of foam blocks, glaring up at Jaxon, who was grinning his ass off. Losing sucked on a normal basis. Losing to him sucked worse.

She punched one of the foam blocks and struggled to sit up. It was like trying to climb out of a pit of marshmallows. Great. Now Jaxon would see her flailing around like a fish out of water. She needed something solid to grab on to. Twisting toward the edge of the pit, she reached for the wall.

Pain, razor sharp, bit into her thigh, making her cry out. *What the hell is that?* She held her breath and tried not to move.

Jaxon appeared at the wall, ready to gloat. "What's wrong?"

"My leg." The sponges shifted, jerking the object sideways. Ripping, wrenching pain stole her breath. She gasped. "Something's...stabbing...me."

Chapter Five

"Stop the joust," Jaxon called out.

Clint and Ivy showed up at the side of the pit.

Jaxon pointed at Clint. "Find Mrs. Anderson."

"How can I help?" Ivy asked.

"Hold her shoulders so she won't sink farther into the pit." Jaxon removed the top layer of blocks. "We need to find out what's in here."

"It's going to be okay." Ivy hooked her arms under Bryn's shoulders. "I've got you."

Sweat slicked Bryn's skin. She took shallow breaths. Not that it helped. Her leg burned like it was coated in acid.

Jaxon removed more blocks, flinging them over his shoulder.

The blocks shifted, forcing the object deeper into her thigh. Bryn roared in pain. She clutched at Ivy. "Pull me out."

Mrs. Anderson arrived. "What's happened?"

"Something's stabbed her leg." Jaxon removed another block and reached the source of her injury. Covered in blood, the tip of a javelin protruded from Bryn's thigh.

"Oh God." *Don't throw up. Don't throw up. Don't throw up.* She focused on Mrs. Anderson's face and took shallow breaths.

"Quentin, get a medic." Mrs. Anderson took Bryn's hand. "We shouldn't move you. We don't know if the femoral artery has been cut."

"My arms are getting tired," Ivy whispered.

Jaxon climbed into the pit and placed one arm under Bryn's lower back and one under her knees. "I've got her weight."

Medic Williams ran into the room with Quentin by her side. She took one look at Bryn. "Don't move her. Let me treat her first." The medic placed a hand on Bryn's forehead.

The familiar sensation of warm honey flowed over her body. When the warmth reached her thigh, the comforting sensation morphed into a blowtorch. Gasping, she dug her nails into Jaxon's forearm. "It burns."

"I'm cauterizing the wound so we can pull the javelin out without too much blood loss," Medic Williams said. "You slept through this part the other times."

"Look at me, Bryn." Jaxon held her gaze. "You can do this."

"Almost done," Medic Williams said. "There. Lift her off."

"On three," Jaxon said. "One, two, three." In a swift motion, he pulled her upward and cradled her to his chest. She wrapped her arms around his neck and held on, ignoring the voice in her head screaming about what this meant. The extra campus security…the cameras…official recognition; none of it changed a thing. Someone was still coming after her and they wouldn't stop until she was dead.

"I'm going to set you down." Jaxon lowered her onto a

soft surface.

She opened her eyes. He'd placed her on one of the mats surrounding the ring where she'd danced with Vivian.

"Bryn, first I need to check and see if the blade was coated with toxins."

Oh God. She hadn't thought of that.

Warmth flowed over her body. "There's no dark mass or strange smell," Medic Williams said. "Rest now."

When the warmth filled the wound, the pain dulled. Her muscles relaxed. Limp with fatigue, she let go and drifted into nothingness.

• • •

Waking in the medical clinic felt all too familiar. Jaxon sitting by her side rather than Zavien—that was different. He'd changed back into his school clothes. His hair appeared damp from a recent shower. Fierce concentration showed on his face as he wrote in a notebook.

"What are you doing?" she asked.

"I'm trying to recall who was on the joust before you. Quentin surveyed the students. Not all of their stories coincide."

"I don't suppose someone left the javelin there by mistake?"

"If it had been anyone else on campus, maybe," Jaxon said. "Since it was you…"

"I know. Wishful thinking."

Jaxon tapped his pen on the page. "Someone had to place the broken javelin in the pit after the last opponent climbed out. While we were talking, someone would've had time to slip it in."

"How could they be sure I'd land on it?"

"The pit is eight feet across. Given that all dragons vary only a few inches in height, the placement wouldn't be hard. Putting it off center by two feet assured a seventy percent chance of bodily contact."

"What Green dragon worked out that formula?"

The grin on Jaxon's face told her she'd guessed correctly. "Mr. Stanton stopped by to see if he could be of any service. I believe he's trying to make up for when you were poisoned in his dorm."

"Did he have any theories?"

"A study of the weapon revealed an expired concealment charm. Whoever placed it in the pit did so while it was invisible."

Javelins weren't something you found lying around. "Where'd it come from?"

"There's a repository for damaged equipment in Mrs. Anderson's office. She said the javelin had been there for months. She didn't notice it missing."

"Sneaky bastards," Bryn muttered.

"Exactly. Now, who do you think is behind this?"

Seriously? "I don't know. A better question is why is this still happening? I mean Alec is dead. And my grandfather recognized me. Shouldn't that give me some sort of political immunity?"

He turned a page in the notebook. "You've been a topic of discussion in the Blue dorm. Not all of it has been positive."

Great. "Let me guess. My grandfather's money doesn't make up for the fact that my father is a Red."

"You're learning. In our Clan, wealth and power count a great deal. Your grandparents have both. You have unusual powers, which fascinate some and repulse others. Most don't believe you'll be allowed to marry. Some think you'd make an interesting mistress."

"That's freaking fantastic," Bryn bit out. "Could you please explain to your dorm mates that I don't need anyone to take care of me and I'm not interested in that sort of arrangement?"

He raised one eyebrow. "Perhaps you should create a flier. I could post it in the first-floor lounge."

"Smart-ass. You do understand how wrong the system is, don't you?"

He didn't respond.

"What do you think your mother is doing when your father is off with another woman?"

"I thought she was unaware." He shifted in his chair. "Knowing otherwise makes me…uncomfortable."

"Uncomfortable. That's it? Shouldn't you be mad at your father?"

He reached to rub his temples. "Technically, he's not doing anything wrong."

"Really?" He couldn't actually believe that. "What about the wives, do they have affairs?"

"Of course not," he snapped.

The irritation in his voice spurred her on. "Are you sure? How do you know?"

Frost shot from his nose.

"I'm not trying to piss you off. It's an honest question. How do you know the affairs are one-sided?"

"You're talking about my mother." Jaxon's tone was arctic.

"Calm down. I'm talking about your social circle, not your mom in particular. How do you know those women are content to be by themselves? How do you know they aren't sleeping with their gardeners out of spite?"

"This is an interesting conversation." Clint walked into

the room, carrying Bryn's book bag.

Jaxon stood. "Thank God you're here. Bryn is trying to give me an aneurysm."

"She does make a valid point," Ivy said.

Jaxon glared at Bryn. "Our gardener is a seventy-year-old female. If I have nightmares, I'm going to call you and describe them in detail."

She felt bad, but not bad enough to let the topic drop. "Feel free to share my theory with your friends. Maybe they'll be faithful to their wives."

Jaxon exited the room, muttering to himself.

"We thought you might want this back." Clint passed Bryn her book bag.

"Thanks."

"How's your leg?" Ivy asked.

"Better now that there's no longer a sharp metal thing jabbing through it."

"Makes sense," Clint said. "Next inquiry, where's Zavien?"

Good question. "I haven't seen him since he left the gym. He said something about running errands at lunch."

About ten minutes later, Zavien bolted through the door. "Are you all right?'

Good. He's worried. "I'm recovering."

"Tell me everything." He sat in the chair Jaxon had occupied.

She launched into the story, leaving out Jaxon's taunts about being the other woman. When she mentioned the blond's role in helping her, Zavien frowned.

"How do you know he wasn't distracting you to give someone time to plant the javelin?"

"He didn't hurt me, he helped me." *Wait a minute. When had Jaxon become one of the good guys?*

Chapter Six

After a quick checkup, Medic Williams released Bryn with a slip excusing her from classes for the rest of the day. Zavien escorted her across campus while Clint and Ivy returned to class. Bryn's leg was stiff, but thanks to the healing power of Quintessence, would be good as new by tomorrow night.

The disgusting sweat-soaked gym clothes had to go. When she reached her room, she made a beeline for the shower.

Clean and dressed, she emerged from her bedroom to find Zavien brooding on the couch. Did he have any insight on who had planted the javelin?

She sat next to him. "What are you thinking?"

"It's not important."

Not the answer she expected. She tried a different tactic. "What errands did you run today?"

"Nola needed to do some shopping in Dragon's Bluff."

He'd ditched her for Nola. Again. Knowing she was being

irrational didn't stop the words from flying out of her mouth. "Did you have fun shopping with Nola while someone tried to turn me into a shish kebab?"

"I've told you before that she's a friend." Zavien reached for her hand.

Not good enough. "When she shows up, you run to her rescue."

"I've come to your rescue on more than one occasion."

He was right. Damn it. "I don't like sharing you. She needs to find her own hero."

Zavien leaned in and pressed his lips against hers. This seemed to be his standard move when he didn't want to talk. She should be mad, but the distraction technique worked. She wrapped her arms around his neck and pulled him closer. Electricity thrummed through her veins.

When he pulled away from her, she sighed.

He kissed her forehead. "This is something I don't share with Nola. I may let her cry on my shoulder, and I might go shopping with her, but I have no desire to kiss her until she melts against me."

"I don't melt."

One corner of his mouth turned up. He brushed her hair aside and skimmed his mouth down her neck until he reached the sensitive skin by her collarbone.

Liquid heat flooded her body. She clamped her lips together to keep from moaning. When he applied his teeth to the area she gave up all pretenses and growled deep in her throat. She felt and heard Zavien chuckle against her skin.

"Maybe I melt a little."

His chest puffed out with pride.

She stuck her tongue out at him.

"That's very mature."

The phone rang, cutting off further comment. She picked up the receiver.

"Is Zavien there?" Smoke shot from Bryn's nostrils. "Just a moment, Nola." She glared at Zavien while he took the phone.

His end of the conversation consisted of yes and no answers. *Is he hiding something from me?* When the conversation ended, Zavien reclaimed his seat on the couch.

Bryn wasn't ready to get all cuddly with him again. "What was that about?"

"She's inventorying the decorations for the fall dance, and there were a few items she couldn't locate."

Jaxon's taunts about the dance came back to her. "You're still taking me to the dance, aren't you?"

"Of course. We'll go with Clint and Ivy. It'll be fun."

She relaxed, leaning against him. Her stomach growled.

"You could never be a ninja." Zavien poked her belly. "Your stomach would give you away."

She batted his hand away. "I'm still recovering from an injury, so I need all the calories I can get. Feed me."

"Want to go to the dining hall?"

"I'd rather not face the masses. Can you pick up something from the café downstairs?"

"I'll be back in ten minutes." He kissed her on the forehead and walked out the door.

Twenty minutes later, Bryn paced the living room. What was taking so long?

Her phone rang. She answered.

"Don't be mad," Zavien said.

"You've obviously done something you know will piss me off or you wouldn't say that."

"Nola found me and insisted I help design new decorations for the dance."

Bryn growled into the phone.

"Be reasonable," Zavien said.

"You ditched me for her again. You were supposed to bring me food."

"I ordered food for you. They were supposed to deliver it to your room."

"They didn't." She slammed the phone down while he argued his case.

Cursing, she exited her room and set out for the café on the first floor, where the cook had no recollection of Zavien placing an order. She bought three submarine sandwiches and a large soda. Back in her room, she ate and fantasized about setting Nola's hair on fire.

Chapter Seven

Over the next few days, Bryn found it harder and harder to contain her jealousy. No matter how irrational it was, she hated that Zavien jumped whenever Nola called. During class, when her mind wandered, she daydreamed about sneaking into Nola's room in the middle of the night and shaving her pretty Barbie head bald.

Zavien appeared at lunch and gave her pie or cookies as part of his extended apology for being a jerk when they'd first met. Whenever they were alone together, he swore Nola was a friend. She so wanted to believe him.

Thursday morning in Elemental Science, Bryn found a yellow mum on her desk. It wasn't just her. Every student had a small potted plant on their desk and a small cup of dirt beside it.

"Are we planting flowers today?" Clint asked.

"Today," Mr. Stanton said from behind his desk, "we are working on using your emissaries as tools. In small doses, you can funnel Quintessence from one thing to another. Observe." He produced a small twister of air in his right hand and directed it toward the fern on his desk. Before their eyes, the twister of air grew while the fern shriveled into a brown husk. Then he directed the twister to the cup of dirt on his desk. A green shoot burst forth from the dirt and grew into a stem with leaves.

Bryn had seen him do this trick before when he'd sucked the life force from a fern and used the Quintessence to change the color of a bird's feathers. Still, it was impressive.

"You should all produce an emissary and use it to draw on the power of your plant. Feel your life force drawing on the plant's life force."

"Makes me feel bad for the plant," Ivy muttered to Clint.

"Maybe you can resuscitate it afterward," Clint said.

Bryn focused and produced a small fireball in her right hand. She held her hand above the mum and concentrated on drawing energy from it. A strange tickling sensation made her palm itch as the mum shriveled and died and her fireball grew. She held the enhanced fireball over the cup of dirt and focused on sending energy down into the soil. *Poof*. Her fireball doubled in size, startling her. *Crap*.

A strange chemical smell filled the air.

Clint's Styrofoam cup had melted on his desk. "This is not as easy as it looks."

Ivy held a ball of lightning in her left hand. With her right hand, she shot tiny sparks into the soil. After a few shocks, a green shoot poked from the soil. "I think I'm doing it."

Maybe Ivy had the right idea. Bryn held her fireball in one hand and focused on sending Quintessence into the cup with the other. The fireball in her hand shrank as the green stem shot out of the dirt. "Good idea, Ivy."

"As some of you have noticed, it's not easy to control how much life force you send to the seed. You can use the two-handed method like Ivy until you achieve better control."

"He should have told us that in the first place." Clint zapped the small pile of dirt on his desk with miniature lightning bolts. The seed popped open and sent out a gnarled leaf.

"That's just sad," Ivy scooped up the malformed plant and tucked its roots into her cup of dirt. "It's okay, little guy." She directed half a dozen sparks into the cup. "I'll take care of you." Both plants in Ivy's cup grew a few inches.

Mr. Stanton came and stood by Ivy's desk. "You seem to be a natural. There are artists who specialize in creating gardens and topiaries. You might want to consider looking into that as a career."

Ivy blushed. Clint's chest puffed out with pride. "That's my girlfriend. The plant whisperer."

· · ·

That night at Stagecraft, Bryn rolled primer onto a set. Rhianna helped, but she wasn't smiling.

"Is something wrong?" Bryn asked.

Rhianna set the roller down. "Rumors are circulating about you and Jaxon."

Bryn snorted. "You can't believe Jaxon and I are involved."

"His behavior toward you has changed."

If she could explain how she'd saved Jaxon's life, this would be so much easier. Sticking to the official version of her time away from school tied her hands. She went with the party line. "We learned to tolerate each other when we went before the Directorate."

"Where did your book bag come from?" Rhianna asked.

That was easier to explain. "It was a gift from Lillith. She bought a similar bag for Jaxon because she liked it so much."

"Why would his mother buy you a gift?"

Crap. Maybe this wasn't so easy.

Jaxon showed up at that moment, so she tossed the ball to his court. "Rhianna asked why your mother bought me a book bag. I don't really know why. Do you?"

Maintaining his cool composure, he ran his hand through his hair. "Either she likes to shop and has a generous nature, or she felt sorry for Bryn because her book bag was subpar."

Bryn flipped him off.

"What? You asked for an explanation. I gave you two. Pick the one you like most."

Rhianna frowned but didn't ask any more questions.

"Those rumors you've been listening to have no basis in truth." Jaxon's tone was dismissive. "I said I'd be discreet. Seeing Bryn would not be discreet. It would be a nightmare for all involved and would more than likely lead to death and dismemberment."

Bryn would've yelled at him, but he spoke the truth.

Rhianna gave a small smile. "I suppose you're right. It's easier to imagine you hacking away at each other with swords rather than being romantically involved."

"Exactly." Jaxon reached for the blond girl's hand.

Rhianna laced her fingers through his. "I think I'm done for the evening. Walk me to my room?"

They walked off together.

Bryn continued painting her section of the set and

allowed her mind to drift. What had Jaxon meant when he said he'd promised to be discreet?

Were he and Rhianna seeing other people? More than likely, he was seeing other people and she was putting up with it.

Asshat.

A hand waved in front of her face. Startled, she jerked backward.

Zavien stood next to her. "I was beginning to think you were having an out-of-body experience."

"Sorry. Lost in thought."

"Care to share?" he asked.

"Nope."

"Finish up and we'll walk back together."

That would be nice, but she'd bet he wouldn't hold her hand. And that bothered her. A lot. After she cleaned up, they exited the building and emerged in the cool night air. Did he put his arm around her shoulders? Of course not. Time to think about something else.

"What color tuxedo are you wearing to the dance?"

"Basic black."

"It would be cool if you could find a bow tie to match my dress."

He snorted. "Colored bow ties are ridiculous. Basic black is classic."

"Clint is wearing a scarlet bow tie to match Ivy's dress."

"He's still in the infatuation stage. A year from now he'll wear a black bow tie."

Wait a minute. She was infatuated with Zavien. Apparently he didn't feel the same. And that sucked.

"What's wrong?" he asked.

Everything, but she couldn't say that. If she opened her mouth right now, all her angst would come flying out. That would be bad. She needed to get away from him. She increased her pace to put some distance between them.

He matched her stride and grabbed her arm. "Tell me what's wrong."

Her eyes grew hot. Damn it. Why did tears have to come with anger? They made her feel weak. "Not here."

His hand fell away from her arm and they walked in silence. When they reached her dorm room, she took a deep breath and tried to find a way to voice her concern without sounding whiny.

"Remember what you said about Clint and the matching bow tie?"

He nodded.

"How do you feel about me?"

"You know how I feel." He leaned in to kiss her.

Whoa. Not this time. She backed up a step. "I need words. If you're not infatuated, then how do you feel?"

Zavien ran his hand down his face. "I chose my words poorly. Clint and his feelings toward Ivy are different from what's happening between us."

Wrong answer. "Why?"

He took her hand in his. "It's different because we started on an even playing field. We met, there was an attraction, and we acted on it. Clint has been chasing Ivy for years. He finally caught her and he'd probably wear a gorilla suit to the dance if she asked."

Her shoulders relaxed. "It's not that you don't care about me, it's that you still have a mind of your own."

"Exactly." He pulled her close and kissed the tip of her

nose. "Better?"

"Yes."

"Good." His lips brushed across hers. She blocked out all doubt about his feelings and enjoyed the kiss.

He maneuvered backward toward the couch. She hoped he remembered to avoid the coffee table. The backward motion stopped and they bumped noses.

"Coffee table?" she asked.

"And I was being so smooth."

She chuckled and walked around the table to reach the couch.

"Pretend that never happened," he said.

"Right. I'll sit here, far away from the treacherous coffee table, and you can kiss me."

"Good plan."

She laughed against his mouth. He retaliated by tickling her ribs. Laughing, she batted his hands away. He pulled her close and kissed her. For the moment, all was right with her world. She vowed to ignore any nagging doubts about his feelings and enjoy what they had.

. . .

Saturday was a strange day. Females from every Clan were working themselves into a frenzy about the dance. When she walked into the dining hall for lunch, a girl she'd never met stopped her.

"Which nail polish do you like best?" the girl asked.

All ten of the girl's nails were painted different colors. "What color is your dress?"

"It's lilac."

Bryn pointed at the girl's index finger, which was painted a dark plum. "I like that one."

The girl rushed off and shoved her hands in front of someone else. In the buffet line, a redheaded female touched Bryn's red, blond, and black striped hair. "Did you do this yourself?"

Time to lie. "No." She piled ravioli on her plate. "I had it done at a salon."

"I don't have time to go to a salon," the girl said. "You're no help at all."

"Sorry." Had everyone gone psycho? It's not like the girls' dates hadn't seen them day in and day out all semester.

After picking two types of pie, Bryn wound her way to their regular table where Clint and Ivy were already sitting. "Have strangers been asking your opinions on their hair and nail polish?"

Ivy nodded. "They need more confidence in their appearance."

Bryn pointed at Ivy's short black hair, which stuck out in all directions. "Not everyone can pull off your hairstyle."

"True." Ivy reached up and ruffled her hair, making it look wilder. "Yesterday in history class two Blue females were debating how to wear their hair. I said they should wear it the way they normally do. You would've thought I suggested they run naked across campus."

Zavien pulled out the chair next to Bryn and joined them. "Who's running naked across campus?"

"Bryn is," Clint responded with a serious face.

Zavien looked at her with raised eyebrows.

"What? I thought you'd be okay with it since it's a political protest against the Directorate."

Clint and Ivy laughed.

"Funny. Very funny." Zavien shook his head.

Bryn gave a dramatic sigh. "I suppose I'll have to settle for attending the dance with a man in a black bow tie."

"They have copper ties at the dress shop," Ivy said.

"Don't go there," Bryn said. "Getting him to agree to take me was hard enough. He can wear a zebra-striped tie if he wants."

"Why don't we meet at Bryn's room before the dance?" Zavien said.

"Works for me." The ravioli on Bryn's fork fell and landed on her blouse.

"Maybe you shouldn't eat at the dance," Zavien said.

Chapter Eight

Zavien was due to meet her in ten minutes. Bryn examined her reflection in the full-length mirror. Her dress rocked. The copper material skimmed across her curves in front and dipped below her waist in back.

Knock knock. Her heart fluttered as she darted into the living room and opened the door.

What. The. Hell?

Bryn blinked. The picture in front of her didn't change. Clint tugged at his bow tie while Ivy bit her lip. Both of her friends seemed nervous. The reason for their discomfort was obvious.

Zavien stood there wearing a classic black tuxedo. He could've been the poster boy for "how to look hot in a tux." The only item out of place was his pink bow tie. A pink bow tie in the exact same shade as Nola's dress. The dress Nola was wearing as she stood next to him.

What was Nola doing here? Why did Zavien bring her

on their date? The matching bow tie couldn't mean Nola was his date. Zavien wouldn't do that to her.

Nola reached for Zavien's hand and smiled at Bryn. "Are we early?"

Afraid of what might come out of her mouth, Bryn shook her head no, and stepped aside to allow the two couples to enter.

No need to panic. There could be a rational reason why he'd brought Nola along. *Right, and the Easter Bunny is real.*

Fire roared in her chest. With effort, she tamped it down. Zavien deserved a chance to explain before she blasted him into a charcoal briquette.

"Bryn, can you cut the tag out of my dress?" Ivy asked. "It's bothering me."

"Sure." She followed Ivy into the bedroom and closed the door.

"Sorry. I would've called to warn you, but there wasn't time." Ivy spoke rapid-fire.

"Why would he bring her? He said he was taking me." Smoke shot from Bryn's nostrils.

"What were his exact words?"

"He said we'd go as a group with you and Clint. He never mentioned Nola."

"Odd wording." Ivy frowned. "I wonder if he planned it this way all along."

"If he did, he's dead." Bryn stalked back into the living room.

Clint's eyes lit up when Ivy entered the room. Zavien didn't bother to look up from the conversation he was having with Nola.

"Zavien, can I speak to you?"

He gave her a casual smile. "Let's talk on the way. I don't want to be late."

Too damn bad. "I'm sorry. This can't wait."

Nola patted Zavien's knee. "We have time."

Bryn headed back to the bedroom with Zavien in tow. She slammed the door and then spoke through clenched teeth. "What's going on?"

"I told you we'd go as a group."

A volcano erupted in her stomach. Sparks shot from her nostrils. "You tricked me."

"I misled you." His tone bordered on condescending. "If I'd suggested you attend with Nola and me, you would've said no."

"Hell yes, I would've said no. Now I'm the pathetic tag-along."

He loosened his tie.

"Nice pink tie, by the way. Very masculine."

"Nola gave it to me tonight. I couldn't think of a polite way to say no."

She poked him hard in the chest. "You don't have a problem telling me no."

He grabbed her hand and rubbed circles on her palm with his thumb. "This isn't as bad as it seems. Nola likes to circulate. I planned on asking you to dance. We can still spend time together."

Like that was the same thing. She jerked her hand away. "Forget it. I'm not going."

"Think about the consequences of your actions. If you don't go, Ivy won't go."

Damn it. He was probably right.

"Fine. I'll go but it would be in your best interest to stay away from me." She flung the bedroom door open and called out. "Why don't we fly from my terrace?"

Knowing her friends would follow, Bryn shifted on the

terrace and flew to the theater building. An orchestral waltz floated through the air. Below her, couples stood in groups waiting for friends or chatting. Bryn circled once around the building, hoping the joy of flight would temper the bitter disappointment of Zavien's betrayal. No such luck. She still wanted to fry the bastard.

Clint and Ivy waited on the theater building steps. Bryn landed, shuffled her feet to maintain balance, shifted, and then followed her friends into the ballroom. Six-foot trees sculpted from copper and bronze metal lined the walls. Some branches were covered in red and yellow leaves. Others held candles. The marble floor reflected the glow of the candles, creating a romantic twilight effect. It was freaking perfect.

Zavien and Nola glided onto the dance floor.

Bryn gritted her teeth.

"What did Zavien say?" Clint asked.

"When he told me we'd go as a group, I thought he meant the four of us. He apparently had planned it this way all along."

"Jerk," Ivy muttered.

"I'd be happy to dance a few songs with you," Clint said.

"Thanks. I don't feel much like dancing. I think I'll check out the food and then disappear to my room."

"We could all go back to your room and order pizza," Ivy said.

Bryn hugged her. "You're a good friend. You've been looking forward to this dance forever. I want you to have fun." A new song started. "Clint, that's your cue."

Clint pulled Ivy onto the dance floor. Bryn stepped into the shadows and watched. All the dancers were matched up by Clan. The couples seemed like mirrored reflections of each other. Golden-skinned blond males danced with golden-skinned blond females. Dark-haired males with dark-haired females. Something in her gut twisted. No matter what she did, she'd never fit in.

Out of the corner of her eye, she saw Nola in Zavien's arms. They appeared like the perfect couple. More than likely, they were. Averting her gaze, she made her way to the nearest door and stepped outside onto the terrace. Leaning against the railing, she inhaled the sweet scent of roses from the garden below.

Footsteps sounded on the flagstones behind her. "Look who we have here."

Fan-freaking-tastic. "Hello, Jaxon."

He came to lean on the railing beside her. "I thought Zavien was taking you to the dance."

"You were right. He lied to me." She turned to face him. "Does that make you happy?"

"A few weeks ago it would've made me happy. Now I feel sorry for you."

Pity from Jaxon. Just what she needed. "If you didn't come to gloat, why are you here?"

"Something about Alec's attack is still bothering me. How—"

"You mean besides the fact that he planned to kill you?"

"Yes, besides that minor detail. How did he know the layout of your grandfather's estate?"

Good question. "I don't know. Are blueprints kept on file somewhere?"

"Probably. My theory is someone gave him the blueprints."

"Who would do that?"

"I don't know. Think about it. See what you come up with." With that parting command, he left.

Now what should she do? It was a nice night. Maybe she'd hide out here until she could sneak off without anyone noticing. And maybe she'd fly to Nola's room, and burn all her pretty flowing dresses. And then she'd fly to Zavien's room and shred his research paper. She knew where the first fifty pages were. They'd make a nice pile of confetti.

"Bryn, I thought I saw you come in." Miss Enid joined her by the railing. "Why are you hiding out here?"

Back to crappy reality. "Have you seen Zavien?"

"No. I thought he'd be with you."

"That makes two of us." Bryn gave a bitter laugh. "The joke's on me. He's with his real date."

"I'm sorry."

"Me, too." She glanced over her shoulder at the dancing couples and shook her head. She couldn't stay here. "Maybe I'll fly to Dragon's Bluff and eat my weight in lemon ice."

Miss Enid's eyes lit up. "Wait here. I know something that will make you smile."

The woman had good intentions. Nothing could make her happy right now. Bryn turned back to the railing and fantasized about running away, just flying off to another country where no one could ever find her.

"Could you only afford half a dress?" a familiar masculine voice asked.

She turned to find her knight, Valmont, striding toward her. He looked handsome in dark pants and a pale blue shirt.

"What are you doing here?"

"Fonzoli's donated lemon ice to the dance. I dropped by to supervise the setup." He glanced toward the dance floor. "I hear Zavien preaches change but is afraid to rock the boat." He stepped closer and took her hand. "His loss is my gain. Would you care to dance?"

Valmont was fun, he enjoyed annoying Zavien, and his single dimple made her smile.

"I'd love to."

He led her onto the dance floor and pulled her close. One of his hands came to rest on her waist. "Did I mention how much I like your dress?"

The devilish gleam in his eye made her chuckle.

"You laugh now. Later, you will be wooed by my charm." He wiggled his eyebrows for effect and she laughed harder.

The song ended. Bryn noticed Valmont's posture stiffen as the next song started. He pulled her against the tide of dancers and then they moved with the flow again.

"What was that about?"

"The spiky-haired nitwit was approaching. If he wants to apologize, you should make him work for it."

"He should've told me the truth… Finding Nola on my doorstep was humiliating."

"He showed up with her at your door?" Valmont's eyes narrowed.

"What are you plotting?"

"If I tell you, you'll be an accomplice."

"Why don't we forget about him for tonight and have fun? Unless there's someplace you have to be." A guy like Valmont must have a girl waiting for him somewhere.

"I'm your knight." His tone held complete sincerity. "My place is by your side for as long as you need me."

Her throat became tight. "Thank you. I'd love it if you'd stay and help me regain my dignity."

"Am I allowed to torment him?"

She didn't even have to think about it. "Hell, yes."

Chapter Nine

Valmont pulled her close and placed her hand on his chest. He rested his free hand on her lower back, where his fingers brushed bare skin. Her heartbeat kicked up a notch. No two ways about it. Her knight was hot. Dark hair and blue eyes were a killer combination. He smelled like soap and sunshine.

"You could forget about Zavien." His voice came close to her ear.

Was he joking? He'd never acted interested in her before. Maybe that's because she'd been with Zavien. Raising her head, she met his gaze.

"Just a thought," he said.

The song ended.

Zavien approached with a wary expression on his face. "Bryn, would you like to dance?"

"Bite me."

"I believe that's a no." Valmont delivered this news in a

cheery tone. "Shall we?" He moved her along to the music while she imagined Zavien's hair going up in flames.

"Tell me what you're thinking," Valmont whispered in her ear.

"I wish my life were simpler."

"Simple is boring."

They swayed in silence until the song ended. Clint and Ivy joined them.

"Are you okay?" Ivy asked.

"I'm managing. Valmont is helping."

"Why don't we get something to drink?" Clint pointed across the room to the tables decorated with ice sculptures shaped like trees, which Nola and Zavien had designed, which made her want to shoot a fireball at them. But setting the room on fire might ruin the evening for the other students.

After grabbing glasses of punch, the foursome wound their way back outside to the terrace.

"It's a perfect night for flying," Bryn said.

"It is," Valmont agreed.

"You don't have wings," Clint said.

Ivy elbowed him.

"What? I wasn't being rude. I'm pretty sure he knows he's not a dragon."

"I fly planes." Valmont grinned at Bryn. "You should come with me some time."

"Bryn, can we talk?" a feminine voice asked.

It couldn't be. Bryn turned around, praying she was wrong. No such luck. "What do you want, Nola?"

"Perhaps it's best if we move away from the others? It's personal." She wandered farther down the terrace.

Bryn shoved her glass of punch at Valmont and joined

Nola.

"This is awkward." Nola's cheeks flushed. "I noticed how upset you were when I showed up with Zavien. When I asked him what the problem was, he said you might have misunderstood his invitation."

That lying, evil rat bastard.

Nola clasped her hands in front of her chest. "You thought he asked you to attend the dance as his date, didn't you?"

At least she didn't have to lie. "I did."

"What you feel for him is a crush. It will pass."

It certainly would. Right after she cremated the son of a bitch. "Did Zavien send you?"

"No, he thinks I'm circulating." Nola placed her hand on Bryn's shoulder. "Zavien has gone out of his way to make sure you're taken care of. You shouldn't mistake his kindness for anything but friendship."

A small growl escaped her throat. "Maybe you should ask Zavien how *kind* he's been to me."

Nola shook her head. "You're young. He's a flirt. I can assure you any interest perceived was your imagination. I best get back. I wouldn't want him to know I spoke with you."

Oh, he was going to hear about this conversation. How dare he explain away her anger as a stupid crush? Flames roared up her throat and her breath came faster. Valmont appeared at her side, holding her drink.

"Thought you might need this. But if you'd rather torch Zavien, I'm okay with that."

She reached for his free hand. "I will literally rip the head off the next person who says his name."

"That would create a terrible mess." He grinned. "But if that's what you want, I'm in."

The punishment for decapitating a student was probably more severe than detention, so she pushed the idea aside. "Better not."

"Let's move on to option two. Do you want to dance?"

"I was about to ask you the same question," Jaxon said. Rhianna stood by his side.

"Why would you ask me to dance?" She pointed at Rhianna. "Are you punishing him for something?"

Rhianna grinned. "As painful as it may be for you, I'd appreciate it if you'd dance with Jaxon. I'm tired of people dropping hints about your matching book bags."

"I don't understand."

"She wants us to dance together to show we're not involved," Jaxon said. "It's her theory that people who carry on affairs in private don't appear together in public."

Hello, irony.

Valmont placed an arm around Bryn's shoulders. "Introduce me to your friends."

"Sorry. Rhianna and Jaxon, this is Valmont, my knight."

Jaxon's eyebrows went up a fraction of an inch. Rhianna pressed her lips together like she was trying not to talk.

"You're dying to ask questions, aren't you?" Bryn chuckled.

Rhianna's cheeks colored. "It wouldn't be polite."

"If we're switching partners, it's my duty to entertain you," Valmont said. "We can dance, and you can ask me anything you like."

Rhianna grinned like a child with a new toy. "I have so many questions."

Valmont led his new partner to the dance floor.

"I don't like him," Jaxon said.

Where had she heard that before? Valmont inspired jealousy wherever he went.

Jaxon placed his hand on Bryn's elbow. "Ready?"

"Can I refuse?"

Rhianna's laughter drifted across the room.

"Let's get this over with before Rhianna starts mooning over your knight."

Bryn bit her lip to keep from laughing. Couples stared as Jaxon placed his hand on her waist and began moving her around the dance floor.

"This might actually work," she said.

"It's ridiculous for people to think we'd be together," he said. "I've no idea how they could be so delusional."

She'd had just about enough rejection for one night. "It's not like I have a third eye."

"You lack basic social skills."

"I do not."

"I've seen you eat."

Since she couldn't argue the point, she stepped on his foot.

He glared at her.

"Sorry, that was an accident." The smile on her face probably damaged her credibility. The smile vanished when Zavien and Nola came into her field of vision.

"Must you let every emotion show on your face?"

"Do you want me to step on your foot again?"

Jaxon sighed. "I'm about to give you sincere advice. Pay attention. Zavien is amusing himself with you. He will end up with Nola. The odds of the Directorate matching your lineage with anyone else's are slim. Stick with your knight."

It wasn't that simple. She couldn't just turn off her feelings for Zavien. Eyes hot with unshed tears, she took a deep breath and focused on not crying.

"Tell me the story of this Valmont guy," Jaxon said.

"Zavien and I were arguing, and he followed me into Fonzoli's where Valmont works. I told the jerk he couldn't sit with me. Valmont was standing in the aisle. When Zavien tried to push by him, Valmont refused to let him pass. He could tell I was upset and he protected me from a perceived threat, which activated the dormant spell all the knights' descendants in Dragon's Bluff carry in their blood and... He became my knight."

"Perhaps Zavien's behavior then should have been a clue."

She managed to step on his feet three more times before the song ended. Valmont showed up with a glowing Rhianna in tow. Jaxon took one look at his girlfriend and scowled at the knight.

"I see what you mean," Valmont stage whispered.

Rhianna giggled.

Jaxon aimed his scowl at Bryn. "All the aggravation in my life leads back to you."

"Then my secret plot is working." She grabbed Valmont's hand. "Can we go to Fonzoli's? I'm starving."

"I have a better idea. I'll cook dinner for you."

"I want a knight," Rhianna said.

"No," Jaxon said, like he was king of the world.

"I know how to get one," Rhianna shot back.

Jaxon gave Valmont a look of loathing. "You don't need a knight. We'll have a chef." He took his girlfriend's hand and led her toward the buffet.

"That was fun." Valmont tugged her toward the exit. "Come on. My car is out back."

Bryn spotted Clint and pointed to Valmont and then pointed out the door. Clint gave a thumbs-up that he understood.

The drive to Dragon's Bluff was exhilarating. Riding in Valmont's cherry-red convertible with the top down and the wind rushing through her hair reminded her of flying. "This car is awesome."

"I figured the car should match the owner."

"Who can argue with that logic?" They sped past the main road into town. The winding side street he chose took them up into the bluffs.

"Where are we going?"

"Did you think I lived at Fonzoli's?"

"No." *Maybe.*

"My grandparents used to live in an apartment above the restaurant before they built their house next door. I lived there for a while with my cousin. The short commute to work was great, but I wanted to be on my own. I bought an old cabin, moved in, and I've been restoring it."

The word "cabin" brought to mind creepy images of animal heads hanging on walls. "How rustic is it?" He had better mention the words "indoor plumbing."

"Wait and see. You're going to love it."

Chapter Ten

Valmont pulled into a gravel driveway that led to a log cabin so old, the wood was bleached with age. Vines climbed up the walls, making it difficult to distinguish the house from surrounding vegetation, as if it had grown from the forest.

Warm yellow light flickered on and glowed from the front windows.

"Do you have a roommate?"

"No. Watch this."

He shifted into reverse and backed the car up, and the lights in the house blinked off. When he pulled forward again, they came on.

"I had a sensor installed in the driveway to turn the lights on."

"Cool."

Once inside, Bryn was relieved to discover there wasn't a single animal head in sight. Thank God. A pair of swords hung on one wall. They weren't dusty antiques. Light glinted off their edges, like they'd just been cleaned.

A beat-up gray couch sat in the living room. On the other side of a half wall, a small table and chairs, which resembled the furniture at Fonzoli's, sat in the kitchen.

"Bringing your work home with you?" Bryn pointed at the table and chairs.

"I may have borrowed those from the back room." He grinned.

She walked farther into the space and saw a two-burner stove set in a black countertop. A black refrigerator, a sink, and oak cabinets completed the kitchen.

"This is great. Did you do all the work yourself?"

"My grandfather helped. He likes to hide here when my grandma has friends over to play canasta." He opened the refrigerator. "Is chicken all right?"

"Sure."

He pulled out a tray of chicken breasts and set them on the counter.

"What can I do to help?" she asked.

"I'm a messy cook." Valmont retrieved a bottle of olive oil from the cabinet. "You can help, but we should find something else for you to wear."

He disappeared down a hallway and came back with a navy sweatshirt and gray sweatpants. "You won't win any fashion contests, but these should work."

Bryn took the clothes and headed down the hall in search of the bathroom. The first door led to a bedroom. The second door revealed a minuscule bathroom—yay for indoor plumbing—but changing in the bedroom would be easier.

Valmont's sweatshirt came down to midthigh. The pants were huge. She cinched in the drawstring waist. The too-long pants had elastic leg openings, so the extra material pooled around her calves and ankles like leg warmers.

Good thing she wasn't trying to impress anyone.

The wooden floor was cool under her bare feet as she padded back into the kitchen, where Valmont had more ingredients gathered on the countertop.

"What can I do?"

He pointed at a pile of tomatoes and zucchini. "Dice those."

She grabbed the knife he'd laid out for her and chopped. *Splat*. One of the tomatoes fought back, squirting juice and seeds on the front of her shirt.

"You were right. Good thing I changed."

He winked. "I'm always right."

She rolled her eyes and chopped the rest of the vegetables, passing them over to Valmont. He added them to the pan of chicken sautéing in olive oil, along with a healthy dose of Italian spices.

"Is that all there is to it?" she asked.

"This by itself would be okay." He reached for a garlic bulb, broke it apart, and then put three cloves through a press. "Now it will be fabulous."

The scent of garlic and Italian spices filled the air.

It smelled fabulous, but their breath afterward wouldn't. It's not like they'd be kissing or anything. Because that was ridiculous. Well, not ridiculous, but she had enough crap to figure out about Zavien without complicating the situation by kissing the smoking-hot knight who was staring at her like he knew exactly what she was thinking.

Her face heated. "Sorry. Did you say something?"

"I asked you to grab the plates. They're in the cabinet

above the sink."

"Sure." She brought two plates to him. He arranged the chicken and vegetables in a pattern, making it attractive. "Before you say it, I know I'm not at work, but if something is worth doing, it's worth doing right."

"That sounds like a knightly thing to say." She took her plate to the table.

He joined her. "More of a family motto."

She realized she didn't know much about him. "Has your family always owned Fonzoli's?"

"The restaurant has been handed down through generations. My grandfather is the head chef, while my father manages the business end of things. Since I graduated from high school last spring, I've been working as a waiter while my grandfather trains me to make all the family recipes. When he retires, I'll become head chef."

It seemed weird to have your whole life planned out at eighteen. Then again, that seemed to be a common theme among dragon society. "Did you ever want to do anything else?"

"No." He grinned. "I love everything about food because it makes people happy. Thank God, my sister loves the business side of the operation and she'll replace my dad one day when he retires. My oldest brother wanted nothing to do with it. He works at the airfield, training pilots. What about your family?"

"My parents own a yoga and martial arts studio."

"Is it true they live as humans?"

Bryn nodded. "I had no idea they were dragons. Flames shooting out of my mouth clued me in something was up."

Valmont laughed and shook his head. "That had to be

a shock."

"A huge shock…but now I can't imagine not living as a dragon. I want to become a medic and use my Quintessence, which I can't do back in the human world."

"Good to know you're staying. I was worried you planned to leave. I don't want to sound like a stalker, but since that dormant spell was activated, I can't imagine not having you within arm's reach, so to speak. The thought of you leaving and going someplace else makes me twitchy."

She was happy to be right where she was, thank you very much, which brought another question to mind. "Not to be rude, but how can you afford your own house when you just graduated from high school?"

"There are two answers to that question. One, these cabins were originally part of the Directorate security system. Before everyone had phones, the knight's descendants who lived here kept watch over the area and reported any threats. Since they are no longer needed in that sense, the Directorate donated the cabins to the town. Any knight's descendant who wants one signs a contract agreeing to care for the property, and we pay a nominal fee. Two: the Directorate pays all the townspeople a livable wage for keeping their secret and promising to fight by their side, if necessary."

"So that's how you can afford a house and an awesome car."

Valmont nodded. "And every job in Dragon's Bluff is well paid. So it's not like on television where lawyers act superior to waiters. Of course, the Blues act superior to everyone, but I think that's genetic."

Bryn chuckled. "I think you're right about that."

Being with Valmont was so easy. She could relax around

him. He flirted enough to make her feel attractive, but not uncomfortable. If he were a dragon, he'd be the perfect guy. Then again, Zavien was a dragon and he was the perfect jackass.

After dinner she noticed a major appliance was missing from the kitchen. "You don't have a dishwasher."

"Yes. I do." He pointed at her. "You can be the dishwasher or the dish drier, your choice."

"Ha ha. I'll dry."

There wasn't much to clean up. As she finished drying the last dish, she yawned.

Valmont checked his watch. "We better head back, it's almost curfew."

Facing reality didn't sound like fun. "Can I hide here?"

Valmont grabbed her hand. "I'll always be here for you."

She wanted to stomp her feet like a toddler. "I'm happy here. If I go back there, I'll have to deal with that jerk."

"If you don't want to deal with the idiot, don't talk to him. Maybe you two will work this out. Maybe you won't. Whatever happens, don't give in too easily or he'll think he can behave this way again."

He wasn't judging her, and she appreciated that. "Thanks. I'll go change."

"Wear my clothes back to school." He gave a cocky grin. "That'll annoy the hell out of him."

She laughed. "Good idea."

"I can only take the high road for so long."

The ride back to campus ended too soon. Valmont insisted on walking her to the dorm, where he held the door open for her.

"Thanks for tonight," she said.

"I live to serve. Call if you need me."

Once in her room, she hung up her dress and kicked off the sweatpants. The sweatshirt was nice and warm…maybe she'd sleep in it. The little voice in her head that called her pathetic could shut the hell up. Valmont's warm fuzzy sweatshirt reminded her someone cared.

She flopped backward onto her bed. Did Zavien care? How the hell would she know? He'd never said the words. How many opportunities had she given him to tell her how he felt? Dozens.

The sadness and depression she'd been holding at bay came rolling in like the tide. Her throat burned and her eyes grew hot. Crying seemed inevitable. Maybe it was best to get it over with.

A knock on the door interrupted her scheduled breakdown. Should she answer it? It could be Clint and Ivy. She padded barefoot into the front room.

"Who is it?"

"It's me," Zavien said. "We need to talk."

Best not to get her hopes up. She took a deep breath and blew it out, wrangling her tear ducts into submission. Crying in front of him wasn't an option. Trying to appear composed, she opened the door and allowed him to enter.

A muscle in his jaw twitched as he studied her outfit. "Nice sweatshirt."

"Nice bow tie." If he wanted a fight, she was happy to oblige.

"You left the dance. Where did you go?" he asked.

"To Valmont's cabin."

His eyes narrowed. "You shouldn't have left. There are still people out there who want to hurt you."

"You hurt me." And now he needed to apologize.

"Aren't you blowing this out of proportion?"

Fire flared in her gut. "You lied to me. What's crazy is that Jaxon told me the truth. He said you wouldn't take me to the dance. How in the hell did he end up being the honest one?"

"I didn't lie," Zavien said. "I never said I'd take you as my date."

"Fine. You're a rat bastard who insinuated you'd take me as your date. Is that more accurate?"

"I told you many times I couldn't take you. You said you'd ask Valmont. I couldn't stand the thought of you with him, so I twisted the truth."

Bryn held out the hem of her sweatshirt. "Look how tonight ended. If you'd been honest with me I'd be happy to see you right now. Instead, I want to rip your head off."

"You don't mean that." He reached out to touch her cheek.

She smacked his hand away. "Yes I do. You told Nola I misunderstood your invitation. You said it was a stupid crush. She went on and on about how I'd misinterpreted your actions."

Zavien went very still. "What did you tell her?"

"Oh my God." Realization punched her in the gut so hard she doubled over. "You're more worried about her finding out about us than you are about my feelings."

He took a step toward her. "That's not true."

"Then what is the truth?"

"Bryn, this is…it's complicated."

No. It wasn't complicated. It was painfully, heart-wrenchingly, agonizingly simple. "You chose her over me—

again."

"You're being ridiculous." He chuckled. "It was a stupid dance."

Her life, everything she believed about him and how he felt about her, was falling apart, and he was laughing. Sadness transformed into heated anger. "Get out."

"You're making too much of this. You don't really want me to leave." His trademark lopsided grin appeared. He was so sure of himself. So sure that she'd come running because he snapped his fingers.

Damn it, Jaxon was right. Zavien was amusing himself. She'd been an idiot.

"Get. Out." White-hot rage flowed through her body. Sparks shot from her nostrils with every breath. She growled and pointed at the door. "Out, now. Before I lose control and burn you to a crisp."

Zavien backed up a step. Healthy fear finally seemed to set in. He yanked open the door and retreated into the hall. "We'll talk tomorrow."

"Come within ten feet of me tomorrow and you'll regret it."

Slamming the door, she leaned against it. How could she have been so wrong about him? Her chest heaved as a volcano roared to life inside her. He'd made her look like a fool, just like her grandmother had warned her he would. The flames built inside her and begged to be released. She focused on cold and snow and lemon ice. Nothing worked. She stumbled through her bedroom and opened the window. Roaring in rage, she blasted the concrete terrace with flames over and over again, until there was nothing left. Numb, she went to bed.

Chapter Eleven

At breakfast Monday morning, Bryn scanned the dining hall, waiting to see if the cowardly asshat would make an appearance. Ivy and Clint seemed to sense she didn't want to talk. They chatted about the weather and homework. She was required to contribute little to the conversation, which was fine with her.

Zavien approached the table carrying a tray.

As his hand touched the chair, Bryn growled. "Try to sit in that chair and you'll never be able to father children."

He paused.

She held up her butter knife. "I'm not joking."

"You need more time." He backed away and sat across the room.

Clint cleared his throat. "Note to self: never piss off Bryn."

She sank into her seat and sipped her coffee without tasting it. What would life without Zavien mean? She could buy her own desserts. Clint and Ivy would go with her to

Dragon's Bluff. It wouldn't be so bad.

Out of habit she reached to touch the dragon locket she normally wore. Her fingers scraped against bare skin. A momentary twinge of panic had her sitting up straighter. Then she remembered. It was under her bed somewhere, where she'd flung it. Still, the emptiness felt wrong.

In Elemental Science, she did her best to focus on Mr. Stanton's lecture. Her mind wouldn't stop replaying the painful loop. *Zavien's gone. Zavien's gone. He never cared.* Sparks shot from her nose. *Zavien's gone. Zavien's gone. I'm an idiot.* Flames shot from her nose. *Whoosh.* Her notebook went up in flames.

"Bryn," Mr. Stanton yelled.

"Sorry."

Snow hit her desk, drowning the fire. She turned to see who'd had her back. Jaxon frowned at her like she was a small child who'd misbehaved.

"Thanks." She ducked her head. This was what her life had been reduced to. Jaxon stepping in to save her. The rest of her classmates not so subtly scooted their desks away from her. None of them made eye contact, like they thought she'd snap at any moment.

Mr. Stanton kept her after class. "I know you're upset, but you must control your fire. I have to fill out a report on any student who can't manage their breath weapon. If your name shows up more than once a month, you're required to see a counselor. You don't want that."

He was trying to help. Since he knew of her relationship with Zavien, maybe he could offer some advice. "What's your opinion of Zavien's behavior?"

Mr. Stanton frowned. "I believe it was unwise of him to

act on his attraction. It's not fair to you. He should've known better."

Not the answer she'd wanted or expected. Unable to speak, she nodded and left.

Miss Enid found her sitting at her usual table during second hour. "I'd ask how you are, but I think that's obvious."

"Zavien didn't apologize. He accused me of over-reacting." She took a shaky breath. "Mr. Stanton said it was wrong for Zavien to start seeing me."

The librarian frowned. "Old men forget what young love is like."

"Young men are idiots."

"Young men aren't good at discussing their feelings."

Smoke drifted from Bryn's nostrils. "I told him how I felt about him. Not once did he say he cared about me."

"He does, but there is always the chance he doesn't feel as strongly as you do."

"My life sucks." Giving up, she laid her head on the table.

Miss Enid patted her shoulder. "Visit Valmont. He makes you smile."

How much trouble would she be in if she skipped the rest of her classes to track down Valmont? She'd probably end up on another list somewhere.

In Basic Movement, she wailed on a Slam Man, imagining the robot-like figure had spiky black hair.

Outside of Clint and Ivy, Jaxon was the only student brave enough to speak to her. He approached when she was stretching out on the mats.

"Why are you letting everyone see your pain? It's undignified."

"Why do you care?"

He shrugged. "I don't. I feel compelled to offer advice since you keep doing things wrong."

She growled at him. Smoke drifted from her mouth as she spoke. "Do you really think pissing me off right now is a good idea?"

"Zavien went to a lot of trouble to mislead you and keep your relationship a secret. Now everyone on campus knows something is going on between you two."

He was right. "I wonder if Nola will figure it out."

"Wait until Stagecraft tomorrow evening and see if she tries to drop a set on your head." Jaxon said.

"Death by crappy scenery. That would be a great way to go." She realized she felt better. "Thanks, Jaxon."

"For what?" He walked away.

The next morning, Zavien sat across the room with Black dragons she didn't know. She managed to keep her expression blank while she ate.

"You look sedated," Clint said. "You're scaring me."

"I'm trying to block everything out. If I set my notebook on fire again, I'll have to see a counselor."

Ivy sighed. "I wish there was something we could do."

In Elemental Science, Bryn managed to keep her fire under control. In Basic Movement she ran on a treadmill until her legs felt like dead weight.

That night in Stagecraft, Bryn painted the top of a set blue to represent the sky. Someone with actual artistic talent would add the forest later.

Rhianna worked next to her. "What happened between you and Zavien?"

Bryn frowned. How much should she share? Rhianna was nice, but they weren't close.

"He misled me about something and he hasn't apologized. He keeps telling me I'm wrong to be upset."

Rhianna dipped her roller in the blue paint. "If you're upset, then he should respect your feelings and do something to make you feel better, rather than telling you you're wrong."

Exactly. "Would you mind pointing that out to him? He doesn't see it that way."

Laughter drifted across the stage. Bryn's gaze shot up to see who was having such a good time. Zavien stood off to the side of the stage with a small group of students, including Nola.

Resentment welled up inside her. Why wouldn't Zavien be having a good time? He'd had friends before she'd come along. He didn't need her, and he probably wouldn't miss her. But she had had three friends and was now down to two.

She slammed her roller into the paint tray. "Can you clean up by yourself? I have to get out of here."

"Sure." Rhianna gave her a sad smile. "I'll tell Ivy you left."

Bryn fled the auditorium and ran down a side hall. She leaned against a wall with her eyes squeezed shut. She would not cry again. She'd cried enough over that jackass. Once her tear ducts were under control, she found the closest exit, shifted into dragon form, and took off into the night sky.

The cool evening air flowed around her body, washing away some of her anger. If she could stay up here for a while, maybe she'd be all right. Then again, she'd have to come down eventually. When she did, she'd need good company. Pumping her wings to gain speed, she aimed for Dragon's Bluff. Valmont would make her feel better. How would she find his cabin from the air? She circled the forested area where she thought his cabin stood. All of the greenery looked the same. Change in plans. Fly to Fonzoli's. If he wasn't working, they'd know how to reach him.

The street in front of the restaurant was empty. She shifted as soon as her claws touched cement and stumbled a few steps. The chilly evening air, which she'd enjoyed in dragon form, gave her goose bumps. Rubbing her arms, she hustled into the restaurant.

The hostess greeted her. "Table for one?"

"Is Valmont working?"

"Yes. Would you like to sit in his section?"

She wanted Valmont to skip out on work and distract her from her sucky life, but she'd take what she could get.

Seated at a table for two, it took ten seconds for Valmont to spot her. He slid into the chair across from her. "Everything all right?"

"No."

His eyebrows drew together. "Can I beat him up now?"

Valmont may have been a descendent of knights, blessed with superior strength and trained to fight dragons, but she wasn't sure he could take on Zavien.

"If I can't beat him up, you can't."

He undid the top few buttons of his work shirt. "Want to get out of here?"

"Yes."

Taking her hand, he pulled her back into the kitchen. "Grandpa, we're going to the cabin."

. . .

Since her last visit to the cabin, he'd added blue throw pillows to the couch. She pointed at them. "Those are new."

"My sister said the couch looked sad. She gave me the

pillows as a housewarming gift. If I keep having her over, I won't have to decorate."

Bryn pointed at the only other decorative item in the cabin. "Did she give you the swords?"

Valmont walked to the fireplace. He pulled down the two swords hanging above the mantel. "No. These are real broadswords. Everyone in Dragon's Bluff receives swords on their sixteenth birthday as a reminder of who we truly are. We train as a way to stay in shape and to keep our skills sharp." He wiggled his eyebrows.

Bryn groaned. "Was that an intentional pun?"

"Sorry, couldn't help myself."

Bryn accepted the sword he held out to her. It wasn't as heavy as she thought it would be. "Can you teach me how to use this?"

"Sure, let's go out back."

"Isn't it too dark?"

"Nope." They stepped out the back door into the twilight. Valmont flipped a switch, and lanterns hanging from the eaves of the house bathed the backyard in warm yellow light. It would have been beautiful except for the fir trees that resembled short telephone poles scattered about the yard. Most of the branches had been cut off, and they were only a bit taller than Valmont.

Bryn pointed at one of the oddities. "Is that some sort of knightly landscaping?"

"No. I want to clear this area to make room for a picnic table and a barbecue grill. Cutting down trees is great for sword practice."

He pointed toward a stump about ten feet away. "Sit over there and watch. You'll understand how knights can defend themselves."

Valmont swung at a branch five inches thick. He cut through the limb like it was made of cream cheese. Swinging the blade in a reverse arc, he sliced through another thick branch.

Maybe he could fight a dragon. "I'm impressed."

He smiled and waved her over. "We're going to focus on your form. Keep both hands on the pommel and swing in fluid figure eights. Do not bring the sword down and hit yourself in the leg."

Being careful, Bryn swung the sword in an awkward figure eight. After a few tries, the movement became more fluid.

"I'm doing it."

"You're ready to chop wood." Valmont stepped well out of range. "Try the smaller branches first."

She aimed at a two-inch branch and the sword passed right through. A six-inch branch met the same fate. *Cool.* Bringing her arm down with force, she sliced diagonally through the trunk of the tree. The top third fell to the pine needles below, stirring the woodsy scent.

Valmont whistled. "Very nice. I don't think I could manage that."

Bryn wiped sweat from her brow and struck a pose. "I'm a badass."

He laughed. "Yes, you are. Want something to drink?"

"Sure."

Back in the kitchen, he showed her the proper way to wipe down a sword. Then they sat at the kitchen table drinking iced tea. Valmont kept her amused with stories about his family.

"Your grandmother did not threaten your grandfather with a meat cleaver over a bottle of olive oil." Bryn laughed.

"Yes, she did." He grinned. "Never mess with an Italian woman's pantry. Things will turn ugly."

Time flew too quickly. Bryn frowned as she glanced at the clock. It was a quarter to nine. "I should go."

"Let me drive you." Valmont pulled the keys from his pocket.

"I can fly back," she said.

"You could. But then I'd worry about you." He stood. "Come on. It'll take less time if you don't argue."

Why am I arguing? If she could hold on to the happy feeling she had around Valmont, life would be so much better. On the ride back to the institute, she willed her good mood to continue. The warm feeling drained away as soon as she stepped foot on campus. Valmont walked her to her dorm with his arm around her shoulders.

When they were within ten feet of her door, she spotted Zavien coming down the sidewalk returning from Stagecraft.

Zavien stalked forward; a deep, rumbling growl came from his throat.

Valmont chuckled. "If seeing her with someone else upsets you, maybe you should've treated her better."

Bryn held her breath as she waited for him to respond. The scent of ozone filling the air meant Zavien was battling for control of his breath weapon—which for Black dragons was lightning. The fact that he was disturbed enough to become unstable meant he cared, right?

"Figure out your apology yet?" Bryn asked.

"What do you want me to say? You know how I feel about Valmont."

Flames banked in Bryn's chest. "I know you're jealous of him." Smoke drifted from her lips. "How do you feel about me?"

Chapter Twelve

"You know I—" Half a dozen students came around the corner of the building, and Zavien snapped his mouth shut.

Oh no he didn't. "What? Now you won't talk to me in public?"

Zavien met her gaze, turned away and entered the dorm.

He would not leave her hanging like this. Damn it. She lurched forward to grab his arm. Valmont's hand anchored her to the sidewalk. "You don't want to do that."

"Why not?"

"He needs to be the one chasing after you, not the other way around."

A low growl escaped her throat. Her knight made sense, but that didn't mean she had to like it.

· · ·

Over the next several days, Bryn caught fleeting glances of Zavien. Whenever she came near, he stormed in the other direction. To take her mind off the cowardly jackass, she decided to start on one of her papers for history class. She could write the papers about anything she wanted, so why not research the time before the Directorate took over? There had to be other hybrids back then. If the folktales she heard were true, the whole point of the arranged marriages was to force dragons to marry within Clans to keep certain powers from coming to light.

If there was even one hybrid who had married and had kids and their kids had kids, then there must be some hybrids still walking around somewhere. Right? According to the folktales she'd heard, Wraith Nightshade had been the most powerful hybrid. He had wielded some sort of mind control or super-charisma. Countless kingdoms had fallen to his charm or his sword. Eventually, his wife had betrayed him and his reign had ended. Why did she do that? If Wraith had been like Ferrin, that would explain it.

After spending several hours in the library, all she had was a bunch of theories and no proof. If there were any records that Wraith had truly existed, they must be kept behind locked doors.

· · ·

By Friday evening, Bryn's anger toward Zavien had transformed into a slow, boiling fury.

Armed with a plate piled high with chicken fingers and fries, she joined Clint and Ivy at their usual table in the dining hall.

Ivy snagged a french fry from her plate. "You look like a volcano ready to blow."

Fair description. "So far I've come up with six ways to kill Zavien and make it look like an accident."

Clint reached across the table and confiscated her butter knife. "Rather than commit murder, why don't you talk to him?"

He could keep the knife. At this point she could kill Zavien with her bare hands. "I've tried. The coward keeps running away."

"We could help you corner him somewhere," Ivy said.

"When you say corner him, it sounds like you're saying kidnap him and tie him to a chair," Clint said.

"Do you have a problem with that?" Ivy asked.

"No." Clint shook his head. "Just making sure we're all on the same page."

Valmont's advice echoed in her head. "Zavien should be the one chasing after me. What if he decides I'm too much trouble? What if he doesn't care enough to make the effort?"

Ivy reached across the table and squeezed Bryn's hand. "Then he's an idiot."

The ache that had taken up a permanent place in her chest throbbed for a moment. "I wish I could erase him from my head."

"Try thinking about something else," Clint said.

Right. Like it was that easy.

After dinner, back in her room, she searched for something to distract her from the sucky state of her love life. Jaxon's question from the dance popped into her mind. How had Alec known the layout of her grandparents' estate? Blueprints must be available somewhere. Either that or someone familiar with the layout had fed Alec information.

If Alec had murdered Jaxon, Lillith, and her, who would

benefit? Alec would achieve his revenge, but who else would profit from his actions? The Directorate would crack down on the entire dragon community. Some dragons would rebel. If the Directorate went too far, it might lead to mutiny or civil war.

The Black dragons who lived in the forest had little love for the Directorate. The Orange dragons believed their decrease in numbers was somehow the governing body's fault. Had the Directorate done something to keep the Orange Clan's population low? The sonic wave Octavius produced in class was impressive. If hundreds of Orange dragons worked together they could probably take out a building or an army.

This was a cheery line of thought. Maybe if she thought of it as a puzzle, she could figure something out. And since she was looking for blueprints, documents that she knew existed, this search should turn out better than her quest for hybrids. And she knew just who to ask for help.

• • •

The next afternoon, Miss Enid led Bryn down a hallway and into a small room lined with file cabinets. "Any building the Directorate approved for construction will be filed here under the owner's name."

Bryn flipped through the alphabetized folders. The folder with her grandparents' surname, Sinclair, was empty. "Is there supposed to be something in here?"

"That is disturbing." Miss Enid rifled through the surrounding files. "I don't know how this could've happened. Blueprints are not to be removed from the library. They're lent out on an hourly basis but must be kept in the building."

"Is there any way to find out who looked at the blueprints last?"

"It should be listed in my computer." Miss Enid exited the room and walked to the front desk. She pulled up a file on her computer and frowned. "The last person to look at the blueprints was Nola."

Nola? Would Nola have given Alec the blueprints? He was her brother. Would she have known of her brother's plans? Did she want Bryn out of the picture so she could have Zavien to herself?

"She knows better than to remove them." The older woman frowned in disapproval.

"What do you mean?"

"Nola studies blueprints all the time. It helps her design the sets for Stagecraft."

That poked a nice big hole in her conspiracy theory. "How long has Nola been doing that?"

Miss Enid's fingers were a blur on the keyboard. "Let's see. Here it is. She started about two years ago."

Too bad. Nola in prison would make reconciling with Zavien much easier. Evil as the idea was, it made her smile. Back to the mystery at hand.

"Is there anyone who could take the blueprints from the library without checking them out?"

Miss Enid pursed her lips. "I suppose a Directorate member could."

Fabulous. Someone on the Directorate might have given Alec the blueprints. Ferrin's name came to mind first. As much as she despised him, he'd never do anything to endanger Jaxon.

"Thanks for your help."

"I'll let you know if the file turns up."

Okay. Now what? Bryn scanned the area for a friendly, or at least not hostile, face. Rhianna studied at one of the long wooden rectangular tables. She'd probably know where Jaxon was. Why should she try to figure this puzzle out on her own?

Rhianna glanced up at Bryn's approach and smiled. "Hello."

"Hi. I wanted to ask Jaxon a question about the Directorate. Is he here with you?"

Rhianna pointed to the midnight-blue book bag hanging on the back of the chair next to her. "He went to look for a book."

"Know which way he went?" Searching for someone in the monstrous library could take all night, and there was no guarantee of success.

"Up to the second floor, I believe."

Which meant he could be anywhere. "I'll ask him another time."

"Thank you," Rhianna said.

"For what?"

"You came to me rather than searching him out on your own. We just quashed those strange rumors about you two, and I'd hate for them to start again."

"How can people be so stupid?" Bryn plopped down in Jaxon's seat. "I'd never sneak around with Jaxon for two reasons: one, because I like you, and two, because he annoys the hell out of me on a regular basis."

Rhianna covered her mouth with her hand as she giggled. "I envy your ability to say what you're feeling."

"You should try it sometime."

"This is a frightening development." Jaxon came toward

them carrying a thick leather-bound book.

"Afraid I'll be a bad influence?" Bryn asked.

"Yes. If you could remove yourself from my seat and stay away from my future wife, I'd appreciate it."

Bryn leaned forward, placing her elbows on the table. "Now I'll have to become best friends with Rhianna to spite you."

Jaxon waved her away from his chair. "Go corrupt someone else. We have homework to finish."

"She wanted to ask you a question." Rhianna stood. "I'll visit with Miss Enid and give you two a moment."

"You can stay," Bryn said.

"Thank you, but I'd like people to witness that I trust you together." Rhianna walked toward Miss Enid's desk.

Bryn told him about the missing blueprints and Nola's habit of checking them out. "Patrons aren't allowed to take blueprints out of the library. Someone did and there's no record of the transaction. Miss Enid believes only a Directorate member could pull that off."

Jaxon frowned. "The Directorate is…political. Another Blue might try to outmaneuver my father in a business deal, but a plot to kill my father's family must've come from outside the Clan."

"That doesn't narrow the field much." There had to be a clue they were missing. "If Alec had succeeded, if he'd killed us, who would've benefited?"

Jaxon leaned against the table and stared off into space. "I'm not sure. Alec was probably in league with the group that's been burning down Directorate members' houses for the past six months."

"We still don't know who the arsonists are." Time to

drop the problem in his lap. "Why don't you think about it and let me know if you come up with anything."

• • •

Dry leaves crunched under Bryn's feet on the walk back to her dorm. Normally she liked fall. Tonight, the dried brown leaves littering the ground seemed discarded and sad. The overcast autumn sky didn't improve her mood. Happy couples walking by holding hands made her heart ache.

It was Saturday. What was she supposed to do tonight? Ivy and Clint had invited her to join them in Dragon's Bluff for dinner. As great as they were about having her around as a third wheel, they deserved some time alone, so she had declined.

A chilly breeze brushed against her neck. Goose bumps broke out on her arms. She needed a scarf. Maybe she should learn how to knit and make her own scarf. Since she was destined to be alone, she might as well start a solitary hobby.

Stupid Zavien.

She kicked a rock and watched it skip across the sidewalk. Her future would consist of knitting and adopting a bunch of cats. Life with cats wouldn't be bad. Maybe she'd knit clothes for the cats and start an upscale cat boutique. Women like Lillith would pay big bucks to outfit their pets in the latest fashion. There, she had a plan.

The sidewalk pitched.

What the hell? Heart racing, Bryn fought to maintain her footing. Zigzag cracks appeared in the cement. A fissure ripped open beneath her feet. Acting on instinct, she shifted to dragon form and took to the air.

Where she'd stood moments before, there was now a gaping trench. What was going on?

A rumbling roar filled the air. Grassy areas rolled and heaved. Trees toppled or sank into fissures. Sidewalks were swallowed whole. Anyone on the ground shifted and took flight.

Was this an earthquake? The other students seemed as confused as she was.

A siren wailed. The piercing noise grated on her frazzled nerves. Did they think that noise helped? Flapping her wings, she flew higher to escape the sound.

From this vantage point, she noticed something strange. None of the buildings were affected. How was that possible? No, wait. There, below her, several fissures raced toward the history building like someone was directing them.

Blue dragons converged in the sky and flocked toward the history building. They positioned themselves in front of the building and exhaled frozen flames at the ground, driving spears of ice deep into the earth, like they were trying to create a dam of ice. What good would that do?

The oncoming fissures closed in and hit the subterranean ice wall with a resounding crack. Shards of ice and dirt shot high into the sky, but the fissures slowed and then stopped a dozen feet from the building.

And then there was silence. Bryn checked the ground. No new fissures appeared. The sidewalks stopped their strange gyrations. Was it over?

Time to find someone with answers. Bryn settled on the ground, where she shifted and searched for a familiar face. Jaxon's friend Quentin stood near the history building.

"Was that an earthquake?"

He shook his head.

"Then what was it?"

Eyes narrowed, he scanned the sky. "It was an attack."

The only dragons capable of attacking in this manner were the Orange Clan, but that made no sense. Neither Octavius nor Vivian could be involved in this. "How did you know what would stop it?"

"We're taught how to defend ourselves against the other Clans." Quentin frowned. "I imagined fighting another male over some offense. I never expected anything like this."

Bryn surveyed the destruction. It looked like someone had taken a giant knife and slashed gaping raw-edged wounds into the grounds. Clumps of dirt and grass were flung all about. Trees lay broken and twisted, or submerged in rifts. Some of the sidewalks disappeared completely. Others were broken into rubble.

It made no sense.

"Why would someone do this?" Bryn asked. "I know the radical Revisionists hate the Directorate, but I thought they were all Black dragons, unless they started recruiting outside their Clan."

Quentin flicked a bit of dirt off his sleeve. "Whoever did this purposely attacked on a weekend evening. Imagine what would've happened if they'd attacked in the middle of a school day. Hundreds of students would've been on the grounds. Many would've been injured. This was a warning. "

Bryn hugged her arms across her chest to ward off a sudden chill. "I don't understand. Why attack the campus?"

"The institute stands for everything the Directorate believes in."

"That means none of us is safe," Bryn said.

Quentin didn't respond.

Chapter Thirteen

All students were required to return to their dormitories and sign in. Teachers were dispatched to Dragon's Bluff to round up anyone off campus. Bryn sat in the first-floor lounge chewing her fingernails and waiting for Clint and Ivy to walk through the door. When her friends crossed the threshold, she ran to hug them.

"I was so worried about you guys."

Ivy sniffled. "We didn't know anything had happened. Mr. Stanton showed up at Fonzoli's and announced that all students were to return to campus and sign in at their dorms." She blinked rapidly. "When I saw…"

Clint pulled her into a hug and kissed the top of her head. "It's all right. We're safe. The Directorate will investigate and figure out what to do."

Clint speaking favorably about the Directorate? That was new. "Do you really trust them to protect you?"

He shoved his hand back through his hair. "The Directorate

is kind of like your parents. You may try to sneak around and break some of their rules, but when things turn ugly you know they'll take care of you."

The way Clint kept his arm wrapped around Ivy sent a pang of envy through Bryn's chest. If Zavien and she were still together, would he put his arms around her? Wait a minute. Where was he?

"Have you seen Zavien?"

Clint and Ivy scanned the room.

"Maybe he was at the theater building." Ivy said.

Bryn pushed her way through the crowd to the front door where people were checking in.

"Has Zavien Blackthorn signed in?"

The woman taking signatures flipped through the pages on her clipboard. "He hasn't. Don't worry. We haven't rounded up everyone from Dragon's Bluff."

Bryn checked her watch. "When should I start to worry?"

"Anyone who isn't accounted for in thirty minutes will be declared missing. Security is searching the campus for anyone who might've fallen in a rift."

She shuddered. What a horrible way to die. Now what? With no other options, she went to sit with Clint and Ivy. Every time the door opened, she checked for spiked black hair.

"If he dies before he has a chance to apologize, I'm going to be pissed."

Ivy patted her arm. "I'm sure he's fine. He'll live to apologize and everything will go back to the way it's supposed to be."

Time crawled. Bryn stared at the clock, willing the hands to move. It felt like she was in a slow-motion sequence from a movie. People around her talked while the sound of her own heart drummed in her ears.

When twenty-five minutes passed, she shot to her feet. "I can't take this anymore." Without a clear idea of what to do, she approached the front door.

The lady with the clipboard gave a sympathetic grin. "Worried about your friend?"

"Yes." Bryn's throat felt tight. "Can I go check with the medics?"

"Sorry, I have orders to keep everyone here."

Bryn growled in frustration. "I have to do something."

The woman looked Bryn up and down. "If I tell you to stay here, you're going to sneak out, aren't you?"

"Yes."

"That's what I thought." She pulled a sheet of paper from her clipboard. "This is a list of students who are unaccounted for. Take it to the medics and find out how many of them are patients and how many are still missing."

Bryn exited the building, shifted, and flew toward the science building where the medics were housed. No sign of Zavien outside. In the medical center, she found Medic Williams and her colleagues treating more than a dozen injured students.

"Bryn, we're spread thin. I could use your help for the minor cuts and scrapes."

"I can do that, but first, I'm supposed to ask if any of these students are being treated."

Medic Williams took the list. "Five of these students are here." With quick efficiency, she checked off the appropriate names. Zavien wasn't among them.

He'd been by her side during most of her trips to the clinic. She'd thought for sure he'd be here. "So, no sign of

Zavien?"

"Don't worry. The professors enlisted some of the older students to search the rifts. I'm sure Zavien is helping." She pointed toward a group of students who sat on a bench in the hallway. "The minor injuries are over there. Ask if they mind you healing them, since you aren't licensed yet. If they have issues, tell them it's a forty-five-minute wait."

Bryn approached a red-haired girl cradling her right arm.

"Medic Williams asked me to help. I've had some training. I can cure minor cuts."

"This doesn't feel minor, but do what you can." The girl extended her arm, which was covered in a blood-soaked towel.

Bryn lifted the cloth and discovered a six-inch laceration on the girl's forearm. She closed her eyes and visualized her life force as a ball of white fire in her chest. Opening her eyes, she pictured the fire flowing down her right arm into her fingertips. As she traced her fingers back and forth over the girl's wound, she imagined the skin undamaged. After a few minutes, the edges of the cut began to come together. The skin closed until all that was left was a pink line.

"Better?" Bryn asked.

The girl's shoulders relaxed. "Much better. Thank you."

"Can you drop this at the Black dragons' dorm on your way out?"

The girl took the paper and left.

A Blue male sat next in line. He held a cloth to a wound on his forehead. Before she could speak, he said, "I'll wait for the real medic."

"Are you sure? It's going to be a while before anyone else can help you."

"Positive."

Jerk. "Your choice. Anyone else want my help?"

A Green male pointed to the girl leaning against his shoulder. "Help her."

The dark-complected girl held out her arms, which were covered in superficial cuts and abrasions. Healing the minor damage was easy. Doing this felt right. This was what she wanted to do. Feeling sure about one thing in her life was a relief.

She healed three other students and sent them on their way, then she checked with the stubborn Blue. "Change your mind yet?"

"No." He scooted away from her like she was about to force herself on him.

"Stop being an ass and let her heal you," a familiar voice ordered.

Jaxon came to stand by her side. His clothes were uncharacteristically wrinkled and mud-splotched, but she didn't see any blood.

"Are you injured?" she asked.

"No. I was sent to check on our missing students." He pointed at the Blue with the head injury. "Heal him so I can take him back to the dorm."

Bryn turned to find the Blue still wearing the expression of disgust, but he dropped the cloth from his forehead. Jaxon must outrank him in some way. The cut was shallow, and she healed it with ease.

Before Jaxon could leave, she said, "Have you seen Zavien?"

The blond gave her a look that was part pity and part scorn.

"Don't judge me," she snapped. "Just answer the question."

"I haven't seen him." Jaxon raised a brow. "Do you think he's asking anyone where you are?"

"Jerk."

He feigned confusion. "Are you referring to me, or Zavien?"

At this point, she didn't know. Making her way over to Medic Williams, Bryn asked, "Heard anything about Zavien?"

The woman didn't look away from the wound she was closing. "No."

"I'm going to find him."

No one tried to stop her. Bryn left the science building and came up short when faced with the devastation to the campus grounds. She closed her eyes and inhaled, hoping to catch Zavien's scent. All she detected was the sharp smell of green grass and the loamy scent of freshly turned earth.

Vivian and Octavius worked to repair the damage. Half a dozen adult Orange dragons labored alongside them.

Where had the Orange dragons come from? Had Octavius contacted his Clan and asked for aid? Mr. Stanton seemed to be supervising the cleanup. Curious, she walked out to meet him.

"Be careful, Bryn. The ground is literally shifting under our feet."

A loud rumble reverberated through the soles of her shoes, and part of a nearby fissure closed.

"Who do you think did this?" she asked.

"We don't know. Octavius and Vivian came to me minutes after the attack. We contacted their Clan and they offered aid."

"The Directorate will blame them," Bryn said.

"At first they will. We'll find out who the real culprits are after an investigation."

"Have you seen Zavien?"

"He helped us look for stragglers earlier. I haven't seen him in a while." Mr. Stanton grabbed Bryn's arm as the ground beneath their feet groaned. "You'd best relocate. This isn't a precise science."

Okay. So he'd seen Zavien, and Zavien hadn't asked about her. Frowning, she stalked toward her dorm.

Inside the student lounge, she spotted Clint and Ivy sitting at the small café. Ivy waved Bryn over, but her expression wasn't happy.

She pulled out a chair and joined her friends. "What's up?"

"I have news you aren't going to like." Ivy patted Bryn's arm, like she was trying to console her. "Zavien came back twenty minutes ago. He saw us, but he didn't stop to visit."

The ugly truth crashed down on her. "He didn't talk to you, which means he didn't bother to ask about me. How could I have been so wrong about him?"

Neither of her friends answered.

"With all these rifts, it wouldn't be difficult to hide his body," Ivy said.

Clint gaped at his girlfriend. "Don't encourage Bryn, or we'll spend our weekends visiting her in jail."

Chapter Fourteen

Suddenly, all the students in the café and lounge started talking at once. Bryn glanced toward the door to see what caused the disturbance.

Valmont strode into the dorm like he belonged there. Light glinted off the broadsword strapped to his thigh. Was it the weapon or his presence in the Black dragons' dorm that caused everyone's interest?

When he reached Bryn, he sat and grabbed her hand. "I came to make sure you were all right."

Damn it. Why couldn't Zavien act like this? "I'm fine." Better, now that he was here.

He studied her. "Fine never means fine. What's up?"

She shrugged.

"If you don't want to talk about it, I'll respect your wishes." He turned to Clint. "What did the spiky-haired nitwit do now?"

"Hey," Bryn shouted.

"You don't have to talk about him if you don't want to," Valmont said, "but I still want to know. Clint?"

"After the attack, Zavien didn't bother to check on us or her," Clint said.

The knight squeezed Bryn's hand. "Sorry about that."

"Why are you sorry?"

"It's my job to protect you. Short of running the idiot through with a sword, I can't think of a way to help."

"There are all those nice deep rifts out there," Ivy muttered. "It would be a shame for them to go to waste."

Valmont raised a brow.

Bryn chuckled. "Ivy volunteered to help throw Zavien's body in a rift."

Valmont tapped his chin like he was thinking. "That's not a bad idea."

"Am I the only sane individual left at this table?" Clint asked.

"If Clint won't let us kill Zavien, I guess we need another plan for the evening," Bryn said.

"All three of you could come out to my cabin," Valmont said.

"I doubt we'll be allowed to leave campus." Bryn's stomach growled. Channeling Quintessence must burn calories like crazy. Eating with friends would be nice. "We could order pizza and eat in my room."

A serious expression crossed Valmont's face. "First, I have a question you must answer with utmost certainty. What is your stance on anchovies?"

She made a yuck face. "Anchovies are disgusting."

"Correct answer."

Twenty minutes later, Bryn sat next to Valmont on her

couch while Clint and Ivy sprawled out on the floor. The situation seemed surreal. It was like someone removed Zavien from a photo and Photoshopped Valmont in his place to restore balance to the picture.

"Why are you frowning?" her knight asked.

Bryn grabbed another slice of pizza while she fabricated a response, because he didn't need to know how strange her brain truly was. "I was wondering who's behind the attack."

"Who has the most to gain from upsetting the Directorate?" Valmont asked.

"Someone who wants to start a revolution," Bryn answered. "I'm not sure who that would be."

Ivy rearranged the pepperoni on her pizza in a symmetrical pattern. "The radical Revisionist dragons in the forest talked about affecting change. I'm pretty sure that's code for 'let's start a revolution.'"

Pizza sauce dribbled down Bryn's chin. She wiped it off with a napkin. "I'm not sure how effective the regular Revisionists' petitions are, but war seems extreme."

"There isn't much middle ground with the Directorate. It's their way or no way," Valmont said. "Maybe war is inevitable."

"That's not a cheery thought." Ivy moved closer to Clint and leaned against him. He kissed her forehead.

Envy shot through Bryn. Zavien should've been here to comfort her.

Warm fingertips brushed against her cheek. "You're not alone," Valmont reminded her. He leaned in and whispered, "I can be whatever you want me to be."

Well, that offer was wide-open to interpretation. He seemed to be waiting for an answer she didn't have. "Thank you. But right now I'm a mess."

He grinned and passed her another napkin. "That statement is true in more ways than one."

She wiped her face. "Better?"

He nodded.

"I'm exhausted." Ivy yawned.

"Stress wears you out." Clint eyed the pizza boxes. "One more piece and then we'll go."

After Clint and Ivy left, Valmont helped clean the mess from dinner. "Need anything else before I go?"

"No. Thanks for coming to check on me."

"If I could, I'd camp outside your door just to make sure you were safe." He sighed. "Knowing you could've been hurt eats away at me. And yes, I know it sounds like I'm obsessed, but since I became your knight, you're my number one focus. I tried asking around for advice, but there hasn't been a citizen of Dragon's Bluff who's stepped forth to protect a dragon in more than a century."

"Why did you intervene that day?"

He clasped her right hand between his and stared at her like she was the most beautiful creature in the world. "There's something about you, something special, something worth fighting for."

Wow. If there ever was a perfect thing for a guy to say, that was it. "Valmont, I—"

"I know you're working through some issues right now." He reached out and tucked a piece of hair behind her ear. "I'll be here when you've figured everything out. Then we can continue this conversation." He leaned in and kissed her on the cheek before he left.

. . .

In Elemental Science on Monday morning, Bryn found a new seating chart on the board. The assignments seemed random. She was in the third row between Quentin and Ivy.

"Notice who's missing?" Quentin asked.

After a quick check of the room, she realized the Orange dragons weren't present.

Mr. Stanton stood and cleared his throat. "After recent events on campus, the Directorate decided to investigate the Orange Clan. Octavius and Vivian will rejoin us once their innocence has been determined."

"They helped fix the rifts," Bryn said. "Why would the Directorate think they did it?"

"I believe they are going with the duck theory," Mr. Stanton replied.

Bryn waited for the punch line. There wasn't one. "You lost me."

"The duck theory is simple. If it looks like a duck and walks like a duck, then it's probably a duck." Mr. Stanton frowned. "The Directorate is investigating the most obvious suspects first."

How would they know which Orange dragons attacked the campus? It's not like ripping open the ground left fingerprints.

"Students, I encourage you not to jump to conclusions. Just because there are a few rogue Orange dragons, that doesn't mean the entire Clan or your classmates are involved."

A low rumble broke out in the class as students growled or whispered.

"I assure you the Directorate has everything under control. New security measures have been taken. It's my duty to inform you that you'll no longer be able to visit

Dragon's Bluff during the week. On the weekends you'll be allowed to leave the institute after signing out at the gate."

More grumbling filled the class as students objected to the restriction.

"I've seated you in an alternating pattern. Given the current climate it seems advisable for us to practice deflecting breath weapons. Pair up and then switch partners."

By the end of class, Bryn felt confident she could defend herself against another student. Fighting off an adult might be another story.

In Basic Movement, she spotted Jaxon and Quentin fighting with swords. "Will you guys come with me to see what they're doing?" Bryn asked Clint and Ivy.

"Sure." Ivy grabbed Clint's hand and pulled him along.

Jaxon and Quentin danced around each other searching for openings. Both moved fluidly and struck with precision. When Jaxon's sword connected with Quentin's shoulder, the two blonds stopped to catch their breath. Quentin handed his sword to Jaxon, nodded at Bryn and her friends and climbed out of the ring.

Jaxon offered the weapon to Bryn. "Want to give it try?"

She climbed into the ring and accepted the thin wooden sword. "I'm not sure what I'm supposed to do with this. Valmont's sword is bigger."

"No man wants to hear that," Clint called out.

Bryn snorted with laughter.

"You've no class at all," Jaxon said.

"Class is overrated." Bryn tested the weight of the sword. "Enlighten me with your superior knowledge."

"Your knight probably has a broadsword. It's an unsophisticated weapon meant for hacking away at the enemy."

Jaxon held out his sword. "This is a rapier. It's a more precise instrument used to stab the opponent."

Bryn waved the sword in a figure eight.

"No." Jaxon came to stand by her side. "Watch. You thrust and retreat. The object is to fatally wound your enemy before he stabs you."

His superior tone annoyed her. "Are you always this obnoxious when you play teacher?"

"Fine. You fight your way. I'll fight mine." He returned to his side of the ring. "First to three touches wins?"

Jaxon might beat her, but she wouldn't back down. "Agreed."

He came at her with a quick thrust. She swung her sword at his weapon to counter the attack. He closed in on her. She tried to block. He feinted left and then stabbed her right shoulder.

"Damn it."

He smiled.

She went on the attack and swung at his torso. He blocked her sword with ease and tapped her forearm.

Smoke shot from her nostrils.

Jaxon chuckled.

She narrowed her eyes and lunged at him. Her sword connected with his ribs, giving her a rush of joy.

He went on the attack. His sword was a blur as he stabbed at her. Pain in her ribs told her he'd connected again. She growled in frustration.

He laughed at her.

Aiming for his head, she swung the sword in a wide arc.

Surprised, he blocked the blow and ripped the sword from her hand. "It's over. You lost. Deal with it."

Bryn growled. She hated losing, especially to Jaxon.

. . .

By Friday night at Stagecraft, Bryn had lost patience with Zavien's duck-and-cover routine. How could she make him talk to her? Sneaking up on him, knocking him unconscious, and tying him to a chair with barbed wire might work. Maybe she'd give it a shot.

Rhianna stood in front of an expanse of canvas with a paintbrush and a can of gray paint.

"What's the assignment tonight?" Bryn asked.

"We're supposed to paint smog along the top." Rhianna demonstrated by painting large gray arcs on the canvas at various angles.

Bryn grabbed a paintbrush and lost herself in the mindless activity.

"Did you love him?" Rhianna asked.

Bryn's hand froze midarc. "Is it that obvious?"

"No. It took me a while to figure out. Love isn't common among Blues. That used to make me sad. Now I don't mind because it looks too painful."

Zavien's laugh drifted across the stage. Unable to stop herself, Bryn turned to locate him. He stood near the black wrought iron staircase, which led to the catwalk. When his gaze met hers, he scowled. She refused to look away. He turned from her and climbed the spiral steps.

"Go after him." Rhianna plucked the paintbrush from Bryn's hand.

"Valmont told me I should wait and make Zavien come to me."

"Has that approach yielded any results?"

"No. The coward runs away every time I come near. I spend my days plotting different ways to murder him."

Rhianna ducked her head. "When Jaxon is obnoxious I fantasize about hitting him with my book bag."

Bryn chuckled. "I've had similar fantasies."

"No matter how irritating Jaxon is, I know he'd be there for me if I needed him. Can you say the same of Zavien?"

Yes...no...she didn't know anymore. Maybe Rhianna was right. She groaned in frustration. "Fine. I'll do it." She'd climb up on the catwalk to talk to Zavien. At least there he couldn't run from her. "Wish me luck." She crossed the stage and ascended the staircase. The wrought iron steps were a blur under her feet. This was the right thing to do.

She cleared the stairs, stepped on the catwalk, and came face-to-face with the one person she didn't want to see. Every muscle in Bryn's body tensed as Nola blocked her path.

"Bryn, we need to talk."

"Wrong. You need to get out of my way."

"You're behaving like a child," Nola said.

"No." Smoke drifted from Bryn's lips. "I'm behaving like someone who was lied to."

"Zavien never lied to you." Nola's voice grew louder. "You misunderstood his invitation. You heard what you wanted to hear."

"If you keep lecturing me, I might tell you the truth. Then we'll see how self-righteous you are."

"What's going on?" Zavien crossed the catwalk and stood behind his future wife. He glared at Bryn like she was the one causing the problem.

"Your friend decided to lecture me about my behavior," Bryn bit out.

"You're acting like a spoiled brat," Nola said. "You were delusional to think he'd be interested in anything beyond friendship."

Flames roared in Bryn's chest. If Zavien didn't come to her defense, it was over. "Zavien, it's now or never. Tell her the truth, or I will."

He ran his hand down his face. "Bryn has a right to be upset. For a brief time, I behaved inappropriately."

His words slammed into her chest, knocking her back a step. She clutched the catwalk railing for support as her world turned upside down.

Nola rounded on him. "How could you?"

"She had a crush on me." He shrugged. "I was flattered."

Rage tightened her fists on the metal railings. "Stop it. Stop making it sound one-sided. You're the one who came to find me before you went shopping with Nola." She smiled at the dark-haired woman. "He stopped by to kiss me before he spent the afternoon with you."

Nola's lips went white with rage.

Zavien said nothing, so Bryn continued. "He pressed me against the wall and kissed me like his life depended on it. Does he kiss you like that?"

Nola's open palm swung at her face.

Bryn grabbed her forearm. "Try that again and I will knock you on your pretentious ass." For emphasis, she shoved Nola backward, right into Zavien's arms.

Not what she wanted to see. "Damn it, Zavien. How did you turn out to be such a disappointment?"

He stepped around Nola and spoke in a tight voice. "You don't understand—"

"You're right. I don't understand. One day you're

kissing me and talking about changing the law so we can be together, and the next day you cut me out of your life. What am I supposed to—"

The catwalk lurched, throwing her off balance.

"What was that?" Bryn looked up and down, trying to assess the threat.

A rough grinding sound filled the air as the entire building shifted. Brick ground against brick. Cables snapped and zinged through the air. The can lights crashed to the stage below. Students screamed. *Holy crap. Was the building under attack?*

Time to get off the catwalk. Bryn turned for the stairs. Her foot touched the top step. *Screech.* The stairs twisted, breaking away from the metal catwalk. There was nothing but air beneath her right foot.

A hand latched onto her arm and yanked hard. She stumbled backward. Zavien pulled her against his body and wrapped his arms around her like she was something precious he needed to protect. She twisted around and buried her face in his chest. His summer rainstorm scent brought tears to her eyes. She'd missed him so much.

A ripping sound filled the air. Sets suspended in the rafters broke loose and crashed down, missing them by inches. Nola screamed. Zavien squeezed Bryn tighter. He was protecting her, choosing her. If they didn't die, maybe life could go back to how it was before, the way it was supposed to be.

The catwalk bucked and pitched sideways, wrenching Bryn from Zavien's arms and launching both of them into the air.

Bryn shifted. Something lashed across her right wing

like a razor blade. Roaring in pain, she veered left, diving past the chaos on the stage and aiming for the seats. She landed in the second level. A quick shift and she tumbled to the floor.

Her heart thudded in her chest. Where was Zavien? Students clogged the aisles in dragon and human form. She climbed on a seat for a better view and spotted Nola and Zavien a few rows over. Crap. She needed him over here, not over there.

A metallic screech filled the air. Bryn whipped her head around to locate the noise. The catwalk crashed down, splintering the stage. Cables snapped and zinged through the air and more can lights fell.

Then, silence.

Dust and mortar drifted everywhere, creating a haze. A ringing sound filled Bryn's ears as her heart fought to return to a normal rhythm. Was it over?

"Everyone out here," Zavien yelled. "Check to see if your friends are present. We need to figure out who's missing."

Students made their way into the seats. Some limped. Most were bleeding. Now that she no longer feared for her life, a stinging pain shot up her right arm. She wiped the blood away, revealing several deep cuts. After taking a moment to center herself, she gathered her life force and healed the wounds.

Where were her friends? She spotted Clint holding Ivy on his lap. Bryn pushed through the crowd to reach them. "Is she okay?"

Clint nodded.

Jaxon appeared at Bryn's side. "Where's Rhianna?"

Bryn pointed at the stage where sets lay tossed about

like a fallen house of cards. "We were working over there before I went up on the catwalk."

Jaxon ran for the stage, and Bryn followed. Together they picked up the wooden sets and moved them aside. Across the stage, other students sifted through the debris searching for friends.

Under a park scene, they found Rhianna. Her body was twisted and one of her legs was bent at an unnatural angle.

Jaxon dropped to his knees. "Rhianna?"

Bile rose in Bryn's throat. She knelt and placed a hand on the girl's forehead and scanned Rhianna's body.

"Her pelvis is broken," Bryn whispered.

"Fix it."

"I don't know how." Tears rolled down her face. She couldn't tell him about Rhianna's spine. Maybe dragons were different from humans. Maybe Quintessence could heal a severed spinal cord.

Chapter Fifteen

"Who needs medical attention?" a male voice called out. Bryn waved at the medics streaming into the room. She stepped aside and waited to hear what the man would say.

The medic squatted next to Rhianna and ran his hands over her body. When his hand passed over her waist, he growled. "Her spine is damaged."

Jaxon seemed to shrink in on himself.

"Can you fix it?" Bryn asked.

The medic sighed. "We can heal it, but damage has already been done."

Jaxon pushed to his feet. "I'll make arrangements for a staff of specialists to treat her. Tell no one of her condition."

The medic nodded and Jaxon left the auditorium.

"Why keep this a secret?" Bryn asked.

The medic ignored her while he healed Rhianna's pelvis. Once he was done, he spoke with a voice full of pity. "If his father finds out, he'll void their marriage petition."

"Bastard."

The medic didn't respond. She took his silence as agreement.

"Bryn." Clint waved from across the room and pointed to the doors leading outside. It must be okay to leave. Should she go with them? What about Zavien? He'd chosen *her* in a time of crisis, but what did that mean?

At the moment, he was in a heated debate with Nola. Neither of them looked happy. If she walked over to him while he was with Nola, nothing good would happen. Frustrated, she growled and moved to join her friends by the exit. They emerged in the cool evening air, and her breath caught in her throat.

Broken glass from the theater building's windows glittered in the moonlight, making the sidewalks look like they were covered in diamonds. Splintered trees were ripped from the ground and tossed about like kindling. Reds dressed in military fashion roamed the campus with eyes narrowed and fists clenched, ready for a fight. The enemy seemed to have slipped away like mist.

"One of the medics said the attack was wind, like tornadoes," Clint said.

"Green dragons attacking the campus?" Ivy said. "That doesn't make sense."

"Whoever it was, they meant to hurt people." Smoke shot from Bryn's nostrils.

They walked toward their dorm in silence. Not telling Clint and Ivy about the incident on the catwalk was making her crazy. But talking about her love life seemed shallow when Rhianna lay injured and the campus was in chaos.

Bryn relaxed when they reached the dorm for about sixty seconds, until she remembered the stairs. Trudging up the stupid stairs to their rooms seemed like too much work after the evening they'd endured, but she didn't feel like tromping back outside, shifting, and flying up to her terrace, either. "This place needs elevators."

Wait a minute. "Why hasn't the campus been made wheelchair-accessible? Isn't it required by law?"

"Maybe human law," Clint said. "Here, it's never been an issue. Medics heal almost all injuries."

"What about those who can't be healed?" Images of Rhianna lying twisted on the floor came to mind. "If a student lost a leg, what would happen?"

"I don't know," Clint said. "I've never seen dragons in wheelchairs unless they were ancient."

There were two possibilities here. Either medics healed everyone, or those who were injured beyond repair were kept out of what Mrs. Silvertrap, the Proper Decorum teacher, referred to as "polite society." Given what Bryn knew of the Directorate, she bet on the second theory.

After a nod to her friends, Bryn headed for her room, where she stripped off her clothes and climbed into the shower. Hot water kneaded her tense muscles while she replayed the events of the evening. Who had attacked the campus? Would Rhianna recover? Where did she stand with Zavien? He'd chosen her in a time of crisis. Would he apologize now so they could start over? The memory of his arms around her made her heart hurt. Could they start over after everything he'd done, or rather not done? He hadn't checked on her after the first attack. He hadn't tried to apologize. He hadn't even admitted what he'd done was wrong.

As usual, there were too many questions and not enough answers. When her skin started to prune, she went to bed.

The alarm woke her the next morning in its usual annoying fashion. Bashing it with her Proper Decorum book didn't bring about the desired results. The alarm survived unscathed. Maybe tonight she'd fly to the top of the dorm and toss it down on the sidewalk to see what would happen.

At breakfast in the dining hall, the only sound was utensils hitting plates. Ivy and Clint greeted her, but they ate in silence. Everyone seemed to be suffering the aftershocks of yesterday's attack. Once again, not the right time to ask them about Zavien.

She sipped her coffee and checked the other tables in the dining hall. No Rhianna and no Jaxon. Had he taken her to a special hospital? Jaxon would hire the best specialist money could buy. Hopefully that would be enough.

• • •

In Elemental Science, the Orange dragons had returned to class. Bryn smiled at Octavius. He nodded, but his expression remained grim.

Mr. Stanton stood behind his desk. The dark circles under his eyes proved he hadn't had a restful evening. "Class, I have a few announcements before we practice our breath weapons. Octavius and Vivian were cleared of all suspicion in regard to the first attack. Since yesterday's attack came in the form of wind, the Directorate is interviewing any Greens capable of higher-level magic." He gave a tight smile. "I was questioned last night and cleared of suspicion."

"Do they have any leads?" Bryn asked.

He shook his head. "They are following all logical paths. In the meantime, more security has been added. The

Directorate is doing everything in its power to keep the campus safe. Now, let's get to work."

After class, on her walk to the library, Bryn passed several groups of Reds, dressed in military uniforms, continuing the cleanup effort. Bits of glass caught the morning light and sparkled in the grass. It would be weeks before they managed to rid the campus of debris. The blank spaces where majestic trees had once dotted the landscape resembled open graves.

In the library, she headed for her usual spot on the third floor. It was in a back corner where there wasn't much traffic, so she was surprised to find a notebook on the table. No book bag hung on the chair, so it didn't seem like the table was occupied. Checking to make sure there was no one in sight, she opened the notebook. On the first page someone had doodled the same drawing over and over again. It looked like a circle around a plus sign. Inside each quarter there was a triangle. Two right side up and two upside-down. One of each triangle had a line through it. She flipped through the pages. There was nothing else in the notebook; no assignments, no names, no more drawings. Weird. If no one came looking for it, she'd drop it off at the front desk on her way out.

Three paragraphs into a five-paragraph essay, Onyx joined her.

"Your protection charm has been restored." He pulled the key from his pocket and placed it on her textbook. The red and blue stones caught the light and winked at her, like they knew something she didn't.

"Thank you." She picked up the key and placed it in her pocket. "Do you have any news on the attacks?"

"No. I believe both of the previous attacks were

warnings. They were meant to shake us up with a minimum of damage. I'm afraid the attacks will increase in severity as time goes on."

That wasn't reassuring. "What now?"

"The Directorate wants to initiate mandatory curfews for everyone. That will lead to more unrest."

"I thought creating unrest was the Revisionists' goal."

He shook his head. "Not like this. We want change, but attacking our fellow dragons isn't part of the plan."

"Is someone trying to start a war?"

"So it would appear." Onyx stood. "Be careful who you speak to about this matter. The Directorate is interviewing anyone they deem a threat. Even though your grandfather recognized you, you're still on that list."

That was a cheery thought.

Bryn made sure to leave time to stop by Miss Enid's desk on the way out of the library. "Someone left this on a table upstairs."

Miss Enid opened the notebook and frowned. She ripped the drawing out and then shredded the paper over and over again until it was confetti.

Not the reaction Bryn expected. "What's wrong?"

Miss Enid leaned in closer. "Did you show this to anyone?"

"No. Why? What does it mean?"

"The four triangles represent earth, water, air, and fire. The circle represents Quintessence."

"And that's bad because…"

"A long time ago, it was used as a symbol for rebellion. A group of dragons from different Clans came together and tried to overthrow the Directorate. They failed, but the symbol has cropped up occasionally when there is unrest. The Directorate banned its use." She tapped her nails on the counter. "The question is, did someone leave this for you as a test, or a message?"

"I don't know. Either way, I'm going to ignore it."

In Basic Movement, Jaxon sought Bryn out. "I need to speak with you in private."

She followed him over to the lockers where the wooden swords were kept.

"Rhianna wants to see you. I'm visiting her after dinner tonight."

"Is she all right?"

"No." Jaxon cleared his throat. "The doctors healed her spinal cord, but her right leg will always be weak."

The tightly controlled pain in his voice brought a lump to Bryn's throat. "Can she walk?"

"Yes." He pretended to search for a sword while he spoke. "But she has a limp."

"Can she fly?"

"The doctors want to continue physical therapy before allowing her to shift."

Losing the ability to fly would be like losing a limb.

"Meet me outside the dining hall at seven." Jaxon slammed the locker door and stalked off.

• • •

At seven, Bryn waited in the appointed spot. Jaxon rounded the corner of a building and came toward her. He made eye contact, but kept walking. She fell into step a few yards behind him. Why was he being so secretive? *Whatever.* This was for Rhianna, so she played along.

He led her down a side walkway that wound through a garden. Raised flower beds edged in decorative bricks were laid out in a complex geometric pattern. During warmer weather, the garden would be beautiful. Now, the brown clumps of dead vegetation dotting the brick-lined flower beds seemed like a monument to death and decay.

Wrapping her arms around herself to ward off a chill, Bryn jogged to catch up. Jaxon waited for her inside a service entrance.

"Rhianna isn't supposed to have visitors," he said.

"Why?"

"The less she's seen, the less others know of her condition."

That didn't sound right. There was something he wasn't saying. She followed him up a flight of stairs. "Where my parents live, it isn't uncommon to see people using canes or wheelchairs."

Jaxon stopped walking. "Humans are more tolerant of imperfection than dragons."

"What does that mean?"

He turned to face her, his lips set in a grim line. "Dragons who are unable to fly often choose isolation."

Flames roared in her chest. "They choose it, or it's forced on them?"

He rubbed the bridge of his nose. "I...I don't know. Come on. Rhianna is expecting us."

Damn the Directorate and their intolerant ways. She followed him up two more flights of stairs. They emerged in a darkened hallway. Jaxon opened the second door on the right and she sneaked in.

Rhianna lay in a hospital bed, her normally golden skin

pale against the white sheets. "Thank you for coming, Bryn. I need your help."

Bryn crossed the room, grabbed her hand, and squeezed. "Name it."

"Jaxon told me how you healed him. I need you to tell me the truth. How badly was I injured?"

"Jaxon didn't tell you?"

"Of course I told her," he snapped. "But I don't know the extent of her residual injuries. The medics healed her as much as possible. You can use your Quintessence to read her. Let us know where we stand."

"Okay." Bryn put her hand on Rhianna's forehead. "I saw the damage to your spinal cord after the accident. Maybe I'll recognize what's been healed. I'm not making any promises. Saving Jaxon's life was the trial run of my powers. Since then, I've only healed cuts and scrapes."

"What?" Jaxon's eyebrows shot up. "You didn't know what you were doing? You could've killed me."

"Medic Williams said you'd die if I didn't try. Besides, it worked. What are you griping about?"

Rhianna giggled.

Bryn stage-whispered, "Your boyfriend is moody."

"Really? I hadn't noticed." Her deadpan response made Bryn laugh.

Jaxon played along, huffing out an exaggerated breath. "I knew you were a bad influence."

The laughter lightened the mood. Bryn closed her eyes. "Here we go."

She scanned Rhianna's body and focused on the point where the spine met the tailbone. There were a few dark spots, but the area, which had been severed, appeared to be fused together.

"I'm no expert, but it looks like they reconnected everything. There are a few dark spots. I'd guess those were bruises. Maybe they need time to heal."

"Try to heal them," Jaxon said.

"Rhianna, it's your call. I don't know if I'd hurt you or help you."

"Try to heal one bruise," Rhianna said.

Bryn gathered a small ball of white light and channeled it into one of the dark spots. After a few moments, she stopped. The bruise remained unchanged.

"Feel any different?"

"What you did felt warm, but I don't think it changed anything." Rhianna sat up and moved to the edge of the bed. Bryn backed out of the way while Jaxon helped Rhianna stand. Once Rhianna was steady, she took a few steps. Her gait was uneven. The girl who used to glide across the floor now shuffled her right foot.

Bryn dug her nails into her palms, but made sure to keep her voice upbeat. "Better or worse?"

"The same," Rhianna whispered.

"Maybe you need more time to recover." Jaxon's tone was hopeful.

"Take me to the roof." Rhianna's voice shook. "I need to know if I can fly."

Jaxon placed his hands on Rhianna's shoulders. "I don't know if that's a good idea."

"If we take you up there, we'll be caught for sure," Bryn said. "Do you want to risk that?"

"I don't care. What can they do to me that's worse than this?"

Good point. Should they risk the roof? There had to be

another way. "Shift in here," Bryn said, "and try to move your wings."

"Is there enough room?" Jaxon asked.

"Let's see." Bryn shifted, being careful to keep her wings tucked to her side. Her tail knocked over the plastic trash can with a muffled *thump*.

Jaxon crossed his arms over his chest and glared. "Must you follow through on every idea that pops into your head?"

"Change back," Rhianna said. "There isn't room for both of us in here."

"I don't know if this is wise," Jaxon said. "If you can't move your wings, what will you do?"

"I need to know." She moved around him in an awkward fashion.

The air around Rhianna shimmered. The scent of cold metal filled the air. Then Rhianna stood in dragon form.

Both wings were intact, thank God. Bryn held her breath as Rhianna extended her wings. Up they both went, but her right wing stopped a foot below its apex. Frost shot from the Blue dragon's nostrils.

"It will be all right." Jaxon moved forward and placed his hand on Rhianna's flank. "You'll be able to fly. After some practice I'm sure you'll be able to gauge how high to lift your left wing."

Rhianna returned to human form. Tears streamed down her face. "Your father…"

Jaxon wrapped his arms around her and made soothing noises. "Don't worry about my father. I promise, I will take care of you, no matter what happens."

Bryn's face heated. This was a painful, private moment. She shouldn't be there. Making as little noise as possible, she backed out of the room.

On the walk back to her dorm, she tried to think through the situation. What would happen to Rhianna if the marriage contract ended? Would she consent to be someone's mistress? Jaxon's words came back to her and his true meaning hit. If the contract were ended, Jaxon would take care of her, meaning he'd keep her as his mistress. In this twisted world of Directorate-controlled relationships, he was trying to do right by her.

What sucked was, that was probably the best Rhianna could hope for.

"Bryn McKenna?" a masculine voice barked.

She froze midstep and whirled around, ready for a fight. One of the new military guards bore down on her.

For a moment, she considered lying but her coloring gave her away. Squaring her shoulders, she tried to appear calm. "I'm Bryn."

The guard looked her up and down, taking her measure. She must have passed the test because he gave a curt nod. "There's a visitor for you at the back gate. The fool claims he's your knight."

"Valmont's at the gate?"

The Red's eyebrows came together. "He really is your knight?"

"Yes." The thought of seeing Valmont was like a soothing balm. "Can he visit, or are we on some sort of lockdown?"

"I'll sign him in." The guard led her across campus. "He can't stay long."

Valmont stood between two auburn-haired guards built like pro wrestlers. While her knight matched their height, they each outweighed him by fifty pounds.

He smiled at her approach, and his single dimple appeared. "Come to save me from military arrest?"

The guards scowled.

"Be nice. They're doing their job."

Valmont addressed the guard by her side. "Am I allowed on campus?"

He pointed at a clipboard hanging by the gate. "Sign in. You can stay for twenty minutes. You must sign out when you leave." He leaned forward so his nose was an inch from Valmont's. "If you don't sign out, I'll have to track you down, and that will annoy me."

"Understood." Valmont grabbed the clipboard and signed.

Bryn took his hand and led him back the way she'd come. "This is a nice surprise."

"I hadn't heard from you, so I wanted to check in."

"Things have been crazy around here." Since it was a nice night, she led him to the steps on the side of the dining hall. "Mind if we sit here?"

"Is there a reason you don't want to take me to your dorm?"

"No." She squeezed his hand. "It's a nice night and I spent all day in classes."

He released her hand and put his arm around her shoulders. "How are you holding up?"

"I'm fine." Her voice grew thick. "Rhianna isn't."

"The sweet blonde from the dance? What happened?"

Bryn leaned into him for comfort and relayed the story of Rhianna's injuries.

"I thought your medics could heal anything."

"I guess not." She blinked to hold back tears. "Now Jaxon's father could void their marriage contract."

Valmont's muscles tensed. "That's wrong."

"I agree." She sniffed. "That's all the sucky news I have. What's new with you?"

"I have acquired a roommate." He chuckled. "My grandfather forgot his wedding anniversary. Until he can figure a way to get back into my grandmother's good graces, he's living with me. The man snores like a chain saw."

"If you want any rest you'll have to help him apologize."

"He's been leaving roses and chocolate on her doorstep every morning for a week."

"That's nice."

"My grandmother doesn't think so. She gives him the evil eye any time he tries to speak to her. Give me a female's perspective. What else should he do?"

"I'm not sure." Then it hit her. "Has he apologized in person, or is he just leaving gifts?"

"I don't know."

"Romantic gestures are good," Bryn said, "but sometimes a girl needs to hear the words."

"Speaking from personal experience, are we?" He arched a brow.

She gave a small shrug. "Maybe."

"Has the spiky-haired nitwit apologized?"

"No, but he was next to me when the theater building was attacked. He chose to protect me over Nola."

Valmont kicked at a pebble on the steps. "Then what happened?"

"Nothing, and it's driving me crazy. I thought he'd find me and apologize, but he hasn't."

"So he'd be upset if you died, but he doesn't want to be seen with you in public."

Bryn elbowed Valmont in the ribs. "Don't spare my feelings."

"Believe it or not, I'm trying to keep you from being hurt again. Just because he doesn't want you dead, doesn't mean he's boyfriend material. If he came to you right now and apologized, what would you do?"

The question caught her off guard. "I don't know. If he'd come to me the day after the dance, I would've taken him back. He didn't check on me after the first attack, but he tried to keep me safe during the second one."

"If you hadn't been next to him during the second attack, do you think he would've checked on you afterward?"

Acid churned in her stomach. "I don't know."

"There you are." The Red dragon with the clipboard stalked toward them.

"Sorry. Has it been twenty minutes?"

"Yes." The guard thrust the clipboard at Valmont. "Sign and go."

The knight didn't seem concerned. He leaned back on his elbows. "You're early. It's been fifteen minutes by my watch."

The Red's jaw muscle twitched.

This could turn ugly. "Valmont, why don't I walk you back to the gate?"

"Fine." Valmont stood and signed the paper on the clipboard. She grabbed her knight's hand and pulled him along.

"If that guard's temper is anything like my father's, you don't want to mess with him."

He leaned in and whispered. "It's my cosmic duty to mess with people. Haven't you figured that out yet?"

"Please don't bait the guards. They are large and angry."

"Fine."

At the gate, he pulled her hand to his lips for a quick kiss. She waved good-bye as he drove off in his red convertible.

Chapter Sixteen

The next morning in the buffet line, Bryn piled her plate high with pancakes. The Blue male behind her raised a brow.

"Food makes me feel better," she said. "Do you have a problem with that?"

"Not as long as there's enough for the rest of us."

She considered nabbing the entire platter of pancakes just to piss him off, but common sense won out.

When she joined her friends at their normal table, Clint glanced up. "Were you able to talk to Zavien before the attack?"

Ivy stole a piece of bacon off her boyfriend's plate. "I thought we agreed to let her bring him up."

He rolled his eyes. "We waited a respectable amount of time. She's probably dying to tell us, but didn't know if it would be appropriate."

"We can add mind reader to your list of character traits." Bryn poured syrup on her pancakes. "When the auditorium was attacked, he chose to protect me over Nola."

"And?" Ivy prompted.

She slashed at her pancakes. "And nothing. He hasn't apologized and I don't think he intends to. As Valmont put it, Zavien would prefer I didn't die, but he doesn't want to be seen with me in public."

"Ouch," Clint muttered around a mouth full of toast.

"Exactly." Bryn ripped open three packets of sugar and poured them into her coffee. "Any suggestions on what I should do now?"

"What do you want from Zavien?" Clint asked. "As a guy, I might be able to tell you if your fantasy has a chance at becoming reality."

Sipping her coffee, she thought about the question. "I want him to apologize for being a colossal ass, and I want him to choose me over Nola."

"Legally, I'm not sure that's an option." Clint said. "His family has entered into a binding contract with Nola's family."

Bryn smacked her fork down on the table. "Then why did the jerk start something with me in the first place?"

"I think he might truly care for you." Ivy grimaced. "Though that probably makes it worse, doesn't it?"

"Yes." If she could flat-out hate him, it'd be easier to let go. "Part of me thinks it isn't his fault, it's the damned Directorate's fault for insisting on arranged marriages. But if he loved me, he'd fight for me. Hell, even Jaxon is fighting for Rhianna."

"What do you mean?" Ivy asked.

Bryn leaned forward. "Yesterday, Jaxon took me to see Rhianna." She told them Rhianna's condition and what

Jaxon had promised. "You can't tell anyone."

"There aren't words for how much that sucks." Clint's eyes narrowed. "Wait a minute. You knew about her condition right after the attack. That's why you asked about wheelchair accessibility."

Time to confess. Sort of. "I knew she was hurt, but I thought the medics could heal her."

"Maybe they still can." Ivy sounded hopeful. "At least Jaxon is stepping up and promising to take care of her. Who knows who she'd end up with otherwise."

"She'd be in the same sucky position I'm in." What a depressing thought.

"Promise not to shoot a fireball at my head for what I'm about to say," Clint said.

Bryn nodded and clenched the edge of the table.

"You could continue your relationship with Zavien in the same manner Jaxon offered to continue his relationship with Rhianna."

Anger burst through Bryn's body like a volcano. Sparks shot from her nostrils.

"Idiot." Ivy punched her boyfriend on the shoulder. "You knew how she'd react to that idea."

Clint nodded. "That's why I included the caveat about not roasting me like a marshmallow." He held his hands up in a sign of surrender. "Realistically, that is the only offer Zavien can make if he comes back. I didn't think you'd be cool with it, but I wanted you to think about it."

Bryn's shoulders slumped. The fight drained out of her body. "I can't believe that's the best I can hope for. My life sucks."

· · ·

By the end of the week, life on campus returned to semi-normal with an undercurrent of anxiety. The Red Militia wandering the campus both reassured and worried Bryn. Did their presence mean the Directorate expected another attack?

No one left any weird drawings for her to find, which was a relief. She considered looking up the symbol online, but was afraid that might set off some internal computer alarm.

Friday night, Bryn holed up in the library hoping to find detailed information about why Alec had hated the Directorate so much. Right before he'd tried to kill her, he'd said the Directorate had stolen his life.

What did that mean? Zavien had told her that Alec's marriage contract had been denied and that was enough reason to hate Ferrin and the Directorate, but was it enough to want to kill Ferrin's family and Bryn?

Miss Enid had tipped her off about where the Directorate housed the records of marriage petitions both approved and denied, which was why she was on the fourth floor of the library in a secluded corner surrounded by musty-smelling books. Some of the books were so old their leather bindings had cracked. Newer books, exact replicas of the ancient ones they were shelved with, held the most recent information. Names of the proposed husband and wife were listed together, along with a notation of whether they were approved or denied. Of course, the information stopped there. A reason for the denials wasn't listed.

She shoved a four-inch-thick leather-bound beast back onto the shelf. Stupid thing must weigh twenty pounds. Had the damn Directorate never heard of computers? They probably recorded information this way to discourage people from looking things up. Too bad for them she had time to kill.

In one of the books, she found where Alec's marriage petition to a girl named Analise Lane was denied. Alec had been offered another choice, which he had refused. What had happened to Analise?

After flipping through a few more books, Bryn found lists of benefactors—the men who kept mistresses—and the women they were involved with. There was only one name paired with each male. At least they were faithful to their mistresses.

Halfway through the book, Bryn found Analise's name next to a male named Castor Wrenright. Her name was crossed out in different-colored ink and a new woman's name was written next to it. What did that mean? Did mistresses get dumped? Talk about adding injury to insult. First you're not good enough to marry and then they break up with you? That would be grounds for murder.

Bryn shook her head. Before she'd come into her power and shifted into a dragon for the first time, she'd never thought about murdering people in such a casual manner. Sure there had been a few snotty girls at her old school she wouldn't have missed if someone had flattened them with a truck, but this new attitude was different. Was her temper worse now, since she could shift into a dragon? She didn't think so. Then again, no one had tried to kill her before. Being poisoned and partially blown up was enough to sharpen anyone's temper.

Fantasizing about killing Zavien didn't mean she'd follow through with it.

What about dragons who did follow through with their instincts? In his Orientation speech, Ferrin had mentioned a student facing incarceration. Furious over the denial of his marriage petition, he'd burned down a Directorate member's home. The Directorate must have its own prison system. Where were the records for that? They must be here somewhere. There was no catalog system for those books that she knew of, or had access to. How could she find them?

And then she saw it. Of course. More color-coding. All the books she'd checked so far that recorded marriage petitions had a midnight-blue binding. A few shelves over, all the books had red bindings. A quick check showed the books with red bindings recorded business deals. Green bindings contained medical records. Black bindings contained endowments given to various arts. White bindings contained family trees.

In the back of each of the books was an index, which allowed you to search by date or name. Maybe she could find Analise's name somewhere and figure out what happened to her.

An hour later, her head hurt, and she was no closer to finding the information she needed. It was like a giant scavenger hunt. She needed help. Clint and Ivy would help, but what if someone found out they were poking around? She wouldn't put it past the Directorate to deny marriage petitions to people who questioned them. Best not to involve her friends. But who did that leave?

. . .

The next day she tracked Jaxon down in Basic Movement and told him about her investigation. He stared at her like she was insane. "You want me to do what?"

She should have known he wouldn't come quietly. Moving closer so the other students couldn't hear, she said, "I want you to help me figure out what happened to Alec's intended."

"And why would I do that?"

"You started this investigation with your questions about Alec and how he knew about my grandfather's estate."

"Yes. And that's why you're supposed to be investigating Alec, not this Analise."

It took effort to keep her voice low. "Whatever happened to Analise is the reason Alec went homicidal. Why was her name crossed out? Are mistresses replaced once they reach a certain age?"

He stared off into space for a moment. "If what I've heard is true, it's a lifelong association."

"So she died?"

"That would be my first guess."

Not good. "We need to find out how she died."

He rolled his eyes. "There's this fabulous invention called the computer."

"Do you think I didn't start there?" Maybe she could appeal to his natural greed. "I bet you twenty bucks her name doesn't bring up any information relevant to her death."

His eyes narrowed. "Fine. Meet me in the library tonight at seven."

• • •

Jaxon used his student password to sign in to one of the library's computers. He scrolled up and down. His jaw muscle twitched as he glared at the screen.

"There isn't any indication this Analise ever existed."

"See. That's why I need help going through the Directorate records. Or you could ask your father."

"Like my father has nothing better to do." He stood and gestured for her to lead the way. "Let's get this over with. I have an essay to write for Elemental Science."

"Essay? What essay?" Had her mind drifted in class and she'd missed an assignment?

"If you read your syllabus, you'd know we have an essay on the multifunctional uses of our breath weapons due next Thursday."

"Don't scare me like that." She whacked him on the arm in the same manner she'd smack Clint.

His entire body stiffened. Eyes narrowed, frost shot from his nose. "Did you just hit me?"

A month ago, this display of temper would've had her preparing for battle. Now, her first instinct was to laugh. She pretended to cough until she was under control.

"Sorry. Would you prefer I not do that?"

"Yes."

"Duly noted. Now, can we go figure out what happened to Analise?"

Bryn showed him the page with Analise's name crossed out. "According to the date their petition was denied, both she and Alec would've been twenty-four. If she finished her bachelor's degree, she could've died any time in the last three years."

Jaxon shook his head. "The girl who took her place

graduated two years ago. Therefore, Analise must've died two years ago."

"What is the average dragon's life span?"

Jaxon glanced at her over the top of his book. "How can you not know that...oh wait...I forgot...you were raised by wolves."

She flipped him off.

He snorted and turned his attention back to medical records book. "Most dragons live to be eighty or ninety. It's rare for someone to die earlier unless they live a dangerous lifestyle."

"Does mistress fall under that heading?"

"No, though there are occasional accidents." He turned a few more pages. "I think I found something. Analise was admitted to the hospital shortly after graduation." He continued reading. "*All* mistresses are admitted to the hospital around the same time." His brow crinkled. "What type of medic is an OBG?"

An uneasy feeling crawled up Bryn's spine. "That's a gynecologist."

Jaxon grimaced and dropped the book.

"Very mature." Bryn grabbed the book and tried to decipher the medical notes. "All of the girls saw the same medic for the same procedure, something called Ovex." She raised a brow at him. "Since you weren't raised by wolves, do you know what that is?"

"Easy enough to find out. You keep digging for information, and I'll go use a computer."

"One of us should've brought a laptop." Bryn flipped more pages as she scanned for Analise's name. All she found was a notation that she had canceled her three-month post-procedure checkup, but would call to reschedule. The second appointment was never mentioned.

She continued to scan the medical records hoping to find another mention of Analise.

Jaxon returned, tight-lipped and narrow-eyed. He threw himself into the chair opposite Bryn and rammed his hands through his hair.

Rather than prod him for information, she waited. He took a deep breath and blew it out. "Ovex is a procedure where a doctor inserts material into a woman's fallopian tubes. Within three months, scarring occurs, which blocks the tubes."

"Why would they…oh my God. Those bastards sterilize their mistresses." Heat flared in her gut. "Did you know about—"

"No," Jaxon cut her off. "I had no idea. I mean…I knew mistresses didn't have children, but I thought it was something they had agreed to."

Smoke shot from her nostrils. "Damn Directorate. What gives them the right?"

He shook his head. "I always believed… I never thought…"

Analise missing her three-month checkup took on a whole new meaning. "What if Analise had gotten pregnant?"

Jaxon's head whipped up. "Impossible. She had the procedure."

"She never went back for the checkup. What if someone helped her reverse the operation?"

His golden complexion paled. "If she had deceived her benefactor and conceived a child… I'd like to say the Directorate would never take a woman's life. But if a woman showed up at my father's door with a bastard child, the shame alone would be enough for him to take extreme measures."

All the air left her lungs. "And you're okay with that?"

"No." He looked down at his fists, clenched on the table. "But there are some acts of betrayal which are unforgivable."

"Are you listening to yourself? The poor woman probably wanted a child. They shouldn't have killed her for that."

Jaxon met her gaze. "They're the Directorate. They can do what they want. Haven't you figured that out by now?"

This was insane. "They can't be all powerful. There has to be some system of checks and balances."

"Do you think your grandfather allows someone to tell him what to do? Do you think it's a coincidence that your father's entire family died in a car crash weeks after he ran off with your mother?"

Chapter Seventeen

The room spun. Her father's family was dead? She hadn't found any record of a McKenna at school, but her dad had been an only child, as were his parents. It made sense that there weren't any cousins wandering around campus. But dead?

Jaxon leaned toward her. "You didn't know?"

She shook her head and tried to think. Was it possible? Could her grandfather do such a thing? She remembered the man's ice-cold stare and shivered.

Jaxon leaned back in his chair. "Which means your father doesn't know."

Son of a bitch. Bryn slumped in her chair as the weight of this new knowledge settled on her chest like a hungry vulture. "What am I supposed to say, 'Merry Christmas, Dad. By the way, did you know your whole family is dead? Oh, and Mom's dad probably killed them. Pass the eggnog.'"

"Perhaps you should wait to make this announcement

until after you open your presents."

Smoke shot from her nostrils. Grabbing the nearest object, she winged her notebook at his head.

He snatched it out of the air before it could make contact. "Just trying to lighten the mood."

"Bad idea." She shot out of her seat. Needing a moment alone, she stalked down the closest aisle.

When she was twenty feet away, she heard the door to the stairs bang open.

"Jaxon Westgate?" a masculine voice asked.

Bryn crept closer so she could peer through the stacks. Two men in dark suits flanked Jaxon. Neither appeared friendly.

Jaxon straightened in his seat and raised a brow at the newcomers. "Hello, gentlemen. Can I help you?"

"Were you working on the computers downstairs a few moments ago?"

"What business is it of yours?"

"Your inquiry triggered an internal alarm." The two men sat on either side of Jaxon, boxing him in. "Why were you looking up information on a certain medical procedure?"

Playing it cool, Jaxon shrugged. "I heard a rumor, and I was curious."

"The Directorate suggests you stop poking around."

With feline grace, Jaxon stood and looked at the two men like they were dirt. "And you represent the Directorate? I find that hard to believe. Do you know who my father is?"

"Of course we do. He'll learn of this situation in his morning report. If you insist on continuing this investigation, something could happen to your friend Rhianna. That would be a shame."

"She's not my friend, she's my intended."

"Not anymore she's not." The man smiled like he relished delivering the news. "Your father voided the contract after discovering her...disability. He contacted her parents, and they've agreed it would be in her best interest to seek a benefactor."

Jaxon cleared his throat. "I'll discuss this with my father. In the meantime, I forbid you to speak to anyone about this matter. Do you understand?"

"Who are you to give us orders?"

"I'm a Westgate." Jaxon emphasized each syllable of his last name. "Unless you want the Directorate to seize your family holdings for the good of the Clan, you will keep your mouths shut." His pronouncement was met by silence, as the two men appeared to reevaluate their authority.

How had Jaxon taken control of the conversation? Impressed despite herself, she watched him stalk away.

Wait a minute. He was leaving her with the suits.

The men stared down at the table. One spotted her book bag.

Crap.

He picked up the bag, flipped it open, and pulled out a notebook. A quick check on her latest assignment and he frowned.

"We know you're here, Miss McKenna."

Not like she could argue with him. If she wanted her book bag back she had to come out.

A hand touched her shoulder. Heart racing, she wheeled around. Zavien stood behind her. "Wait here. I'll take care of this."

Where the hell had he come from? Was he here by coincidence, or had he been spying on her?

Zavien walked out to meet the men, like nothing was

wrong. "Gentlemen, I'm grateful you found my book bag."

"*Your* book bag?" The larger of the two men laughed. "You expect us to believe this is yours?"

"Yes." The tone of Zavien's voice changed into something more commanding. "Jaxon acted alone. No one else was here. Do you understand?"

The two men blinked.

Wait a minute. Zavien was *pushing* them, like he'd hypnotized her when they'd first met. She really needed to learn how to do that.

Zavien grabbed her book bag, tossed it down a nearby aisle, and then turned back to the men. In a normal tone of voice, he said, "Excuse me. I was looking for Jaxon Westgate and his friend Quentin. Have you seen either of them?"

The men looked at the table. "Jaxon was here."

"Was he with a friend?"

"No. He was alone."

Zavien nodded. "Thanks, I'll have to catch up with him later."

The two men headed toward the stairs.

Bryn retrieved her book bag and joined Zavien where he was flipping through the books open on the table. She wanted to say something…but what?

"Thanks for helping."

"What were you and Jaxon looking for?"

"We were trying to figure out why Alec wanted to kill us."

He closed the books and started returning them to the shelves. "He loved Analise. Losing her drove him over the edge."

"Wait. Do you mean the marriage petition being denied

or after the Directorate had her killed?"

Zavien frowned. "What are you talking about?"

She recapped her and Jaxon's discovery. "If we knew where the obituaries were kept, we could find out for sure."

Zavien stalked down an aisle to a shelf full of books with silver bindings. "I researched an artist's death once. The records are here." He pulled volumes off the shelf and thumbed through them until he found the one he wanted. "It says here she died in a car accident."

"Seems to be a lot of that going around. I don't suppose it says if the accident was Directorate-sanctioned."

Zavien shook his head and reshelved the books. "Do not go down this path."

"Don't you want to know?"

"Even if you find out someone had her killed, it won't bring her back. It will just land you in trouble. What would've happened if I hadn't been here to *push* those guards?"

Time for the gloves to come off. "Sorry you don't approve. Since you ran out on me, I had to improvise."

His friendly facade cracked. "I didn't run out on you. You broke our deal."

"What deal?"

"I told you our relationship had to stay secret."

"Wrong." Smoke shot from her nostrils. "You told me you'd fight to change the law so we could be together. Then you walked away from me."

"I didn't walk away from you when the theater building was attacked." His expression softened. He reached out and brushed his fingertips down her cheek, staring into her eyes.

Bryn sighed. Memories of his arms around her and his mouth pressed against hers rose up and made it hard to think. Damn it, how could he still have this effect on her?

He moved closer. "I chose you that night."

"Yes. You did." Angry tears filled her eyes. "Then you proceeded to ignore me, *again*. My God, it's like you have a split personality."

"Do you have any idea how my actions hurt Nola? I wanted to find you afterward, but Nola warned me away. What was I supposed to do?"

"Stop whining and act like a man." Jaxon's voice came from behind them.

Zavien whirled around. "Don't lecture me about acting like a man. You ran off and left Bryn with those Directorate lackeys."

Jaxon made eye contact with Bryn. "Sorry. I thought they would follow me out."

"They saw my book bag."

"How'd you leave things with them?" Jaxon asked.

"I took care of it," Zavien said. "I *pushed* them into thinking you were alone."

"And why were you here in this secluded area of the library in the first place?" Jaxon asked.

"Good question." Bryn crossed her arms and waited.

"Onyx asked me to meet him here." Zavien frowned. "But he didn't show up."

The small part of her heart that had held out hope he'd been following her so he could talk to her, crumbled into dust. "So, you were here on business and just happened to run into me." She took a deep breath. "If you'd never run into me would you have ever come to talk to me?"

"I— " His gaze shot to Jaxon. "Do you mind?"

Jaxon retreated a dozen feet back to the table, where he

packed up his things.

Zavien sighed. "I care about you, but right now, things are complicated."

Wow. He was doing great until the "but." "What does that mean?"

"It means I'm beholden to Nola and her family. It means I can't necessarily do what I want. It means I—"

"Sorry I'm late." Onyx strode down the aisle with a determined look on his face. "Bryn, will you excuse us? Zavien and I have business to attend to."

Bryn grabbed Zavien's arm. "Finish what you were going to say."

"We don't have time for this. Zavien, come with me." Onyx turned back the way he'd come.

"I have to go." Zavien pulled away from her.

"Seriously?" He was going to leave her hanging like this, again?

He hurried after Onyx without looking back. She stood there, dumbfounded.

Chapter Eighteen

On the walk back to her dorm, she tried to make sense of the information she'd gained. Alec had wanted to end both the Westgate and Sinclair lines by murdering Jaxon, Lillith, and her in order to steal Ferrin's and her grandfather's future—just like they'd stolen his future with Analise, first by denying the marriage petition, and then by arranging her death in a car accident. That was one mystery solved.

Then there was the revelation about her dad's parents' suspicious deaths right after he ran off with her mom. The scariest part was, she could imagine her grandfather orchestrating the whole thing as revenge. What was she supposed to do with that information? As usual, she was left with more questions than answers. Funny how Zavien was the least of her concerns right now.

Could she do anything to help Rhianna? Who would Jaxon be paired with now that Rhianna was undesirable?

The last question brought her to a screeching halt. She

prayed that her grandmother and Lillith wouldn't have any influence over who Jaxon would be paired with.

"There you are." Ivy's voice brought her out of her nightmare haze.

"Hi, guys."

Clint and Ivy walked toward her hand in hand.

"Where've you been?" Clint asked.

She should keep them out of the loop, but she wasn't that strong. "I asked Jaxon to help me investigate some Directorate business."

Ivy opened her mouth to speak.

"The reason I didn't ask you guys was because I knew it could land us in trouble. And it did. Two of the Directorate's goons showed up to threaten us."

Clint's brows drew together. "Threatened how?"

"They tried to intimidate Jaxon, but he went all Westgate on them."

Ivy snorted. "You mean he went all superior and obnoxious?"

"It was kind of funny." Bryn shoved her hands in her pockets. "And then it wasn't." She told them about Zavien showing up and his stupid claim that she'd broken their deal. "He griped about how much trouble he was in with Nola."

"He needs to grow a pair," Clint said.

"Jaxon said the same thing. In a more upper-class way, of course."

"And?" Ivy asked.

"Zavien said he cares about me, but things are *complicated*. Like I don't know that already. Idiot. He didn't even stay, he just ran off with Onyx." She kicked at a rock on the sidewalk. "So here I am, pissed off at Zavien, and the Directorate, and pretty much any male who isn't Clint or Jaxon." She knew what she needed to do. "It's time for me to focus on something else. If Zavien wants to talk to me, he can come find me. I'm done with all this drama."

Clint scratched his chin. "Speaking of moving on to something new, you don't think your grandmother will — "

"Don't say it." Bryn clapped her hands over her ears.

Ivy laughed. "Come on. It's almost curfew."

After parting ways with her friends, Bryn paced her dorm room. Before tonight, she hadn't loved the idea that the Directorate kept watch over everyone. But now, it was super creepy.

• • •

News of Rhianna's change in station spread across campus by dinner the next day. Jaxon growled, literally, at anyone who mentioned it. Outside the dining hall, she witnessed him arguing with another Blue.

"If you ever refer to Rhianna as 'damaged' again, I'll make sure your marriage contract is denied."

"You don't have that kind of power," the other Blue shot back.

Not smart.

Jaxon's eyes went flat and hard. The lines of his face seemed to sharpen. He moved to stand toe to toe with the other Blue, who no longer seemed so sure of himself.

"If you cross me, I will do all within my power to make your life a living hell." Frost shot from Jaxon's lips with every word.

The other Blue's gaze darted back and forth, checking to see if anyone planned on stepping in. All the other students in the vicinity seemed to find their shoes or the sky interesting. None returned the boy's gaze. Shoulders slumped, the Blue kept his gaze down. "I apologize for my rude comment."

"And?" Jaxon leaned in forcing the boy to retreat a step.

"And it will never happen again." Apology complete, the young man bolted down the sidewalk, shifted, and took to the air.

Jaxon glanced around at the students who'd witnessed the incident. "Feel free to share this with your friends."

The other students scattered like leaves in the wind. When his gaze landed on Bryn, she grinned at him. "I never thought I'd say these words, but I'm proud of you."

He rolled his eyes. "Now my life is complete."

. . .

Bryn entered the dining hall and almost tripped over her own feet because Zavien stood last in line at the buffet. It was almost like fate was mocking her. She walked up and stood in line behind him, just to see what would happen.

No response.

Un-freaking-believable.

He didn't even know she was there. If you'd asked her a month ago, she would have said she could've felt his presence as soon as he walked into a room. She'd assumed he felt the same way. Apparently not.

When he shifted positions to grab a plate, he caught sight of her and froze. Tension filled the air. Her pulse spiked. If he didn't at least say hello to her, she'd do her damnedest to slam his face into the giant serving bowl of mac and cheese.

"Hello, Bryn." He moved forward in line.

Okay. He'd spoken to her. He'd spoken to her like he'd speak to any other student or teacher. His tone screamed, *You are not special. You mean nothing to me.*

She grabbed a plate and followed along. "So we're back to casual small talk? Should I ask how you feel about the weather?"

A muscle in his jaw twitched. He scooped out a helping of mashed potatoes and put it on his plate. "I'm trying to be polite."

She grabbed a spoonful of mac and cheese and smacked it onto her plate. "How does one go from, 'I'll work to change the laws so we can be together' to 'I'm trying to be polite'? Because I'm still stuck in the 'What the hell happened to the guy who acted like he loved me?' stage."

Zavien set his plate down and met her gaze. "You want to do this here?"

"No. I don't. Let's go for a walk, and talk somewhere private."

"No point. Let's get this over with." He sighed. "I need you to understand. I never lied to you. The idea of changing the marriage law...maybe I was lying to myself, hoping it was possible." He gave her a sad smile. "I am sorry. I never meant to hurt you, but our relationship was a mistake. There are certain things...things I cannot change. I will always care about you, but it's best if we go our separate ways."

And now she had closure. She'd known it was over, but hearing him say it still made her heart hurt. She'd trusted him. Believed in him. To her horror, angry tears filled her eyes.

Zavien reached for her. "Bryn?"

"Don't." She shoved her plate onto the buffet and backed

away from him. She would not do the whole girlie-crying-thing here, in front of everyone. As soon as she cleared the door, she shifted and took to the sky. Pumping her wings, she drove herself upward and broke through the clouds. There was no fire waiting to be released; there was only disillusionment and disappointment. All this time, she'd held out a tiny bit of hope that he'd apologize and come back to her.

Stupid. Stupid. Stupid. With every downward thrust of her wings, she tried to escape the chant in her head. It wouldn't go away. *Stupid. Stupid. Stupid.* She was a stupid girl who'd believed what she wanted to believe.

Her grandmother's warning came screaming back to her. "Only those you love can truly hurt you."

How right she'd been.

Chapter Nineteen

Escape. She needed to escape this sadness. Taking in great gulps of air, she put as much distance between herself and reality as possible. She pushed her wings harder until her muscles screamed and the sky itself seemed to press down on her. Spots flashed in front of her eyes.

The school was a mere speck below her. She was as high as she could comfortably go. It wasn't far enough to escape her problems.

What should she do now?

No way in hell was she going back to school. Dragon's Bluff was off to the right somewhere. Hoping for distraction, she aimed for the town, determined to find the rock formation it was named for.

Would she be punished for leaving school without permission? Probably. Not that it mattered. Right now she just needed some alone time to sort herself out. She descended below the clouds and breathing came easier. It still felt like an elephant sat on her chest, but that had nothing to do with physiology. Off in the distance, the bluffs rose above the town. Pulling her wings in, she dove for the cliffs. From up here, none of the rocks resembled a dragon.

She circled the area and skimmed the ground until she found what she wanted. The pile of rocks took on dragon features the closer she flew. Reducing her speed, she landed, digging her claws into the grass and ripping up sod. She walked around the formation. It did appear to be a dragon turned to stone. When Ivy had told her the tale of a dragon who had mourned the knight she loved and turned to stone by his graveside, she'd thought it a colorful legend.

Shifting to human form, she traced her fingers over the individual scales carved into the rock. The grave marker next to the dragon added to the realism of the tale. Inscribed on the stone were the words, "My knight. My love. My life."

Could someone die of a broken heart? If the ache in her chest was any indication, it could happen. Angry tears rolled down her face. She attempted to shut down the waterworks. *Why bother?* If there was ever a good place to cry over love gone wrong, this was it.

She backed up to the stone dragon's flank and slid to the ground. Pulling her knees to her chest, she gave into grief. Losing Zavien meant more than losing a boyfriend. She'd lost her mentor and her best friend.

"There you are."

Her head jerked up at the sound of the familiar masculine voice. "Jaxon? What are you doing here?"

"I'm here because your friends are slow, both in their flying and in their thinking skills." He glanced at the gravestone and pursed his lips. "Why isn't your knight out here searching for you?"

"I guess because he doesn't know I left campus. Why are you here?"

"Your friends accosted me and insisted I chase you, since they had no hope of catching you. Let's go."

"Where?"

"Back to campus."

No freaking way. "I don't want to go back to campus."

"What you want is irrelevant." His eyes narrowed.

Inappropriate laughter bubbled out of her throat. "That's the story of my life."

He crossed his arms over his chest and glared at her like she was a dog who'd peed on the carpet. "I was on my way to see Rhianna when your friends sidetracked me. Unlike you, she has real problems."

Now she *felt* like a dog who had peed on the carpet. Standing up, she dusted off her clothes. "Thanks for throwing that in my face. Now I feel much better."

"I don't know why you're upset about Zavien. You should have seen this coming."

Fire rose in her throat. "Excuse me?"

"You've known from the beginning that his contract was in place."

"He told me they were friends. I believed him when he said he'd work to change the law."

Jaxon shook his head. "Nice line. Most guys stick to 'Let's take a ride in my Lamborghini,' or 'We should spend the weekend on my family's yacht.'"

Zavien wouldn't do that. "You're wrong. He cared about me."

"Not enough, it seems. Come on. Let's go."

Smoke shot from her nostrils. She closed her eyes and thought of snow. The flames in her gut died down, but she still wanted to roast Jaxon.

If it weren't for Rhianna waiting for him, she'd drag out the argument to delay returning.

"Fine." She shifted and flew back toward school. Where should she go? Would Clint and Ivy still be in the dining hall? She definitely didn't want to go back there. Maybe she'd just go back to her room.

Jaxon veered off toward the Blue dorm. Bryn's stomach growled, reminding her she hadn't eaten. First she'd stop in her room, and then she'd order a pizza. Maybe two pizzas.

Landing on her terrace, she pitched forward and caught herself with her wings. After shifting, she pushed open the window and heard voices. Creeping into the room, she peeked around the doorframe. Clint and Ivy sat on the couch. The spicy aroma of pizza made her mouth water.

Stepping through the doorway, she gave a lame smile. "Hi, guys."

Ivy swooped over and pulled her into a hug. "I'm so sorry."

With those three words, the waterworks started again. Bryn squeezed Ivy and then stepped back. "Thanks for being here." She sniffled and wiped at her face with the back of her hand.

"Here." Clint handed her a box of tissues. "Now I'm going to escape while you and Ivy do the whole crying thing."

Bryn nodded. "Thanks for the Kleenex."

Clint made a hasty exit. Ivy pulled Bryn to the couch.

Bryn relayed the conversation with Zavien between bites of pizza. "I just feel so stupid for believing him in the first place." She groaned in frustration. "And I expected more from him. What's worse is Jaxon thinks all Zavien's talk about changing the law was a line."

A growl emerged from Ivy's throat. "If we ever find out that's true, I'll help you kill him and hide his body."

"Thank you."

"That's what best friends are for."

• • •

Bryn lay in bed that night contemplating her screwed-up situation. Clint and Ivy were wonderful, and they would continue to be there for her, but Zavien's bowing out left a huge hole in her life. What would she do with the time she used to spend with him?

She turned on her side and punched her pillow into shape and tried to focus on positive things. Maybe she could visit Valmont tomorrow, because he made her happy. And Christmas was coming up. That was good. She loved Christmas shopping. Maybe she'd focus on her relationship with her grandparents. She didn't need a guy in her life. She just needed to focus on her own life. There, she had a plan.

• • •

Dragon's Bluff bustled with activity. Shoppers carried bags decorated with Christmas trees. A mood of cheeriness permeated the air. Something she hadn't felt on campus since the first attack. On the walk to Fonzoli's, she people-watched.

A familiar blond woman stared into a boutique window that featured baby clothes. The high collar of the woman's coat obscured the lower portion of her face. And what would

Jaxon's mother Lillith be doing looking at baby clothes anyway?

When she was within five feet of the woman, Lillith looked up and smiled. "Bryn, how are you?"

"I'm good. How are you?"

"I'm wonderful." Lillith pointed to the window. "Which pajamas do you like best?"

Snowflakes dotted one pair of blue footy pajamas, and frogs decorated a green pair.

"Since it's almost Christmas, I'd go with the snowflakes."

"My thoughts exactly." Lillith glowed with happiness.

Life with Ferrin couldn't be responsible. Maybe it was the holiday season or recreational pharmaceuticals.

"Then again, maybe I'll buy both and have *W*s embroidered on the collar."

"*W* as in Westgate?" That was weird. "Aren't they a little small for Jaxon?"

Lillith laughed. "They're not for Jaxon. They're for his brother."

Jaxon had never mentioned a brother. Lillith grinned and placed a hand over her abdomen. The pieces fell into place.

"You're pregnant?" Bryn asked.

"Isn't it wonderful?"

Holy crap! That meant she'd slept with Ferrin. Bryn swallowed her automatic response of *Ewwww, gross* and went with "Congratulations."

She didn't like to acknowledge her own parents'…interactions…much less someone else's.

"Thank you." Lillith glanced around. "It makes me feel guilty to be so happy, in light of the recent sad news about

Rhianna."

Bryn's good mood burst like a balloon hit with a dart. "Can't you talk Ferrin into—"

Lillith shook her head. "There's not a person in the world who can talk Ferrin into anything. Jaxon told me of his plan to take care of Rhianna. Even though she won't have the life she wanted, her future isn't in question. Hopefully that will provide some consolation."

It wouldn't be enough consolation. About that, Bryn was sure. Time to change the subject before Lillith mentioned pairing *her* up with Jaxon. "I was headed to Fonzoli's for lunch if you'd like to—"

"Mother?" Jaxon approached with a wary look on his face.

Lillith smiled. "There you are. I was doing a little shopping before lunch."

"With Bryn?" Jaxon's eyes went to the display of baby clothes in the window. His brow furrowed and then his face colored. "Dear God, Bryn, how could you be so stupid?"

"What?"

He moved in close and spoke in a low voice. "Did you forget about Analise? What do you think the Directorate will do when they learn about your condition?"

The moron thought she was pregnant? She couldn't wait to see his expression when he realized the truth. She put her hand on his chest and pushed him back a step. "While I appreciate your concern for my well-being, I'm not the one shopping for baby clothes." She bit her lip to keep from laughing as confusion wrinkled his brow. Then his gaze darted to his mother, and his face paled.

"Mother?"

"Are you going to call her stupid?" Bryn asked.

"Of course not," Jaxon snapped. He squared his shoulders. "Congratulations, Mother. I presume this is a happy occurrence?"

"Yes." Lillith reached for his hand. "How would you feel about a baby brother?"

He looked at his shoes while he spoke. "I suppose it's too late to suggest you adopt another kitten, instead?" His tone was dry, but there was truth in his words.

Lillith laughed. "Too late, but don't worry. You'll always be the firstborn male and your father's heir."

"Until the baby plots to overthrow you," Bryn muttered.

Jaxon shot her a look that could melt glass. "Shouldn't you be running along to meet your knight?"

"Bryn invited us to have lunch with her. Isn't that sweet?" Lillith reached for the door to the shop. "But first I want to order some clothes."

When she'd asked Lillith to join her for lunch, Jaxon hadn't been part of the plan. "Now that I know you won't be eating alone, I'll be on my way."

"I insist you have lunch with us." Lillith held the door wide. "In you go. Both of you. First we shop. Then we eat."

Jaxon reached for the door handle. "Ladies first, Mother. I suppose you should enter as well, Bryn."

"Just for that, I'm going to buy matching monogrammed sweaters for you and your baby brother." She wasn't sure this store made such things, but they had to exist online somewhere. "I'm sure you'd look great in a blue sweater with choo-choo trains or a Disney character."

Lillith winked at Bryn. "I know a store where they sell footy pajamas for grownups and babies. Wouldn't it be adorable if Jaxon and his brother wore matching pajamas for our family Christmas photo?"

The image of Jaxon in Elmo footy pajamas had Bryn snorting with laughter. Lillith's laughter tinkled like silver bells.

Jaxon pursed his lips. "I'll wait right here."

Bryn followed along behind Lillith, oohing and ahhing at the baby clothes. That part was easy. What she needed was an escape plan. While Lillith was wonderful, having lunch with Jaxon wasn't what she needed today. Or any day. God forbid it put ideas in Lillith's head about the future.

When it was time to pay for the clothes, Bryn made a show of checking her watch. "I'd no idea it was so late. Time for homework. I better go."

"What about lunch?" Lillith's eyes filled with tears. Real tears.

And now she'd made a pregnant woman cry. A new low. "Right. Lunch. I forgot. Lunch would be great."

"Good." Lillith retrieved a handkerchief from her handbag. "Sorry about this. I'm a bit emotional."

"Not a problem." Crap. How could she ditch Jaxon without abandoning Lillith? No ideas came to mind. And she still needed to see Valmont. "Want to eat at Fonzoli's?"

• • •

Jaxon muttered under his breath as they walked down the sidewalk toward their lunch destination.

"What was that, Jaxon?" his mother asked.

"I said, 'Do you think Father would approve of us being seen together, in public, with Bryn?'"

What was she, a social leper? If she didn't fear Lillith

bursting into tears, she'd insult him right back.

"Your father isn't here." Lillith pulled out her cell phone. "Though three *is* an awkward number. I know who should join us."

Bryn tensed as Lillith dialed. Who was she calling?

"May I speak to Mrs. Sinclair?"

Crap. Not her grandmother.

Jaxon turned to her with terror in his eyes. "Stop this," he whispered.

"What do you want me to do?" she whispered back. "Tackle your pregnant mom and wrestle the phone away from her?"

Maybe her grandmother wouldn't be able to join them.

"Good afternoon, Marie. It's Lillith. Sorry for the late notice, but Jaxon and I ran into Bryn in Dragon's Bluff and we planned to lunch at Fonzoli's. Would you like to join us?"

Jaxon grabbed Bryn's arm, holding her in place while Lillith kept walking. "Leave. Now."

"I can't just run off." She jerked her arm from his grasp. "Pretend you're sick or something."

"Westgates never run from a conflict."

"But it's okay if I scurry off."

"You have no family reputation to uphold," Jaxon shot back.

"Now I'm staying, just to spite you." She moved faster and caught up with Lillith.

"That's wonderful, Marie. We'll see you soon." Lillith tucked her cell phone back into her pocket. "Your grandmother will meet us at the restaurant."

"That's great." She tried to sound happy. "This will give me a chance to finalize our plans for Christmas Eve."

When they reached the restaurant, Bryn scanned the

room for Valmont. He appeared from the kitchen wiping his hands on a white-and-red checked towel. His eyes focused on her within seconds. He smiled like she was the best thing he'd seen all day.

Happy warmth filled her chest as he crossed the room to meet her. His gaze took in Jaxon and Lillith. When he reached her, he put his arm around her shoulders in a proprietary manner, which gave her a warm fuzzy feeling.

"I'm off work in an hour. Want to go Christmas shopping?" Valmont asked, like Jaxon and his mother weren't standing there.

"Sure. I'm having lunch with Jaxon, Lillith, and my grandmother. After that I don't have any plans."

Valmont squeezed her shoulders and then removed his arm. "You'll need a table for four. Would you like to sit by the windows up front or would you prefer a quiet table in the back?"

Jaxon said, "In the back," at the same time his mom said, "By the windows, please."

Valmont made a show of looking back and forth between Jaxon and his mother. "Sorry, I think she outranks you."

Lillith grinned like a Cheshire cat as Valmont led them to a table by the front windows. "Is this to your liking?" he asked.

"This is perfect." Lillith sat when Valmont pulled out her chair. "How do you know Bryn?"

"I'm her knight," Valmont stated, like it was the most common thing in the world.

Lillith's eyebrows shot up. "How did this come to be?"

"An obnoxious individual threatened Bryn, and I interceded," Valmont said as he passed out menus.

Thank God he didn't go into details. Today was supposed to be about forgetting Zavien, not dredging up old memories.

"Why don't I bring a round of iced tea and some toasted ravioli while you wait for the rest of your party?"

Bryn's stomach growled. Toasted ravioli sounded wonderful.

• • •

Jaxon sat ramrod straight in his chair, eyeing the front door like he expected Godzilla to come charging in. Given a meeting with Godzilla or her grandmother, Bryn wasn't sure whom she'd choose. At least Godzilla wasn't trying to fix her up with Jaxon.

What would she say when her grandmother walked in? How should she behave? She had no clue. "Lillith, this is awkward, but how should I act when my grandmother comes in? I hug my parents, but my grandmother doesn't seem like the hugging type."

Jaxon snorted.

Lillith pretended not to hear him. "If you were close, it would be proper to kiss her on the cheek."

She'd spent limited time with her grandmother. "Close" wasn't a word she'd use to describe their relationship. "I'm not sure we're there yet."

"I suggest you follow her lead. If she leans in, kiss her on the cheek. If not, then a light touch on her shoulder would be appropriate."

Like she didn't have enough to be nervous about. When Valmont returned with drinks and two trays of ravioli, she considered kissing him.

He winked at her. "I knew you'd be hungry."

"You're the best knight ever." She unrolled the napkin containing her utensils and speared a ravioli with her fork. A quick dunk into marinara sauce, and she popped the ravioli in her mouth. It was crunchy, spicy Italian bliss. She was working her way through her sixth ravioli when conversation died down around them.

Marie Sinclair entered the establishment and heads turned. Fonzoli's probably wasn't on the list of restaurants her grandmother visited on a regular basis. Wearing a crisp dove-gray suit, her grandmother broadcast power and influence. Bryn resisted the urge to apologize for her gray sweatshirt and jeans.

Jaxon stood to pull out her grandmother's chair.

"Mrs. Sinclair, how nice to see you again."

"Thank you. It's lovely to see you and your mother as well." Her grandmother sat and turned to Bryn. Expectation and challenge clear on her face.

"Hello, Grandmother." Hoping for the best, Bryn leaned in and pecked her grandmother on the cheek. "It's nice to see you."

A genuine smile lit the older woman's face. "Thank you. It's nice to see you, too."

Okay. That went better than expected. Now what?

Valmont appeared next to Bryn. "Mrs. Sinclair, may I bring you something to drink while you study the menu?"

"I'll have a glass of white wine and the pasta primavera."

Since she probably shouldn't eat an entire pizza in front of her grandmother, what was the easiest, least-likely-to-drip-on-her-shirt meal she could order? Best to choose something she could eat with a knife and fork.

"Bryn?"

An escape route wasn't within Valmont's power, so she decided on two pepperoni calzones.

After everyone placed their orders, her grandmother said, "We should discuss our plans for Christmas Eve."

It was hard to discuss something she knew nothing about. "What time do you usually have dinner?"

"Dinner is served at eight. Of course the orchestra starts playing at six."

Wait. What? "You're having an orchestra?"

Her grandmother sighed. "I tried to convince your grandfather we should go with a three-string quartet, but he had other ideas."

Three-string quartet? What had she gotten herself into? "When I hear 'Christmas Eve dinner,' I imagine sitting down to eat with a few family members. What do you mean when you say it?"

Her grandmother blinked. "I'm referring to our annual Christmas Eve ball."

A ball...as in Cinderella-riding-in-a-horse-drawn-carriage kind of ball? *Where is my fairy godmother when I need one?* What in the heck would she wear?

"I've never been to a ball," seemed like the only rational response.

Jaxon snorted.

Bryn's grandmother turned her steely gaze on him. "Did you have something to add to the conversation, young man?"

"No. Sorry. That was rude of me. I can't imagine a life where you've never been to a Christmas ball."

Bryn imagined beaning him in the head with a ravioli.

but then she realized this wasn't about Jaxon. It was about mending fences with her grandparents. Keeping her voice calm and even, she ignored Jaxon and addressed her grandmother. "A ball sounds fun. I assume people dance and eat. What else happens?"

"After dinner, we adjourn to a separate ballroom where everyone opens one present. The rest are saved for Christmas morning."

Okay. Her grandparents had more than one ballroom. Interesting. Did she need to buy presents for her grandparents? What could you buy for people who had two freaking ballrooms?

"I love watching the little ones open their presents." Lillith's hand drifted to her stomach. "It will be a few years before Asher figures out how Christmas works."

"Asher?" Bryn's grandmother asked.

Lillith practically glowed. "I'm expecting a boy."

"Congratulations." Her grandmother held up her wine in a toast. "I hope he brings you as much joy as Jaxon has."

Bryn snorted.

Jaxon glared at her.

Bryn tried to look repentant, but ended up laughing. "Sorry. It's just that I don't associate you with joy."

"He wasn't always this intense," Lillith said. "You should have seen him when he was three. He walked around clutching this bear—"

"Mother." Jaxon sounded like he was moments from exploding.

Lillith reached over and ruffled his hair. The mutinous expression on his face almost made Bryn choke on the ravioli she'd popped into her mouth. "Bryn needs to know you're not always this serious. After all, if the Directorate approves your lineage—"

"Here's your food." Valmont passed out entrées, oblivious to what he'd interrupted.

"Anything else I can get for you?" he asked.

"Strychnine, or a noose," Jaxon muttered.

"Sorry, you have to call ahead for special orders." Valmont touched Bryn's shoulder and gave a reassuring squeeze. "I'll rescue you if things turn ugly."

"Thanks."

Her grandmother watched Valmont walk away. "Are you friends with the waiter?"

"He's my knight."

"You do seem to foster relationships with the most inappropriate people." Her grandmother's tone was frosty.

Fire rose in Bryn's throat. Concentrating, she pushed it back down. After taking a drink of her ice water, she cut into the calzone. "Valmont is one of the most honorable people I know. If anything bad were to happen, I know I could trust him to be on my side."

"And you couldn't trust me?" Her grandmother's tone was flat and cold.

Just like that, lunch went to hell. Bryn set her fork down and gave her grandmother her full attention. "If I played my role according to polite society, this is the part where I'd declare my undying trust in you. However, I was raised to be honest. The truth is, I don't know you well enough to answer that question. I'm sorry if this starts us out on the wrong foot."

Lillith and Jaxon both looked like they were ready to duck and cover. Had she ruined everything?

"Although my daughter is to blame for your lack of social skills, at least she instilled in you a good moral code. While I don't like your answer, I appreciate your honesty."

Bryn's shoulders slumped in relief.

"Do sit up straight, and try to keep your elbows off the table."

After adjusting her posture, Bryn tackled the next thorny topic of conversation. "Are my parents invited to dinner Christmas Eve?"

Sipping her wine, her grandmother stared off into the distance. Was she remembering Christmases past? Had there ever been a happy Christmas Eve at her grandmother's house? They probably hadn't stayed up all night eating cookies and stringing popcorn.

"Your grandfather and I decided it might be best if your parents came for a private visit on a different day."

That was convenient. She gripped her fork tighter and tried to keep the snark out of her voice. "Any day in particular?"

"A day between Christmas and New Year's would be ideal. You can discuss it with them when you return home for the holidays, and then we'll make plans."

Strain showed around her grandmother's eyes. Giving this inch must've cost her a lot.

"Thank you for agreeing to see them."

Her grandmother nodded. "On to more important business. Do you have an appropriate gown for the ball?"

She had the copper dress she'd worn to the fall dance. Not a happy memory. God forbid she wear a dress her grandmother deemed inappropriate. Best to ask for help. "What type of gown are we talking about?"

"We should go shopping together." Lillith announced like it was a fabulous idea.

If the woman weren't with child, Bryn would've kicked her.

"I agree." Bryn's grandmother tilted her head and studied Lillith. "Are you feeling well enough to go shopping after lunch, or do you require rest?"

"I'm fine." Lillith turned to Bryn. "I know you planned to Christmas shop with your knight. Perhaps you can reschedule?"

Noooooo. She wanted to spend time with Valmont. Now it appeared she'd have to spend the day with her grandmother and Lillith.

"I'm sure your friend will understand." From the set of her grandmother's jaw, saying no wasn't an option.

Bryn pushed her chair back from the table. "Why don't I go chat with him right now?" She headed for the kitchen door and waited for Valmont to appear. He finished taking an order at a table across the room and then headed her way.

"In need of a rescue?" he asked.

"Yes, but I don't think it would help my relationship with my grandmother. She wants to go shopping after lunch. Could I meet you later?"

"Sure." He reached over and brushed a crumb off her chin. "Why don't you come back after you finish shopping?"

"Thanks for understanding."

"Part understanding. Part fear. Your grandmother is one scary woman."

Chapter Twenty

After lunch, Bryn followed her grandmother, Lillith, and a mutinous Jaxon to a small dress store off the main street.

"I didn't know there were stores back here," Bryn said.

"It's not a store, it's a boutique." Rather than reach for the door handle, her grandmother pressed what looked like a doorbell. The saleswoman glanced up from the cash register when she heard the bell and flew across the room to unlock the doors.

"Mrs. Sinclair, how lovely to see you." Jaxon and his mother walked in. "And the Westgates—it's always a pleasure when you stop by. What can I help you with today?"

With all that sucking up, the woman must work on commission.

"I need a Christmas gown for my granddaughter."

The saleswoman glanced at the door, like she was searching for another person. Bryn cleared her throat, and the woman put the puzzle pieces together. "Sorry, I expected someone more…"

"Blond?" Bryn said with a grin.

"Yes." She swallowed and seemed to regain her composure. "Come with me. I'm sure we have something perfect for you."

Right.

The woman whisked her off to a dressing room and then returned with a dozen dresses. Wait. Not dresses. They were gowns…actual ball gowns made of what she knew had to be real silk. Every single one had ruffles or sequins or lace. The bodices were stiff and the skirts were floor length.

None of them looked like something her grandmother might wear. Was this a test?

"Excuse me, I need to ask my grandmother a question." She stuck her head out of the dressing room. "Do the gowns have to be so…frilly?"

"Frilly?" Her grandmother frowned. "What do you mean?"

"The dresses are age appropriate," the saleslady said.

"I'm sure these dresses would be lovely for someone else. I'd prefer something without ruffles, or lace, or sequins." She looked at her grandmother. "Unless you disagree. I've never been to a ball before, so maybe I don't understand what's expected."

Her grandmother shot the saleslady a look that would've reduced a small child to tears. "Remove those gowns from the dressing room and find Bryn a strapless silk sheath dress in a dignified color."

"Of course. My mistake." The saleslady scurried off to do as her grandmother asked. When she was out of hearing range, Bryn said, "One of the dresses had ruffles and lace *and* sequins. I think there might have been some feathers mixed in as well." She shuddered. "It was awful."

"Was it lavender?" Lillith asked.

Bryn nodded.

"That dress has been here forever. I think they've been trying to pawn it off on some poor girl for the last twenty years."

The saleslady returned with a handful of dresses. Tight-lipped, she hung them in the dressing room and then retreated to the cash register.

Bryn examined her choices. This was more like it.

There was an emerald sleeveless gown that resembled something an actress might wear on the red carpet. Could she pull it off? Only one way to find out. Stripping out of her clothes, Bryn slid into the whisper soft silk. She checked the three-way mirror and did a small happy dance. The dress fit like a glove. The knee-length slit allowed her to walk without shuffling her feet.

She stepped out of the dressing room. "What do you think?"

Lillith clapped her hands together. "It's lovely."

Head tilted to the side, her grandmother scanned Bryn from head to toe. "Turn around."

Ignoring the resentment she felt at being ordered around like a puppy, Bryn did as her grandmother asked. When she completed the rotation she expected to find her grandmother nodding in approval. This was not the case.

"Tell me those tattoos aren't permanent," her grandmother said.

Bryn's throat grew tight. Zavien had drawn the tattoos with permanent marker. Bryn used her skill with Quintessence to keep them vibrant, thereby avoiding needles. She'd requested the image of the Blue and Red dragons, head to tail in a yin-yang circle, because it represented who she was. Zavien had added a small black dragon on her right shoulder signifying she was an honorary Black dragon. She could remove the black dragon, but the yin-yang dragons representing her mixed parentage stayed.

"Do you dislike tattoos in general, or mine in particular?"

"Both." Shoulders squared, her grandmother appeared ready to do battle.

Bryn took a deep breath and blew it out. There were going to be bumps in this road to reunion, but in the end it would be worth it. Hopefully. "If you can give a little, I'll give a little. The yin-yang dragons stay, and I'll make the smaller one disappear."

"I'd prefer it the other way around." Her grandmother straightened the sleeve of her blouse.

"It represents who I am." Bryn smoothed her hands over the skirt of the gown. "Even if I remove the tattoo, people will know who my parents are. I won't hide my heritage to make others comfortable."

Fingers drumming on the armrest of the couch, her grandmother's lips set in a thin line. "Fine. Now, let's talk about your hair color, or colors. Perhaps you could pick one?"

That did it. Bryn concentrated and shifted the Quintessence in her body to color her hair neon green. "Like this, you mean?"

Lillith seemed overcome by a coughing fit, to hide her laughter.

Her grandmother reached up to rub the bridge of her nose. "You *are* your mother's daughter. Aren't you?"

"I am." Maybe this wasn't going to work. A hollow feeling settled in her stomach. "If you want someone to smile and nod, I'm not your girl."

"You're the only granddaughter I have. My hope is you'll mature and grow out of this odd hair phase. For now, change your hair back, and eliminate the smaller tattoo." Her grandmother turned to face the saleslady. "We need shoes and a small, tasteful handbag."

"Emerald green is such a lovely color." Lillith touched Jaxon's shoulder. "A bow tie in that color would be striking with your black tuxedo."

"No." Jaxon spoke in a voice that mimicked his father's.

Lillith snatched her hand back like she'd been burned. Her eyes filled with tears.

Jaxon sighed. "I'm sorry, Mother. I didn't mean to sound harsh. Rhianna is still my date, and my bow tie will match her gown."

Damn it. There Jaxon went again, doing something nice.

"I appreciate your loyalty, young man, but the argument is pointless," Bryn's grandmother said. "This morning I received word Rhianna and her family will be traveling to Europe over the holidays. Be that as it may, the tradition of matching bow ties to gowns may be appropriate for school dances, but not for an actual ball."

Lillith sniffled. "Ferrin matches his ties to my gowns."

Her grandmother gave a tight smile. "I see. Perhaps I am old-fashioned in my thinking. If you wish to buy Jaxon the matching emerald bow tie, please do."

"I don't believe Father would find an emerald bow tie amusing. If you'll excuse me, I have homework to complete." Jaxon headed for the door, pushing it open so hard it bounced against the wall and rattled the glass in the windowpanes.

"He has a temper like his father," Lillith said.

"Which is why I wish you'd stop trying to fix us up. If you

keep pushing Jaxon and me together, one of us won't come out alive."

Bryn's grandmother rose and came toward her until they were arm's length apart. "Do you enjoy flying?"

Was this a trick question? "Yes."

"Do you still want to become a medic?"

Not knowing what was coming, Bryn nodded and waited for her grandmother to move in for the kill.

"And do you think your parents enjoy their isolation? Don't they miss flying?"

She'd never thought of her parents in those terms before. When did they have time to fly? The simple fact that she'd never suspected they were anything but human told her how infrequent their flights must have been. A weight of sadness pressed on her heart.

"I can see it in your eyes. You realize now what they gave up. You will marry whomever the Directorate chooses if you wish to live this life."

"Are you trying to blackmail me?"

"No." Her grandmother reached to cup her chin. "I'm trying to save you. Understand this: marriage is a legal contract that produces children. Nothing more. Love isn't part of the equation."

Bryn felt her nails digging into her palms and unclenched her fists. "Did you ever love your husband?"

"No. And I'm better off for it." Leaning in, her grandmother pressed a light kiss on her cheek. "I'll have your gown delivered to our estate. You can dress there before the ball."

Her grandmother exited the boutique.

"She's right, you know," Lillith said.

The blond woman looked so fragile sitting on the couch

alone.

Bryn joined her. "Right about what?"

"It's better not to love someone who can't love you back." Lillith sighed and averted her gaze. "When my contract with Ferrin was approved, I thought myself the luckiest girl in the world. He was so handsome. When he came to call on me at school, he was the perfect gentleman. All my classmates were jealous.

"It wasn't until we were married that I noticed his lack of warmth. At first, I thought I'd done something wrong. Gradually I came to realize he'd never recovered from your mother's defection. I could never live up to her memory. So I stopped trying."

Not knowing what else to say, Bryn went with her gut. "I'm sorry."

"I'm not. I have a good life. My son loves me. And I have another child on the way. I'm happy. You could be happy with Jaxon."

It was difficult to swallow over the lump in her throat. Lillith and her grandmother meant well, but a loveless life would never be enough. "There is no way Ferrin will allow me to marry Jaxon." *Thank God.* "It's silly to discuss this."

"A few weeks ago, I would've agreed. Rhianna's accident opened a door for you. Jaxon is handsome, smart, and loyal."

Bryn sat back and crossed her arms over her chest. "He's stubborn and he has a foul temper."

A slow grin spread across Lillith's face. "Must be like looking in a mirror."

Not like she could argue that point. "Fine. Our temperaments are similar. That alone should be reason for us not to marry. Think about how obnoxious your grandchildren would be."

"I know you respect my son," Lillith went on, ignoring Bryn's argument. "And he respects you. That is a good foundation for a relationship."

This conversation was going nowhere. Bryn pushed to her feet. "Believe what you will. I'm going to change out of this dress, go back to Fonzoli's and spend time with Valmont."

When she reached the restaurant there was a line out the door of people waiting to be seated. Crap. Maybe she could sneak in the back. The door to the kitchen stood wide open to let the heat out. Should she go in?

Valmont's grandfather saw her and waved her inside, spouting something in Italian. The only word she understood was "Valmont."

The door to the dining room swung open and Valmont strode in. Just seeing him made her feel better. When he looked up and grinned, her stress melted away. His single dimple was like therapy. The hug he pulled her into felt heavenly. He smelled like Italian spices.

"Come with me. I want to show you something." He grabbed her hand like it was the most normal thing in the world and led her through a door at the back of the kitchen and up a flight of narrow wooden stairs.

"Where are we going?"

"My secret sanctuary." At the top of the stairs, Valmont produced a key from his shirt pocket and unlocked the door before gesturing for Bryn to go in. "Ladies first."

A strange sense of déjà vu came over her. Jaxon had said those same words outside the baby clothing store, but hadn't meant them. Jerk. Valmont meant it.

The polished oak floors and walls of the attic room gleamed in the light. A marble-topped table sat in the middle of the room. The matching chairs were black cast-iron with gray cushions. She blinked. It was patio furniture.

A glider swing sat in the far corner of the room with matching chairs. Colorful pots of roses and other flowers were scattered around the room on small tables or lined up against the baseboards. Their sweet scents permeated the room. "It's a garden. How's that possible?"

"Look up," Valmont said.

The roof was punctuated with rows of windows. There were so many, and so evenly spaced, the ceiling resembled a checkerboard made of light and dark squares.

"I love it."

"My grandmother loves to garden, so my grandfather built this room as a wedding gift so she would always have a garden no matter the season."

"It's beautiful."

"Why don't you pick a chair, and I'll go fix us a couple of cappuccinos."

"Sounds good." She wandered the room smelling different flowers. Several roses were in full bloom, and half a dozen buds appeared ready to burst. She touched a red rose, channeling a bit of Quintessence into the soil. The buds burst open and their fragrance filled the air.

Maybe she could become a florist or a gardener. Beautiful flowers made people happy. If she was a florist or a gardener, she could move back to the human world and leave this entire mess behind. But then she wouldn't be able to fly whenever she wanted or become a medic. Damn her grandmother for putting those thoughts into her head.

The sound of Valmont's footsteps on the stairs kept her from trying her skills on another plant. He entered the room carrying a small tray with two steaming cups of cappuccino, sugar, and cream.

She inhaled the rich coffee scent. "That smells fabulous."

Once they were seated at the table, he seemed content to drink his coffee in silence. After a few minutes, she couldn't take the quiet. "What does your family do for Christmas?"

"I have a sister and an older brother who are married. Between them they have three boys and two girls. Christmas Eve, my parents, siblings, and all the assorted nieces and nephews squeeze into my grandparents' house, eat until we're about to burst, and then have a ping-pong tournament."

"Ping-pong?"

He grinned. "My grandmother is the undefeated champion."

"That sounds nice."

"What does your family do?"

"Normally, my parents and I string popcorn to decorate the tree, bake cookies, and play board games. This year, I'm trying to make nice with my grandmother, so I'm going to her house."

Valmont cringed. "Sorry to hear that."

She laughed. "It's funny. If you'd asked me six months ago if I wanted to wear a gown and attend a Christmas Eve ball, I would've jumped at the chance. Now all I want to do is go home."

"You could come play ping-pong with us. I guarantee the food and the company will be better."

In her mind she could see herself laughing and eating dinner with Valmont's family. "Wish I could. But if I want to have any sort of relationship with my grandparents, I must go to the ball." She shook her head. "My life is the weirdest fairy tale ever."

Crash. Glass rained down on them. Bryn jumped back, knocking her chair over as a baseball-sized piece of hail smacked into the table.

"What the hell?" She met Valmont's gaze. They both glanced up.

Crash. Crash. Crash. Glass flew as hail smashed through the windows. Valmont lunged for her, and together, they ran for the stairs. Once they were on the landing, he slammed the door to the greenhouse room. The crashing sound was muffled, but the pounding on the roof grew louder. People in the restaurant screamed. Valmont and Bryn ran down the stairs.

Valmont's grandfather was shouting in Italian, and waving his hands directing customers who'd been in the dining room to cram into the kitchen. The back door had been shut, and wooden shutters had been closed in front of the windows.

Bryn ran to look in the dining room. Two girls huddled under a table, crying. They couldn't have been more than six years old. Where was their mom? Hail flew in through the gaping hole where the window used to be and smacked down on the table, splintering the wood.

"Valmont, I'm going to blow fire at that window to keep the hail away while you grab those girls. All right?"

"Give me a minute." He ran back into the kitchen and came out with a pot on his head. He placed one on her head and held a smaller pot in each hand.

"Good thinking," she said. "Ready?"

"Let's go."

She took a deep breath and thought of the idiots who were playing with peoples' lives. Fire roared in her gut and up her throat. She inhaled and then blasted a stream of fire over the table at the window, slowly walking toward it. As the hailstones hit her flames, they hissed and melted into steam. Valmont, keeping low to the ground, ran to the girls and put the makeshift helmets on their heads. With one girl under each arm, he ran back to the kitchen.

Once they were safe, Bryn moved toward the window.

"Bryn, what are you doing?"

Answering him would mean stopping her flames. The anger fueling her pyrotechnics raged inside her. She kept going until she reached the window and checked the street. Crouched against walls and in doorways, dragons of every color used their breath weapons to keep the hail at bay. None of them appeared to need her help, so she stayed where she was.

The hail banging on the rooftops was deafening. Then, as if someone threw a switch, the hail stopped. Ears ringing, Bryn turned to find Valmont behind her wearing a soup pot on his head. The pissed-off expression he wore, combined with his odd headgear, made her laugh.

"What's so funny?" The pot shifted so it covered his eyes. "Oh." He pulled the pot off and took hers off, too. "I suppose that did look ridiculous."

"But it was smart." She pointed back toward the kitchen. "Are the girls okay?"

A solemn look crossed his face. "Their mom told them not to leave the table while she ran down the street to buy something. Unfortunately, they listened too well."

"Do you think their mom is okay?"

"I hope so." People started filtering out of the kitchen, picking up their belongings and righting the tables and chairs. "I better get a broom."

"Wait." Bryn pointed to a group of Green dragons. "You three. Use your wind to push all the debris into a pile."

The girl in the group opened her mouth, but Bryn cut her off. "Do it now."

One of the Green males cleared his throat. "If everyone would go back in the kitchen for a moment, we'll clean this up."

Bryn and Valmont returned to the kitchen as well, but stood in the doorway to supervise. The Greens directed wind from their hands to push all the debris into the back corner. In five minutes, they'd cleared the floor.

"Thank you." Valmont nodded to the Greens. "Much appreciated." He pointed at the waist-high pile of glass and splintered wood. "I'm going to need a bigger dustpan."

The rest of the patrons cleared out.

"I'll drive you back to school," Valmont said. "I'm sure they'll be checking to make sure all the students are safe."

"Please tell me your car is safe in a garage." The idea of his cherry-red convertible banged to pieces made her ill.

"It is, but I'll drive my dad's truck, in case the hail comes again."

"Maybe you should keep some soup pots in the trunk of your car for emergencies."

· · ·

After Valmont dropped her off, she signed in at the back gate and headed to her dorm, intent on finding Clint and Ivy. They were waiting for her in the first-floor lounge. Ivy zoomed across the room to hug her.

"From now on, we're all going places together." Ivy's

voice shook.

Bryn hugged her friend back. "I was inside at Fonzoli's. I'm okay." She stepped back from Ivy. "Where were you guys?"

Ivy blushed. "We were studying."

Right. "Did anyone get hurt?"

"You didn't hear?" Clint asked.

The hair on the back of her neck stood up. "Hear what?"

"The hail came on so fast...students who were flying got beaten up pretty bad. Garrett...the hailstones..." Clint cleared his throat and looked away. "He's lost the use of his right wing."

"No." Bryn didn't feel her legs give out, but the next thing she knew, she was sitting on the floor. This could not be happening. "In Dragon's Bluff, it wasn't so bad. Windows were smashed, but everyone found shelter."

"Everyone to your rooms, please." A guard bellowed from the front door. Dark circles ringed his eyes, like he was recovering from a broken nose. "If any of your friends are missing let the staff or one of us know."

Bryn rushed over to him. "Can I help the medics?"

Pain shone from the man's eyes. "It is my understanding that those who are still injured are beyond help."

Tears flooded her eyes. What would happen to Garrett and anyone else who was permanently injured? Before she could ask, the guard turned and left.

Bryn, Ivy, and Clint all stayed in her room together that night. The next morning, classes were canceled and the dining hall was closed. Students were to stay in their dorms and eat at the first-floor cafés.

An air of disbelief and misery seemed to float through

the first-floor lounge where Bryn, Clint, and Ivy sat picking at their breakfast of submarine sandwiches.

"Okay. In the big scheme of things, I know this is petty, but I miss eggs and bacon." Clint picked the onions off his sandwich.

"Thank God they have coffee." Bryn sipped her second cup. She could eat anything for breakfast as long as caffeine was part of the deal.

"We've had wind, ice, and earthquakes. Does that mean fire or lightning is next?" Ivy asked.

Fire was self-explanatory. "What form will lightning take? A giant storm, or bolts of electricity zapping everything?"

"If you were still privileged enough to be enrolled in history class, you'd know that Black dragons used storms to cover their attacks. It's a two-for-one whammy. Drench everything with water and then light it up."

"So it's electrocution or fire. Great." Bryn finished off her bag of chips. None of this made sense. "Have the Clans ever worked together before to attack the Directorate?"

"That's the weird thing," Clint said, "or one of the weirdest of all the weird things going on right now. The Clans have always played their separate roles."

"Not true," Ivy said. "The Clans fought among themselves and against each other when they were trying to keep territories, before the Accords were drawn up. Each Clan settled in a specific territory and sent a representative to marry into another Clan."

"This sounds vaguely familiar." Bryn rolled her eyes. She'd been kicked out of history class over this topic. The teacher had claimed that crossbreeding couldn't produce a functional shape-shifting dragon, even though Bryn had been sitting right in front of her. *Wait a minute.* She scooted closer to her friends so she wouldn't be overheard. "I heard a folk tale that those dragons who married into other Clans had children with unusual powers and that one of them, Wraith Nightshade, tried to take over everything and make himself king. In the end, he was killed, and that's when the Directorate was formed to make sure nothing like that happened again."

"And if that's true, if any of those hybrid kids survived and married, they'd produce more hybrids." Clint glanced around. "We probably shouldn't be talking about this out here."

"Okay, no more hybrid talk." Bryn leaned back in her seat. "Why are these attacks happening? Why are they hurting students? We have no power. If someone is pissed off at the people in control, why aren't they going after them?"

Ivy shoved her sandwich away. "My best guess is they want to scare our parents, so they'll demand the Directorate do something. And if the Directorate fails, our parents, or some of them at least, will rebel."

Doubtful. Most of the dragons seemed to bow down to the Directorate pretty readily. Even Zavien, who was supposed to be the leader of the student Revisionists, was just an errand boy who delivered petitions to the Directorate. And that's when it hit her. She hadn't thought to ask about Zavien since she'd gotten back. Was that bad or good?

"What do you think the Directorate's next move will be?" Bryn asked.

"I imagine they'll find a way for us to go back to classes tomorrow," Clint said, "but I doubt we'll be able to go to Dragon's Bluff for a while, or go flying."

"I wonder if they'll still let us go home for Christmas next week," Ivy said. "I mean, they have to, right?"

"Of course." Clint put his arm around Ivy's shoulders. "Do you think the Directorate wants to deal with a bunch of surly teenagers griping about missing Christmas?"

"They're attacking the school because we're like sitting ducks here. We're probably safer spread out in different cities," Bryn said.

Clint and Ivy gave her the "you don't have a clue" look, which she hadn't seen in a while and hadn't missed. "What? You all live in some color-coded apartment complex?"

"No." Ivy leaned into Clint. "The Blues stick to their estates, which are scattered in the forest surrounding the institute. Clint and I live in a town about twenty minutes from here called Lakeview Hills."

"Because there are hills that overlook a lake?" Bryn asked.

"Yes. It's a bunch of three-bedroom houses and parks. The business district is one town over in Emberville. A lot of dragons live in apartments or condos close to where they work. There are a few small villages mixed in throughout the forest. I mean really small, like just a mom-and-pop store and a gas station with one blinking stoplight."

"So dragons mostly populate small areas and keep to themselves." Speaking of people keeping to themselves, Bryn needed to email her parents and break the news about Christmas Eve.

"What's wrong?" Ivy asked.

"I have to tell my parents I won't be home for Christmas Eve. It's always been just the three of us." The depth of her parents' isolation finally became clear to her. "I never thought about it before. How lonely they must be."

"Do they seem lonely?" Clint asked. "Because the way you described them, they seemed happy."

"I thought they were. Now I realize they've never had any close friends."

"Given a choice of marrying Ferrin or keeping to yourself, which would you choose?" Ivy asked.

"Good point." Maybe she was projecting her own feelings on her parents. They'd never seemed unhappy when she was growing up. "I think I'll call them tonight to tell them about Christmas."

Later that night in her room, she made the call. No one answered, so she left a message and decided to email them. She explained that she'd come home on the twenty-second, fly back to her grandparents' estate for the Christmas Eve ball, and then come home later that night so she'd be there to open presents Christmas morning. After sending the email, she waited for a reply. None came. They were probably out Christmas shopping.

That brought a puzzle to mind. How could she shop if she wasn't allowed to leave campus? If she had a credit card, she could shop online. She crossed her fingers for luck and pulled out her Dragon's Bluff credit card. Sure enough, there was a Web address, which allowed her to shop online at several stores. First she needed to check her balance. Her parents didn't have that much to give her. Before she tried to order Christmas presents, she should check her limit.

After typing in her information, she gaped at the screen. The number for her account had far too many zeros at the end. She checked her account's history and saw the modest balance she'd begun with. The extreme jump in her funds had come after her grandparents had recognized her. *Huh…* *That was weird.* It was nice that they were willing to help out with her expenses, but why hadn't they mentioned it?

She'd ask her grandmother about it later. Right now, she'd shop. First, she ordered a giant tin of caramel corn from Snacks Galore and several frozen pizzas from Fonzoli's to be shipped to her parents.

Now, what to get Clint and Ivy? An art set would work for Ivy. For Clint, she bought a T-shirt that looked like a tuxedo jacket and shirt when you put it on. Since he'd made such a big deal out of hating to wear a tuxedo to the dance, maybe he'd find it funny. Guys were hard to buy for. That left Valmont and her grandparents to shop for. For Valmont, she found a rug that would match the pillows his sister gave him as a housewarming gift for his cabin. For her grandparents… she had no clue. What did you buy people who had two ballrooms?

After scrolling through multiple Web pages, she settled on a gardening club membership for her grandmother, which sent one plant a month in the mail. Gardening was the only hobby she knew her grandmother had. For her grandfather, she bought a dessert-of-the-month-club membership, since he seemed to like food as much as she did. Was that lame? Probably, but it would do until she came up with a better idea.

The next morning, Bryn didn't know if she had class or not. She showered and dressed just in case. When she wandered down to the café for breakfast, it was empty. A sign posted in the café informed her classes would resume at normal times and the dining hall was open. "Nice of them to let us all know."

Should she run and knock on Ivy's door? Ivy and Clint coming down the stairs answered that question. They checked out the café. Bryn pointed at the sign.

"Okay." Clint yawned and walked toward the front door of the dorm with Ivy in tow.

The mood in the dining hall was cautiously optimistic. Students talked about leaving school at the end of the week.

"How did your parents take the news about Christmas Eve?" Ivy asked as they filled their plates at the buffet.

Bryn drenched her pancakes in syrup before adding a pile of bacon to her plate. "They haven't answered yet. I don't know if they're busy, or if they don't know how to respond." A nervous feeling plagued her stomach. That didn't stop her from eating her weight in pancakes. As her mom once told her, when she'd explained that dragons could eat as much as they want and not gain weight, there are few problems in life sugar and fat can't solve.

"How are you getting home?" Clint asked.

Bryn paused with her fork halfway to her mouth. "I hadn't thought of that. Zavien and Garrett flew with me the first time." Zavien was out of the picture. Garrett, well, he wouldn't be flying anywhere. She pushed her food away. "Has there been any news on Garrett?"

"They allowed the injured students to leave school early for the holidays," Clint said.

Allowed to leave? Probably more like shooed them out of sight. Sadness for Garrett and Rhianna slammed into her chest. "It's all so wrong."

They finished breakfast in silence.

Chapter Twenty-One

They'd taken their seats in Elemental Science when a commotion broke out in the hallway. Bryn turned to find her grandmother standing in the classroom doorway. Tears streaked the older woman's face. "Bryn, come with me."

Something was wrong, like end-of-the-world wrong, because nothing would make her grandmother openly show emotions except…no… She wouldn't go there. It had to be something else.

She checked with Mr. Stanton. He gestured that she should go.

Pushing away from her desk, it took effort to move toward her grandmother. "What's wrong?"

"Not here." Her grandmother walked down the hall and into a classroom where two Reds stood flanking her grandfather. The frown lines etched in his face made him look like he was carved from stone.

Her grandmother sat at a student desk, like the weight

of an ugly truth bore down on her, making it too hard to stand. Bryn backed up to a chair and sat. "My parents…"

"Bryn." Her grandfather cleared his throat. "There's no easy way to say this. A bomb, disguised as a Christmas present, was delivered to their apartment late last night. They were killed instantly."

"No." He had to be wrong. Her parents couldn't be gone. She was going home tomorrow… They were going to decorate the tree, and string popcorn, and bake cookies, and play Battleship. Her dad would win like he always did, and she would roll her eyes at his victory dance while her mom laughed.

"I am sorry." Her grandfather's voice wavered.

No… No… No. Heat built inside her body. This couldn't be happening. Her parents weren't involved in dragon politics. They were innocent. Anger banked the flames in her gut. Her breathing came faster, and something crawled up the back of her throat and for a moment she thought she might vomit, and then sparks shot from her nostrils with every exhalation and all she could taste was smoke.

She wanted to scream…yell…demand answers…and she could do none of those things without spewing flames. Pushing to her feet, she stumbled over to an open window, took a deep breath, opened her mouth and roared her grief in blazing flames over and over again until her throat felt raw and exhaustion dropped her to the floor.

And it wasn't enough. Pain raged inside her, but her spark was gone. Her flame exhausted. Everything. Gone.

On her knees, she stared out at the afternoon sky. It was still blue. Students walked around campus going about their lives.

"How does everything keep going?" Bryn asked.

"It just does." Her grandmother stood by her side. "Even though you think the entire world should come to a screeching halt. It keeps turning, which is damn annoying."

Choking back a laugh, Bryn took the hand her grandmother offered. Holding out one last hope, she addressed her grandfather. "Could there be... Is there any chance you're wrong?"

"I wish there was," he said, "but no."

The injustice of it cut at her insides. "Why? My parents didn't have anything to do with any of this."

"I know." Her grandfather straightened his shoulders. "Life isn't fair. As I'm sure you've learned."

"Can I see...is there..." Too horrific, the words wouldn't come.

"The bomb leveled your parents' apartment and half the city block around it. Believe me when I say there is nothing left to see but a crater in the ground. Whoever did this made sure there wasn't any DNA evidence left for the police to find. Nothing to identify your parents as anything other than human." He stood. "From now on, your home is with us."

"Thank you." She felt hollow and empty, like someone had scraped her guts out with an ice cream scoop.

The next hour was a blur. Her grandmother and one of the Red guards accompanied her back to Mr. Stanton's class, where she explained the situation to Clint and Ivy. They barely had time to hug her before she was escorted to her room to pack her belongings.

Her grandmother rambled on about not worrying about missing homework assignments. Like she gave a crap about homework right now. Nothing mattered right now. Nothing except finding the people who'd done this and exacting revenge. She'd never believed herself capable of murder. And now she wouldn't give a second thought to digging her talons into the murderers' chests and ripping out their hearts. More than that, she would enjoy it.

Funny what you learn about yourself during times of stress.

Once she'd packed, the guard ushered her and her grandparents into an SUV driven by another guard. Other students, mostly Blues, were being shuffled into similar cars.

"Everyone is afraid." No one answered or confirmed her suspicions. "Are my friends safe?"

"You mean the Black dragons from your class?" her grandmother asked.

Bryn nodded.

"As long as they don't have relatives on the Directorate, they should be fine."

That was good. Bryn stared out the window of the SUV, watching the trees go by, consumed by one thought. "When we find out who murdered my parents, what happens to them?"

"No trial. No explanations. No excuses," her grandmother said. "They die."

Chapter Twenty-Two

Good to know her grandmother was on board with the revenge plan.

The SUV bounced over a rut in the tree-lined road leading to her grandparents' estate. Bryn grasped her seat belt, needing to hold on to something. Which was funny, because with her parents gone, what did she have left to hold on to?

Time to block things out for a while. Hoping for sleep, Bryn closed her eyes as the SUV continued winding through the forest. When the motion stopped, Bryn woke. One look out the window showed that the building—she couldn't think of it as a house—was as monstrous as she remembered. Five stories high, built of pale gray stone, it would've made a great set for a vampire movie.

Would this ever feel like home? Probably not. She followed her grandparents through the giant front door and into the main hall. The marble floors and granite walls of the foyer didn't broadcast a warm welcome. Goose bumps pebbled her arms.

Up a marble staircase they went, to the second floor landing, where they stopped. *Now what?*

"I have Directorate business to attend to. I'll see you both at dinner." Her grandfather continued up the stairs to the third floor.

"I thought we'd choose your rooms." Her grandmother gestured toward the right. "There are several suites in my wing that would be suitable."

"Okay." Rooms? As in more than one? Whatever. As long as it had a bed and a dresser, she'd be fine.

The only sound in the house was the clicking of their heels on the marble tile. This silence, this nothingness, would drive her crazy. She'd need a radio or a television for sure. They reached a door on the right hand side, and her grandmother gestured that she should enter. "Go on."

Bryn grasped the doorknob and froze. "Are we sure there aren't any bombs wired to the doors this time?" The last time she'd been here a bomb had blown her across the room, fractured both her legs and her pelvis, and burned off her eyebrows. Even though the medics had been able to heal her with Quintessence, it wasn't an experience she wanted to repeat.

"Security did a sweep of the house this morning."

"Good." She pushed the door open and stepped inside. The room was decorated in peach ruffles and cream lace. Ick. Staying in this room would give her a toothache. She made eye contact with her grandmother. "It's lovely, but…"

Her grandmother raised an eyebrow in challenge.

"It's a little too…"

"Frilly?" her grandmother asked.

"Exactly."

"Then let's move on." Farther down the hall, they came to a door with a brass doorknob.

Bryn opened the door. The plain blue and beige color scheme lacked flair, but it was better than that froufrou nightmare. "This works for me."

"There is one more set of rooms I'd like you to see before you choose."

Was this a test? Would she be forced to spend the day playing musical bedrooms? All she wanted was to go to sleep and block out the nightmare her life had become. But apparently, that wasn't on the agenda. She followed her grandmother around the corner and up a flight of stairs that ended at a small landing. The door to this room was decorated with carvings of a forest.

"Cool door." She pushed it open and gasped. Light spilled in from the floor-to-ceiling windows and reflected off the polished dark wood floor. The room was decorated in every hue of autumn leaves. "It's like a forest in here."

"Your grandfather didn't understand when I discussed this with the interior decorator, but I think it turned out quite well."

"It's so warm and inviting." Oops. "Not that the rest of your house isn't warm and inviting."

"Stop backpedaling. Your grandfather chose intimidating and cold decorations for the main part of the house. He achieved what he set out to do. I prefer more warmth." She turned for the door. "Come. I'll show you my rooms."

Interesting. Maybe her grandmother wasn't as cold as she'd first thought. Back down the small set of stairs, they took a side hall and went up another flight, which dead-ended at a landing. Pride was evident in her grandmother's face when she opened the door and ushered Bryn inside.

"Wow." Sunshine spilled into this room, lighting up the amber and evergreen decor. Not a ruffle or scrap of lace in sight. Everything was simple clean lines.

Suspicion confirmed. "The frilly peach room was a test, wasn't it?"

"Maybe." Her grandmother pointed to another doorway. "This room is my favorite."

One wall made entirely of glass turned the small sitting area into a greenhouse. Orchids and other flowering plants lined shelves and tables, releasing a sweet floral sent. Two brown leather wingback chairs and a bookcase were the only other items in the room.

"This is amazing."

"Do you have any interest in gardening?" Her grandmother picked up a brass pitcher and watered a pale pink orchid.

"I'd be happy to learn. We never had a yard." *Bam.* Pain ripped through her gut. There was no yard…no apartment… no home to return to…no parents. Just a wrenching, cold ache. She grabbed at the wall. *Breathe. Breathe. Breathe. Suck in a breath, and exhale. Push the flames down.* Setting her grandmother's favorite room on fire wouldn't improve the situation.

Once she was under control, she straightened. "Sorry… it just hit me again."

Her grandmother nodded. "And it will, over and over again. This isn't the first time I lost your mother."

She'd never thought of it that way—the pain her mom had caused when she ran away and abandoned her own family.

Still, her mom had tried to mend fences. She'd sent letters. Made an effort. Had pride kept her grandmother from forgiving her mother? These were questions Bryn needed to ask, but now wasn't the time.

"Sit," her grandmother said in a tone that wasn't a request.

What now? Bryn sank into one of the chairs and waited.

"You must promise me something." She reached over and placed her hand on Bryn's. "You must promise me you will never run away. If you wish to leave, you are free to do so. But you cannot disappear in the middle of the night."

"I promise." She wouldn't do that to her grandmother, or anyone, for that matter.

"That's settled then." The vulnerable look on her grandmother's face disappeared as if a mask slid into place. She stood and headed for the door. "We'll have lunch while your belongings are placed in your new room."

Apparently the touchy-feely moment was over.

Bryn followed her grandmother back out into the main hall and tried to orient herself. "My rooms are that way?" she asked.

Her grandmother nodded.

"Good. I might need a map to figure out the rest of this place." Which reminded her, she'd never found an answer about what happened to the blueprints of the house. Focusing on the puzzle gave her something to think about besides her parents.

"How did Alec know the layout of your estate?"

Her grandmother stopped midstride. "That's quite the topic change."

"Jaxon asked me that question a while ago. We both

think it's odd that Alec knew about the security elevator and the best place to drag two unconscious victims." Jaxon and his mother drugged, bound, and gagged like two life-size rag dolls was an image she couldn't get out of her head.

"Your grandfather and I discussed this. He thinks someone could have taken the blueprints from the school's library."

"We checked into that, and they're not there."

"We removed them."

One mystery solved. They continued walking. How far was the dining room? Her feet ached. Stupid high heels. Realizing this was something she had control over, she stepped out of her shoes, picked them up, and continued walking.

The glacial look her grandmother gave her told her exactly how she felt about Bryn's actions.

"I'll put them back on before we enter the dining room." That was all she was willing to concede.

"And you won't indulge in this behavior in front of your grandfather or any guests."

Funny how her grandfather fell into the same category as guests. Figuring out her grandparents' odd relationship could be a full-time hobby.

"So, you removed the blueprints after the attack?" Bryn asked.

"Yes."

"Did you question Nola since she was the last to have them?"

"Are you asking that question as a rational individual or as a woman resentful of her former suitor's chosen mate?"

Her grandmother didn't pull any punches. "Both."

"Do you still harbor feelings for Zavien?"

"Does bitter disappointment count?"

Her grandmother laughed. It wasn't a happy sound. "'Live and learn' is one of those painfully obvious adages."

When they reached the dining room, her grandmother stopped and pointed at Bryn's feet. *The shoes. Right.* She slipped on the painful black heels and entered what her grandmother referred to as the small dining room, which meant the table could seat sixteen people. At the moment, it was set for eight. Four plates on one end and four on the other. What was with the segregated dining?

"Who's joining us?" Bryn asked.

"I'm never sure. Sometimes your grandfather has Directorate members dine with us. I find it's better to be over-prepared."

A maid Bryn had met before, named Abigail, wheeled a cart into the room and served chicken and asparagus covered in some sort of cream sauce. Rather than ask what it was, and risk looking stupid in her grandmother's eyes, she dug in. It tasted like Alfredo sauce. *Yum.*

Her grandfather and Jaxon's father, Ferrin, joined them halfway through lunch. Out of habit, Bryn braced for an attack.

Neither her grandfather nor Ferrin paid the slightest bit of attention to her or her grandmother. They continued discussing something about security issues while they ate.

"Is it always like this?" Bryn nodded toward her grandfather.

"Like what?" her grandmother asked.

Seriously? "Does he"—she pointed to her grandfather— "bring Directorate members in for lunch and ignore you and everyone else in the room?"

"Mostly."

"Then why eat in the same room?" It didn't make sense.

"Because this is where Abigail serves lunch."

Okay, then. What to talk about now? Her brain went back to their previous conversation. "You never answered me before. Was Nola questioned about the blueprints?"

"She likes to plan her sets based on real blueprints to make them more realistic."

Bryn snorted. All three adults in the room shot her disapproving looks.

"What? I've painted those sets. If Nola uses blueprints as inspiration, then something is lost in the translation."

"What are you going on about?" Ferrin asked.

"How did Alec know the layout of the estate well enough to attack us that night? Nola was the last to check out the blueprints. Alec was her brother."

"Do you think the Directorate is ignorant of those facts?" Ferrin asked.

"Before you continue talking to me like I'm an idiot, you should know your son was the one who suggested this line of investigation." That shut the jerk up.

Her grandfather gave her a sideways glance. Was he mad at her? Too bad. She would wear uncomfortable shoes and do her best to act like the young lady her grandparents wanted her to be, but when Ferrin came into the equation, all bets were off.

"You'll have to forgive Bryn. She's distraught over the death of her parents." Her grandfather's tone was flat and even. He observed Ferrin like he was waiting for a reaction. Did he suspect Ferrin of killing her parents? When her mom had jilted Ferrin and run away with her dad—a middle-class Red dragon—Ferrin had been furious. Would he seek revenge in this manner, knowing it would be blamed on the brewing civil war? Maybe.

"My condolences." Ferrin's tone was tight, like the words strangled him.

She nodded in response. Her throat grew tight and her eyes burned. And she'd be damned if she'd cry in front of him. Setting her fork down, she pushed away from the table. "May I be excused?"

"Of course," her grandmother said. "I'll send Abigail to check on you in a while."

Chapter Twenty-Three

Bryn paced back and forth at the foot of her bed. It felt like a crater the size of the Grand Canyon had been ripped open in her chest. She'd cried on and off for the last half hour.

Her mind screamed that her parents couldn't just be… gone. Maybe they'd escaped the explosion. They were smart. Maybe they realized the package was a bomb and flew away before it exploded. There had to be at least a 1 percent chance they had escaped.

Pound. Pound. Pound. It felt like someone was hitting her in the head with a hammer. Scratch that. It felt like someone was inside her skull trying to break out. Maybe a hot shower and comfortable clothes would help.

Half an hour later, she wore a pair of her favorite comfy jeans and Valmont's sweatshirt, which she'd never returned. If anyone could comfort her right now, it was Valmont. In fact, he would consider it his duty as her knight.

She grabbed the phone on her nightstand. No dial tone.

Crap. She wanted to call Fonzoli's and at least speak to Valmont, if she couldn't see him.

Maybe the phone was unplugged. She followed the cord to the wall. Nope, it was plugged in. She picked up the phone and pressed zero, just to see what would happen. Nothing. Her grandparents had more money than Fort Knox; it's not like someone cut off their phone service because they hadn't paid the bill on time.

Ring. Ring.

Bryn jumped from the unexpected noise. She picked up the phone. "Hello?"

"Did you require something?" a feminine voice asked.

"I was trying to make a phone call."

"My name is Rindy. I'm the operator for Sinclair Estates. I can place a call for you."

That wasn't weird at all. "I can call myself, if you tell me how to make the phone work."

"It's no trouble," Rindy chirped.

This wasn't worth the argument right now. "I was trying to call Fonzoli's restaurant."

"I can have the chef prepare anything you like."

"Thank you. I wanted to speak to a person at Fonzoli's named Valmont. Not order food." Although now that she thought about it, pizza sounded good.

"I'll put the call through for you; please stay on the line."

"Sure." Why was making a simple call so difficult? Did her grandparents not trust her with a phone? Was this their way of monitoring who she spoke to?

"Hello, Bryn." Valmont's relaxed tone washed over her and she loosened her death grip on the phone.

"Hey. Can we meet somewhere?" she asked.

"Sure, I can pick you up in fifteen minutes."

"I'm at my grandparents' place." And now that she thought about it, she wasn't sure of the directions to the estate. Both times she'd come here, she'd slept in the car. "We may have to ask Rindy to give you directions."

"Don't worry, Fonzoli's has catered dinner parties for your grandparents before. I know the way. It'll take half an hour. Do you want me to bring some lemon ice?"

"You are the best knight ever."

He chuckled. "I'll see you soon."

She hung up and changed into nicer jeans and a blue turtleneck shirt. The mirror above her dresser reflected a girl in serious need of some makeup. So she darkened her lips and eyelashes with Quintessence. Directing her life force through her body to change her coloring seemed second nature now.

Was there anything else she needed to do before Valmont arrived? Crap. Should she have asked her grandmother's permission before inviting someone over? Should she go knock on her grandmother's door? And then it came to her. She picked up the phone and dialed zero.

"Hello, this is Rindy. How can I help you?"

Geez, did this lady read from a script? "Rindy, this is Bryn. I wanted to speak to my grandmother, but wasn't sure if I should call before I go knock on her door."

"I'll call her private line. Please hold."

This place was like a freaking hotel. Private lines and operators. *Who lives like this?*

"Bryn?" Her grandmother sounded annoyed.

"Sorry if I interrupted something. I wanted to let you know that I called my friend Valmont and he's coming over for a visit."

"Oh." That single syllable spoke volumes. Was it the visit or Valmont that she objected to?

"Do I need to ask before I have friends visit?"

"It would be nice if you made me aware before the fact rather than after."

"Okay." The silence stretched out. "I'll do that next time. Do I need to call the guards to let them know he's coming?"

"I'll take care of it."

"Thank—" *Click.* Her grandmother hung up before she could get the entire word out.

Don't be mad. Your grandmother is set in her ways. Maybe she should ask for a manual of appropriate behavior. Of course, that might just tick her grandmother off more.

. . .

Bryn checked the clock on her dresser. Time to walk down to the entry hall. Would she bump into her grandfather or Ferrin along the way? Her grandfather probably wouldn't approve of her socializing with the caterer. Ferrin would more than likely make some snide comment. Maybe Valmont would be offended on her behalf. Maybe he'd run Ferrin through with a sword. A life with Jaxon would be much easier if his evil, vindictive father were out of the picture.

Oh. My. God. Had she just thought what she thought she thought? A life with Jaxon? She shivered and hurried out the door. In the entry hall, a Red dragon stood guarding the front door. In his human form, he was tall, broad-shouldered, and built like a pro wrestler, just like her dad had been.

Bam. Right in the gut. She clutched at her stomach and

turned away.

"Are you all right, Miss?" the guard asked.

No. And she never would be, but her grandmother would want her to stick with the politely accepted answer, so she sucked it up and said what she should. "I'm fine. Thanks."

He glanced around the foyer like he was checking for spies. Once he thought he was in the clear, he said, "Your father, he was a good man."

Tears filled her eyes. She couldn't speak over the lump in her throat. So she nodded.

A knock on the door had the guard turning with purpose.

He glanced back at Bryn. "I'll need you to confirm your friend's identity before allowing him to enter."

"Okay."

Her stomach flipped in anticipation. Valmont would make everything better, or at least as good as things could be.

The guard swung the door open. Valmont stood there wearing black pants and a white shirt, which was his uniform at Fonzoli's. His dark hair was mussed and his blue eyes held concern. Did he already know what she was about to tell him?

"That's my knight." She walked toward him.

"Can I come in?" he asked the guard in the most respectful tone she'd heard him use toward an authority figure. He must know her grandparents' private guards weren't to be trifled with.

The guard stepped aside. Valmont crossed the room and pulled Bryn into a hug. She inhaled his scent; he smelled like sunshine and leather with a dash of Italian spices. Wrapped in the warmth of his arms, the world seemed like a better place.

"I heard there's been trouble, but I'm not sure what's going on," he whispered.

Bryn looked up at him. As soon as she opened her mouth to explain, to tell him that her parents were gone, the tears would come. She couldn't do that in the foyer of the main hall. "Let me show you my new rooms. We can talk there."

"Rooms?" Valmont said. "As in more than one?"

Bryn rolled her eyes. "I believe it's called a suite. I have a living room and a small library connected to my bedroom. It's pretty cool."

"It's bigger than my cabin, isn't it?"

Bryn stopped walking and thought about it. "Embarrassingly enough, I think it is."

Valmont glanced around the hall, checking out the other doors. "What are all these rooms?"

Did he care, or was he trying to occupy her mind? Not that it mattered. "I can find my way to my rooms, a dining room, the foyer, and my grandmother's rooms. Besides that, I have no idea what's where." She leaned in and whispered, "And I've no idea why two people need this much space."

When they reached her suite, he stood in the living room, shaking his head. "This is amazing."

"It's pretty awesome." She pointed at the paper bag he carried. "Is that lemon ice?"

"As requested." He pointed at the couch. "Should we sit here, or is there a dining room table hiding in your closet?"

"Your guess is as good as mine. I just moved in this morning." Her voice wavered.

He pulled her to the couch. "You can tell me when you're ready. Whatever it is, I'm here for you literally and figuratively."

Maybe ripping it off like a bandage would be best. She opened her mouth to speak, but the words wouldn't come. She cleared her throat. "My parents are…" Saying it made it more real and a thousand times more painful. "There was a bomb," she choked out. "They're gone."

And then it was like a dam broke open inside her. She was sobbing and Valmont was holding her and making soothing noises that didn't do any good, because how could they? Her parents were dead. She'd never see them again. No more pancakes for breakfast. No more Battleship tournaments with her dad. No more anything, ever again. It was impossible for her brain to accept that her parents had just ceased to exist, and in their place was this giant aching void of sorrow. She sobbed until her throat was raw.

Valmont shifted, and then a wad of napkins appeared in front of her face. "I'm sure there's Kleenex or silk handkerchiefs around here someplace, but for now this is the best I can do."

She managed a smile. "Thanks." The paper napkins were rough against her skin. Her face felt windburned from all the salt in her tears. "I better go splash some water on my face."

Valmont nodded. She looked at him and realized his shirt was wet through. "Sorry about that."

"I'll live." He said the words, and then his smile faltered. "I'm sorry. That—"

"It's okay." Her eyes burned. "I'll be back in a minute."

After splashing her face with cold water, she checked the mirror. Wow. Those actresses in movies who cried and managed to look pretty afterward must be super talented. Her eyes were red-rimmed and bloodshot. Her nose was tomato red and her cheeks looked as windburned as they felt. Looking like crap when she felt like crap didn't seem fair. A girl should be able to catch a break somewhere. Wait a minute. She channeled Quintessence to her face and returned her cheeks to normal color. Her eyes she didn't want to mess with.

Valmont's sweatshirt hung on the hook on the back of the bathroom door where she'd left it when she'd changed earlier. Would he want to change out of his tear-soaked and *dear God please don't let it be* snot-stained shirt into something drier? She'd offer it to him and see what he thought.

When she went back into the living room area, Valmont was whispering into his cell phone. Who was he calling? Was he trying to keep something from her?

Feeling wrong about what she was going to do but doing it anyway, she walked up behind him quietly and listened as best she could.

"Yes, Grandfather. I know. There isn't much we can do about it now. Yes. I'll ask her. No…no, that isn't an option at this point. I'll stop by on my way to the cabin. No. You don't have to meet me there. Yes…yes… Fine, if you insist, bring a tray of cannelloni."

Feeling guilty for eavesdropping, she walked into his line of sight. "Talking to your grandpa?"

"Yes. He heard that several students' family's had been attacked. He called to see if he could offer any assistance. The man thinks everything can be fixed with food."

Thank God. He wasn't involved in some plot. Just dealing with an overprotective grandfather, which was nice. "Most of time food helps."

She held the sweatshirt out to him. "Since I cried all

over you, I thought you might want to change."

He glanced down at his shirt. "Good idea." He pointed back the way she came. "Bathroom is this way?"

"Yes. Don't be surprised if all the lemon ice is gone by the time you get back."

She picked up the carryout container of lemon ice. It looked like the containers ice cream came in from the store. Curious, she checked the bottom of the container. It read, "Lemon Gelato, New York, NY."

Disappointment settled on her shoulders like a heavy blanket. Which was ridiculous. Did it matter than Valmont's family didn't make the lemon ice from scratch like the rest of their food? She said a small prayer that they did make the rest of their food from scratch. If she rifled through the restaurant storage area and found giant industrial-sized containers of Ragu, she'd be completely disillusioned.

It didn't matter where the lemon ice was made. Valmont brought it to her because he cared, so love went into it even if it didn't come from Fonzoli's kitchen.

When the guy she was thinking about strolled toward her wearing the sweatshirt she'd had on hours before, all doubt vanished from her mind. Valmont was a good guy. It didn't matter where the lemon ice came from or whom he'd been talking to on the phone.

"I expected half of that to be gone by now."

"I could lie and say I was waiting to share, but I was lost in thought." She opened the bag and pulled out a plastic spoon the size of a ladle.

"Is this supposed to be a comment on how much I eat?"

He grinned and took the large spoon from her. "I thought it might make you laugh. There are regular spoons in the bottom of the bag." He grabbed the bag, reached inside, and then frowned. "I threw real spoons in here. Maybe they fell out in my car."

Should she eat with the ladle-sized spoon? If she was by herself, she might. "I could call Rindy, the magical fairy who knows all, and ask her where my grandparents keep their spoons."

"Good idea. From the outside of the house, I know where the kitchen is located. From in here, I haven't a clue."

A quick call to Rindy had Abigail the maid at their door five minutes later with a pushcart loaded with utensils, drinks, and snacks.

"Wow." Bryn looked over the platter of fruit and cheese, the plate of cookies, and the bowl of popcorn. Several types of soda and bottled water also sat on the cart.

"Thanks, Abigail. This is awesome."

She inclined her head. "If you need anything else, you can reach the kitchen by dialing three-six-six-three."

"I better write that down." Bryn stepped away from the door.

"No need to write it down." Abigail grinned like she knew a secret. "It spells food. Your grandfather is a clever man."

"Yes, he is." Bryn watched as Abigail left the room and closed the door behind her. She grabbed two spoons off the cart, tossing one to Valmont. "What would you like to drink?"

He came over to investigate and picked up a bottle labeled LIME FIZZY WATER. "The name alone makes me want to try it. How about you?"

Her first instinct was to go for a soda. She checked the other options and picked up a pretty pink bottle. "I'll try the strawberry fizzy water."

They settled back on the couch with the lemon ice set between them. Bryn took a bite. The cold, tangy sweetness melted in her mouth. Thank God it still tasted as good as she remembered, even though it wasn't made here in town. "How did you end up buying lemon gelato from New York?"

"My grandfather vacationed there once. Said it put his lemon gelato to shame. He's refused to serve anything else ever since."

A knock sounded on her door. Before she could stand and open it, the door opened. Her grandfather stood in the doorway frowning. "What is he doing here?"

Could her grandfather make Valmont feel less welcome? "He's my friend."

"He's staff. You can't be friends with the staff."

And it was on. "He's my friend and my knight, and he's not your staff."

"You don't need a knight," her grandfather said. "No one has a knight anymore. It's archaic. Release him from his bond."

"No." She stared her grandfather down, refusing to blink.

The jerk grinned. "Good to know you fight for what you believe in."

And with that he left.

Bryn stared after him and then turned to Valmont. "What the hell was that?"

"I think it was a test, and you passed with flying colors."

"It's frightening to think his blood runs in my veins."

"Could be worse. Imagine how Jaxon feels."

Bryn laughed. "Sharing blood with Ferrin. That *is* a terrible reality."

"Speaking of Jaxon," Valmont said, "why were you

having lunch with him the other day?"

Hoping to show him how stupid she thought the whole Jaxon fix-up idea was, she rolled her eyes. "Since my grandparents recognized me, my grandfather wants me to marry and have grandkids and all that crap."

Valmont bit his lip like he was trying not to laugh. She glared at him. "I see you've connected the dots."

Laughter poured out of Valmont's mouth. It was a warm, rich sound, and surprisingly enough, it didn't make her angry. In fact, she joined in.

He regained control but still grinned like an idiot. "That is the funniest thing I've ever heard. You and Jaxon, together. I imagine neither Jaxon nor his father are amused by the idea."

"My grandmother and Jaxon's mother, Lillith, are behind it. Ferrin would have me assassinated before he allowed me to marry his son. I might prefer that myself."

"Why is your grandmother scheming with Lillith? Shouldn't Jaxon's contract already be in place?"

"It was." And the story wasn't funny anymore. "Rhianna didn't fully recover from her injury after the attack on the theater building, so Ferrin, being the utter asshat that he is, voided their agreement."

"That's awful. What will she do?"

"Jaxon, who has turned out not to be a *total* asshat, promised he'd take care of her no matter what. Which is admirable, but it shouldn't have to be that way. I don't see why it's an issue."

"Jaxon is more honorable than I thought." Valmont reached for her hand. "When will you know if you've been approved for an arranged marriage?"

"No idea. I try not to think about it. It's all so weird. A

few months ago, I was a normal girl living a normal life in a public high school. My biggest worry was who I'd sit next to at lunch. Now it seems like I'm living in a foreign country on the brink of a war. A lot of people hate me. Some of them are trying to kill me. If I live, there's a chance, however slim, that I'll be forced into an arranged marriage, which has nothing to do with actually loving or even liking the person. My grandmother told me marriage is a legal contract that produces children. Nothing more. I can't believe that. My parents are happy, I can't—"

Oh, God. Doubling over, she breathed through the pain in her chest. Her parents were dead. She didn't have any more tears.

Breathe in. Breathe out. Breathe in. Breathe out. She sat up and met Valmont's gaze.

He reached over and pulled her close so she could lay her head on his chest. "You forgot for a moment." He wasn't asking a question. He just knew. Which was nice. It made things easier.

"When will I stop forgetting?" she asked. "Because it hurts…a lot."

"I'm not sure."

Leaning against his solid chest, she felt warm and safe. He stroked his hand up and down her back.

What little energy she had left drained out of her body. "Do you mind if I close my eyes for a little bit?"

"No. Go ahead."

"Thank you."

Chapter Twenty-Four

After Valmont left, Bryn found herself back in the small dining room for dinner, sitting at the stupid table that could seat sixteen people, with only her grandparents for company. Her grandmother sat at one end of the rectangular table and her grandfather sat at the other. She was in the middle, which felt like no-man's-land.

Were her grandparents mad at her? Was that why no one was talking? Or was this how they ate every day? After ten minutes of listening to utensils hitting plates, she couldn't take it anymore.

"Is this normal?" she asked.

"What are you referring to?" her grandfather asked.

"This." Bryn pointed from one end of the table to another. "Do you always sit at opposite ends of the room and not talk?"

They both gave her blank stares. Great. "If it's just the two of you, why don't you sit at a smaller table? If it's just the three of us we could still sit at a smaller table. Or at least we could talk."

"What would you like to talk about?" her grandfather asked.

Okay. She'd walked right into that one. "For starters, what did you do today?"

Her grandfather wiped his face with the linen napkin and sat back in his chair. "I reviewed plans for a better defense system at school."

She was surprised he was willing to share. "What did you come up with?" Short of a giant dome placed over the school, she couldn't figure out how they would stop any further attacks.

"I can't divulge that information." His eyes narrowed. "You were there during the attacks. What can you tell me about them?"

She sipped her water and thought about the best way to present information to her grandfather. She should probably keep the smart-ass comments to a minimum.

"Well, the first time the campus was attacked, I thought it was an earthquake. It was only afterward that I realized someone had attacked using sonic waves." She remembered Octavius mentioning the Orange Clan's dwindling numbers. "There are only two Orange dragons at school and they were cleared of charges. What happened to the Orange dragons? Why are there so few of them?"

Her grandfather frowned. "That is a good question. I don't have the answer."

"So, the Directorate didn't do anything to decrease their population?"

Her grandfather leveled a glare at her that could have

melted steel. "Where did you hear such nonsense?"

"Uhm, from the one Orange male student at the institute? Because the Orange dragons' breath weapon, sonic waves, are so powerful, he thinks someone is keeping their population small. Could he be right?"

"That's ridiculous."

She couldn't help noticing he didn't answer the question. Maybe it was time to change the topic. "The second time the campus was attacked, I was in the theater building. The building twisted and shook like we were having a tornado, and then it just stopped."

"That's when Rhianna was injured." Her grandfather stated this like it was a boring fact. Like he didn't care or feel any empathy toward the girl Bryn had begun to think of as a friend.

"I don't understand why Ferrin voided the contract between Jaxon and Rhianna. So she has a limp. Big deal. It's not genetic. She won't pass it to their children. Other dragons were injured. What's happening to them?"

"The Directorate offers anyone who isn't comfortable with returning to school a private tutor."

Smoke shot from Bryn's nostrils. "The only reason someone wouldn't be comfortable returning to school is because the Directorate and other dragons tell them they shouldn't be seen in public. What's the deal with dragons' insistence on physical perfection? There are tons of people who survive and flourish with all sorts of disabilities. Look at Stephen Hawking. He's the smartest man on the planet and he isn't physically perfect."

"He's a *man*." Her grandfather emphasized the last word. "We aren't men. We are creatures, animals, it is our instinct to cull the weak from the herd. We can't risk a dragon passing on inferior genes."

And now her head was going to explode. "So if a dragon is injured during an attack the Directorate failed to prevent, injured by an enemy the Directorate failed to protect them from, that makes them weak? How is that logical?"

"Strong dragons will find a way to escape the attack or fight back." Her grandfather said this like it actually made sense.

"So Rhianna is weak because she failed to predict that sets held in the rafters would crash down on her and sever her spinal cord? Garrett is weak because he failed to predict that giant hailstones would be shot through the sky, ripping into his wings? Do you not see how screwed up that logic is?"

"That's how it has always been," her grandmother said. "Like we discussed before. If you plan to live among us, you must learn our ways. You don't have to agree with them. But you can't publicly express an opinion against the Directorate. Someone is trying to splinter us off into Clans, which is a battle tactic so they can pick us off one group at a time. We must present a united front or we'll appear to be easy targets."

Okay. What her grandmother said made some sense, except for the one gaping hole. "If you were out flying and someone shot a giant hailstone through your wing, that wouldn't make you weak, it would make you unlucky. You can't punish people for things they have no control over."

"This isn't open to debate," her grandfather said in his "I am God" voice.

"Your house was attacked during the Directorate meeting. Your guests were kidnapped and almost killed. Does that mean you're weak?"

Her grandfather's posture stiffened. His expression went hard and flat.

Time to backpedal before they shipped her belongings to a dark corner of the basement. "I'm not saying you're weak. I'm saying your logic of blaming the victim is wrong. The fact that this house was attacked shouldn't reflect badly upon you."

"But it does," her grandfather said. "And I have taken precautions so I won't appear weak ever again."

Wow. Logic didn't have much effect on this guy.

"Maybe we should agree to disagree," Bryn said.

"You're the one who wanted to talk in the first place." Her grandfather went back to eating his meal.

True. Maybe silence was better.

· · ·

After dinner Bryn returned to her room just to get away from the possibility of any more annoying conversations with her grandfather. His "cull the herd" mentality was total crap. What she needed was a good book to take her mind off all this insanity, so she wandered down to the library. Thinking about going into the library was one thing; actually stepping foot in the room where a month or so ago she'd nearly died proved a bit more difficult.

The room looked different than she remembered it. There was still a sitting area in front of the fireplace, but the large mahogany table that occupied the back half of the room had been replaced by a desk. Palms sweating, she crossed the threshold and ignored the uptick in her heartbeat. Nothing would happen to her here. It was just a room.

The floor-to-ceiling bookshelves held an assortment of books. Some looked stiff and new, like they'd never been opened. Others had cracked leather bindings and were huge tomes like the books from the school library. A book with a golden spine and "Tales of Time" written in silver lettering caught her attention. She grabbed the book and leafed through it. Short stories about different dragons filled the pages. Interesting.

She laid it on the desk and searched for more books about historical dragons that might hold some information about hybrids. Her grandfather wouldn't allow any anti-Directorate books in his library, but she might find some references to hybrids.

"What are you doing in here?" her grandfather's voice boomed through the room.

Don't panic. Don't show fear. Don't give a smart-ass answer. She closed the book she'd been reading and turned to face him. "I thought I'd find something to read."

He stalked toward her. "In my office?"

Well, crap. "The last time I was here, this was a library. I didn't realize you'd turned it into your office." Sure, there were folders stacked on the desk and an ashtray, but the room certainly didn't look lived in.

"It's one of my offices." His eyes narrowed as he picked up *Tales of Time*. "Why did you choose this?"

No way would she utter the term "hybrid" in his presence. "I have to write three five-page term papers on the history of dragons. The history text is dry. I thought there might be something interesting in here to inspire me."

"If you're looking for inspiration"—he walked to the

shelves and selected a brown leather book from the top shelf—"try this."

The book was easily eight inches thick. Bryn grabbed it and read the title, *Directorate Law, Volume I.* If it was written in legal terminology, she'd have to pass. Flipping to the first text-covered page, she read an account of a trial. A Black dragon had been accused of stealing artwork from a Blue's office. Testimonies were given. The art was never found, but the Black dragon was given the choice of creating a series of portraits for the Blue or being incarcerated for a month. He chose incarceration. That was strange.

"Are you confused by his choice?" her grandfather asked.

Geez, did he have these cases memorized? "Yes."

"Later, it was found that one of the maids had taken the paintings. For lying and stealing from her employer, she was sentenced to five years in jail. The Black dragon who had been wronged was given a new studio stocked with art supplies."

"If the Black dragon didn't do it, why did they put him in jail in the first place?"

"He seemed the most likely suspect, but you're missing the most important part. The Black dragon could have taken the blame for stealing the paintings, done the commissioned work without pay, and gone on with his life. Instead, he told the truth, maintained his innocence, and proved himself honorable by not taking the liar's way out."

The twisted logic made her head hurt. "So he was rewarded for choosing jail time he didn't deserve rather than lying and essentially paying a fine of free portraits."

"Yes," her grandfather said. "Loyalty and honor are

more important than taking the easy way out."

He seemed to expect some sort of response. "I'm not sure what you want me to say."

"I don't want you to say anything. I want you to understand our belief system and act accordingly."

The phone on his desk rang, saving her from coming up with some sort of response. She used that chance to escape, opting to leave the books behind, afraid he might quiz her on the court cases later.

...

The next morning, Bryn woke late. It was the first time since coming to school that the damn stress-inducing alarm clock hadn't woken her. Talk about a bonus. Of course, after Christmas break, she'd have to return to school and deal with it again. But this was a nice sabbatical.

Okay, she was awake. Now what? Would her grandmother call and ask her to come down to breakfast? Could she go have breakfast by herself somewhere? That sounded nice. In this ginormous house there had to be a quiet room with a normal-sized kitchen table somewhere.

Rather than wander for hours, she decided to ask Rindy, the all-knowing phone fairy. After dialing and waiting for the call back, she learned there were tables in a sunroom on the third floor. Abigail would have breakfast waiting for her in thirty minutes. Having money didn't necessarily make you happy, but it certainly made life easier.

After a quick shower, she dressed in jeans and a nice blouse (as a concession to her grandmother). Until she was told there was a formal dress code in the house, she would continue to wear tennis shoes and jeans.

Silence met her when she walked down the hallway. Her tennis shoes made no sound. Why have such a giant house for two people? From her conversations with her grandparents yesterday, everything seemed to be about keeping up appearances.

Living your entire life that way would be exhausting. She'd do her best to keep her grandparents happy, but there were limits. People could think what they wanted. She didn't give a rat's ass.

Almost every room she passed had a closed door. Was there a living room somewhere, a place to sit and watch TV or listen to music? There were five freaking stories in this mansion. There had to be a television somewhere.

When she came to the stairs, she looked up and down to see if anyone else was around. Nope. She was by herself. Wanting to burn off some anxiety, she jogged up the stairs to the third-floor landing. The back wall of the landing was floor-to-ceiling windows. Trees and manicured greenery went on for as far as she could see. If she were in charge, she'd put a table and chairs right here to enjoy the view. How isolated were they out here? Maybe she'd ask Valmont to bring her a map.

Rindy had said the sunroom was the second door on the left after the landing. When she entered the room, she spotted Abigail collapsed on the floor next to the food cart.

Chapter Twenty-Five

Bryn scanned the area for someone who might jump out at her as she ran to kneel next to the maid.

"Abigail?" She turned the woman's body over. Her eyes were wide open, her pupils dilated. Should she try to heal her or find a phone and call for help?

What if time was of the essence? She focused on her life force, imagining it as a small sun glowing in her chest. Once it burned brightly enough, she placed her hand on Abigail's forehead and pushed her life force into Abigail's body like Medic Williams had taught her to do with Jaxon. The familiar claustrophobic feeling hit as she channeled Quintessence into Abigail's veins, feeling for what was wrong.

There was no head trauma. The plush carpet must've cushioned the woman's fall. She pushed deeper. What was that sickening sweet scent? God, it was awful, like rotten meat. Where was it coming from? And then she saw it, an odd grayish substance in Abigail's blood. That had to be poison.

She directed her Quintessence in the form of fire to burn the disgusting substance. In a few minutes the gray was gone, and the rotten meat smell went with it. Bryn withdrew her life force from Abigail's body. Nervous, she watched as Abigail came to, blinked, and looked around.

"What happened?"

Bryn helped her sit up. "I came in here and found you passed out on the floor. Do you feel okay now?"

"I think so." She tried to stand and wobbled a bit.

"You should sit." Bryn pulled a chair over. "What's the last thing you remember?"

Abigail sank into the chair. "I came in, opened the curtains, and set the table." She pointed at the table set for one. Then I checked the food to make sure it was hot." Abigail blushed. "Don't tell your grandmother, but I ate a few strawberries. I've been up since five and…"

"You don't have to justify why you were hungry." Bryn walked over to the dish of strawberries set on the table. "Are these the strawberries you ate?"

"No. I filled your dish, and then ate the extras before I put the plate back on the cart."

Bryn stabbed a berry with a fork and sniffed it. The faint odor of rotten meat made her gag. "These are drugged or poisoned. We'll explain what happened, and then my grandmother can have them tested."

Abigail wrung her hands. "Please. I've worked here for years. I don't want to be fired."

Seriously? Her grandmother would fire someone over eating extra food? Abigail would know better than she did. "Fine. Let's say I came in while you were dishing out the strawberries. I said it would be a shame for the extras to go to waste and suggested you eat them. Does that work?"

"Your grandmother will yell at you for fraternizing with the staff."

"I think my grandma is going to be yelling at me about a lot of things. I don't mind. Now, as soon as you fell, I used Quintessence to help you. Okay?"

Abigail nodded. "Thank you."

Bryn walked over to a phone set on a side table. "Here we go." She spoke to Rindy, and her grandparents swooped into the sun room five minutes later, looking beyond pissed off.

"Tell me everything," her grandfather said.

Bryn shared the story she and Abigail had set up. Her grandfather grilled Abigail on who prepared the food.

"The new chef prepared everything," Abigail said.

"We didn't hire a new chef." Her grandfather pulled a cell phone from his pocket and stomped from the room shouting orders. Her grandmother headed for the door, signaling that Bryn and Abigail should follow.

In the kitchen, the staff gave a description of the new chef. He'd shown up that morning claiming to be substituting for the normal chef, who was out due to the birth of his son.

"Call his house, make sure he's okay," Bryn said, to no one in particular.

Her grandmother looked at her like this was an odd request.

"The last time someone tried to kill me, they killed the plumber to take his place." How could her grandparents have forgotten that?

"Maybe this is just food poisoning?" Abigail said like

she wished it were true.

"No. I'm sure it's people trying to kill me, again." *Bam. Bam. Bam.* Her head pounded like a mariachi band was playing inside it. "Funny that I'm getting used to this."

"I am not." Her grandmother spit the words out.

A man cleared his throat. "Pierre is at home. His wife had a baby boy. They're all okay."

"He's fired," her grandfather roared.

"You can't fire him because the temp agency sent a bad guy in his place. Fire the temp agency, not the man who has a wife and child to support," Bryn shouted.

"Don't tell me how to handle my staff." Her grandfather spoke through clenched teeth.

"They're not just your staff. They're people with lives and families. They matter. You can't just move them around like they're pieces on a chessboard."

The only sound in the room was the clock ticking on the wall. Everyone looked ready to duck and cover, even her grandmother.

"You are an ungrateful brat," her grandfather said.

"You're inconsiderate and narrow-minded," Bryn spat back.

Her grandmother looked ready to burst a blood vessel. "That's enough. Both of you need to learn to control your tongues and your tempers. The problem here is that someone made an attempt on your granddaughter's life under your roof. Again. Focus on that. You can work out your personality differences later."

It was on the tip of her tongue to say that it wasn't her personality that was the problem, but since she didn't want to be kicked out, she offered him an olive branch.

"I'm sorry. I don't mean to be disrespectful. It's just… I thought I was safe. It's unsettling to find out these people are organized enough to come after me so quickly. It's only my second day here. How did they even know where to find me?"

"I imagine news of your parents' passing has made its way through the social network," her grandmother said. "People would have heard you left campus with us. It was only logical to surmise that you'd stay here."

Bryn kept her gaze on her grandfather. Waiting for some acknowledgment that she'd apologized. He didn't so much as twitch an eyebrow in her direction. What had she expected? Common civility? She could hear her grandfather claiming that he wasn't common. The idea made her laugh.

"What about this situation do you find amusing?" her grandfather asked.

"Sometimes you have to laugh or cry. I'm choosing to laugh."

"None of this is funny." Her grandmother stalked over to the refrigerator and yanked the door open. "I want all this food removed and the entire kitchen sanitized." She pointed at Abigail. "Give the guards a description of the culprit and then go see a medic to make sure you're okay."

Abigail scurried from the room.

Her grandmother gave orders and handed out assignments to the staff. After everyone had a task to carry out, her grandmother turned to her husband. "I presume you will speak with the guard and the Directorate about this."

"Of course."

Bryn's stomach growled loudly enough for her grandparents to hear. They both regarded her with distaste.

"I didn't eat yet this morning. Since you're getting rid of all the food here, maybe I'll fly into Dragon's Bluff for breakfast."

She expected an argument. Her grandmother surprised her by saying, "Let's take the car instead."

"Okay."

"First you need to change into something more suitable."

Crap.

Fifteen minutes later, she and her grandmother sat in the backseat of a large black SUV driven by one of the Red guards. Bryn had changed per her grandmother's request into a dress, but she'd worn flats rather than heels. They were black patent leather, so it's not like they were casual.

"Is there any place we can have pancakes?" Bryn asked. Carbs were her go-to comfort food. Right now she wanted a dozen drenched in maple syrup and butter.

"Take us to Suzette's," her grandmother told the driver.

She'd never heard of the place. "Is that a restaurant in Dragon's Bluff?"

"It's more of a tearoom, but they do serve a nice break- fast. Maybe if I bring your grandfather a box of muffins, he won't be so testy for the rest of the day."

Should she apologize for arguing with her grandfather? Nope. She'd already apologized once. It hacked her off that he hadn't acknowledged the effort she'd made.

"In the past, when you two have fought, has he ever apologized or recognized an apology from you?"

Her grandmother chuckled. It wasn't a happy sound. "Ephram Sinclair has never apologized to anyone for anything."

Chapter Twenty-Six

"How's that possible? He must've made mistakes at some point in his life."

"Mistakes, he has made, but he hasn't seen them as such. Your grandfather is a very confident man. He thinks he knows what's best for everyone."

"Is that a side effect of being on the Directorate?" Oh shit, did she say that out loud?

This time her grandmother laughed for real. "I believe it is. When it comes to dealing with Blue males, it's best to let them think they are in control. Yelling at him was risky. You shouldn't do it again. If he had kicked you out, there would be no second chance."

"How do you deal with his attitude? I'd shoot a fireball at his head."

"Believe me, there have been times I've wanted to. But there's a lot to be said for keeping the peace. Like I told you once before, he goes his way, and I go mine. It's just…

easier."

. . .

When they reached Dragon's Bluff, the guard parked in a lot across the street from a bakery.

"Are we having doughnuts for breakfast?" Bryn asked.

"No." Her grandmother exited the vehicle and waited for Bryn to join her. "Suzette's is just down the street. Before we eat, we're going to visit a bakery. I need to decide on a dessert for the Christmas ball."

When it came to Christmas, there was only one dessert that mattered. "Does the bakery make Christmas cookies?"

"I suppose they could."

Her grandmother didn't sound that interested.

"If they don't, could we buy some ingredients to make Christmas cookies?" Sadness welled up inside her but she pushed it down.

"You want to bake your own cookies?" Her grandmother looked at her like she was speaking a foreign language.

Patience. "The only thing better than eating Christmas cookies is baking them."

Her grandmother nodded. "We'll see what we can do."

They crossed the street. It was a pretty winter day with crisp weather and a cloudless sky. The light posts in front of the shop were decorated with silver snowflakes. "I wonder if it will snow for Christmas?"

At home, she'd had a few white Christmases. Her eyes grew hot. She sniffled and tried not to think about what had been. Too late. Images flooded her mind. Her dad dressing up like Santa Claus. Waking Christmas mornings and running to find the reindeer food they'd left on the fire escape gone. Stringing popcorn while watching *Rudolph* on television. Her dad singing all the songs, badly off tune. *Bam. Bam. Bam.* The hits kept coming.

She clutched at the light post she stood next to because it was within reach. It was real. Everything else was gone. Her entire life. Gone. Everything good, *gone gone gone.*

Bryn became aware that she was sitting on the ground and her grandmother was yelling at her. "Bryn, what is it? Are you sick?"

Strong hands grabbed Bryn by the shoulders and pulled her to her feet. Jaxon stared into her face. "What's wrong?"

"It can't be Christmas without them." And then she burst into tears.

Lillith appeared by Jaxon's side. "I'm sorry for your loss."

People kept saying that, but it didn't do her any damn good.

Her grandmother passed her a lace-edged handkerchief. Bryn took it and dabbed at her face, but the tears kept coming.

"You're not going to stop crying, are you?" Jaxon said.

"I'm not doing it on purpose." She took a deep breath and blew it out. Didn't help.

"Perhaps we could sit somewhere and have a cup of tea," Lillith suggested. "Suzette's is just around the corner."

"God, no." Jaxon backed up a step.

The look of utter horror on his face turned Bryn's tears to laughter. How bad could the tearoom be?

Her grandmother stepped into her line of sight. "Do you feel up to eating, or should we go home?"

The last thing she wanted to do was go stare at the

walls of her bedroom. She sniffled and dabbed at her eyes. "Breakfast sounds good." Wanting to prove she was okay, she added, "And we can shop for desserts afterward."

"So we're going to the teahouse?" Lillith's face lit up with excitement. "I've been craving sweets, and they have the best cherry pie."

Jaxon picked up the shopping bags he'd been carrying. "Why don't I take our bags home, and you can stay and have a nice visit."

"But you love the cherry pie at Suzette's." Lillith sounded like she might cry. Was she acting or was she experiencing hormonal mood swings?

The way Jaxon sighed and gave a resigned nod hinted at one answer over the other.

Lillith and her grandmother took the lead. Bryn and Jaxon walked behind them.

"So your mom is a little mood-swingy right now?"

Jaxon snorted. "I'm not sure you should comment on someone else's mental stability."

Bryn came to a dead halt. "Have you reverted back to the asshat you used to be? Because a little notice would've been nice."

He rounded on her. "I am not the problem here. You, my mother, and that god-awful flower-infested tearoom are the problem."

"You're this upset about a tearoom? Now who's emotionally unstable?"

"My mother dragged me there every Sunday afternoon from the time I was five until I was ten. Believe me, the pie doesn't make up for the agonizing conversations I was forced to endure about china patterns and tablecloths."

She almost felt sorry for him. Almost, but not quite. "Does my grandmother strike you as the type to chat about china patterns?"

"They all talk about china patterns. Like it's mandatory."

"I promise I won't engage in any dish-related conversations." She pointed toward her grandmother. "We better catch up."

"I'm not going." Jaxon took a step backward. "Tell my mother I left to check on a gift."

Before she could argue the point, he took off like a man fleeing death. Fierce Jaxon traumatized by a girlie tearoom seemed absurd. Whatever. She hurried to catch up to her grandmother. They were waiting outside the tearoom.

"Where's Jaxon?" Lillith asked.

Please don't let her cry. "He said he needed to check on a Christmas present."

"Oh, well I guess it's just the three of us." Lillith entered Suzette's.

The dining room at Suzette's looked like a florist's shop had exploded. Floral carpet, floral wallpaper, floral tablecloths, and dear God, there were even floral dishes.

Yet the place was packed. Women of all Clans sat in small groups. There were a few dispirited young men who seemed to have been dragged there by their mothers. The males all had the same get-me-the-hell-out-of-here look on their faces.

Bryn blinked and then checked her grandmother's expression.

"Something you wanted to say?" Her grandmother looked like the cat that had swallowed the canary.

How to be diplomatic about this? "This doesn't look like a place you would enjoy. The decor is…busy."

The hostess met them, grinning like she was in on the joke. "It must be your granddaughter's first time with us."

"Yes," her grandmother said. "She isn't known for her subtle ways. I'm waiting for her to make a comment."

Bryn crossed her arms over her chest. "If they have pancakes, I can deal with the froufrou decorations."

"We'll do froufrou next time," her grandmother said.

"This way." The hostess led the three of them to a side door and down a hallway that led to a room that was the complete opposite of the floral nightmare up front. The walls were a soothing pale blue, the tablecloths were cream-colored, and the floor was polished hardwood. Not a froufrou item in sight.

"Is this more to your taste?" her grandmother asked after the hostess seated them.

Bryn stared around the room. Several women nodded in their direction. Her grandmother and Lillith nodded back.

A waitress brought them menus. Once Bryn saw the words "blueberry pancakes," she was good to go. After they placed their order, she settled back in her seat. "What's the deal with the fake front room?"

"Sometimes you want a place to get away from the men in your life," her grandmother said, "a place they fear to tread."

"The flowery room is a front for the real restaurant?"

"Exactly. For generations, women have dragged their sons and grandsons into Suzette's. Once they're grown men, they never come looking for us here again. As you can see from Jaxon's reaction, it works."

"That is sneaky and brilliant." Bryn had a new respect for her fellow dragons' feminine ingenuity. "Who thought of this?"

"A couple of Green dragons came together with the idea and approached the Blue women's league asking them to finance the operation." Lillith picked up her menu and turned the pages.

"And the men have never suspected anything?"

"They all want out the front door so badly, they never investigate anything else," her grandmother said. "All the women take turns eating in the floral farce once a month. That way the room is always full."

Their food arrived, and Bryn worked her way through the pancakes in the most ladylike way she could manage. Which meant she only dripped syrup on her dress three times.

"We need to work on your etiquette," her grandmother said.

Bryn dabbed at the front of her dress with a wet napkin. At least the syrup didn't show on the dark-colored dress. Time for a topic change. "What's next on the agenda?"

Lillith sighed in satisfaction. "I finished my shopping, so I believe I'm going home to rest."

"Perhaps we should go home, too."

"But we were supposed to shop for desserts." She cringed at the thought of going back to her room and staring at the walls.

"Yes. Well, you weren't supposed to scare the life out of me." Her grandmother's words were harsh, but her tone was soft. She touched Bryn's shoulder. "You might need rest."

"Rest won't fix the problem. Nothing will fix it, but keeping busy might help me cope. I'll try to keep the breakdowns to a minimum."

After a visit to the bakery to discuss dessert options, Bryn and her grandmother returned to the car. The driver sat in the front seat reading a book. Did he have to stay by the car like he was he on call? She needed to figure out how this system worked.

And that made her think of something she couldn't believe she'd forgotten. When would she get her driver's license?

"Will I have driver's training classes at the institute?" Bryn asked as they took the winding road back into the forest to her grandparents' estate.

"Why would you need to learn how to drive? One of the drivers can take you anywhere you need to go."

Drivers? As in more than one? Wow. "At my old school" — she stopped short of saying "human school" — "everyone takes driver's training classes. It's mandatory before you can take the driver's test and get your license."

"That isn't part of the institute's curriculum."

And apparently that topic was over. Okay. Maybe she'd ask Valmont to teach her to drive.

"We need to talk about what happened today," her grandmother said.

"About what?"

"I understand you're grieving, but what happened today is unacceptable. If you can't cope better than that, then we might need to speak with a medic about helping you relax."

Seriously? "First off, I didn't plan it. Second, I'm not ashamed of grieving for my parents."

Her grandmother's lips set in a thin line. "Grief is meant to be acted on in private, not in public."

"I'm so sorry. I'll be sure to schedule my next breakdown for a time that's more correct by your standards."

The rest of the ride was a frosty affair. Her grandmother was angry. She got that, but how could the woman not understand how hard this was? She couldn't adjust to her parents' deaths overnight.

Over the next few days, Bryn did her best to meet her grandmother's expectations. Not that they interacted much. Her grandmother's time seemed to be taken up with planning the Christmas Eve ball. Her grandfather appeared at meals and kept mostly to himself.

Desperate for something to do, Bryn decided to investigate the mansion, avoiding any and all rooms with desks, lest she tread on her grandfather's territory again. She started in her grandmother's wing. She found a ton of guest bedrooms, some sitting rooms, and the occasional bathroom. None of the rooms were super interesting.

When she came across books, she investigated them, but most were about interior decorating or maintaining a proper staff. She knew her mother's old rooms had to be around somewhere, but didn't feel like she could ask. She suspected the rooms where Alec had taken Jaxon and Lillith after he'd drugged them were her mother's, simply because they'd been neglected. The smell of mold and dust had only been outdone by the gasoline Alec had poured on the furniture to prevent her from using her fire. What had her grandparents done after the attack? They couldn't leave gasoline-soaked furniture sitting around. For all she knew, the entire suite was probably destroyed during the battle. Searching through rooms kept her occupied in between meals with her grandparents.

One evening, she found a side stairwell that had a light that didn't work. Very odd. Somehow, throughout this giant mansion, the staff kept everything dust-free and well lit. Could she have finally found a way to reach her mother's old rooms?

Producing a flame in her right hand for light, she ascended the staircase, which ended at a landing crowded with boxes and cleaning supplies. A door stood ajar. Her heart beat faster. She pushed the door open wide enough to enter and sighed in disappointment. Whatever this space might once have been, it had been wiped clean. No furniture, no light fixtures, no carpets or anything filled the space. Although when she looked at the ceiling she could see bare wires hanging down where lights used to be.

Her footsteps echoed through the room and she realized it opened up into a much larger space. On the far wall she saw the elevator doors, which meant the way she'd come in had been the bedroom area, and she was now out in the larger sitting room area backward of the way she'd seen it on the night she'd faced Alec.

She headed back into the bedroom area, hoping to find a closet that might still hold some remnant of her mother, some proof that she'd existed. The closet in the bedroom proved to be empty and freshly painted like the rest of the room. It was long and narrow like a short hallway. At the very end, on the right side, Bryn saw the outline of another door half the size of a regular door, like something that might lead to an attic. She turned the knob and pulled, discovering that it had been painted shut. She yanked harder, and it came open. Kneeling down, she peered inside. Stairs, there were stairs. She crawled through and then stood, brushing dust off the front of her jeans. And there was a lot of dust. The cleanup effort hadn't extended this far.

Bryn climbed the half flight of stairs and came to a small room with a pitched ceiling. Her breath caught in her throat. Pictures of her parents when they were still in school were tacked onto a makeshift bulletin board. She crossed the space and traced her fingers over the photos of her dad smiling with such love she had no doubt it was her mom taking the picture, and photos of her mom grinning like she was the happiest woman in the world. Under the photos there was a stack of books. Bryn picked one up and recognized them as part of the Legends series from the library, about a time when dragons could fall in love and marry without Directorate interference.

She opened the top book, unpinned the pictures, and carefully slid the photos between the pages to keep them safe. A piece of paper fell out of the book. She picked it up and saw a familiar circle divided into four sections, each section containing a triangle...the symbol for rebellion. She flipped through the pages in the remaining books, hoping to find more notes. But there was nothing. Had her mother drawn the symbol because she'd seen it somewhere, or did it mean something else? She could imagine her mother sitting up here, reading about people falling in love and fantasizing about running away. Now that she'd met her grandparents and lived in this world, she realized what courage it had taken for her mom and dad to do what they did. She was proud of them.

It was nearing dinnertime. Bryn decided to take the books and photos and hide them in her room. Not that she should have to hide them, but if her mom had taken the trouble to do so, she felt like she should continue the tradition. There might be other photos of her mom in the house, but she'd yet to see any, and her grandmother had never offered to show her where they might be kept. So she wanted to keep these photos safe. The drawing didn't seem like something she should carry around. Since it had belonged to her mother, she wouldn't feel right throwing it away. Instead, she slid the piece of paper behind the bulletin board.

She made it back to her room without encountering anyone. She used a damp cloth to clean the dust from the books, and then she put them in her book bag. If asked, she could say they came from the library, not that she expected anyone to go through her bag. Once that was done, she changed and freshened up before going to dinner.

During dinner, she listened to her grandmother talk about details for the Christmas Eve ball. She did her best to smile and nod in all the right places. If her reactions were off, her grandmother didn't seem to notice.

Chapter Twenty-Seven

While she'd dreaded Christmas Eve for the sadness it would bring, she was grateful when it finally arrived. The ball could be fun. At least she'd see other people.

Bryn checked her reflection in the full-length mirror. The strapless emerald gown her grandmother had bought her fit like a glove, but not in a skanky way. It skimmed over her curves, looking like it had been made for her.

The dress was good. Her red, blond, and black-streaked hair? That was another story. *Pick a color, any color.* Per her grandmother's request, she planned to tone down her hair for the big event. What color should she choose?

All the guests at the ball would be other members of the Blue Clan, which meant they'd all be blond. Once again, she wouldn't blend. Would it be worth the consequences to use Quintessence to stripe her hair red and green? Probably not. She ran her fingers through her hair and sighed.

Every guest at the ball would be craning their neck to

see if the Sinclairs' granddaughter was up to their standards. And the answer to that question would be a great big fat no. She didn't have their manners, which Jaxon delighted in pointing out to her. She didn't have their grace, which is why she opted for silk ballet flats rather than the heels her grandmother favored. What she did have was a screw-all-of-you attitude and the ability to roast anyone who pissed her off.

Though it might be better to save those extremes as a last resort. For now, she'd deal with her hair. Just to see what it would look like, she colored her hair platinum blond. With her fair complexion, she looked anemic. Option number two, she switched back to her original strawberry blond. Too boring.

She returned her hair to red and blond stripes without the black stripes. There, she'd given up one color for her grandmother. That would have to be enough.

A knock sounded on her bedroom door.

"Come in."

Her grandmother entered looking regal in an ice-blue gown that matched her eyes.

"You look beautiful." Bryn meant it.

Her grandmother gave a genuine smile. "Thank you. You look lovely as well." Her gaze traveled to Bryn's hair. "I see you reduced your hair coloring to two. Maybe you could pick one for this evening?"

"I tried. Nothing looked right. I did get rid of the black for you."

"For that I'm grateful." Her grandmother tilted her head. "With your coloring, you should go for a darker blond. Give it a try for me. If you don't like it, you can change it back."

Why not? She focused and shifted her hair color to a dark honey blond. The image in the mirror surprised her. It worked.

"What do you think?" her grandmother asked.

If it had been her idea, she'd like it more. "It works, but…" How to phrase this without ticking her grandmother off? "I don't want people to think I'm trying to be something I'm not. Does that make sense?"

Her grandmother walked forward and touched the hair on Bryn's right temple. "Add a red streak here."

It worked. The cherry-red stripe gave a nod to her parentage but managed to appear sophisticated rather than punk rockish. "Good call. I like it."

"Me, too. Now come with me and we'll pick some jewelry to go with your gown."

Since Zavien had turned out to be a cowardly jerk, she'd stopped wearing the necklace he'd given her. The key with the protection charm Onyx gave her hung from a thin gold chain around her neck. The key itself was less than an inch long.

"I don't like to take off my protection charm." She followed her grandmother down the hall to a room that had a keypad rather than a doorknob.

Her grandmother entered a long series of numbers and the door popped open. "If you must wear it, I imagine we can find a way to conceal it."

Bryn entered the room and stood with her mouth hanging open. It was a jewelry thief's dream. Display cases full of necklaces, rings, earrings, and bracelets lined the walls. There were separate cases for diamonds, sapphires, emeralds, and rubies. "Holy crap. All of this is yours?"

"It's been handed down through generations," her grandmother said.

Bryn stood still, afraid if she touched anything an alarm would go off.

Her grandmother walked over to a case and retrieved an emerald necklace with stones the size of pennies. "I think this would look lovely with your gown."

Bad idea. "I don't think so."

"You don't like it?"

"What? No. I love it. But I could lose it or break it or do something stupid with it. You shouldn't trust me with something that valuable."

"You're being ridiculous. Nothing will happen to the necklace as long as you leave it on."

Yeah, because weird crap didn't happen to her on a regular basis. Still, the necklace was gorgeous. Bryn let her grandmother fasten it around her neck. The stones were cool at first, but they warmed to her body heat. She checked a nearby mirror. "I feel like a princess in a fairy tale." Too bad fairy tales never ended well.

"You'll need to take your other necklace off."

Bryn unhooked the chain and removed the small gold key. Now what? The strapless bra she'd struggled into in order to wear this dress fit like a vise. She turned away from her grandmother and slid the key into her bra.

"I think I'm ready." Wait a minute. "Besides keeping my elbows off the table and don't chew with my mouth open, are there any rules I should know about?"

"Never disagree with someone even if they say something ridiculous, just smile and say, 'That's an interesting perspective,' or 'I've never thought of it that way.'"

"So, no shooting fireballs at anyone's head?" She was only half joking.

"No. Not unless I request it."

"That takes some of the fun out of it. Just so you know, if anyone insults my parents, I will fight back."

"If anyone says something to offend you, come find me. I'll have them escorted from the ball and have their names removed from next year's guest list. In our social circles, this ball is the highlight of the season. A threat from me will carry far more weight than the threat of a fireball from you."

"Yes, but shooting a ball of flames at them would make me feel much better than having them banned from your party."

"No fireballs in the house," her grandmother said. "The only exception is if you're defending yourself."

Chapter Twenty-Eight

Christmas trees decorated with poinsettia flowers flanked the door to the ballroom. Each tree had a gold star at the top that sparkled in the light. Inside the ballroom, round tables were scattered around two-thirds of the room, while the center of the floor was left open for dancing. Not that anyone would ask her to dance. She should've invited Valmont.

An orchestral version of "Deck the Halls" played softly in the background. Correction. The orchestra on the stage at the far side of the room played "Deck the Halls." All the instruments appeared to have dampers on them. If her grandfather didn't want the music to be loud, why didn't he hire a smaller group of musicians? Wait. She knew the answer. In her grandfather's world, bigger, which meant more expensive, was better.

Bryn felt someone staring at her. She tuned back in to her surroundings and realized her grandmother was waiting for a response. "It's beautiful."

A smile of pride lit her grandmother's face. "I'm glad you like it."

If her grandmother had been a Red dragon, she would've been an interior decorator. Since she didn't need to work, she threw fabulous, well-decorated parties instead.

"It's tradition for us to greet the guests as they enter." Her grandmother headed back to stand a dozen feet inside the doorway.

"Does that we include me?" *Please say no.*

"It most definitely does." Her grandmother pointed to the space next to her.

Great. Bryn took up her appointed post. "What do I do?" If this involved any of that weird air-kissing like they showed on television when rich people got together, she was out.

"If you were a man, you'd shake everyone's hand. Since you're not, you hold your hands clasped at your waist, smile at everyone, and thank them for coming."

She'd rather help the staff do the dishes. "Isn't it weird for me to thank them for coming when they don't know who I am, and I don't know them?"

"Everyone will know who you are. And you'll know who they are because I'll introduce you."

"Sounds like fun," she lied.

People filtered into the ballroom in an orderly line. Bryn did her best to smile and nod during the introductions. If her grandparents hadn't been next to her, half the people wouldn't have said anything to her except to call her mean names. This was going to be a fabulous evening.

Once everyone entered the room, her grandmother pointed to a table near the orchestra. "Let's have a drink and enjoy the orchestra for a moment before your grandfather welcomes everyone."

Hadn't they just done that? *Whatever.* She followed her grandmother to the appropriate table, smiling at anyone who looked her way. A few smiled back; most pretended not to see her. Fine. Not like it mattered.

Once she made it to the table, a waiter came around with glasses of tea and wine. When the waiter asked which she would like, she said tea. Although if there ever was an occasion to start drinking alcohol, sitting in a ballroom where the friendliest face she'd see all night would be Jaxon's definitely qualified.

Their table was set for eight. Name cards warning her who would be joining them would've been nice. "Who will sit with us?"

"Whoever we ask to sit with us." Her grandmother scanned the room and gave a slight nod to someone. Bryn tried to figure out who her grandmother was communicating with. Lillith and Jaxon approached the table. Lillith beamed while Jaxon appeared wary. What was that saying about the devil you know is better than the devil you don't know?

"You've outdone yourself this year," Lillith said. "It's beautiful."

"Thank you." Her grandmother zeroed in on Jaxon. "Don't you have anything to say?"

He froze for a second, and then regained his composure. "Did you commission the gold and diamond stars for the trees flanking the door?"

"I did." Her grandmother smiled.

"They are works of art that I'm sure your friends will be copying for their own holiday celebrations."

Number one: What orifice had Jaxon pulled that from?

Number two: The freaking stars were made of actual diamonds and gold?

"Where's Ferrin?" her grandmother asked.

Who cares? If they were lucky, he'd been unable to attend.

Jaxon's eyes darted around like he was checking the room for exits. Like he'd rather be anywhere other than where he was. "Mother, why don't I go let Father know where you'll be sitting?"

"Your father knows where to find *us*." Lillith touched Jaxon's shoulder. "Why don't you and Bryn go mingle with some of your friends?"

Jaxon arched an eyebrow at Bryn.

"Are you trying to telepathically communicate that my friends aren't here?" Bryn asked.

"I didn't say a word." Jaxon managed to sound confused.

"Right."

He pointed at Bryn's head. "Why did you change your hair?"

She grinned at him. "Before you ask that, wouldn't it be polite for you to tell me how lovely I look?"

Her grandmother puffed up with pride. "I knew my genes were in there somewhere."

Bryn laughed.

Jaxon's nostrils flared.

"Oh, come on. It was funny." Why was he being such a jerk? Maybe she should throw him a bone. "I wanted to try something different with my hair for the ball."

"Two colors rather than three was a good choice."

If he didn't knock off the attitude, she'd touch him, focus her Quintessence, and do her damnedest to turn his hair flamingo pink.

"If you'll excuse me," Jaxon said, "I see someone I need to speak to."

"Young man, be the gentleman your mother raised you to be," her grandmother said. "Go introduce my granddaughter to your social circle."

Could Jaxon ignore a direct order from her grandmother? She didn't think so. Her grandfather seemed to outrank Ferrin by age, if not by money, and the ability to scheme and blackmail his fellow Directorate members. It made sense that her grandmother would outrank Lillith and Jaxon.

"Fine." Jaxon pasted a polite smile on his face. "Bryn, would you like to mingle?"

She'd rather eat cockroaches, but that didn't seem like an answer her grandmother would appreciate. "Thank you. That sounds lovely." This fake socialite crap wasn't so hard after all. *Lie through my teeth and I'm good to go.*

As soon as they were a few feet from the table, out of the hearing of her grandmother, Bryn said, "So what does mingle mean? Small talk? Discussing how much money someone spent on their latest fur-lined yacht? Clue me in."

"Why would anyone want a yacht lined with fur?"

"It was meant to be an absurd example." She clipped off the end of the sentence where she referred to him as an idiot.

"Like a yacht with diamond chandeliers?" he asked.

"Yes. Why?"

They wove between tables toward Jaxon's friend Quentin and several other Blues she didn't recognize.

"Because your grandfather has one."

What? "If that's true, I'm going to learn how to drive it and leave it in a port somewhere as a donation to a charity for kids with cancer."

Jaxon came to a dead halt. "Why would you do that?"

"Because anyone who has enough money to buy a yacht with diamond chandeliers has enough money to help people."

"Why would dragons help humans when they could help other dragons?"

Whack. His question was like a Nerf bat upside the head. She'd been raised to believe she was human. Weird to think she no longer belonged in that category. Not like she'd try to explain that to Jaxon.

"I think you should help anyone who needs help, human or dragon. That's beside the point. No one needs diamond chandeliers."

"Your grandfather thinks otherwise, and I suggest you never repeat what you said to me in front of him or anyone else."

They reached a gathering of three couples. Quentin was the only person Bryn recognized.

She smiled and nodded when people said hello. She smiled while the boys talked about what sports cars they hoped to get for Christmas. She smiled while the girls talked about platinum jewelry versus gold jewelry. Did she fit in either conversation? No. So she smiled and nodded and pretended to give a crap, because that's what her grandmother wanted her to do.

When the orchestra started a song at full volume, everyone stopped talking and headed to their tables. She followed the Stepford maneuver, grateful to escape the boring conversation.

Once everyone was seated, her grandfather headed up to the stage and took a microphone. "Thank you all for coming this evening. In unsure times like these, it's good to know who your friends are." Polite applause sounded. All Bryn could think of was that war quote she'd heard in a movie, "Keep your friends close and your enemies closer." Was that what her grandfather was doing? More than likely he was showing off his exorbitant wealth. Later, she'd have to ask why her grandparents were the ones to host the ball. It must have some meaning. Probably "my bank account is bigger than yours."

Her grandfather waited for the applause to die down. "I'd like to wish all of you a wonderful holiday season." The orchestra flared to life again, and her grandfather bowed to more applause.

Rather than joining Lillith, Jaxon, her grandmother, and her, he walked over to a table where several men, including Ferrin, sat.

"Isn't he sitting with us?" Bryn asked.

"He'll join us later. It's hard to keep his mind off business for long." Her grandmother didn't seem to mind.

Two women her grandmother's age approached the table and asked to join them. There was the standard polite round of introductions. Then the women started to talk about the difficulty of hiring reliable caterers for the holiday. *Yawn.*

How had her mom put up with all this high-society crap? The stray thought made her heart ache.

Jaxon stared off into the distance while maintaining a polite smile and an occasional nod. He must have practiced this act from toddlerhood.

Since he was here, she might as well ask him how all this worked.

"Jaxon, what happens next?"

"What do you mean?"

She gestured in a circle to include the entire ballroom. "We eat, and then what happens?"

He looked like he was trying not to roll his eyes. "After everyone has eaten, there will be dancing. During that time, I will be hiding on the terrace behind a large plant. As will anyone who has any common sense."

She laughed at the idea of him hiding behind the Christmas decorations. "Why hide? No one forces you to dance, do they?"

"Wait and see. Your grandmother will politely suggest you dance with someone so you can network with them. If Rhianna were here — "

The anger in his voice and the way he bit off the sentence made her heart hurt.

He cleared his throat and looked away. "Her parents dragged her off to Europe without allowing us to say good-bye."

"I'm sorry." She leaned in. "She'll be back at school after the holiday break, won't she?"

His eyes were hard and flat. "I'm not sure."

Fire roared in her gut, and she tasted smoke in the back of her throat. What was happening to Rhianna and the other students who were now less than perfect was wrong.

She closed her eyes and took a slow measured breath, thinking about ice and snow and cold things to put out the fire. Setting her grandmother's Christmas ball ablaze wouldn't win her any favors.

Their food arrived. Bryn examined the plate of prime rib in front of her and checked to see what everyone else was doing. No one ate yet. Were they waiting for the entire ballroom to be served? *Who knew?* A better question, why hadn't she chosen wine instead of tea?

Five minutes later, her grandmother picked up her fork and knife and cut into the entrée. Everyone else did the same. Out of the corner of her eye, Bryn saw people at other tables pick up their utensils. It was like a ripple effect.

Bryn chewed, nodded, and smiled. When the plates were cleared, she craved sugar cookies with icing. Every year, she and her mom would make sugar cookie dough and cut out candy canes and stars. Her dad would take small balls of dough and make lopsided snowmen whose appearance did not improve with baking.

A wave of sadness swamped her, threatening to drown her where she sat. She took a deep breath and pushed the sadness away. *Don't think about it. Time to focus on the present.*

Everyone around her seemed so damn happy. Even Jaxon was chatting with his mother. Everyone had family, except for her. Okay, that wasn't fair to her grandparents, but it would take a long time before they could fill the void left by her parents. And the sadness rolled in again. She needed to get out of here.

"Excuse me." She pushed away from the table and headed out the door to a side hall where the restrooms for guests were located. She took a turn down a different hall and headed out onto a terrace decorated with twinkling lights designed to look like snowflakes.

Gripping the edge of the railing, she stared up at the stars, willing her tear ducts to behave. Her grandmother would never forgive her if she caused a scene at the Christmas ball. The night air was cool and the terrace was quiet. It was nice to get away from people. Maybe she could hide out here for the rest of the night.

Footsteps sounded behind her. Was it Jaxon or her grandmother coming to check on her?

"Out here by yourself?" a masculine voice asked.

She turned to find a young man smiling at her in a way that set her trouble meter on high alert, but he was one of her grandparent's guests, so he couldn't be too scary, right? The terrace, which had seemed nice and insulated from prying eyes, now seemed too secluded.

"I just came out for a breath of fresh air. I'm not used to being around so many people. I better get back before my grandmother sends someone to look for me." Babbling, she moved toward the door, but he blocked her path.

"It's too late for that."

Chapter Twenty-Nine

She laughed like he was making a joke, but held her palms face out, ready to blast him with fire if need be. "If you'll excuse me." She went to squeeze by him.

He grabbed her arm. "Stay here with me."

She backed away from him, trying to yank her arm from his viselike grip. Focusing on the rage over her parents' death, she blasted foot-high flames from her free hand. "Let go. Now."

He dropped her arm, laughing like this had been a joke. "Sorry, I didn't mean to frighten you."

"You didn't scare me. You pissed me off. There's a difference. Don't do it again."

"Bryn, your grandmother sent me to find you. They're serving dessert and she knew you wouldn't want to miss it." Jaxon stood in the doorway, speaking to Bryn, but with his gaze locked on the man who'd grabbed her. "Taven, I'm surprised to see you here. I wasn't aware that your family had been invited back to the Sinclairs' estate."

"Just this year." Taven flashed a fake smile. "My parents declined, but I decided to accept the invitation on their behalf. To bury the hatchet, as they say."

He wanted to bury the hatchet all right, in her skull. Maintaining her irritated expression, she headed inside at a slow pace. No way would she let him know he'd frightened her. Jaxon caught up with her a dozen feet down the hall.

"Who was that creep?" she asked.

"Someone you'd do well to stay away from." Jaxon looked around like he thought they might be followed. "Why were you speaking with him?"

"I was getting some fresh air, and he found me. Not the other way around." She rubbed her arm where he'd grabbed her. "Should I tell my grandmother about this?"

"Absolutely not. You'll go back in there, make a big fuss over the dessert your grandmother chose for you, and pretend everything is wonderful. I'll find your grandfather and tell him what happened. He'll deal with it how he sees fit." As they reached the door back into the ballroom, Jaxon said, "Try not to do anything stupid for the rest of the evening."

She glared at his back as he headed across the ballroom toward the table where her grandfather sat surrounded by his Directorate cronies.

Her grandmother's face lit up when she saw Bryn. "Jaxon didn't spoil the surprise, did he?"

"No." Bryn glanced at waiters entering the ballroom carrying covered trays. They stopped at her grandmother's table first and set the silver platter on the table. With a flourish, her grandmother lifted the dome. Underneath,

Christmas cookies in all varieties and colors decorated the plate. There were chocolate chip, oatmeal, Russian teacakes, and something covered in cinnamon.

"Tell me those are snickerdoodles," Bryn said.

"Although the name is undignified, those have always been my favorite," her grandmother said.

Happy at having a bit of her Christmas tradition restored, Bryn grabbed a snickerdoodle and took a bite. It was cinnamon sweet vanilla goodness. "These are awesome."

Other people at the table grabbed a cookie apiece and politely ate. Bryn grabbed one of each and piled them on her plate.

Jaxon returned to the table, took notice of her plate, and shook his head.

She just grinned and ate her way through a dozen cookies. Even though she could've eaten more, she stopped. To her grandmother, she leaned over and said, "Please tell me there will be more of these in the kitchen later tonight."

"There should be three dozen set aside for our personal use." Her grandmother smiled, obviously happy that Bryn was happy.

"Thank you."

The orchestral music swelled in the background, and Bryn saw her grandfather approaching the table. Was he finally coming to join them? It was about time.

He came around the table and held his hand out toward his wife. "Are you ready, Marie?"

"Yes." Her grandmother actually smiled.

They walked away hand in hand.

"What's that about?" she asked Jaxon.

He gave her a long-suffering look. "Why am I your

personal ambassador for the Christmas ball tonight?"

"Because I find your personality so delightful." She batted her eyelashes at him. "Now answer the question."

"They are walking toward the dance floor. The orchestra is playing a song. What do you think will happen next?"

"Oh." That made sense. "You don't have to be so condescending."

"I strive to be just condescending enough, but sometimes the balance is hard to maintain."

If they weren't in the middle of a ballroom surrounded by her grandparents' friends and associates, she would've flipped him off. As it was, she didn't bother to respond.

On the dance floor, her grandparents took a traditional dance pose and the orchestra launched into a romantic rendition of "Blue Christmas." Was that supposed to be a joke?

Her grandparents moved together with the ease of a couple who'd slow-danced together for fifty years. Funny how they looked so perfect together, when they actually lived as what? Friends? No, that wasn't the right term. More like business partners or associates. The lack of love in their relationship seemed sad. Before, she'd wondered how her mother could walk away from everything. Now she knew. It was simple. True love trumped everything.

Would she have a chance to experience true love? She'd loved Zavien, or at least she thought she had. Just because he hadn't returned her feelings didn't mean hers hadn't been real. Looking back on it, she could see the times she'd made comments about being willing to run away with him. He'd never, not once, said anything similar. Which made her feel stupid now.

Applause broke out around her, bringing her back to the moment. She clapped along with everyone else as her grandparents acknowledged the applause with slight nods of their heads.

Jaxon stood. "I'm going to visit the men's room, and then I plan to hide on the terrace."

Was he serious? Apparently so, because he took off like a shot.

His mother turned around from her conversation and frowned. "Where's Jaxon?"

"I believe he ran to the restroom." Should she follow his lead?

"When he returns, you two should dance." Lillith said it like it was a fabulous idea. Bryn was pretty sure Jaxon would rather do a rendition of "I'm a Little Teapot" while wearing nothing but black socks and a Viking helmet than dance with her.

Not wanting to upset Lillith, she smiled and nodded. Her grandmother would be proud.

Ferrin came toward the table. The smile that lit Lillith's face made Bryn's heart hurt. Did Lillith harbor feelings for Ferrin? She'd claimed she was happy with a son who loved her and another one on the way. Was that true?

Bryn didn't want to make eye contact with Ferrin, so she reached for another cookie while Lillith floated out of her chair to the dance floor. More and more couples joined her grandparents. Blonds dancing with blonds, as far as the eye could see. Always being the odd man out sucked. Maybe she should follow Jaxon's lead and hide on a terrace. Then again, there were whack jobs like Taven on the terraces.

All she wanted to do was go hide in her room with a

platter of cookies, but her grandmother would be hurt if she left the party early. That meant she had two choices. Sit here by herself and pretend it didn't bother her that everyone else was dancing, or find a safe place to hide and kill some time while she waited for the orchestra to stop playing.

First, she'd retreat to the restrooms, and then she'd figure out a good hiding spot. The restroom off the ballroom reminded her of the restroom at a theater. There were multiple stalls and sinks. Most of them were in use at the moment, so she waited in line. Which didn't bother her, because it killed more time. The woman in front of her glanced back to see who had joined the queue and frowned.

Great.

After leaving the restroom, Bryn walked the edge of the ballroom pretending to study the various Christmas trees lining the walls.

Jaxon stood across the room talking with Quentin and a few other guys. If there had been any females in the group, she might have joined him. With just males, it would be beyond awkward.

Now what? Out of ideas, she headed back to her table. Dang it. The table was empty. Everyone must be dancing. Which would look more pathetic—sitting by herself or standing off to the side by herself?

She'd sell a kidney on the black market for a friendly face at this point. Since there were none in sight, she opted for sitting at the table where she had the consolation of Christmas cookies.

With every cookie she ate, her mood sank.

Christmas Eve. All her life it had meant a cozy home, stringing popcorn, and watching *Rudolph*. Now it meant attending a ball where she was tolerated, but not welcomed. God, maybe she'd be better off living somewhere by herself, pretending to be human. With her love of food, she could become a chef or a baker. But then, she'd never be able to share who she truly was with anyone. That sounded lonelier than being ignored by hundreds of shape-shifting dragons.

In time, would they come to accept her? Did she care one way or another? Best-case scenario, she could live in Dragon's Bluff with Valmont or his family. They were all warm, loving people who thought food made everything better. She liked that logic.

"Excuse me." A Blue male she didn't know stood in front of her. He glanced back at a group of males who were snickering.

Her internal alarm went off. Odds were this wouldn't end well.

"Yes?" she braced herself.

"I was wondering if you'd like to dance?" The tone of his voice screamed, *I am a jerk.*

"One question: Are you the joke or am I?"

He blinked. "I don't know what you're talking about."

She pointed at his friends. "Are they laughing at you for asking me to dance? Or are they laughing at me, because they think I'll be stupid enough to believe you actually want to dance with me?"

The polite expression melted from his face, leaving behind a cold sneer. "You're not stupid, are you?"

"No."

"You realize this is probably the only chance you'll have to dance tonight."

That hurt a little bit because it was probably true. She gave him a go-screw-yourself smile. "Then I'd rather not dance."

He mumbled something under his breath that sounded a lot like "bitch," but she couldn't prove it. And as much as she'd like to shoot a fireball at his head, she refrained.

When he reached his friends, he said something that made them laugh. What was he telling them? The idea that he'd be the one controlling what people thought had happened made her stomach churn. It's not like she could counteract the rumors. Who did she know to talk to? Think. Damn it. Jaxon might help. Then again, he might just be pissed off she asked. Clenching her fists, she drank the last of her tea and resisted the urge to wing the empty glass across the room at her tormenter's head.

A waitress came to refill her drink. Bryn was surprised to see it was Abigail. "Hello. How are you feeling?"

"I'm fine. Thanks to you." Abigail grinned. "How are you enjoying the party?"

"It's amazing. But do you know who that young man is over there?"

Abigail glanced toward the jerk in question. "He's Liam Eldridge, son of a Directorate member."

"He asked me to dance as a joke, and now he's over there laughing it up with his friends. I'm not sure how to handle it."

"Don't worry, jerks like him always get their comeuppance one way or another." She patted Bryn on the shoulder. "Forget about him. Go find someone nice to dance with."

Easier said than done. "Thanks, I might try that." Bryn sipped her tea and watched as Abigail walked over to another member of the waitstaff, an elderly woman Bryn didn't know. The woman hovered around the table where

Liam and his friends sat. What was she doing?

The elderly server lifted a pitcher of iced tea to refill Liam's glass. Abigail walked behind the woman and jostled her so that she lurched forward, dumping the entire pitcher of tea onto Liam's lap.

His outraged growl ripped through the ballroom. The elderly woman backed up apologizing. He opened his mouth like he was going to verbally rip her apart. Then he noticed everyone staring, and forced a tight smile.

The woman continued to apologize. He nodded and said something about it not being a big deal. Bryn ducked her head and sipped her tea when his gaze swept in her direction. Hopefully he wouldn't connect the incident with her. Whoever the elderly woman was, Bryn was going to send her the mother of all gift cards from Fonzoli's.

Jaxon and Quentin approached from across the room. Jaxon shot her an *I know what you did* look. She played innocent and hoped it was a convincing act.

Her grandmother returned to the table a short time later. "I wish you would dance."

Laughter may not have been the appropriate response, but Bryn couldn't help it. "That would require someone asking me."

"But I saw Liam over here talking to you. Didn't he ask you to dance?"

Was her grandmother fishing for a confession? How much should she tell her? Time to lay her cards on the table.

"He did ask me to dance, but he wasn't sincere." She told her grandmother about her conversation with the jerk.

"Well." Her grandmother did not appear pleased. "That is disappointing. His father is one of your grandfather's allies. I'd expect him to think of the consequences his actions might bring to his father's interactions in the Directorate."

Okay. Bryn's feelings weren't important. How this would reflect on Liam's father and her grandfather were the concern. Did Blue dragons have their feelings removed at birth, or what?

"Are you responsible for Liam's need to change clothing?" her grandmother asked.

She wasn't about to admit to anything just yet. "If I were, how would you feel about that?"

"If you had orchestrated the event, I would request that you not use household staff to sabotage our guests." A slow grin spread across her grandmother's face. "But I would applaud your resourcefulness. Now, we need to develop your circle of allies, and Jaxon is going to help."

Oh, God.

Her grandmother stared at Jaxon until he could probably feel the laser-like intensity sinking into his skull. He turned with a resigned look on his face and walked toward the table like a man approaching the gallows.

"Did you need something, Mrs. Sinclair?"

"Yes, Jaxon. I would appreciate it if you'd ask my grand-daughter to dance."

"Of course." He turned to Bryn. "Would you like to dance?"

"My grandmother would like us to. Is that the same thing?"

"Yes." Her grandmother's tone was teasing with a bit of edge. "Go out there and pretend to enjoy each other's company."

"Let's get this over with." Jaxon took her hand and they moved onto the crowded dance floor. "You're responsible for what happened to Liam, aren't you?"

"Karma is responsible for what happened to him."

Jaxon shook his head, but he was smiling.

"Are you friends with him?" she asked.

"No. Quite the opposite. His father and mine rarely agree, and he always acts so smug. It's annoying."

Jaxon's calling someone else smug caught her off guard, and she laughed.

He glared at her. "What's so funny?"

"Nothing." She tried to maintain a straight face, but couldn't.

"Are you saying I act like him?"

"You used to act like him. Now you're not nearly as annoying." He did not look appeased. "Now you're downright charming. Warm and fuzzy, almost."

He laughed and gave her a fake haughty look. "I'm a Westgate. We don't do warm and fuzzy. It's against our genetic code."

"Someone at your house better do warm and fuzzy, because your mother is only going to become more hormonal."

"I'm counting down the days until we return to school. She's redecorating the entire estate to make it baby-safe. My father pointed out that the baby won't be walking for a year, and she burst into tears. Now he's ordering every babyproofing item on the internet and having the staff install them. She even put them in my room. It's absurd."

"It's nice that your dad is trying to help her."

"Please. He runs out the door on Directorate business at every opportunity, leaving me to pretend to be interested in baby blankets and strollers."

"I wouldn't mind spending time with your mom." *Where had that come from?*

"Why would you want to spend time with her?"

"I like your mom." And it's not like she had a mom of her own to hang around. "Don't worry, this isn't a plot to walk you down the aisle. I could use a friend right now, and it sounds like she could, too. Unless you want to spend time looking at baby clothes."

"No. You're more than welcome to take over that duty. I'll tell her you asked about decorations for the nursery, and she'll take it from there, I'm sure."

The song ended, and Jaxon stepped away from her. Another girl caught his eye, and he abandoned Bryn without another word. And it bothered her. Not that he was dancing with someone else, but that they'd been having a friendly, or so she thought, conversation, and he must have been counting the minutes until he could dance with someone else.

She stood there, unsure of what to do as couples started dancing around her. Did anyone else approach and ask her to dance? Of course not.

Fine. Holding her head high, she walked back to her table, which was empty again, damn it. Time to visit the bathroom. And she'd do it with a smile on her face. No reason for people to see that she'd been tossed aside again.

The losses in her life kept adding up. Zavien had been her emotional rock. Now he was gone. Her parents…best not to think about that right now. That left her with Jaxon. She'd been stupid enough to think they might be friends. He'd just proven that they might be allies, but nothing more.

Somehow, being rejected by her former nemesis was the final straw for the evening. She was done. If there were any way to have her feelings removed, at this point she'd be willing to look into it.

Chapter Thirty

How long could she hide in a bathroom stall before people noticed or someone came looking for her? Ten minutes ago she'd taken refuge in the ladies' room. After five minutes of hiding in the stall, she came out and washed her hands multiple times.

Time to suck it up and head back out to the damn party where she felt like a social leper. She grabbed the door handle, and then backed up as it swung inward.

"There you are," her grandmother said. "I was beginning to worry about you. Are you all right?"

"I'm fine." That was a big fat lie.

"It's time for us to adjourn to the small ballroom to open gifts."

Aw, crap. She'd left the gift certificates for the gardening club and dessert-of-the-month at school. "I left your gifts in my dorm room."

"Don't worry, we can send for them later." She waved

Bryn out into the hall.

"What happens after the gift opening?" Was it too much to hope that everyone would go home so she could collapse in bed?

"After the presents are opened, we say good-night and guests are free to leave or mingle for a while longer over hot cocoa."

Was she included in the list of people allowed to leave? The only way to find out was to ask. "Does that mean I can go lie down? I'm exhausted."

"Normally, the answer would be no. But I know you've had a hard time this evening, so you can leave when the guests do."

"Thank you."

"All right now. Chin up. We are going to walk into that ballroom smiling like we don't have a care in the world. Understand?"

No, but that didn't matter right now. "One smiling grand-daughter, coming up."

Plastering a grin on her face, she accompanied her grand-mother into the small ballroom, where families congregated around individual Christmas trees. It looked like a scene out of a movie rather than something in real life.

Her grandfather stood there surveying his domain like the lord and master he thought he was. "You're late," he said without changing his facial expression—like a ventriloquist who could talk through a fake smile.

"No harm done." Her grandmother reached down and pulled a shoe box–sized rectangular package from under the tree and handed it to him.

Why did he get the first gift? You'd think they'd let the

little kids go first.

He carefully opened the package without ripping the paper. Inside was a box of cigars that reeked from three feet away.

"Thank you, Marie. This is perfect. I was running low."

"You're welcome."

Stepford wasn't a strong enough description for this exchange. Disingenuous might be better. Was this the same thing her grandfather said to her grandmother every year?

Her grandfather pulled a small blue velvet jeweler's box from his pocket and handed it to his wife. She popped the lid and smiled a smile that didn't reach her eyes. Turning the box so Bryn could see, she said, "Aren't they lovely?"

The teardrop sapphire-and-diamond earrings were amazing, but they didn't seem to mean anything to either of her grandparents.

"They're beautiful," Bryn said. She wanted to add, *and you people are crazy*, but that wouldn't help the situation.

Her grandfather nodded, like her response was appropriate. He pulled a long thin blue velvet box from his other pocket and handed it to Bryn. The plant-of-the-month and dessert-of-the-month club memberships she'd bought for them seemed vastly inappropriate now.

Popping the lid open on the box, her breath caught in her throat. A sapphire-and-diamond bracelet winked at her from the box. "It's gorgeous."

Both grandparents seemed pleased by her reaction.

"Let's see what it looks like on." Her grandmother removed the bracelet from the box and fastened it around Bryn's left wrist, where it fit snugly enough that it couldn't come off over her hand. She moved her wrist back and forth in the light, watching the stones sparkle.

"I love it. Thank you." Without thinking about it, she leaned in and kissed her grandmother on the cheek and then did the same thing to her grandfather. He appeared embarrassed, but something in his expression softened.

Were they not supposed to do public displays of affection? She didn't care right now. "You'll probably think my gifts for you are lame. I can tell you what they are if you want, or you can be surprised."

"What did you buy?" her grandfather asked.

"Since you seem to like food as much as I do, I bought you a dessert-of-the-month-club membership." She shrugged. "You're kind of hard to buy for since you seem to own everything already."

He grinned.

To her grandmother she said, "I knew you loved gardening, so I bought a plant-of-the-month-club membership for you. I hope that's not stupid."

"I think it's thoughtful," her grandmother said. "And we can take care of the plants together so I can teach you how to garden."

"I'd like that."

"I'm not sharing my dessert," her grandfather said in a deadpan tone.

Bryn laughed. For a moment, all was right in her world, or if not right, at least not bad.

Waitstaff rolled in silver carts covered with steaming china cups of hot cocoa. Half of the drinks had a large marshmallow floating in the chocolate-colored liquid. The others were plain.

The scent of chocolate mingled with the fresh-cut-pine

scent of the trees and created a happy smell.

"Cocoa?" her grandmother asked.

"Yes." Bryn headed toward a cart and arrived at the same time as Jaxon, who actually wore a genuine smile on his face.

"Was Santa good to you this year?" she asked.

He held out a set of car keys dangling from a key fob with an emblem she didn't recognize.

"You got a car?"

He looked at her like she had two heads. "Not just a car, it's a Bugatti Veyron. There are only three hundred made a year."

Okay. So it was a fancy elite snobby car. "Oh, that's great." She tried not to laugh, but he continued to glare at her.

"I'm sorry. I don't know anything about cars. I'm sure yours is the best car ever invented and everyone will be jealous. There, is that better?"

"That's what you should've said the first time." He reached for a cup of cocoa with a marshmallow and offered it to her. "I assume this is what you want."

"How did you know?"

"I've seen you eat. 'Less is more' isn't an adage that applies to your diet."

She opened her mouth to argue and then stopped. "You're right."

"Your grandmother takes hers plain." He handed her another cup, which she accepted with her left hand. He didn't let go of the cup.

"Are you planning on taking it back?" she asked.

His breath caught. "That's a Vanleigh."

"What's a Vanleigh?"

"Your bracelet is a Vanleigh." He released the cup and then pointed to the bracelet. "See the signature *V* on the clasp?"

She set the cocoa down to look at the mark he indicated. "Does that mean this is a limited edition one-in-three-hundred bracelet that your friends will be jealous of?"

"No. It means it's a one-of-a-kind bracelet that most of the women in this room would kill to have. And you had no idea." He shook his head like he was astounded.

"Do you know what I see when I look at this bracelet?"

"I hate to ask."

"I see a pretty bracelet that sparkles when I do this." She moved her wrist back and forth so it caught the light. "The person who made it, or how much it cost, doesn't matter."

Jaxon dramatically touched his forehead. "Take that back before my head explodes."

Boom!

The teacups on the tray rattled. The Christmas trees shook, and everyone froze.

"I don't suppose that's fireworks?" *Please, please, please let it be fireworks.*

Kaboom! Boom. Boom.

"It's lightning," Jaxon said. He set his cocoa back on the cart and scanned the room. Bryn shoved her china cups on the cart and ran to her grandparents.

"Is this another attack?" she asked her grandfather.

"So it would appear. Marie, take all the women and children into one of the stormproofed rooms. I'll gather our forces and launch a counterattack."

"It's Christmas Eve, damn it." Bryn said to no one in

particular.

"They don't appear to care. Come with me," her grandmother said.

No way. She wasn't a sit-on-the-sidelines-and-let-the-men-fight-for-her kind of girl.

"Bryn." Jaxon grabbed her arm and spun her around. He placed his white-lipped mother's hand into Bryn's hand. "Take care of my mother."

Double damn it. "Sure." She looked at Lillith's terrified face. "It's okay. We're going somewhere safe."

"I can't lose this baby, too." Lillith's eyes were huge.

As if by some unspoken word, all the women gathered in the center of the room while the men stalked the perimeter.

"If you'd all follow me, we'll head into the storm shelter," her grandmother announced in an "Isn't this a lovely change of events" voice.

Bryn put her arm around Lillith's shoulders and guided her along behind her grandmother. She wanted to ask questions, like, is this a storm shelter or some kind of bunker they'd had built in case of attack? Asking that question might upset Lillith even more. What had Lillith meant when she said she couldn't lose this baby, too? Had she lost other babies? How far along was Lillith and how delicate was a dragon pregnancy? She knew humans had to be careful to avoid certain things during pregnancy, but she had no idea how their dragon counterparts worked.

She itched to join the men in the ballroom, to help plan a counterattack. Even if she didn't fight, she wanted to know what was going on. Damn Jaxon for putting her in this position.

Chapter Thirty-One

They walked down a hallway toward the library and then turned down a smaller hall, which led to a set of enclosed stairs.

"Be careful on the stairs," her grandmother called out. "They aren't very wide, and we don't want anyone to fall."

The steps ended in a well-lit room, or rather, many rooms which flowed into one another through giant archways. There were several sets of couches and chairs in various areas. Floor-to-ceiling bookshelves covered one wall, and a row of shelves contained toys for children of all ages. At the far end of the room, wait staff set trays of cocoa out on what looked like an enormous buffet table. Platters of cookies and bottled drinks were also set out along the buffet.

"Is this some sort of bunker?" she asked her grandmother.

"It's a shelter that can keep out weather or enemies, as the need arises." She cleared her throat and spoke in a loud voice. "Please help yourself to cocoa or snacks and make yourself comfortable. Children, help yourselves to the toys. We have our own fully stocked kitchen. If you'd like anything besides what is being served on the buffet, just ask.

"Bryn, come with me," her grandmother said in a normal tone of voice.

She followed, bringing Lillith with her. They stopped at a set of cream-colored couches. Once they were seated, her grandmother took Lillith's hand.

"This shelter has enough food and provisions to last six months. The walls are designed to be earthquake-proof so that even an Orange dragon can't blast through. You and your baby are safe."

Lillith blew out a shaking breath. "Thank you. I know it's ridiculous, but twice before this I lost—"

"No need to explain," her grandmother said. "I understand better than you know."

Her grandmother had lost a baby, too? *What the hell?*

"Can I get either of you anything?" Bryn asked.

"Why don't you bring us some cookies and cocoa," her grandmother said.

Bryn did as she was asked. After she approached the buffet, other women did the same. Had that been her grandmother's plan?

Back at the couches, Bryn kicked off her shoes, which made her grandmother's eyebrows shoot up.

"If it weren't for my current obligation, I'd be up there helping with the counterattack. Consider shoes off to be a small rebellion by comparison."

"Then it's good Jaxon asked you to take care of me," Lillith said. Her color seemed to be returning.

"If he hadn't, I would've dragged you down here kicking

and screaming," her grandmother said. "And I could do it."

"I have no doubt about that." Bryn laughed. "Now I know where my stubborn streak comes from."

The sound of women talking and eating drifted through the room. Bryn glared up at the ceiling. "We can't even hear what's going on, can we?"

"Sonic wave–proofing has the side effect of soundproofing. Which isn't bad."

Unless you wanted to know what was going on. Bryn tried to focus on what she could do, which was talk to Lillith and keep her calm.

"Have you picked out a theme for your nursery?" she asked.

"Theme?" her grandmother said. "What do you mean?"

Okay, so she'd never decorated a nursery herself, but she'd seen nurseries on television and seen the things for sale in the stores. "You know, some people decorate with ducks or Disney characters."

Lillith pressed her lips together like she was trying not to say something.

"Most of the nurseries I've seen are decorated either blue or pink," her grandmother said, "None of them had a theme."

"Jaxon's room had the cutest teddy bear theme," Lillith gushed. "Ferrin didn't think it was masculine enough but I loved it."

Bryn filed that information away for later. For right now, she'd keep Lillith talking to keep both their minds off the attack. "Have you picked out something for Asher yet?"

"I can't decide. There are so many cute things but I can't ask Ferrin, because he'll say none of them are masculine enough, and Jaxon practically runs from the room whenever I ask him to look at anything baby-related."

"I'd be happy to look at baby things with you. It sounds like fun."

"Really?" Lillith grinned like she'd just received the best Christmas present. "That would be wonderful. Maybe we could go shopping one day and have lunch."

"I'd like that." The funny thing was, she meant it. Lillith was fun to hang around with and she laughed at Ferrin's pretentiousness. How she lived with the man without killing him was a mystery.

Lillith leaned back on the couch and sighed. "Would it be all right if I closed my eyes for a bit?"

"Of course," her grandmother said. "There are bedrooms down the hall if you'd like to lie down."

"Thank you, but this will do just fine." Lillith kicked off her shoes and tucked her feet up underneath her.

"I'm going to make the rounds and check on all my guests. Bryn, why don't you stay here with Lillith so I know you won't wander off."

"Yes, ma'am. I can do that." Her grandmother floated from group to group, checking on the women and children scattered throughout the shelter. Through all of it, she remained calm and composed, projecting confidence like there wasn't a thing to worry about. How did she do that?

Lillith's breathing became regular. Now that she was asleep, could Bryn run upstairs to check on the situation? Not without her grandmother finding out and kicking her butt. So she stayed where she was, working her way through the plate of cookies.

Were Clint and Ivy having a fun Christmas Eve?

They lived next door to each other, so they were probably celebrating together. Valmont was probably knee-deep in homemade food. What else had he told her they did on Christmas Eve? Some kind of tournament. Ping-pong, that was it. His family had a ping-pong tournament. Which was kind of strange, but in a fun, wholesome family values kind of way.

What she wouldn't give to have Valmont here right now. Not that she couldn't stand on her own two feet, but having backup in the form of a handsome knight would be a bonus.

Boredom and a full stomach made her eyelids heavy. How long had they been down here? An hour? Women and children slept on the couches. Her grandmother sat across the room speaking with the ladies who'd shared their table during dinner. They looked to be the same age as her grandmother. Maybe they were her friends.

Falling asleep on the sidelines while Jaxon fought upstairs was not an option. Time for caffeine. Standing up, she made her way over to the buffet and asked for coffee. While she was there, she grabbed another plate of cookies.

Now what? Polite conversation with strangers would be awkward. She walked over to a bookshelf and spotted a sudoku book. Maybe that would keep her mind off how little control she had at the moment.

Five completed puzzles later, a phone rang. Everyone turned toward the sound. The phone, which Bryn had overlooked, hung on the wall by the entrance into the shelter. Keeping a sedate pace, Bryn's grandmother crossed to the phone and answered it as if it were any other phone call.

Bryn moved to the edge of her seat, clutching a throw

pillow while she watched her grandmother. The set of her jaw and her relaxed stance gave nothing away. After hanging up, she turned to face everyone.

"The attack is over. The Directorate has everything under control. Even though they feel it's safe to return to your homes, you are all invited to stay the night. We have more than enough bedrooms for everyone's comfort."

Women picked up their children and headed toward the steps. No one ran or panicked. They walked at a leisurely pace. All she wanted to do was race upstairs and demand answers. Was she the only female who'd wanted to fight? How was that possible? Ivy would've joined the battle if she were here. Was it a Clan thing or a class thing?

Who knew? Either way, it was damn irritating.

A hand touched her arm. "Don't march upstairs demanding answers," Lillith said. "Even though the men will appear calm and act as if they have everything under control, they'll still be on high alert. I'm sure your grandfather is ready to rip someone's head off over this incident. His Christmas Ball was disturbed by an act of war."

"Act of war?" Chill bumps broke out on Bryn's arms.

"What else would you call attacking the estate where every single Directorate member is known to be?"

She hadn't thought of it that way. "Will you stay the night?"

"Ferrin will make that decision, and I'll let him because it will give him the sense that he is in complete control of something. A Blue male with wounded pride is one of the most dangerous creatures on the planet. Remember that in your dealings with Jaxon."

"Are you afraid of your husband?" Uh-oh. Boredom must've turned off her filter.

Lillith stared off in thought. Which was scarier than an outright answer. "I never fear for my safety or Jaxon's. However, I do fear for the safety of others."

And suddenly Ferrin seemed scarier than he'd ever been. Great.

Bryn stood. "The crowd has cleared. We better go find Jaxon before he accuses me of losing you."

Chapter Thirty-Two

As they climbed the steps back up to the main area of the house, a cold feeling skittered down Bryn's spine. Was the house damaged, or the grounds ripped up like at school? Whoever was behind these attacks seemed to have dragons from every Clan. How was that possible? The first attack on campus came in the form of sonic waves, then they'd used wind, directing tornado-like gusts to attack the theater building. In Dragon's Bluff, the attack had come in the form of giant hail. Tonight had been the Black dragons' weapon, lightning. That only left the Reds' weapon, fire. Whenever the next attack came, would it come in the form of flames?

On the way back to the ballroom, everything appeared normal. Had they panicked over nothing? The smell of burned wires drifted through the air. Lillith's grip on her arm prevented Bryn from running ahead.

Inside the ballroom, Bryn found the source of the smell. Christmas trees lay on their sides, with their branches burned and broken. Ice, or maybe glass, glittered on the ballroom floor. Most of the floor-to-ceiling cathedral windows were missing their panes or were left with jagged remnants of glass.

Had the attack been centered on the ballroom? If it had, that meant the attackers knew when and where everyone would be at a certain time. Men stood in groups with their heads together, talking heatedly. Blood spotted their dress shirts, and in a few places it puddled on the floor.

She approached a man she didn't know who was seated on the floor, clutching his arm against his body. Blood soaked through his shirtsleeve.

"If you're hurt, I can help you. I've had some training as a medic."

Indecision showed in his eyes.

"Jaxon Westgate trusted me to heal his classmates." Maybe that would sway him.

He pulled the sleeve of his shirt up, revealing a jagged tear, like a talon had ripped through his skin. Bryn sat on the floor next to him and focused her life force, visualizing it as a small sun glowing in her chest. Then she directed the flow of Quintessence through her right arm and out of her fingertips. Tracing her fingers back and forth over the torn skin, she visualized the raw edges pulling together, the muscles knitting themselves back together.

Concentrating on healing the young man, she didn't pay attention to anything else. When the cut was healed, she smiled up at him.

"Thank you." His words were sincere.

She nodded and pushed to her feet. That's when she noticed everyone staring at her. And she did mean everyone, even her grandparents. Nothing like a captive audience.

"Does anyone else need help? I can't heal broken bones yet, but I'm good with flesh wounds."

You could have heard a leaf hit the grass.

"Over here." A woman pointed to her son.

"I'm fine, Mother," the young man protested.

"You're not. I won't have you bleeding all the way home." She pointed to her son's face. Blood soaked through a handkerchief he held to his forehead. "If you would be so kind as to take care of him."

"Humor your mother," Bryn said. "And remove the handkerchief so I can see what I'm dealing with."

Resigned, the boy did as he was told. Healing him was easy.

"Thank you." The woman held out her hand. "I'm Mrs. Everson. Do have your grandmother call me for lunch one day. My treat."

"Thank you."

Someone tapped Bryn on the shoulder. Another woman asked Bryn to heal her husband. She made her way around the ballroom healing half a dozen males who had refused to ask for help, but accepted it when their wives or mothers insisted. All the women extended offers of lunch or tea.

When there was no one left to heal, Bryn located her grandmother, who was saying good-bye to guests. One look at Bryn and her eyes went wide. "Please tell me that's not your blood."

Bryn glanced down at the crimson spattering her emerald gown. "It's not mine. Sorry I ruined the dress, but I did receive several invitations for lunch and tea."

"Then it was a fair trade. Now, help me say good-bye to everyone."

Bryn did as her grandmother asked. The funny thing was, now more people looked her in the eye when they spoke to her.

Where was her grandfather? He was probably off doing Directorate business while her grandmother covered PR. An hour later, the last guest was shown out the door. Feet aching, all Bryn wanted to do was collapse in bed. "Any chance we can find out what happened tonight?"

"Your grandfather will tell us what happened when he is ready. It would be best if we went to bed."

She was halfway back to her room when someone called her name. "Bryn."

Crap. She recognized that voice. What did her grandfather want? She turned with a polite expression on her face that became harder to maintain as her grandfather stalked toward her.

When he was within arm's reach, he placed his hand on her shoulder. "What you did tonight…healing Clan members… it's not something a Blue would do."

Uh-oh.

"You are not the granddaughter I dreamed of having, but tonight you proved you're worthy of our Clan, and I am proud of you."

Warmth filled Bryn's chest. "Thank you."

• • •

The next morning, Bryn rolled over and stared at the clock. It was 8:00 a.m. on Christmas morning. And for the first time ever, it meant nothing to her.

She curled up in a ball and hugged her pillow, remembering Christmas mornings past: waking as early as possible, running into the living room to see what Santa had left for her. When she was older and her belief in Santa had faded, Christmas morning meant ripping open presents and eating pancakes dyed red and green like Christmas ornaments. Then they'd watched Christmas movies or played in the snow.

Tears soaked her pillow and a pounding started at the base of her skull. She sighed. This was getting her nowhere. Time to shower, dress, and find out what the hell had happened last night. Where would her grandmother be this morning? Should she call the operator and ask? Hopefully, Rindy the all-knowing phone fairy had Christmas morning off. Not wanting to find out for sure, Bryn headed to the dining room. There would be food there, if nothing else.

Her grandmother sat sipping coffee and reading a gardening magazine. "Good morning, Bryn. I wondered if I should send someone to wake you, but decided after last night, you could use all the sleep you could manage."

"Thanks. This is the latest I've slept since I came to school, thanks to that stupid alarm in my dorm room."

"I never cared for those alarms myself." Her grandmother pointed to the sideboard, which held covered dishes. "Abigail left food warming for you. Or we could order something fresh if you like."

Bryn poured herself a cup of coffee and went to investigate her options. Time to play what's-under-the-covered-dish. Under the first lid, Christmas cookies. No need to go any further.

She'd worked her way through four chocolate chip cookies before asking the question burning in her brain. "Any news about last night?"

Her grandmother set the gardening magazine down. "We know that someone attacked our estate to make a statement, to try to show that we weren't in control. We mobilized and launched a counterattack. Minor injuries were sustained on our side. Your grandfather believes the other side suffered several casualties."

Was that a good thing? "Do they know who the other side is?" Since these attacks had started, the identity of the rebels had remained a mystery.

"There are indications Black and Orange dragons were among those fighting against us last night."

"I understand thinking it was Black dragons due to the lightning, but why Orange?"

"Because of the wings they found."

And the chocolate chip cookies were about to come back up. "Wings? They found severed wings?"

Her grandmother nodded. "Orange and Black wings, and various other body parts. Disturbing, isn't it?"

That was an understatement. "What happens now?"

"If my instincts are correct, the Directorate will declare the attack on our home an act of war."

"You are correct, Marie." Her grandfather strode into the room, poured himself a cup of coffee, and sat at the head of the table.

That didn't sound good. "What does that mean, an act of war?"

"It means," her grandfather said, "that the Directorate will declare martial law to keep the population safe until we can neutralize this threat. An eight p.m. curfew will be put into effect. Everyone will be advised to travel in pairs or groups rather than alone."

She remembered her conversation with Onyx. "Someone once told me the attacks would continue until the Directorate limited everyone's freedom to a point where they would fight back, creating a civil war."

Smack. Her grandfather's coffee cup hit the table. "Who told you that?"

Uh-oh. "I think he was just theorizing the reasons behind the attacks, not saying it was a good idea."

"His name. Now," her grandfather roared.

"Onyx." While she didn't trust the guy, she didn't think he was behind this.

"That man has been a thorn in the Directorate's side for years, but I don't believe he'd attack in the open this way. He prefers to chip away at the foundation to try to undermine us from within."

Wait a minute. "Is Onyx a member of the Directorate?"

"Unfortunately, yes. A few decades ago we decided to expand the Directorate beyond our own Clan."

"But you don't invite them to your Christmas party?" Bryn asked.

"No. The party is a celebration within our Clan, not a Directorate gathering."

"Does that mean the attack was aimed at the Blue Clan rather than the Directorate?" Bryn retrieved the plate of cookies she had pushed away moments before.

"That is an interesting question," her grandmother said.

"It makes no difference who the attack was aimed at." Her grandfather pounded his fist on the table. "It was aimed at my home, where ninety percent of the Directorate members were known to be."

That brought up another question. "Did they specifically attack the ballroom because they knew we'd all be there at that time?"

"I believe that was their intention. The rest of the estate suffered only minor damage."

Chapter Thirty-Three

Abigail entered the dining room and stood a few feet inside the doorway. Bryn's grandmother acknowledged her with a questioning look.

"There's a call for Bryn from Valmont Fonzoli."

"Really?" That was the best news she'd had in a while. A quick check of the dining room didn't produce a phone. "Where should I take the call?"

"There's a phone in the sitting room down the hall," her grandmother said. "Abigail will show you."

Hopping out of her chair, Bryn followed Abigail to a room on the right. At this point, she was as happy to escape the dining room as she was to speak with Valmont. Sitting on a wingback chair, she grabbed the phone. "Hello, Valmont?"

"Merry Christmas, Bryn." Warmth came through his words.

"Merry Christmas to you, too. What's up?"

"If you aren't busy with your grandparents today, can

you come over for lunch?"

Muscles she didn't realize were tense, relaxed. "That sounds fantastic. Hold on while I ask my grandmother."

Laying the phone on its side, she dashed back to the dining room. They had to say yes. She needed to be out of this house for a while, someplace where she could relax.

She skidded through the doorway and met her grandparents' speculative gazes. "Valmont's family invited me for lunch. Is that okay?"

"Yes," her grandmother said at the same time her grandfather said, "No."

"We were attacked yesterday," her grandfather said.

"Yes. We were," her grandmother said. "And now it's our job to make it seem as though we are unaffected. You will declare your act of war, but we should continue on with our everyday lives. Don't you agree?"

Her grandfather stared up at the ceiling like he was mulling over her grandmother's logic. "It's an interesting tactic."

"And we don't have anything planned until six." Her grandmother turned to Bryn. "You may go, just be back in time for Christmas dinner."

"Thank you." Wow. She'd never seen her grandmother argue with her grandfather before—and win. Interesting development. She ran back to the phone and told Valmont the good news.

"I'll be there to pick you up in ten minutes," Valmont said.

"I thought it took thirty minutes for you to get here."

"I figured you'd say yes, so I left the house about twenty minutes ago."

She laughed. "Be nice to the guards when you check in.

There was some trouble here last night and they'll all be on high alert."

"What trouble?"

Was she allowed to say anything? Who knew? "I'll explain when you get here."

She said her good-byes and ran up to her room to freshen up and change into jeans, a sweater, and tennis shoes. Valmont wouldn't care what she wore, so she could be herself, which was nice.

Should she change her hair back? Her current look seemed to make her grandmother happy, so she'd leave it for now. Maybe she'd ask Valmont's opinion.

By the time she made it to the foyer, Valmont was waiting by the door next to one of the guards. She was relieved to see that the guard didn't look annoyed.

Valmont's ice-blue eyes were full of mischief. He smiled, which made his single dimple show. In an evergreen-colored button-down shirt and jeans, he looked awesome. Her heartbeat sped up as she grinned back at him.

"I like the new hair." He wiggled his eyebrows.

"Thank you."

Once they were out the door and in his car, the world seemed like a brighter place. Being around Valmont made her feel almost normal again. Driving along the forested road with the top down on his cherry-red convertible and the heat blasting to keep them warm, she listened to the sound of the winter wind rustling in the leaves.

"How are things going with your grandparents?" he asked.

She didn't want to talk about the bad part of last night. Better to go with something more general. "I feel like I've been playing dress-up. I keep waiting for someone to come up, point at me, and scream 'imposter.'"

"You are the Sinclairs' granddaughter. You're not an imposter."

"Literally, that's true. But I'm not the granddaughter everyone else expects me to be. I'm not Blue through and through."

"So you're not true blue?" He laughed.

She shook her head. "That was bad. But yes, I'm not a true Blue. At the Christmas Eve ball, I kept sneaking off to the bathroom so I didn't have to sit at the table by myself while everyone else socialized with people they've known all their lives. It sucked."

"What sucks is that your grandparents didn't see that coming and arrange for someone to keep you company." He reached over and grabbed her hand. "I would've volunteered."

That meant a lot. "Thank you. If it wasn't Christmas Eve, I would've called and asked you to come save me."

"You can call me at any time, Christmas Eve or not. I'll always be there for you."

He spoke so passionately, she believed him. Would her grandparents let her bring Valmont as her date somewhere? If she asked they'd probably claim it wasn't appropriate, which meant next time she wouldn't ask. She'd just show up with him and hope her grandparents played nice.

"How was your Christmas Eve?" She didn't want today to be all about her. The world didn't revolve around her. It would be nice to get lost in someone else's life for a while.

"My grandmother is still the reigning champion of ping-pong. I swear the woman puts drugs in the lasagna to slow the rest of us down. Either that or she takes something to speed herself up." He grinned. "She might give you a hard time."

"What? Why?"

"She wanted you to stop by on Christmas Eve. I told her you weren't available, but she doesn't like taking no for an answer."

Light filtered through the trees as they came to a less dense area of the forest. The scent of evergreens filled the air. She took a deep breath. "It smells like Christmas."

They chatted easily on the rest of the drive to Dragon's Bluff. Feeling comfortable around Valmont, after feeling so out of place for days, was a relief.

When they pulled onto the main road, Bryn admired all the Christmas decorations, until she realized each store had the same wreath in the exact same place. "What's with the Stepford decorations?"

"What do you mean?"

"Every store already has the same-colored awning and the same style of lettering, and now they have the same wreath in the exact spots on each door."

"The official line is that uniformity creates harmony. The truth is your Directorate is anal about everything being perfect and exactly the way it has been for the last one hundred and fifty years." He pulled into the lot behind Fonzoli's. The scent of garlic and Italian herbs mingled with the sweet scent of vanilla.

"Is your grandmother baking cookies?"

Valmont opened his door and then came around to open hers. "My grandmother is baking every cookie known to man. When I left she was working on Italian wedding cake cookies."

"Are those the little round balls covered in powdered sugar?"

"Yes. She rolls some of them in cocoa just to add variety."

Yum. "I think your grandmother and I will get along just fine."

"She'll love you, because unlike some of the other females who come for Christmas, you have a healthy appetite."

Right on cue, her stomach growled. "Take me to the food. I'm ready to bond with your grandmother."

Valmont kept his arm around her shoulders as they bypassed the back entrance to the kitchen to a part of the building she'd never visited. There was a covered front porch sporting a Christmas tree with twinkling lights.

"Is this your grandparents' house?"

He nodded. "Members of the Fonzoli family have lived here for generations." They went up the front steps and he held the door open for her. She entered into a living room where no one paid the slightest attention to her. Two younger boys played a video game on the TV. A girl sat on the navy-blue couch with a cat on her lap as she read a book.

They continued into the house. Halfway down the hall, a man who looked like an older version of Valmont greeted her with a grin. "You must be Bryn."

"I am."

"Bryn, this is my dad."

"Nice to meet you." Bryn took the hand he offered and shook it.

"Nice to meet you, too." He leaned toward Valmont. "I need to go pick up your mom's gift. If she asks where I am, tell her I went to bring in some firewood."

"Okay." Valmont shook his head as his dad walked away.

"Before I left to come pick you up, my mom sneaked out to grab my father's gift."

"That's cute." Seeing married people who actually liked each other was a rarity.

Valmont placed his hand on her lower back and propelled her forward through another door into the dining room. A large oak plank table with every type of chair pulled up to it practically groaned with food. Lasagna, garlic bread, turkey, sweet potatoes, green beans, and a half dozen other dishes sat in the middle of the table. It looked so homey, just the type of atmosphere she longed for but no longer had.

A woman with salt-and-pepper curls wearing an apron covered in flour came into the dining room. She spotted Valmont and hustled toward them.

Bryn found herself enveloped in a pastry-scented hug. "I'm so glad you could come. Valmont speaks well of you. It's time we met."

"I'm glad to meet you, too. Whatever you're baking smells fabulous. Valmont swore you wouldn't think badly of me if I ate too much."

"Finally." His grandmother pulled her into another hug. "A girl who eats."

Why couldn't her grandmother be more like this? Guilt followed that thought like a smack to the head. Her grandmother was trying. She was just a different species. Literally.

"Come into the kitchen. Keep me company while I finish up." She couldn't have refused if she wanted to, with the way Valmont's grandmother had latched onto her elbow.

"Sure." She moved forward, and it took her a moment to realize Valmont wasn't moving along with her.

"Valmont?" What the heck was he doing?

"I promised my grandpa I'd go grab a few bottles of wine from the restaurant. I'll be back in one minute."

The kitchen looked like it had been through a war and lost. Flour was sprinkled on the soapstone countertops and in some places on the hardwood floor. Canisters were open, with their lids nowhere to be seen. Dirty mixing bowls were piled three deep in the sink. Spice bottles sat with the lids flipped up, like they were waiting to be used.

Bryn's grandmother would have been appalled, but it felt nice, cozy, lived in.

"Have a seat and help yourself to a cookie."

She sat while his grandmother watched. This was starting to feel weird, like a job interview. Valmont needed to get back here soon. She picked a star-shaped cookie and took a bite. Bitter licorice flavor filled her mouth. Ugh. It was all she could do not to spit it out. Who put licorice in cookies?

Valmont's grandmother turned and reached into a cabinet with her back toward Bryn. If there had been a napkin on the table she'd have spit the nasty concoction out. No drink. No napkin. She swallowed, trying not to grimace.

Valmont's grandmother joined her at the table, giving her a mug of something steaming hot. "Have some tea, dear."

"Thank you." Bryn put the cup to her mouth, concentrated on cold, and exhaled frost into the mug.

"That's a handy trick."

Bryn sipped and smiled. Once the god-awful licorice taste was gone, she lowered the mug to the table. "My grandmother wouldn't approve, but it's handy to produce your own ice sometimes."

"That's what I need to speak with you about."

"My grandmother?"

"No." She gave a tight smile. "The fact that you're different."

Where was this going? "You mean that I'm a hybrid dragon or that I'm a dragon at all?"

"You being a dragon. It concerns me. When it comes to Valmont." The sweet maternal tone was gone. She pointed at Bryn, like she'd caught her doing something wrong. "What's going on between you two, I don't approve."

Chapter Thirty-Four

And the gloves were off. Bryn leaned back in her seat. "What do you think is going on between us?"

"I may be old, but I'm not blind. The boy cares for you in a way you'll never be able to care for him. I want you to release him from his bond and go back to your own kind."

"Wow. You're more like my grandmother than I thought." Bryn smacked her mug down on the table. "For your information, I do care about Valmont. Is the situation complicated? Yes. Do I have any idea what the hell I'm doing? No. All I know is that in the last month I lost someone I thought would always be there for me, and then I lost my parents. I'm living with people who I'm bound to disappoint because I'll never be the person they want me to be." Fire banked in her gut. She focused on cold to change the flames to ice. Frost shot from her nose as she exhaled. "Valmont is one of the only good things left in my life, so until he tells me he doesn't want me around, I'm not going anywhere." She pushed her chair farther from the table and stood. "And for the record, your cookies suck."

The kitchen, which had seemed warm and cozy, now seemed stifling. She needed to escape, to run outside and leave this disaster behind. She turned to the door. Valmont stood there gripping the doorframe like he wanted to tear the house down board by board.

"Time for me to leave." She brushed past him and ran out the front door. Now what? Did she head to his car presuming he'd give her a ride home? She couldn't just sit in his car and wait. What if he wasn't coming? What his grandmother said wasn't untrue. Was she being selfish by holding on to Valmont?

With no other idea of what to do, she stalked down Main Street. If he didn't come after her, she'd fly home. *Damn it, why isn't he coming after me?*

And just like that, all the fight drained out of her. She sat down on the curb of the sidewalk and doubled over with her head on her knees. If he didn't come after her…she couldn't take one more loss. Not one more.

The sound of footsteps approaching made her raise her head. Eyebrows slammed together, lips set in a grim line, Valmont looked mad. Was he angry at her?

"Come with me." His tone wasn't exactly friendly, though he wasn't telling her to go away. She stood and followed him back to his car, where he opened the door for her. *That was a good sign, right?*

They drove in silence. Every second without any words from him had her digging her nails deeper into her palms. She didn't bother to ask where they were going. He was taking her home or up to his cabin. When he turned into the woods down the way they'd taken when she'd visited his cabin before, her body sagged with relief.

"Thank you."

"For what?" he asked.

"For not sending me straight back to my grandparents' house."

"What my grandmother said…" He huffed out a breath. "She had no right. I had no idea you were walking into an ambush. I'm just so—" He smacked the steering wheel.

When they arrived at his cabin, it was exactly like she remembered. Anyone who didn't know where they were going could drive right by it. The vegetation had been allowed to grow over the structure until it was camouflaged. It wasn't until he drove past the sensor in the driveway and warm yellow light shone through the living room windows that you were even sure the cabin was there.

Valmont came around and opened her door. He held her hand on the walk up to the front door. Once they were inside, he pointed at the rug in front of the couch. "I forgot to thank you for the Christmas present."

"I'm glad you like it."

"I'm sorry, but your present is at my grandparents' house."

"That's okay." She was disappointed, but there wasn't a chance in hell she'd step foot in his grandmother's house again.

He led her to the couch. Seated so that their thighs brushed against each other, Valmont put his arm around Bryn's shoulders. She leaned into his solid warmth. What did she want? She wanted Valmont as a friend and maybe more than that. Before, he'd said he'd be there for her in whatever way she needed. Was it unfair to encourage his affections? It's not like she was toying with him. She liked him, needed him in her life. Her grandparents would try their hardest to set her up with the standard arranged marriage. And her grandmother and Lillith would try to arrange something between her and Jaxon. While she might not hate Jaxon anymore, she knew he'd never see her as datable, and as handsome as he was, she wanted to hit him over the head with a bat most of the time.

Closing her eyes, she asked the question she wasn't sure she wanted an answer to. "What are we doing?"

"I don't know." He chuckled. "Being the only knight called to duty in generations doesn't leave me with a mentor to talk to. The statue up on the hill isn't much help."

"Do you think the legend is true?" Bryn asked.

"Yes." There wasn't a bit of doubt in his voice. "Open your eyes." She did as he asked. His gaze was like an ice-blue tractor beam pulling her in. "I don't want to lose you, but I don't want to do anything to push you away. Tell me what you're thinking."

"I can't lose you. What I said to your grandmother was true. Right now, you're my rock. You're the one person I can count on."

He dropped his gaze and spoke in a soft voice. "Your grandparents, they're trying to set up an arranged marriage for you. Do you want that?"

"No." She didn't even have to think about it. "I want to be with someone I love, not someone the Directorate deems as my compatible mate."

"Good." He looked up. "Then there's only one suitable answer."

"What?"

"This." He leaned in, giving her time to back out if she wasn't interested. Did she want him to kiss her? Hell, yes.

Was it wrong? Right now it didn't feel wrong. Letting her eyes flutter shut, she moved toward him; his warm breath feathered across her lips and—

Knock knock knock.

Startled, Bryn jerked backward.

"Of all the lousy timing." Valmont shot to his feet, stalked across the room, and yanked the door open. From her vantage point on the couch, Bryn saw the last person she expected to show up at Valmont's cabin. "Jaxon? What are you doing here?"

"My mother had a craving for cannoli. She asked me to pick some up from Fonzoli's. The old woman who answered the door refused to give it to me unless I flew up here to speak with Bryn." Jaxon shot her an evil glare. "She said, if you both don't come back for Christmas lunch she will call Bryn's grandmother. I don't know what is going on between you two, and I don't care." He tossed a cell phone to Valmont. "Call the old lady. Tell her I delivered the message and I'll be there in five minutes to pick up my order."

Valmont stared at Jaxon like he was insane.

"My mother is pregnant, irrational, and more than likely crying. Make the call."

Valmont dialed.

"Why isn't your father picking up the cannoli for your mother?" Bryn asked.

"She asked him, and he volunteered me for the job," Jaxon bit out.

She wanted to ask if he now agreed that his father was a jerk, but thought that might end in bloodshed.

Valmont hung up and tossed the phone back to Jaxon. "She doubled your order, no charge."

"How kind of her." Jaxon stepped outside the cabin, shifted, and took flight.

Valmont slammed the door and then turned to lean his back against it.

"Do we have to go back?" Seeing his grandmother again, who had looked all warm and loving on the outside, but was mean and conniving on the inside, was just too much. She'd had such hopes for a warm family dinner, something to replace a bit of what she'd lost. While her own grandparents meant well, most of the time, they didn't do warm and loving. Maybe warm and loving wasn't part of dragon culture. It certainly didn't seem to be part of her life.

"We don't have to go back, unless you find the idea of your grandmother teaming up with mine as terrifying as I do."

"That *is* one scary thought."

"Then we have to go back."

Once they were parked back at Fonzoli's, Bryn balked. "I can't go back in there with you."

"Why not?"

She grabbed his hand and squeezed. "It's stupid, but I can't take any more rejection. When I came here today, I thought I'd find a place where I was welcomed, where I could belong." Bitter laughter poured from her throat.

He slid over and put his arm around her shoulders. "You're welcome here. My grandmother's overprotective of me. I don't like what she did, but it's over. Can't we go inside, ignore everyone, and have a nice meal?"

Every instinct told her no. Should she do it for him? He would do anything for her. She knew that. What did it say about her that she wouldn't do the same? Did it mean his grandmother was right? That settled it. She'd go inside and pretend to have a nice time if for no other reason than to show his grandmother she was wrong. Because she needed his grandmother to be wrong.

"Am I allowed to shoot fireballs at anyone who is mean to me?"

He tapped his chin like he was thinking about it. "That might set the house on fire, and that would put a damper on Christmas. You could accidentally cough up a snowball if you want."

"I guess that will have to do."

His grandmother watched them walk up to the doorway, but stood blocking the entrance with her arms crossed over her chest. "You are a rude, headstrong girl."

What the hell? Could she insult his grandmother back? Was that allowed?

"You're being rude to my guest," Valmont said in a quiet voice. "Are we invited in for lunch or not?"

His grandmother narrowed her eyes, but stepped aside, muttering something in Italian. Valmont stiffened.

"What did she say?" Bryn asked.

"It's not worth repeating." Valmont put his arm around her shoulders and pulled her into a hug, kissing the top of her head.

She leaned into his warmth, knowing what she needed to do and not wanting to do it. She lifted her face to meet his gaze. "There isn't a single way I can imagine this lunch ending well. I should go."

Maybe he'd disagree with her. A spark of hope flared in her gut, or maybe that was just residual anger.

"Unfortunately, I think you're right. I'll drive you back."

"No. Stay and have a nice lunch with the members of your family that don't hate me." She shot his grandmother a look. "I'll fly back. I need the exercise to burn off some of this anger."

"Are you sure you know how to get back to your grandparents' estate?"

She laughed and pointed to the east. "Fly that way until I see the obscenely large house that reeks of money and tradition?"

"That sounds about right." His single dimple appeared. As long as he still cared about her, things seemed okay.

She stepped outside, gave a small wave, and then shifted. It might have been immature, but she took a moment to glare at his grandmother and growl. Then she pushed off the ground and took flight. Straight up into the air, she pumped her wings and reveled in the sensation of freedom that flying always brought. In dragon form, she could fly anywhere, do anything. If only there was a place she wanted to go. Maybe someday she and Valmont would take a trip together.

From the cloudy sky, she studied the layout of Dragon's Bluff, and the winding road leading out of town to Valmont's cabin. Farther off into the forest toward the east lay her grandparents' estate. It wasn't visible, but she knew it was there.

Allowing the wind to carry away her anger, she flew toward her destination. Was anyone else out enjoying the cool December weather, or were they all inside spending Christmas with their families? Best not to go down that path. Thinking about her parents, about what she'd never have again if Valmont's grandmother was any indication, would lead to tears. If she cried, it would be behind closed doors where no one could interpret her feelings as weakness.

Wait. Where had that thought come from? If she wanted to cry, she'd cry wherever she wanted to. Who cared what other dragons thought? Her grandparents would care. Jaxon would care. Damn it all if her Blue genes weren't starting to make her care, too. Must be some type of inbred instinct. Her friends had told her that Blues were notoriously proud, but loyal to a fault, which meant revenge was the first option for some of them.

So what if everyone else had a cozy family to spend time with. She'd do just fine with her grandparents, Valmont, and her friends. What other choice did she have?

Something registered in her peripheral vision. Blinking, she turned and checked for company. It must have been a bird. Being cautious, she circled, like she was enjoying her flight, without a concern in the world.

Blip. There it was again. Someone was watching her, she was sure of it. Maybe flying by herself when there were people attacking Directorate members families wasn't the best idea, but Jaxon had been out by himself, so it must be okay. Right?

Hoping to keep the element of surprise, she drove up into the air and rolled like she was playing around. From this higher vantage point, she saw nothing.

Was she paranoid?

Blip. Damn it. Someone was playing games with her or stalking her. Either way, she didn't plan to stick around and find out. Tucking her wings to her body, she dove down, building up speed before she curved back up again. Flying the way a dolphin would swim. Pretending to play while she flew as fast as she could.

She banked the flames in her gut, in case she needed to shoot a fireball at someone's head. As bad as her afternoon had gone, she'd shoot a fireball at any dragon who approached and apologize later, if need be.

Pumping her wings, she drove up and dove down. Her breath came faster as she repeated this maneuver again and again. Was she being too predictable? She performed a diving roll on the next downward dive. There in the distance, she could see the lights glowing from her grandparents' estate. In five minutes she'd be inside, drinking hot cocoa, eating cookies that didn't suck, and laughing about all of this.

Blip. Blip. Two Black dragons appeared out of nowhere, a hundred yards out, flanking her on either side. This time, they didn't disappear; they kept pace with her. Keeping their distance, but making sure they were seen. What did that mean?

She didn't recognize the human features that flashed across their faces. Both were male. That was all she knew for sure. Giving up on pretending they weren't creeping her out, she focused all her attention on outflying them. She was the fastest flyer on campus. Time to give up pretenses and outrun the creepy bastards.

Push. Push. Push. Her wing muscles ached with exertion. The tendons burned. Just a few more minutes; she could do this. She had to do this. Her life might depend on it. The Black dragons couldn't keep up. The one on the left dropped out of sight, and then the one on the right.

The forest below her thinned out. Thank God, she was at the edge of her grandparents' estate. Almost home. Wait. Had she just thought of this place as home?

Bam. Her wings. She couldn't move her wings. Lashing

out with teeth and claws, she tore at whatever ensnared her. Fire crawled up her throat; she inhaled and spouted flames all around her, roaring in frustration as she plummeted to the ground.

What was binding her? A spell? A net? Her wings bent at an unnatural angle. Pain, so much pain, she couldn't breathe. Shift. Maybe she could escape in human form. Get out of whatever held her and then shift back and fly away. She shifted to human form. The net, she could see it now. With holes large enough to crawl through. Struggling, she wiggled through an opening.

Shouts came from all around her. The ground came up fast. The net still held her calves. No more time. She shifted back, praying the net would break from the strain. Pain, burning searing pain as the net sliced into her flank like a razor. With the last of her energy, she shifted back to human form, slammed into the ground, and the world went black.

. . .

Noise filtered through the fuzziness of her head. Was someone talking? Saying her name? Had she been captured? Doing her best to lie still, she played dead and listened.

Wait a minute, shouldn't she be in pain? All she felt was numb. Warmth surrounded her, but she felt nothing. Opening her eyes to slits, she tried to focus. Green. Green filled her vision.

"I think she's coming to," a voice said.

"Bryn?" She felt pressure on her hand. Someone was holding it. "Bryn? What in the hell were you thinking?"

Wait. That voice she recognized. She opened her eyes.

More green, and then the green was gone. In its place a watercolor version of her grandmother. "You're blurry."

"You've had a head injury. Your vision will improve," a different voice said.

There was the green again. It was scrubs. Medics wore green scrubs. A Green dragon was wearing green scrubs. Laughter bubbled from her throat.

"This isn't funny." Her grandmother again. And she sounded furious. "Do you have any idea…? You could have died."

Warmth flowed into Bryn's veins; she recognized the Quintessence at work. The fog in her brain cleared a bit.

"That's better." She focused on her grandmother. "Who attacked me?"

"No one attacked you, you fool. You flew onto the estate, unannounced, and set off the new security system," a male voice said.

Oh, hell. She recognized that voice. "Screw you, Ferrin." Seemed like the least offensive answer she could come up with.

"Leave this room," her grandmother said.

"What? I don't think I can walk."

"Not you, Bryn. You won't be going anywhere for a long time. You're grounded. Ferrin Westgate, leave this room before I have you escorted out."

Bryn giggled. "My grandmother is a badass."

Several people laughed. Bryn didn't know if her grandmother was one of them. Warmth flowed through her body again, and she drifted off to sleep.

Sometime later, Bryn felt something wet on her forehead. Blinking, she opened her eyes. "What's going on?"

"I'm trying to make you presentable," her grandmother said. "You're a mess."

"I feel better." And she did. Her vision had cleared, and the numbness from before had transformed into a mild headache.

"Do you feel good enough to answer some questions?"

"Sure."

"Why were you flying hell-bent onto the estate like someone was chasing you?"

She told her grandmother about the two Black dragons she'd seen.

"Why did you take a chance flying alone at all? Why didn't your knight escort you home?"

"Because his grandmother is an evil woman who makes disgusting cookies." She relayed the events of the day, leaving out the part about the almost-kiss with Valmont.

"Not the day you'd hoped for, was it?" her grandmother said.

"No." And then she remembered what day it was. "Sorry about ruining Christmas dinner."

"We can have Christmas dinner tomorrow night."

Bryn's stomach growled as if to protest that statement.

Her grandmother laughed. "Or we could have dinner now, if you like."

Food sounded good, but showering and dressing in real clothes did not. "Can we have Abigail bring food here? I don't know if I'm up for the hike to the dining room."

"Of course." Her grandmother reached for the phone on Bryn's nightstand and called someone in the kitchen. Once that was taken care of, she eyed Bryn and shook her head. "If you ever go out flying alone again, I will wring your neck. Do you understand?"

"Yes." Her face heated. "I wasn't thinking clearly. I just wanted to come home."

Her grandmother's expression softened. "You don't know how much it means to me to hear you call this your home."

"Thanks, for everything." Bryn didn't know what else to say.

"We're family. Remember, family always comes first." She gave an evil grin. "If you want, I could have a health inspector shut Fonzoli's down for a week or two."

That was a terrible idea, but Bryn played along. "Tempting, but it would stress Valmont out as much as his grandmother, so we better not."

Ten minutes later, Abigail showed up with a cart bearing turkey, ham, hot rolls, and all the food Bryn associated with Christmas. Half an hour later, she'd stuffed herself full and could barely keep her eyes open.

"Go to sleep." Her grandmother leaned down and kissed her forehead.

Bryn drifted off with the sound of plates and cutlery being loaded onto the cart. That must be Abigail packing up the food. Her grandmother left the room. It occurred to her that the warm family she'd been searching for, the day she'd hoped for, had sort of come true right here.

• • •

Bryn opened her eyes and felt like she was swimming through fog. Why did she feel like hell? What day was it? She wasn't sure. All she knew was that she felt gritty and her teeth felt furry and she wanted a shower right now.

Off with the covers, and holy crap. Bright pink lines ran up and down both her legs. Bright pink lines meant recently healed wounds. Her brain sputtered and choked and then it hit her. The new security system. The net. She traced her pointer finger down the line that cut across her thigh and then down another one that ran the length of her calf. They would fade, with time. If she focused her Quintessence she could probably make them disappear, or at least make them a lighter color. Maybe later. She pushed to the side of the bed and sat up. Bracing herself, she rose to her feet and tested her legs. They held her weight. She was stiff, but that was about it. Thank God for medics, or she probably wouldn't be here.

She padded barefoot across the warm wooden floor to the bathroom, where she stripped off her clothes and tossed them in the trash. Avoiding catching sight of herself in the full-length mirror on the back of the bathroom door, she climbed in the shower and blissed out under the hot water. When her fingers were pruney, she exited the shower and dried off with a thick fluffy white towel, the kind she imagined they had at luxury hotels. Not that she'd ever been to a luxury hotel, but she'd seen hotel bathrooms in movies.

Dressed in her blue bra and underwear decorated with goldfish, she checked herself out in the mirror. Her animal-themed underwear normally made her smile, but the bright pink lines wrapping all the way around her body drained any humor from her brain. Water flooded her mouth and prickly heat broke out on her skin. She leaned against the cool marble of the sink and took a few slow breaths. She'd almost died. And she had no one to blame but herself. The nets. The feeling of terror…the panic she felt when the nets tightened…no one deserved that.

She splashed her face with cold water. Best not to think about that right now. Time to dress and head down to breakfast.

Her closet held a surprise. Next to the standard skirts and blouses she had to wear to school and the jeans and T-shirts she wore in her room and on the weekends, new clothes hung. To say the new clothes made her old clothes look like dirt was an understatement.

She pulled a black turtleneck dress made of the softest material she'd ever felt off the hanger and over her head. It settled against her skin like a cloud, making her smile. It felt like she was wearing a hug. Underneath where the dress had hung was a large shoebox. Inside, she found black leather boots that came up to the hem of the dress. She checked the mirror. For someone who'd almost been sliced and diced less than twenty-four hours ago, she looked awesome. Who knew clothes could make you feel this good?

She focused on her life force, directing a small amount of quintessence to darken her lips a shade and add some color to her cheeks. The black dress just begged for a black stripe in her hair. She missed her tricolored locks. The dark golden blond her grandmother had suggested with the single inch-thick red stripe was pretty. She focused on a quarter-inch-wide section next to the red stripe and changed it to black. There. That looked good, and it wasn't too obnoxious. Hopefully her grandmother would approve.

Where would her grandmother be? Rather than hunting through the house, she picked up the phone and asked Rindy. Armed with the information on her grandmother's whereabouts, she headed for the atrium on the second floor.

Her grandparents sat on opposite sides of one of the square white wrought iron tables in center of the atrium, which was decorated with so many of her grandmother's plants it looked like an indoor garden.

The heels of her boots clicked on the marble floor as she approached, causing both her grandparents to look up.

Her grandmother gave a nod of approval. "I knew that outfit would be perfect for you."

A small glow of pride filled Bryn's chest. Approval from her grandmother meant a lot. "Thank you for the clothes. I love this dress. It's the softest thing I've ever worn."

"Of course it's soft, it's cashmere." Her grandmother grinned. "One of the reasons I love winter is you can wear cashmere as often as you want."

Bryn took a seat on an empty side of the square table. "I was never a sweater person, but this may change my mind." She picked up a white china pot that sat in the center of the table and poured herself what she thought was a cup of coffee. The brown liquid that came out was too light in color.

"What is this?"

"It's tea," her grandfather stated in an annoyed tone.

"Why is it tea?" She meant it as a joke, sort of. Tea was good, but it lacked the amount of caffeine she craved first thing in the morning.

Her grandfather folded his paper in half and laid it beside his plate. "You don't like tea?"

"I do." And apparently she needed to this morning, because her grandfather wasn't a happy camper. "I normally have coffee at breakfast and tea later in the day, that's all. No big deal." She could just drink twice as much tea to make up for the caffeine.

Abigail appeared by Bryn's shoulder and set a plate of pancakes on her place mat. "Thank you. These look wonderful." The maple syrup scent had her stomach rumbling. She grabbed a fork and dug in. The pancakes were maple syrup, butter-coated carbohydrate joy.

Focused on inhaling her pancakes, it took a moment for her to realize that neither of her grandparents was speaking. She stopped midchew and noticed the expectant look on both their faces. She swallowed and wiped her mouth just in case she had maple syrup dribbling down her chin.

"Sorry, did you say something?"

"I asked why you felt the need to add another color to your hair?" her grandfather said.

This was about her hair? What was the big deal? "It matches my dress." No need to go into the story of how Clint and Ivy had first approached her due to her striped hair, which resembled something a Black dragon might do. It had provided her with something in common with their Clan. She didn't want to give that up completely for fear her friends would think she'd forgotten them or moved on.

"So if your dress were purple, you'd have a purple streak?" her grandfather snapped.

It was almost like he was trying to pick a fight. Bryn caught her grandmother's gaze and saw the slight shake of her head. Was this a test?

"When I first came to school, I added black stripes to my blond-and-red-striped hair because I liked the way it looked. Now it doesn't look right without a little bit of black." Maybe he'd buy that answer and leave her alone.

"I'd appreciate it if you didn't experiment with your

coloring any more. Unlike your Black dragon friends, it's not something Blue dragons do. We're proud of who we are. Changing your appearance signals you might not feel the same way."

Wow. What was his problem? She could see by the lines around her grandmother's mouth that she was worried this conversation was about to turn ugly.

Sitting back in her chair, Bryn crossed her arms over her chest. "I'm not sure what you're fishing for. Are you asking if I'm proud of my heritage? Are you testing me to see if you can start a fight? Are you pissed off because of what happened last night? Give me a clue and we can head in the right direction."

Her grandmother turned away, looking like she was trying not to say something, or maybe trying not to laugh. At this point it was anyone's guess.

Narrowing his eyes, her grandfather said, "You want the direct approach, fine. I don't like the black stripe in your hair. The red stripe is bad enough, but I'm willing to tolerate it. The black stripe must go."

Taking orders had never been her strong suit. "I don't suppose you'd consider asking nicely?"

He leaned forward in a menacing manner. "This is my version of asking nicely."

Laughter was the only way to save face. So she laughed and was relieved when he joined in. Then she closed her eyes, focused her Quintessence and changed the black stripe in her hair back to golden blond. "There, does that meet with your approval?"

"Yes." He picked up his paper, snapped it open, and effectively ended their conversation.

Bryn shot her grandmother a sideways glance. "Anything you'd like to get off your chest about my appearance?"

"I want to burn all of your jeans," her grandmother said. "But I won't. I figure if I restock your wardrobe with beautiful alternatives such as this dress, you won't want to wear them anymore."

"Good plan." Bryn poured more syrup on her pancakes. "Not sure it will work, but it's a good plan."

"Oh, I didn't meant to interrupt breakfast," a feminine voice said.

Bryn glanced up. Lillith came toward them, practically glowing with maternal warmth. Jaxon followed along behind her, his eyes scanning the room like he was checking for something to use as a weapon.

"We were having a late brunch." Her grandfather stood, folding his paper and placing it under his arm. "Why don't you join Bryn and Marie?"

"We're not chasing you off, are we?" Lillith asked.

"No. I was on my way out." He turned to Jaxon. "Would you like to join me in my law library? I'm drafting a new writ. It would be a good learning experience for you."

Jaxon's chest puffed out with pride. "Thank you, sir. I would be honored to join you."

When had he turned into such a suck-up? And why were Lillith and her grandmother exchanging knowing glances?

Once the males were out of hearing range, Bryn said, "What was that about?"

Lillith poured herself a cup of tea. "That was your grandfather showing his approval of Jaxon as a future Directorate member."

"I thought Jaxon was automatically on the Directorate since his dad is speaker."

"Your grandfather's approval is what's important." Lillith placed her hand over the tiny baby bump that was starting to show and sipped her tea in utter contentment.

"It means the alliance between our families is growing stronger." Her grandmother looked quite pleased with the situation.

Oh, hell. It meant she was one step closer to a marriage contract with Jaxon. She shoved her plate aside and laid her head on the table. Knowing her grandmother would only lecture her if she verbally objected, she decided body language showing abject frustration would have to do.

"Personality-wise, Jaxon is one of the more considerate Blue males," Lillith said.

Bryn lifted her head. "That isn't saying much." Sitting up, she asked the question she couldn't ask in public or in front of her grandfather. "Don't get mad at me, but why are the Blue males so crabby, and why do the women of this Clan put up with so much crap from them?"

Chapter Thirty-Five

Lillith smacked her hand over her mouth rather than spew tea across the table, while her grandmother gave Bryn a look that almost made her run from the room.

"I did say don't be mad," she reminded her grandmother. "It's not meant to be an insult to you. It's just that I've seen the way dragons from other Clans act, and the males aren't nearly as" — she searched for a word and couldn't find one — "as sure that they are right about everything all of the time. And before you say it, I know never to ask a question like this in front of anyone else but the two of you."

"That fact does not reassure me." Her grandmother leaned in. "Never ask a question of this nature when we are anywhere but in my rooms. If the staff overheard you…well, I hate to think about your grandfather's reaction."

"Okay. But can you answer the question?"

"We are the ruling class, which means we behave differently from the rest of the Clans. Men like your grandfather make laws that affect the fabric of our society. Much the same way you want a medic to believe they are capable of performing miraculous acts of healing, your grandfather and the other Blue males must believe they are capable of ruling our society."

Did that make sense? She wasn't sure. "Lillith, what's your take on the situation?"

"I agree with your grandmother. To make the decisions they have to make, they must believe they know what is best. It makes them difficult to live with at times, but I know Ferrin and your grandfather would do anything within their power to protect us and make sure we're safe."

"It's just not..." Bryn searched for a word. "Democratic."

"I never claimed it was." Her grandmother picked up the teapot and poured. "You're thinking like a human. You need to think like a dragon."

And there it was. Once again, she was reminded that she didn't fit in. She used to fantasize about living in Dragon's Bluff with Valmont, but *that* bubble had burst after the confrontation with his grandmother. Where did that leave her?

"One of the good things about Ferrin always being off to run the world is I'm able to do what I want around the house."

That didn't sound like a wonderful way to live. It sounded lonely.

"Speaking of doing what I want around the house," Lillith said, "I was hoping the two of you would go shopping with me to look at baby clothes."

"Sounds like fun." Just to be contrary, Bryn added, "Should we send for Jaxon?"

Lillith actually looked conflicted. "I know he'll hate to miss out on spending the day with us, but I think what he's doing now is more important."

Half an hour later Bryn sat in the backseat of one of her grandparents' many SUVs on her way to Dragon's Bluff. Didn't these people worry about gas mileage or the environment?

"Bryn, did you hear me?" her grandmother said.

Oops. "No, sorry, my mind was drifting."

"What were you thinking about?"

This was one of those times where a partial truth would be for the best. "I was thinking about cars and learning to drive."

"Jaxon has his license." Pride was evident in Lillith's voice.

What was the dragon equivalent of the DMV? Dragon of motor vehicles rather than department of motor vehicles? "Good for him. I'm not sure how the whole driver's license thing works."

Lillith blinked. "His father taught him how to drive, and he took the driver's test. How else would it work?"

"Where did he take the test?"

"He scheduled an appointment with the transportation director. I'm not sure where they went driving." Then it was like a lightbulb went off in Lillith's mind. "We should ask Jaxon to teach you to drive."

That had bad idea written all over it. "I'm not sure I'm ready for lessons yet."

Her grandmother nodded, but said nothing. Great. Now if she ever mentioned wanting to learn how to drive, she'd be stuck with Jaxon as a teacher. Talk about a lose-lose situation.

They rode in silence until the driver dropped them off

in front of a baby boutique. As far as Bryn could tell, the difference between a store and a boutique was anyone could enter a store, but you had to be buzzed into a boutique. Did the boutiques ever refuse to let anyone in? Maybe you had to make a certain amount of money before they thought you were worth their time.

Inside the store, Lillith kept picking up baby blankets and saying, "Isn't this adorable?"

Bryn figured it was her role to smile and nod. Which was fine. She could do that. Her grandmother disappeared into another part of the store. Lillith didn't seem to notice.

A flash of color across the aisle caught Bryn's eye, and she investigated. Rainbow-colored fish swam on a bright blue ocean of a blanket. She picked it up and carried it back to Lillith. "Look at this. It's bright and happy."

"It's cute." Lillith scanned the store. "Where did you find it?"

Bryn led Lillith over to the section with the ocean-themed mobile and bassinet.

"The bed is a bit much." Lillith ran her fingers over the mobile. "But I love this."

Bryn's grandmother returned with a pale blue gift bag in hand. "If you promise not to cry, you may open this here."

"I make no such promise." Lillith took the bag and pulled out a pale blue blanket. The middle was soft and fuzzy, but the edges were bound in a silky blue material. The border was decorated with snowflakes.

"It's lovely." Lillith sniffled.

"They have the matching mobile if you'd like to see it." Her grandmother pointed to middle of the boutique. "It's over there."

Lillith shoved the ocean blanket back at Bryn and walked off to investigate the snow-themed section.

"Oh, dear. Now she's looking at that tacky snowman mobile." Her grandmother took off after Lillith.

Manipulate much? Bryn folded the fish blanket and placed it back on the shelf.

One thing for sure, she had a whole new appreciation for her grandmother's ability to corral people into doing what she thought best.

While Lillith and her grandmother were busy picking out snowflake-themed bedding and decorations, Bryn snuck over to the section with items already in gift boxes. A silver baby rattle would make a cute gift for Lillith. They had to be planning a baby shower, right? Didn't all females, no matter the species, come together to celebrate new babies?

"We offer monogramming services," said the saleslady who'd crept up behind Bryn.

Trying not to look like the woman had startled her, Bryn held out the rattle. "Can you put Westgate on the rattle, or is that too long?"

The saleslady took the silver rattle, which was shaped like a miniature barbell, from Bryn. "We'll make it work. Should I put this on your grandmother's account?"

That's when she realized not a single item in the store had a price tag. The phrase "If you have to ask, you can't afford it" took on new meaning. Her grandmother wouldn't care if she put something on her account. Right? Then again, she did like to be made aware of things ahead of time. Bryn dug her Dragon's Bluff credit card out of her purse. The card worked at every store and restaurant in Dragon's Bluff. Hopefully that meant it worked at boutiques, too.

The saleslady accepted the card without looking at Bryn like she was an idiot, so the card must be okay. Thank goodness. Bryn wandered over to where her grandmother was showing off a mobile with snowflakes. Lillith clutched a mobile featuring snowmen wearing multicolored scarves.

"There you are. Help us pick out a mobile for Asher," her grandmother said. "I think this snowflake mobile is timeless and classic."

"But I like the snowmen." Lillith sounded on the verge of another set of hormonal tears.

Disagreeing with her grandmother wasn't a good idea. Lillith's bottom lip quivered. "Why not buy both? You can change them in and out so the baby won't be bored."

"Oh, I like that idea." Lillith turned to find a saleslady. One was already walking in their direction with a patient smile plastered on her face. Dealing with women who were liable to burst into tears at any moment could make this job not so much fun.

Bryn's grandmother leaned close. "That was very diplomatic of you."

Time to score some points. "I was afraid she'd cry if I told her I liked the snowflake one better."

Her grandmother puffed up with pride. "Good to know you inherited my taste."

Right. "I bought a silver rattle that they're going to monogram. Speaking of which, I need to get my card back from the saleslady."

"Next time just put it on my account," her grandmother said. "Then you don't have to worry about carrying around a card."

. . .

When it was time for lunch, Lillith suggested Fonzoli's. "I've been craving Italian food."

Would Valmont be working? Should she ask for him? Valmont's evil grandma wouldn't poison her food if she was with other people, right?

They'd barely cleared the restaurant door when Valmont appeared out of nowhere. One minute Bryn was standing by the hostess desk. The next minute Valmont was grabbing her hand.

"Pardon me while I borrow your granddaughter." He tugged her back toward the kitchen, not waiting for an acknowledgment from her grandmother.

"What's going on?" Bryn asked.

He didn't answer her, just kept leading her through the kitchen and out the back door to a small enclosed patio with a porch swing. "Sit."

"Since when did you become so bossy?" She sat, preferring to think of it as her own idea.

He sank down on the swing next to her, putting his arm around her. Leaning into him was instinctual. It felt like a weight lifted off her shoulders. She felt his muscles relax.

"There. That's much better." He pushed with his foot, setting the swing in motion. "Now, tell me about your Christmas dinner. We can compare notes, see who had the worst evening."

"I don't want to play that game right now." She laid her head on his shoulder. "This is the most content I've felt in days."

"Fair enough." The swing creaked as they rocked back

and forth.

She listened to his heartbeat, counting ten repetitions. "I'd love to stay here all day, but I think my grandmother might come looking for me."

"Can you stay for a visit after you eat?" he asked.

"My answer is yes. We'll have to see what my lunch partners say."

He squeezed her closer for a moment and then released her. "Too bad we can't just run away together."

His words hit a target she didn't know existed. She'd said the same words to Zavien several times. He'd never responded in kind. Did Valmont love her? Did she love him? One thing for sure, she wouldn't leave him hanging.

"That's a nice fantasy, but I couldn't do that to my grandparents."

He leaned in close, so his mouth was next to her ear. "Maybe we could just run away for a weekend?"

His hot breath on her ear sent happy shivers through her body. She wanted to kiss him. Was that the same thing as love?

"A weekend retreat would be wonderful." She didn't turn her head to meet his gaze, because their lips would be too close, too tempting. Even though she wanted to, kissing him and then heading inside for lunch with her grandmother would not work. She pushed to her feet and then offered him her hand. "You stole me, and I will not face the consequences alone."

He chuckled. "I'm not sure who's scarier, your grandmother in a foul mood, or Mrs. Westgate and her tears."

"It's a toss-up."

Back in the dining room, Valmont escorted Bryn to the

table by the window where the rest of her party sat. And somehow her party had grown by one. Bryn stopped in her tracks and said, "Wait. I changed my mind. Let's go back."

Jaxon scowled at her from where he sat by his mother.

"I didn't know you were joining us," Bryn said.

"Neither did I." His tone was clipped.

Valmont pulled a chair out for Bryn. She sat and reached for her glass of ice water. "Did you have a productive morning with my grandfather?"

"Small talk?" Jaxon raised a brow. "Is that what we've sunk to?"

Bryn looked at her grandmother. "I deserve points for trying."

"Why don't I bring you a few appetizers while you study the menu?" Valmont suggested, backing away from the table.

"At least he's smart enough to retreat." Jaxon leaned back in his chair, like he was trying to put distance between himself and the three women.

Bryn's grandmother shot him a disapproving look. "I'm not sure why you're unhappy with our company, but you will sit up and speak in a respectful tone."

Jaxon straightened in his chair, but the sour grapes look on his face didn't change. He pointed at Bryn. "Do you know why your grandfather really wanted to speak with me?"

What was he getting at? "I assumed he was teaching you the secret Directorate member handshake and taking you on a tour of the clubhouse."

"After your grandfather discussed legal issues and demonstrated how they were recorded in the ledgers, he showed me a book of marriage contracts where he already had our names written in for a request of lineage check."

Valmont arrived at that moment bearing trays of cheese sticks and toasted ravioli. He froze with the platters halfway to the table. "What?"

Jaxon actually laughed. "Please, run away with her. I'll pay you."

"That's it." Bryn's grandmother spoke in an ice-cold tone that cut through the room. "Jaxon Westgate, if you ever slight my granddaughter again, you will regret it."

Okay. Jaxon had been a jerk, but he'd been joking. Sort of. Maybe that wasn't the root of her grandmother's concern.

Bryn touched her grandmother's arm. "I promise I will never run away."

White-lipped, her grandmother nodded.

Nervous laughter bubbled from Bryn's throat. "Even if the Directorate sticks me with Jaxon, I won't run away. I may have my knight run him through with a broadsword, but I won't run away."

Her grandmother glanced at Valmont. "You may have your uses, after all."

Valmont grinned. "I live to serve."

Chapter Thirty-Six

Bryn was surprised when Rhianna called her the next day. "I was wondering if I could visit you this evening."

"Sure. Is everything all right?"

"I'll see you at seven," Rhianna responded like she hadn't heard Bryn's question, and then hung up.

Later that night, Rhianna sat on the couch in Bryn's rooms, hugging a throw pillow to her chest. "Sorry to bother you, but I didn't know anyone else besides you and Jaxon I could talk to about this."

"You can always talk to me," Bryn said. "That's what friends are for."

Rhianna released her grip on the pillow and laid it flat on her lap. "Rather than returning to school, the Directorate suggested I might be more comfortable at home with a private tutor."

That was bullshit. "Tell them they can take their suggestion and shove it up their narrow-minded—"

"Stop." Rhianna laughed. "Finish that sentence and I'll never be able to keep a straight face around a Directorate member again."

"Did they ban you from campus?" Bryn asked.

"No. Technically, I could return to school with you."

"You are going back, end of story."

"What if none of the other injured students come back?" Rhianna's voice wavered. "I don't want to stand out any more than I already do."

"We'll just have to make sure the other students know they have a choice to come back."

"Some may not want to," Rhianna said. "I felt sorry for myself, until I heard the extent of some of the other students' injuries. I'll fly crooked but at least I can still fly."

"Exactly, and you can still think and learn and do all the things a student should do. So, we need a plan. What's the best way to reach everyone and ask if they want to return? And how can we do this without the Directorate hearing about it?"

"Good question." Rhianna stared at the fireplace for a moment. The corners of her mouth turned up. "I bet Lillith would do it for us."

"Why would she?" It's not like she ever stood up to Ferrin, or as Bryn thought of him, the asshat extraordinaire.

"We can appeal to Lillith's maternal instincts. We'll tell her student morale is low due to the attacks and the threat of war, and we wanted to invite all the students to some sort of 'welcome back to school' party. That way everyone, even the injured students, will receive an invitation to return to the institute."

"That just might work. As long as it's not a dance," Bryn

said, "I'm in."

Some of the light left Rhianna's eyes. "No argument there."

Great thing to say to someone with a permanent limp. "Okay, I'm now a nominee for the jerk-of-the-year club. Sorry about that. It's just that my relationship with Zavien ended at one dance. And an act of war happened at the only other dance I've attended."

"Maybe we should leave the type of celebration up to Lillith."

There was one major flaw in this plan. "My grandmother would never speak to me again if she wasn't asked to plan a major event."

"Then I'll say it was my idea. I'll contact Lillith, and suggest she ask your grandmother for help."

"Won't this fall apart when Ferrin hears about it?"

"If Lillith wasn't pregnant, and likely to burst into tears at any given moment, yes." Rhianna laughed. "Blue males, alpha males like Ferrin, back down from nothing, except upsetting a pregnant female. Heirs are how they control the world after they're gone."

Bryn's phone rang. "I wonder who that is?" She crossed the room and answered the phone.

"Come down to the small dining room, immediately," her grandmother said.

"Something is wrong." Bryn ran out the door with Rhianna following behind her.

Covered in soot, his clothes singed, Valmont paced in front of the buffet while her grandmother stood off to the side talking on the phone.

"Valmont?" She shot across the room. "What's happened?"

"Dragon's Bluff. It's burning. We need your help."

"What can I do?" Bryn asked.

"Come back with me. Use your ice to douse the flames."

"Wait," her grandmother ordered, then she went back to shouting at someone on the phone.

"Are you hurt?" Bryn ran her hands down his arms, checking for injuries under his soot-blackened shirt.

"I'm fine, but we need to hurry." His gaze darted to her grandmother.

She was torn. The worry on Valmont's face ate away at her. She wanted to shift, take flight, and get to Dragon's Bluff as soon as possible. But her grandmother had told her to wait. And she didn't want to set off the security system that had almost sliced her to ribbons the last time she'd encountered it.

Her grandmother slammed the phone down. "Word is out. Every available Blue will fly to Dragon's Bluff as soon as possible."

"Including us, right?" Bryn's muscles coiled tight, ready to shift.

"On one condition. You stay with me and follow my orders." Her grandmother pointed at Valmont. "Are you prepared to fulfill your vow as a knight, to protect my granddaughter at all costs?"

Valmont stood straighter. "Yes."

"Come this way." Her grandmother hustled from the room and down a side hall. They ran after her. Rhianna's uneven stride rang out on the marble floor.

"In here." Inside the room, armor, lances, and saddles were displayed on the wall. Valmont went straight to a suit of chain mail and slid it on over his shirt. Next he grabbed a lance and tested its weight.

Her grandmother went over to a pair of floor-to-ceiling windows and unhooked latches that allowed the pair to swing open like a set of doors, which happened to be on the third floor of the house.

Bryn shifted. Valmont placed a saddle on her back. It fit between her shoulder blades like it belonged there. He pushed an end table next to Bryn, climbed up, and settled on her back. A ripple of power ran through her body.

"You're glowing." Rhianna said.

Must be some sort of magic from their bond. Whatever it was, it felt right.

"Bryn, you need to change your scales to all Blue so someone doesn't mistake you for the enemy," her grandmother said.

Bryn closed her eyes, sent a silent apology to her father for abandoning his heritage, and imagined her scales changing from red with blue tips to solid blue. She opened her eyes and looked to her grandmother for assurance.

"Good. Now stay in tight formation. The security system has been disarmed in the south corner." Her grandmother launched herself out into the night sky. Rhianna went next.

"I'm ready," Valmont said.

Bryn dived out into the darkness, catching the updraft. A strange energy flowed through her veins, making her feel invincible. The scent of smoke hit her nostrils and sparks drifted through the sky.

Her grandmother's pace left Rhianna falling behind. Bryn slowed.

"No," Rhianna growled. "Go on."

Bryn caught up to her grandmother while keeping a lookout for enemies. How would she tell friend from foe?

"Valmont, did you see who did this?"

"No. They took out our communications system first. Then the fireballs came. By the time we figured it out…" His voice broke. "Those of us with cars took off to seek help."

Fire roared inside her body, and that was not what she needed now. Snow. Think snow and ice and cold. She focused on the fire inside her body and changed it to frozen flames.

They cleared the forest. Blue dragons dove through the air, shooting sleet and snow at houses. Her grandmother veered left, to an area of homes engulfed in flames. Bryn followed, exhaling sleet at a cottage roof, beating back the flames. She continued on, house after house. The soot and smoke drifted thick in the air, stinging her eyes and blurring her vision.

Shapes darted through the sky blasting ice and fire, while she followed along behind her grandmother exhaling sleet to douse the flames.

"Dive," Valmont shouted.

Obeying her knight's order was pure instinct. Tucking her wings to her side, she sped toward the street. Fire blasted the area she'd occupied moments before. Banking and twisting to the right, she shot frozen flames at the Red dragon circling above her. He dodged left, wobbled and then rolled back toward her, with one wing iced over.

Inhaling, she blasted him again, aiming for his free wing. The Red roared in frustration, flailing and flapping his wings to break the ice.

And she didn't know what to do next. She wanted to drive him away, not kill him. Taking another breath, she prepared to blast him again.

Out of nowhere another Blue swooped in, bit down on

the Red's neck and roared in triumph as blood filled the sky and rained down on her and Valmont.

Oh God. Oh God. Oh God. She was going to be sick.

"Bryn," Valmont yelled. "Over there."

She turned and saw a woman clutching a baby to her chest, surrounded by walls of flame. Saving people. That she could do. Exhaling sleet, she doused the flames on one side, giving the woman an escape route. Screams came from her right. Two girls huddled together under a tree that was on fire. A man rolled on the ground, his clothes aflame. She sprayed the man with sleet and then moved on to the girls.

All around her, people kept screaming. Valmont acted as her personal navigator, helping her avoid surprise aerial attacks and directing her where she was needed most. She did her best to save everyone she could. Inside her, fury raged. Who would do this? These were people, innocent people who shouldn't be used as pawns in a dragon war.

"Bryn, over here. Now."

She recognized her grandmother's voice and followed orders. Her grandmother was building a wall of ice to keep flames from crossing a road to an undamaged section of town. Bryn reinforced the wall as her grandmother built it, exhaling ice until her throat felt raw. By the time they were done, she could barely flap her wings.

"What's wrong?" Valmont asked as she set down on the ground.

"Tired," she said. "So tired."

Her grandmother landed next to her. "You've overexerted yourself. You need to eat. Follow me."

She started to shift, but her grandmother took flight, so she pushed off the ground and forced her wings up and down, traveling to the edge of the forest, where she gagged. Deer, cows, pigs, and any other animals killed in the fire lay lined up like a bizarre buffet.

"No way." She closed her eyes.

"Eat," her grandmother ordered.

"I could shift." Bryn said. "I'm sure—"

"Think of it as a big hamburger," Valmont said.

"Are you serious?" Had he lost his mind?

"The others are doing it."

Bryn looked and saw several Blues chomping down on deer and cows. And her stomach growled...oh gross...now the deer looked good. Wait, what was she thinking? She couldn't eat Bambi....saliva pooled in her mouth.

"It's in your nature." Valmont said. "You are a carnivore and a predator."

Okay. True. And the deer was already dead. But still... could she really do this? Roaring in frustration, she settled down by a small deer, grabbed it in her jaws, flipped it and swallowed it whole. She tensed, waiting for it to come back up.

"Everything all right?" Valmont asked.

"Besides being disgusted with myself, I'm fine."

The Blues spent the next hour putting out fires. The enemy, whoever they were, had retreated. Once the flames were extinguished, all the refugees gathered on Main Street. Bryn, her grandmother, and other Blues joined them.

"Can we shift back?" Bryn asked. "Because I really want to brush my teeth." She could swear there was deer fur stuck between her molars.

"Not yet," her grandmother said. "We'll wait for the Directorate's order."

The freaking Directorate. Which had failed to protect people she cared about. *Again.*

Wait. Had she said that out loud? Because people were staring. But if she'd said it out loud, her grandmother would have had a fit, so that wasn't it. "Any idea why I'm the main attraction?"

"You're the only dragon with a knight," Rhianna said.

"And I'm spectacularly handsome," Valmont added.

Bryn laughed. "That you are. Are you all right?"

"Tired and hungry and mad as hell, but other than that, I'm great."

Bryn's grandfather stalked down the street in human form.

"That's our signal that it's safe to shift back," her grandmother said.

Valmont hopped off her back and removed the saddle. A strange sense of loss overcame Bryn, like she'd lost a piece of herself. She shifted and held a hand out toward Valmont. "Do you feel it?"

He dropped the saddle and pulled her into a hug, whispering into her ear, "Being linked to you felt right. Now I miss you."

"Bryn." Her grandfather's tone was like the crack of a whip.

She stepped away, expecting her grandfather to blast her about inappropriate behavior.

"Come with me." He headed down the street.

Hopefully he wasn't taking her somewhere to yell at her in private. But he'd never been shy about yelling at her before, so what the hell did he want? Only one way to find out. She followed him down a side street and then wished she hadn't.

Bodies. There were human bodies and dragon bodies

lined up on the street. Burned bodies. Bodies with severed wings. Body parts still oozing blood with ragged flesh hanging off broken bones. Coupled with the sickening smell of burned flesh, it was all too much. Prickly heat broke out on her skin. She gagged. Oh God. She could not throw up. She closed her eyes and focused on not projectile vomiting deer parts all over the road.

"Bryn," her grandfather roared.

"I need a minute." Slow, even breaths. She could do this. Her grandfather was asking for her help. She needed to be up to the task or he'd never take her seriously again. "Okay. I'm good." She jogged over to where he stood by a Red dragon's corpse.

"I want you to use your healing abilities to scan this dragon. Tell me what he is."

What was he talking about? Then she saw it. The red scales weren't charred in places like she'd thought at first sight. The black color was uniform on each scale, like a pattern. Like the way she looked in her natural state when her scales were red with blue tips.

Maybe she wasn't the only crossbred dragon after all.

Chapter Thirty-Seven

Now she understood. Squatting down, she focused her life force, like a small sun in her chest. Then, trying not to freak out about what she was doing, she placed her hand on the corpse's flank. His scales were still warm. Not sure how this worked with someone who wasn't alive, she pushed a tiny bit of her life force into the creature's body.

It hurt. Physically and mentally. There was no responding life force, so her Quintessence felt like it was caught in a vise. She held her breath to keep from crying out and forced her way into the cells, coaxing them to return to human form. The cells vibrated. She withdrew her life force and stared down at the boy lying prone on the street. Tears filled her eyes. He was no older than she was. Maybe eighteen at the most. His hair was the auburn color of a Red dragon, but his eyes, which stared unseeing into the night sky, weren't green as they should have been. They were brown. His skin was missing the trademark freckles of a Red dragon. Instead, he had the ivory skin of a Black dragon.

"Black and Red," Bryn whispered.

Her grandfather grabbed the boy's left wrist and ripped open the scorched sleeve of his shirt, revealing a tattoo on his forearm. A circle divided into four parts, each part containing a triangle.

Her grandfather let loose with a string of profanities she didn't think a man like him would know, much less use. Retreating seemed like a great idea, but he might think she was weak, so she held her ground.

"What did you find?" Ferrin appeared by her grandfather's side and looked at the boy on the ground. "Another abomination bearing that mark."

Offended at the abomination part, Bryn bit her tongue because she didn't want to look like she was siding with the enemy.

"It's the third one we've found tonight," her grandfather said.

Whoa. "What does that mean?"

"It means there is a secret community of dragons somewhere, breeding and plotting against us," her grandfather said. "I will give you one chance, and one chance only to answer this question." His gaze settled on Bryn with a level of fury that made her mouth go dry. "Did you or your parents know of any other runaway dragons?"

"No." And now he'd pissed her off. "My parents kept to themselves, and I thought I was human until flames shot out of my mouth."

"Imbecile," Ferrin muttered loud enough for her to hear.

Bryn moved toward him, sticking her finger in his face. "You needed *my* help to figure this out. If I'm an imbecile, what does that make you?"

Ferrin growled, and the air around him shimmered.

"We don't have time for this." Her grandfather grabbed Bryn's arm and yanked her out of Ferrin's personal space. "Go back to your grandmother." He squeezed her arm, hard enough to leave a mark. "And not a word about what we found here."

Just when she'd started to like the guy. She pulled her arm from his grip. "Fine. What's the official Directorate version of events, or do you want me to make up my own lie?"

"I asked if you could ID the bodies as fellow students from school," her grandfather said. "They were too badly burned for you to recognize."

Scary how easy the lies rolled off his tongue. She stomped back toward her grandmother. She now knew which of her grandparents to trust and which one to stay away from.

Her grandmother stood next to Rhianna and Jaxon. Where was Valmont? When he'd dismounted and she had shifted back, the missing of him had been a physical ache. Now she was twitchy, like an alcoholic who needed a drink. Where was he? She needed to know he was safe.

"What was that about?" Jaxon asked, pointing back the way she'd come.

"The *official* truth is my grandfather and your father wanted to see if I recognized any of the bodies. They were too badly charred for them to be sure."

Jaxon's eyes narrowed. "That's a lie."

"I told you. It's the *official truth*. If you have questions, direct them to your father. On to more important things. Where's Valmont?"

"He went to check on his family," her grandmother said.

"And before you get any ideas, the answer is no. You may not go look for him."

"No offense, but I've about reached my limit of people telling me what to do."

"But you will listen to me, anyway," her grandmother said, "because I am trying to keep you safe."

"Way to play the guilt card." Bryn crossed her arms over her chest and indulged in a bit of pouting.

"What happens now?" Rhianna asked. "And if you say we wait for the Directorate to give us permission to leave, I'll start acting like Bryn."

Her grandmother laughed. Bryn joined in.

"I think it's safe for us to fly home." Her grandmother glanced around. "Rhianna, you should return with us. Jaxon, would you like to accompany us back to the estate? I'm sure your father will end up there eventually."

Was she asking Jaxon to come along as protection, or to keep him from flying home alone?

"I appreciate the invitation, but I need to return home and check on my mother."

"Of course."

Jaxon shifted and took flight.

Bryn's grandmother touched her on the shoulder. "When we return to the house, you will tell me what really happened."

"Don't worry, I planned on it."

Rhianna cleared her throat and gave Bryn puppy-dog eyes. Great. She didn't want to keep secrets from her friend, but what could she do?

"While Bryn speaks to me in private, you may wait in the hall outside my door," her grandmother said. "I trust you won't eavesdrop."

Okay. Her grandmother officially rocked.

"I would never consider such a thing," Rhianna said.

Valmont marched toward Bryn. Soot streaked his handsome face. Resolution showed in his ice-blue eyes. He appeared tired, determined, and unbelievably hot. Wow. So not the time for her hormones to kick in.

Her knight smiled, like he knew what she was thinking. If the connection between them had resulted in some type of mind meld where he could read her thoughts, she was in trouble.

Rather than stopping in front of her, he kept coming and wrapped his arms around her in a protective embrace. She returned the hug and a happy warmth flowed through her veins. Like they belonged together.

"Does this mean you missed me?" She spoke into his chest because she was afraid if she looked up at him, they would be in perfect alignment for a first kiss. A kiss she craved right now, but not in front of her grandmother and the entire town, or what was left of it.

Valmont pressed his lips to the top of her head. "Being away from you made me nervous. Like I was abandoning my post."

This time she did look up at him. "I'm a post? Because that isn't a flattering description."

He laughed. "Sorry. That didn't come out as I intended. I feel like my place is by your side."

"I know what you mean." She reached up and rubbed a streak of soot off his cheek. "Doing battle, facing an enemy together, I think it increased our bond."

He leaned down and whispered, "If we weren't in the middle of the street surrounded by people, and your grandmother who is looking at me like I'm a fly she'd like to swat, I'd investigate other ways we could bond."

Did it matter that they were surrounded by people? Because kissing him sounded like the best idea she'd had in a long time. "You could come back to the estate with us."

He released her and backed up a step. "Any other time, I'd be happy to join you, but I need to see to my family."

"Are they all right?"

His eyes darkened. "My grandparents and parents were lucky. They suffered minor burns. My nephews are still unaccounted for."

Her heart dropped. "Is someone keeping track of who's missing?"

"A few Green dragons who were dining at Fonzoli's figured out a system to take roll, using the town business roster and house numbers."

Good. If anyone could figure this out, the Green dragons could.

"Is there anything I can do to help?" Everywhere she looked, buildings smoldered, soot filled the air, and people coughed or cried, hugging their family members close.

"For selfish reasons, I'd like you to stay within arm's reach. As far as the town goes, I'm not sure where to start."

"Me either." Who could she ask? "Come with me." Taking Valmont's hand, because she needed to touch him, she approached her grandmother. "I don't suppose there's a master plan of where to house the people of Dragon's Bluff or how to help them after an attack."

Her grandmother's brow wrinkled. "I'm not sure. If anyone would know, it would be Mr. Stanton."

The head of the Green Clan on campus, Mr. Stanton

would be the best person to find. Or maybe Miss Enid, the librarian. "Is there any way to contact him?" Bryn asked.

"None. The phone towers and the power station were disabled before the attack." Valmont gave a bitter laugh. "I wonder if they had Green dragons on their side."

"Whoever did this, we will find them and they will pay," her grandmother said. "Once we return home, I'll call Mr. Stanton and ask if he can be of help. If nothing else, I'm sure he can find a way to restore your phone lines and power."

Chapter Thirty-Eight

Back at the estate, in her grandmother's rooms, Bryn explained what happened with her grandfather and what she'd seen.

"There are other crossbred dragons?" Her grandmother shook her head. "How is that possible?"

It was on the tip of Bryn's tongue to say other people must have hated the arranged marriage laws as much as she did, but she refrained.

Rhianna, who stood just outside the open doorway, laughed. "I know why your mom ran away from Ferrin. I'm trying to figure out who is as obnoxious as he is, and I can't come up with anyone."

Bryn laughed. Her grandmother didn't.

"Sorry." Time to change the subject. "What did Mr. Stanton say when you called him?"

"He and a dozen of his Clan were going to convene in Dragon's Bluff within the hour to figure out the best way to help everyone."

"That's good." Bone-tired, Bryn yawned. "I'm not sure if I need to eat or go to bed."

"I wouldn't mind some real food." Rhianna grimaced. "I swear I can still taste cow fur."

"You'll adjust to eating in dragon form," her grandmother said. "Rhianna, I think it's best if you stayed the night. I'll inform your parents and have a guest room down the hall from Bryn prepared for you." Her grandmother yawned. "I believe I'll turn in for the evening. Bryn, why don't you have Abigail bring a cart up to your room? I'd rather you weren't wandering around the mansion with your grandfather in the mood he's likely to be in when he returns."

"Good idea."

"And Bryn?"

"Yes."

"The tattoo you saw. Do you know what it means?"

She didn't want to lie to her grandmother. "I thought those were symbols for the elements."

"Alone they are, but together like that they are a symbol for treason. Do you understand why I'm telling you this?"

"Because you don't want me doodling it in a notebook?" Bryn joked.

"No notebooks, no tattoos, no anything. Understand?"

"Yes, ma'am."

Bryn headed for her bedroom, called Abigail, ordered pizza, and changed into her pajamas while she waited for Rhianna to return from her guest room. By the time Rhianna came back, the pizza had been delivered.

"What took you so long?" Bryn stacked two pieces of pepperoni pizza on top of each other and bit into spicy, cheesy bliss.

"I called Jaxon to see if he was all right."

"Why wouldn't he be?"

Rhianna cut her pizza into bite-sized pieces with a knife and fork. "Tonight, you were privy to Directorate information, and he was not. I could tell it bothered him."

And just like that, it hit Bryn. "You care about him, don't you?"

She gave a sad smile. "When our lineage check was approved, I thought he was a suitable match. I respected him. I never expected to feel anything more than that. But, ever since my accident, I've seen a different side of him. It seems the height of irony that I am developing feelings for the male I'm no longer allowed to marry." Tears sparkled in her eyes. "And the girl who will marry the boy I'm falling in love with is my friend."

Bryn slumped back against the couch. "I have no words for how sorry I am about all this. Does it help that I don't want him? Because I don't. You know that. Right?"

"I know, and he's not interested in you, either."

"Good, because I don't want to lose you as a friend."

. . .

The next morning, Bryn woke to someone rooting around in her closet. "Who's there?"

Abigail poked her head out. "Sorry to disturb you. Your grandmother suggested I pack your things for school."

Bryn's head was fuzzy. Rubbing grit from her eyes, she tried to remember what day it was. That was right, she returned to school tomorrow.

Good. She wanted to go back to being the old Bryn with

striped hair who wore jeans and tennis shoes. Twenty bucks said Abigail wouldn't pack a single pair of jeans. She'd have to check the bags before she left.

Hopping out of bed, Bryn grabbed a robe. "Did my grandmother give you a message for me?" She didn't want to wander around the house and risk bumping into her grandfather, who she no longer trusted and had no desire to see.

"She said you should come to the atrium for breakfast."

"Thank you."

Thirty minutes later, Bryn found her grandmother sitting in the atrium with Lillith. The white wrought iron table was set for three, with a platter of bagels and muffins in the middle. *Where was Rhianna?*

"Good morning." Bryn sat, poured herself a cup of coffee, and grabbed a cinnamon swirl bagel. She glanced around. No toaster in sight, so she sliced the bagel and placed it cut side down on her palm. Concentrating, she shot a quick blast of flames from her palm and *ta da*, one toasted bagel.

Lillith giggled while her grandmother shook her head, but there was a smile on her face.

"Anyone else want a toasted bagel?" Bryn asked.

"I've already eaten," Lillith said. "Otherwise I'd say yes."

"Grandmother?"

"No, thank you. And don't do that—"

"In front of my grandfather." Bryn finished the sentence for her.

"Exactly," her grandmother said.

"Did Rhianna already eat?" Bryn asked.

"Jaxon picked her up this morning. They were going to spend the day together," Lillith said.

"That's nice." One, because it would make Rhianna happy, and two, because it meant Bryn wouldn't be blessed with his presence.

"We should talk about the welcome-back-to-school gala that your grandmother and I are planning." Lillith beamed with excitement.

Rhianna's plan must have worked. "What's a gala?" Bryn asked.

"It's an occasion marking a special event," her grandmother said. "In this case, we'll be celebrating the students' return to school after the holidays and the start of a new, safer year at school."

Bryn believed the first part, but doubted the second. "That sounds great."

"I'm glad to hear you say that. Since Lillith and I planned the event it's only right you and Jaxon act as hosts at the party."

Oh, hell. "I don't suppose this is something I can argue my way out of."

"No." Her grandmother and Lillith responded at the same time in the same smug tone.

"Great. Hosting with Jaxon. I can't wait."

. . .

That night as she fell asleep, Bryn reviewed all the weird twists and turns her life had taken.

Due to her skill with Quintessence and her ability to heal those injured at the Christmas Eve ball, she was no longer despised by all Blues. And more importantly, her grandfather was proud of her. While he wouldn't win any contests for being warm and fuzzy, his approval meant a lot, and her grandmother had turned out to be more warm and loving than Bryn ever thought possible. There would be bumps in the road as they moved forward, but she was happy and grateful they were part of her life.

Plus she'd beaten the Directorate at their own game. Using her connections, she'd found a way to work around their stupid "cull the herd" mentality, through the welcome-back-to-school gala. All those students who'd been injured in the attacks and were now considered less than perfect were going to receive an official invitation to return to school. Some might not want to come back, but at least now they had an option.

Returning to school and seeing Zavien would be strange, but that bridge was definitely burned. Then there was Valmont. Fighting together in Dragon's Bluff had intensified their bond and the attraction between them. She had no idea where that would or could lead.

One fascinating fact she knew for sure, other hybrids existed and she was going to find them.

Acknowledgments

There are several people to thank for bringing this book to life. I'd like to thank my husband for putting up with my particular brand of insanity. I'd like to thank my family for being supportive. A special acknowledgment goes to my mother, who went above and beyond by approaching total strangers, telling them about my book and offering them swag. Finally, I'd like to thank Erin Molta and Stacy Abrams for their editing expertise and Entangled Publishing for taking a chance on my dragons.

About the Author

Chris Cannon lives in Southern Illinois with her husband and her three dogs: Pete the shih-tzu who sleeps on her desk while she writes, Molly the ever-shedding yellow lab, and Tyson the sandwich-stealing German Shepherd Beagle.

She believes coffee is the Elixir of Life. Most evenings after work, you can find her sucking down caffeine and reading or writing a fire-breathing paranormal adventure. You can find her online at www.chriscannonauthor.com.

CPSIA information can be obtained at www.ICGtesting.com
Printed in the USA
LVOW10s1744061015

457153LV00016B/611/P

9 781507 568101